Justin Myers grew up in Shipley, Yorkshire, and now lives in London. He spent years quietly working in journalism and largely being ignored (which he was more or less fine with), before unexpectedly finding success when he began writing under the pseudonym The Guyliner, perhaps becoming best known for his playful reviews of the *Guardian*'s Blind Date feature. His writing has appeared all over the place and he's been a weekly columnist for British *GQ* since 2016. *The Fake-Up* is his third novel.

Follow Justin online at:
@theguyliner
www.theguyliner.com

Justin Myers

THE FAKE UP

SPHERE

SPHERE

First published in Great Britain in 2022 by Sphere
This paperback edition published in 2023 by Sphere

1 3 5 7 9 10 8 6 4 2

Copyright © Justin Myers 2022

The moral right of the author has been asserted.
Patti Lupone quote from *Elle* article 'Patti Lupone Wants
to Sign Your Stimulus Check' May 12, 2020.

A CIP catalogue record for this book is available from the British Library.

ISBN 978-0-7515-8349-6

Typeset in Perpetua by M Rules
Printed and bound in Great Britain by Clays Ltd, Elcograf S.p.A.

Papers used by Sphere are from well-managed forests
and other responsible sources.

Sphere
An imprint of
Little, Brown Book Group
Carmelite House
50 Victoria Embankment
London EC4Y 0DZ

An Hachette UK Company
www.hachette.co.uk

www.littlebrown.co.uk

For Paul.
Thank you, Larry.

*They can say you're a flaming
asshole, but they can't deny talent*

PATTI LuPONE

PART ONE.

One.

In the three years Dylan had been occupying the third row, third seat along from the right, at Flo's gigs, he'd never been late. He'd dropped a glass, he'd sneezed uncontrollably during a ballad, and he'd fended off a handbag attack from a drunk woman who thought he'd stolen her purse, but he'd never been late. Until today. All because of the word 'salubrious'. He'd been rolling it round his tongue all day, going over his lines for Monday's audition. This was a big one: a soap. No, hang on, *City Royal* was a continuing drama, that was it. He knew the scene off by heart, save for one stumbling block: 'salubrious'. Saburious. Salubricant. Salubitous. All nonsense words, falling out of his mouth whenever he tried to say it right. Cause of death: salubrious.

As he hopped on the bus to the station, rocked back and forth on the train, darted along the pavement, leapt dramatically over puddles and failed to keep his umbrella right side out – he chanted it over and over. Finally, he chucked himself through the door of the bar and quickly scanned the room for his assigned seat. Maybe Flo hadn't remembered to tell them – this was a new venue, an unpaid tryout for a regular gig. Dylan knew Flo really wanted this, which by default meant he wanted it badly, too.

He scooted along the still-unoccupied row and looked around. It was far more — oh, well, what do you know, a use for it at last — salubrious than her usual venue, where he spent one Thursday night a month watching her and Elijah perform. Giant vases of exotic-looking flowers, shiny pillars, plush velvet curtains draped everywhere — and an archway festooned with glimmering lights that led to the hotel next door. The place was dripping with money and the opulence and polite hostility that came with it. The back of Dylan's neck prickled with nervous sweat as his gaze swept over the bar's patrons: at least two real fur coats, some ill-advised surgical butchery, and a general air of disdain. He self-consciously tapped his wallet through the denim of his jeans — he'd have to make one drink last. They probably didn't even serve pints.

Flo had been nervous about performing here. This crowd could smell fear, thrived on it. Why on earth had she agreed to it? Then Dylan remembered, thanks to a light commotion and the sound of seats shifting. Estelle, Flo's best friend since their days of pigtails and sleepovers, had arrived. Tall and imperious, blond hair gleaming from its third blow-dry of the day, she strode regally to the front, a smaller entourage than usual trailing behind. Estelle didn't usually come to these gigs — her diary was packed tighter than a champion-ship game of Tetris — but her talent for pulling strings had won Elijah and Flo this slot tonight. This was a very Estelle kind of venue. If this went well, it would mean regular and decent money, rather than the haphazard schedules and grubby banknotes of Flo's usual gigs. Estelle was here not just for encouragement, perhaps, but as a reminder she was useful.

Dylan sank into his seat to avoid being seen, but it was no good; Estelle could sniff someone born in the wrong postcode a million miles away. She turned and smiled – like Maleficent browsing a takeaway menu – and beckoned him over. Not wanting to shout and draw attention, he shook his head and pointed at the seat. Estelle's eyes narrowed, pretending not to get it.

'What?' she brayed through the general hubbub like she was wired to the amp. 'Join us!'

She was only asking so she wouldn't look like she was leaving him out, and possibly because ordering people around was her favourite form of cardio. 'I can't,' Dylan said, awkwardly checking nobody else was looking. 'I always sit here, you know?'

'We've never been here before!' Estelle trilled back. 'What are you talking about? Come *along*.'

The 'same-seat promise' had been Dylan's idea, way back after that first time he'd come to see Flo play at her favourite venue, the cheerful little pub in Putney, to five rows of punters. Initially he'd pledged to always be front row, but soon tired of sitting alongside the kind of people who insist on sitting in the front row, so instead arranged to go third row, third seat from the right so, if she needed to, she could always find him. Dylan did his ridiculous mime again and Estelle rolled her eyes and lowered into her seat like it was a throne.

The main lights went down. The stage began to glow as the small curtain lifted to reveal Flo, looking calm and composed – though Dylan knew her stomach would be in full jacuzzi mode. She stood poker-straight, looking beyond them all, like her eyes were searching for a star in a distant sky. Her hair was pulled back from her face, a few free wisps either side — 'strategic,' she'd always say, 'so I don't look too severe, like Miss Trunchbull.' Beside her, on a stool designed for only one pert buttcheek at a time, Elijah, guitar in hand. Dylan's heart clawed its way to his throat, not just from pride but nerves — sometimes Elijah insisted on playing his own material, and it was an acquired taste, like drinking crude oil. Dylan breathed deeply and Flo did the same, as if he were breathing for her. And she was away. Flo sang as she always did, like — well, okay, cliché but seriously — an absolute angel, the entire room in the palm of her hand, bathing in the fluorescent rays of her star power. Seriously, when Flo sang, socks were knocked off, worlds rocked, minds blown. Dylan had watched it happen over and over. She could make anything sound good — even Elijah's klutzy, primary-school-level poetry masquerading as intensity. Flo closed her eyes at first, head tilted back, but as she gained confidence, once a chorus or two was out of the way, she'd look right into the audience, daring them to stare, her eyes round and powerful as she relieved them of every last crumb of emotion. Eventually, as she always did, she glanced over, smiling to find him there, relieved, yes, but also, she always claimed, somehow able to take her voice to the next level. It was celestial.

Whatever they did, there was always a deep connection between them — even when far apart, Dylan could sense if something wasn't right. He never felt more in sync with Flo than he did when she was performing. It was like when he was a kid and flew for the first time — he was convinced only his concentration stopped the plane from nosediving. He'd spur her on, help her hit high notes with telepathy – okay, she could hit them without his help, but she'd told him it was the same when she watched him on stage. It was definitely true that his performance stank way less if she was in the audience.

Dylan watched Flo belt out Elijah's rudimentary lyrics, felt her anguish that singing, like acting for him, would only be a hobby or side hustle, not how they made a living, even though it was her reason for living. These were the moments he understood her best. Everything was about that stage. She was in another realm. He was the same when she watched him, too – taken away, possessed by the person he was meant to be.

Once they'd taken their bows, Elijah and Flo went to chat with the entertainment manager while Dylan made his way over to Estelle and . . . who was it this time? He recognised a couple. Vérité, definitely, maybe Bea too, Toby, yes, and . . . was that Binky? No, Buffy? He wouldn't use names, just to be sure. Flo's circle of friends was largely intact since their days at one of London's poshest and most academically brilliant schools, and like the cast of a theatre company, different people became main players in rotation, depending on popularity, usually decided by Estelle.

'Dylan, how are you?' said Estelle, not waiting for a response. 'Flo said you have a new acting job. Can't wait to hear about it!'

'Well, not quite . . .'

'You know, Barnaby and I were talking to this splendid guy who's an understudy in the West End. We were wondering, maybe you could try that? Looks like terrific fun.'

Shame there were no walls nearby to hit his head off.

'Actually being an understudy doesn't just happen, it's a very coveted—'

'I'm sure you'll get something worthwhile soon.' Estelle impatiently thwacked her gloves into her palm. 'She was amazing, wasn't she? Even Elijah's song about strippers didn't drag her down.'

They'd been good, that was true, but Flo would've been much more amazing by herself, with her *own* material.

'Here she is!' Estelle called across the room to Flo, now in her specs and scanning the crowd for familiar hairstyles. Elijah hung behind, chewing gum. 'Floria! Floria!' Estelle's voice had a knack of getting everyone to turn round. Flo approached, face reddening, and patiently accepted air kisses before settling into a full smooch with Dylan. Estelle tittered sharply. 'Honestly, it's like a wildlife documentary.'

They disentangled, whereupon Dylan reached into his jacket, pulling out a bunch of tired-looking flowers.

Flo laughed. 'Oh *gorgeous*! Some actually look half-dead. Well done!'

Estelle gasped. 'I've never understood this horrendous flower ritual.'

Dylan winked at Flo. The first time he'd seen her play, he'd wanted to make a big gesture and almost emptied his account on a huge bouquet. She'd been grateful but confessed, 'I'm more a supermarket flowers kind of girl, don't worry.' Now, after every gig, he met her with a Tesco bouquet. The more pathetic the blooms, the more hilarious she found it.

Flo smiled brightly at her friends. 'Thank you for coming.'

Estelle smiled and smoothed down the sleeves of Flo's dress like she was her mother. 'Barnaby sends apologies; he's overseeing the dismantling of a giant snow globe.'

Dylan looked around at everybody's faces. Nobody flinched. Estelle's trust-fund boyfriend was king of disastrous start-ups, and always doing something strange in the name of brand awareness. 'How did it go?' he said. 'What did the bossman say?'

Elijah shrugged. 'There was, like, some feedback on costume. I wasn't really listening. Flo?'

Flo's eye twitched almost imperceptibly. 'Oh, fine,' she said, through a tight smile. 'Few things to iron out. He'll be in touch. Shall we?'

They stepped outside, all gasping at the cold January air, more out of habit than anything.

'Drink?' said Estelle. 'Quick debrief?' She saw Dylan checking his phone. Seven missed calls. Two furious messages, one all in capitals. 'Unless you have somewhere to be?'

Dylan shook his head without breaking eye contact. 'I have a prior engagement, work-related.' He could almost hear Estelle's eyebrow rising, like a creaking hinge. 'You go, Flo, I'll see you at home.'

He steeled himself for a quick round of gushing goodbyes, and Estelle's stiff, arctic hug – but Flo was already walking away, toward the Tube.

'I can't,' Flo called behind her. 'Sorry. Anyway, it's Fortnightlies this week.' The 'Fortnightlies' were their regular wine-fuelled catchup which, if he wasn't working at the bar, Dylan dutifully attended. Well, *endured*.

'But . . . I thought it might be nice.' Estelle looked hurt.

'Oh it would,' said Flo, blowing a kiss but not breaking her stride. 'I've got stocktaking at the shop tomorrow and Mummy might drop in so . . .'

'Okay, gorgeous girl.' Estelle's car keys jangled in her

hand; she didn't hang around for excuses. 'Sorry I can't give you a lift – you know I don't go east.'

Dylan locked eyes with Flo. There was more to this. He looked at his phone. Voicemail logjam. He sighed, running to catch up with Flo, snaking his arm round her waist, pulling him into her. Her coat smelled of her special perfume, the one she wore for best or, on occasion, sex; his body tingled in recognition. Then, as the light pouring from the station hit her eyes, he saw she was crying.

'What is it?'

Flo turned to face him, burying her head in his neck. She didn't make a sound but he felt the choking sobs. Finally, the heaving breaths became spaced further apart and she withdrew, her eyes swollen. 'They want me to dress . . . differently. More leg, he said, more . . . I can't even say it, I feel sick. *Tits* and teeth!'

Dylan felt his stomach tightening. 'I'll kill him. I'll rip his balls off.'

Flo flapped her hands anxiously. 'God, no, don't. It wasn't just that . . . he didn't like the material.'

'Why didn't you do more of your own stuff?'

Flo looked at the floor. Another swell of tears was coming. 'I didn't get a chance. Elijah knows the guy from . . . I can't remember . . .'

Dylan could hazard a guess they each had the same old school tie stuffed into a bedroom drawer. The only use Dylan's school tie had ever been was keeping his battered suitcase from bursting open. 'Please let me choke this man.'

Flo smiled but shook her head. 'I want to go home.'

Dylan held her close. 'Okay, let's go.'

'No, you have your party, it's important. Anyway, Lois will be waiting. We both know how she hates that.'

For the hundredth time, Dylan wished he'd never let slip that he'd briefly dated Lois at drama school; he could see the memory flash across Flo's face every time she said her name. But, Flo was right: Lois would be waiting and, yes, she really hated it. Right on cue, Dylan's phone vibrated again. He could practically feel Lois's anger – he was surprised he couldn't hear her, actually, bawling into her long-suffering iPhone with its shattered screen: 'Pick up, for chrissakes.' Everything would be fine. Important people were always late; important actors and directors even more so. Lois was prone to arriving so early to events, they'd often been mistaken for waiting staff – sometimes, Dylan was tempted to take the silver tray and earn a few extra quid.

But now he knew the truth about tonight, he didn't want to leave Flo's side. Plus, he needed to get into the flat before her and take down the crude homemade congratulatory bunting, not to mention unhook the booby-trapped door set to rain glitter as she entered. Tonight was not a night for glitter.

On the Tube, Flo rested her head on Dylan's shoulder, both ignoring the armrest prodding into their sides. He hated to see her like this. There was only one thing for it: happy place therapy. It worked every time. Kind of.

'Remember those narrow streets? All that walking?' He was trying to lure her memory back to their first holiday together, well, their only holiday together so far, as money was tight even before they moved into the flat. Santorini.

'You never let go of my hand all day.'

'Little day trips,' Dylan murmured, keeping his voice low, knowing she liked that. 'The beaches. Gazing at the horizon. I've never felt so free.'

Flo nuzzled in even further. 'So hot. So exciting. I don't think I'd ever enjoyed a couples holiday before then.'

Dylan kissed her forehead. His only foreign trips up to that point had been low-grade getaways in hostels; he was terrified of spending money on something you couldn't eat or wear until he met Flo. She'd been to Santorini before, with her family, and she'd inherited her dad's passion for wine. Dylan had been an enthusiastic student, he loved listening to her endless supply of facts and trivia, learning about his surroundings, the food they ate.

'You were so refreshing,' said Flo, as she always did. 'Treated me like an equal, no, let me take the lead. I thought maybe you were just some boy on his best behaviour.' She looked up now. Eyes locked. He was powerless. 'I thought eventually you'd have to drop the act, until I realised you were an actual nice guy, not a pretend one.'

Dylan blushed at the compliment. He still remembered that final night, word for word. What if they could stay there for ever, he'd said, what would they do? Dylan imagined running a tiny, cute hotel, teaching the local kids a bit of drama, while Flo could sing in a little café they would somehow manage to buy. 'I never realised *Mamma Mia* was such a big influence on me.'

Sitting on the balcony, a bottle of wine between them, the air had been thick with possibility. For a second, Dylan had wondered how Flo would answer if he proposed, shocked to find himself even thinking it. He'd taken her hand; she'd looked slightly terrified. 'I want it to be like this all the time. You make me a better person. You make me feel brighter. In a clever way, I mean. I'm always learning.'

She'd laughed and told him he *was* clever. 'When you're in the bathroom, I have to google some of the words you use.'

'But not about *stuff*. I'm not cultured. I don't travel. I'm, like, totally in awe of you, you know.'

'I know!' She'd laughed again. 'We've got the "same-seat promise" to prove it.'

'I can't promise every day will be like this.'

'I don't want every day to be like this. My hair can't take the sea water.'

'I'll put you first. And I'll cook!'

'What are you asking me, monsieur?'

'Can we save up? Move in together?'

Now, as their train chugged into their stop, she took his hand and whispered, 'I'm so glad I said yes.'

Dylan tried to get ahead of Flo on the endless, twisty staircase that led to their tiny flat in the loft. Dylan and Flo often wondered how the landlord had managed to get all their furniture up it. They'd decided it had probably just grown out of mould. He pleaded with Flo to wait outside but she ignored him and flung the door open, bouncing straight into the lounge, in prime position for the bucket of glittery confetti – an eye-watering £5 from the grotty, antiquated post office on the corner – to tumble onto her head. She screamed, then laughed and picked up the bucket – originally used for a fried chicken takeaway two nights earlier – emptying the last of the shiny stars, hearts and crescent moons over herself.

'I washed it first,' said Dylan. Flo's eyes took in the hastily pinned-up, homemade bunting, trying to work out what the shapes were supposed to be. 'My attempt at Grammys,' he said, embarrassed by his lacklustre art skills.

Flo smiled. 'And these?' She pointed at another string of newspaper bunting, little statuettes breaking up the word

C O N A G R A T U L A T I O N S – only now did Dylan notice the extra 'A'.

'Oscars. I couldn't remember what Brit awards looked like and my phone was out of data.'

'Love it.'

'I wish there was reason to celebrate.'

'There is.' She walked the four short paces it took to cross their living room and planted an exaggerated smacker on his lips. 'Let's celebrate that I'll never gig at that shitty hotel.'

She was clearly still replaying the conversation with the creepy manager in her head, but Dylan felt her decompress as she sat on the sofa and sipped her beer, pretending to be engrossed in the TV. This wasn't the first disappointing gig she'd had to recover from: he knew to leave her alone for a good half hour. He stood in the kitchenette along one wall of their poky living area, with its sloping ceiling that sometimes felt like it was pinning them to the carpet. They'd done what they could with lighting, and throws – Flo borrowing her mother's interior-design ethic of 'cover it in fabric and hope nobody notices how uncomfortable everything is'. Not that Flo would ever let her mum see the place. Any FaceTime conversations took place by the window, sky being the one backdrop her mother couldn't criticise. Despite their best efforts, it was still a hovel, and not even in a romantic way. There was a sign on the letterbox saying NO JUNK MAIL, but in truth a few leaflets and a selection of takeaway menus might have livened up the place. But it was all they could afford – well, all *Dylan* could afford, once they'd agreed on splitting all bills, with no help from anyone else. Dylan wanted one place where he could shut the door and leave Flo's parents' chequebook on the other side.

Dylan's phone throbbed one last time. He'd deal with Lois tomorrow. He looked at the clock, pulled the last two beers out of the fridge, handed one to Flo, and slumped onto the sofa, reaching down for Flo's guitar. Time was up.

'Let's do a top five.'

Flo shook her head. 'Not really in the mood.'

Top Five was a game they'd play during any lull in conversation, waiting for their starter in a restaurant, or when sick of watching TV. Anything could be a top five: top five drinks you could never touch again because they reminded you of a hangover; top five actors you'd want to tell you your label was sticking out of your jacket; top five ice-cream flavours; top five excuses for being late. It also came in handy if one of them needed lifting out of a bad mood. It had never failed Dylan yet. 'Go on. I'll make it easy. Top five things to do if you're bored. Free things, I mean. No scooting off to Mexico on a private jet.'

Flo hesitated, considering resistance. 'Okay.' Result. 'In at five, read a book.' This was true. Flo was never far from a stack of novels. One pile doubled as a bedside table, and was home to coffee mugs and yesterday's chewing gum. 'And four, that'd be . . . I was going to say TV but I hate TV.'

Dylan pretended to thwack her with a cushion. 'What if I'm on it?'

He was glad when Flo shrugged away the obvious answer, that he never was, and said, 'If you're on it, I would love TV. Obviously. I'd superglue my eyes open. Okay, so long as Monsieur Dylan Fox is amid the *dramatis personae*, number four is watch TV.'

'Right. Three?'

'Cook. Anything. It's therapeutic. Even making a sandwich.'

'Does that mean . . . ?'

'No, I'm not making you a sandwich. As for two, that would be sex.'

Dylan gasped exaggeratedly, like he was fourth row from the back at the panto. 'Only number two? Sex with me – actual *moi* – is in second place?'

'Yeah, if I'm bored, I'm not always horny. What if you're not here? Number one always has to be available. That's what makes it number one.'

'Horny? Lovely.' He knew where this was going. 'And in top spot?'

'Um . . . well, number one is to play a song. Sing, I mean.'

Dylan applauded and grabbed her guitar from beside the sofa. 'Ding ding ding! You win the special prize. Play something. For me. What you working on?'

Flo pulled a face – an automatic reaction of modesty, not because she didn't want to play. 'Go to the party. Isn't some big director going to be there?'

Dylan imagined the bollocking he'd get from Lois for standing her up, and his agent, Priya, for not flinging himself in front of influential people enough. Regardless, Flo's sad face needed fixing. 'Lois texted, said it was a bust,' he lied. 'She's the most famous person there.'

Flo's face brightened. 'I've got the bones of something but . . . it's not good.'

She always said this; she was always wrong. 'If you'd rather not, I understand.' He pretended to reach for his phone, knowing she'd rather play him something crap than watch him disappear down a social-media wormhole.

She played a verse and the beginnings of a chorus; Dylan was rapt. It was a song about letting time slip through your fingers, trying to grasp what you really want.

'Well?'

Dylan thought carefully before he responded; he didn't want to explain her own song to her or steer her off course. 'I sense disappointment. Wistfulness.' He knew what it was about, but didn't want to say. 'Like a . . . like a heart crying out to be noticed. Am I right?'

Flo nodded.

'I wish you'd ditch Elijah. Sing this stuff for yourself.' He'd told her many times she was too loyal for her own good.

'I know. I've known him a long time, and . . . he's not too bad, really.'

Elijah was bearable and nothing more. At least he'd finally given up asking Dylan if he could score any weed in time for his next twee middle-class music festival.

'This isn't autobiographical, or anything,' said Flo, idly tapping her guitar. 'Just channelling my . . . frustration into something people will relate to.'

'It's brilliant,' Dylan replied, truthfully. 'Pop it on your YouTube? Little acoustic number?'

Flo snorted. 'My seventy-four followers don't want rough cuts. Well, except the one who keeps commenting "Feet pics? *Please?*" under everything I post.'

'This very keen follower does.' Dylan picked up his phone and stood to adjust the lamp with the knackered-but-charming velvet shade that they'd rescued from a jumble sale. It threw off the most flattering light; Flo was bathed in a warm and welcoming glow. 'We don't have to publish if you don't like it.' He saw her make her mind up, sitting up straight, smoothing down her eyebrows, sweeping fallen strands of her hair behind her ears. 'If all else fails, I'll film your feet for half an hour. Ask for donations.'

'It may come to that,' she laughed, waiting for his nod before starting to play.

There was always a certain energy between the two of them when Flo played her music at home. Super-charged. It wasn't unusual for one or both of them to get a little hot under the collar and, sure enough, each made their move and they had sex on the sofa. 'I know it sounds corny,' said Dylan, unable to stop the words tumbling from his mouth, reddening with every syllable, 'but . . . that was incredible. Every time feels like the first time.'

Flo laughed so hard she started coughing. He laughed too, but felt silly. He knew he shouldn't have said it.

'It *does* sound corny.' Flo reached for a cushion and lightly thwacked him with it, sensing his embarrassment. 'Never stop telling me what you're thinking, even if it's factually incorrect.'

'How do you mean?'

'It's definitely not like the first time, thank God.' Flo sighed at the memory. 'Remember . . . after . . . I was still trying to get my head straight and wondering what to do next, like should we snuggle, should I go home, fix my make-up or . . . whatever.'

'Yes?'

'You came back from the bathroom and you'd put on this . . . I don't know, like a Cyberman helmet, and you walked into the bedroom and said you were grateful for our "earthly intermingling" but you had to return to your home planet.'

'Oh. Shit, sorry. That was Max's, of course, not mine.' Dylan cringed, remembering Flo's horrified face as she gathered the covers right up to her neck, the joke not landing as he'd hoped. He always did that, got nervous around big feelings, so made a joke. 'Maybe it's like the second time, then?'

'Yes, just like it.' She laughed. 'One question, though . . . when you were . . . I'm not sure you realised, but just then, when you were about to come . . .'

'What?'

Flo chewed her lip. 'It was pretty weird but . . . why on earth did you shout out "salubrious"?'

Two.

Flo loved to tell people the story of how they met. Not because it was especially romantic, or even unlikely, just that it was different from everyone else's origin story. All her friends had been matched up by antsy parents, forced into uncomfortable fours at supper clubs, or had met at weddings, with table plans more carefully orchestrated and agonised over than the mobilisation of troops on D-Day.

She still remembered, crystal-clear, looking up as she heard the tinkle of the bell above the shop door – usually a major irritant – and being surprised not to see the regular kind of rich, thin person searching for artisan candles or bamboo yoga wear. Instead, the universe had brought her Dylan, slightly awkward-looking, but very handsome, eyes darting all over, trying not to look at the fitness gear, or the crystals, or the dainty pottery, in case he accidentally committed to buying it with eyes alone. He needed a good luck card, he said. So quaint. She'd directed him to the small display of greeting cards and notelets, all made by people her mother knew, and stocked as a favour. She was glad she'd dusted them that morning, but noticed one or two yellowing at the corners. Thankfully, her mother had already stopped calling by the shop. He picked the most feminine of the lot, she'd noticed with a tinge of regret that surprised her. The best part was, he seemed to notice, because he quickly told her it was for an ex – Lois, she now knew.

They talked a little: he worked in the bar opposite, the Consulate. Not his kind of place, but his best friend was manager and gave him time off for auditions – an actor! This information wasn't being volunteered just to make conversation; this man – no names exchanged yet – was showing an interest. She'd never been in the bar before; Flo's mum called it a 'joint', like it was a strip club or seedy disco, not a fairly boring place popular among pleasant, if air-headed, west Londoners.

That night, Flo sailed past bronzed millionaires, beaming starlets, and a few boorish lads who'd mistaken cocaine for a personality, walked up to the bar and, juddering with nervous energy, held out her hand and said, like they'd seen each other only seconds earlier, not hours, 'By the way, I'm Floria, but you can call me Flo.'

'Enchanté.' His face had broken into a broad grin. 'I'm Dylan. Call me whatever you want. What can I get you?'

Boom. They'd both felt it, they confessed later. Proper thunderbolt stuff, she'd always say when telling it. Flo had read about this kind of relationship in the novels she used to hide under the counter at the shop during quiet spells; love like this wasn't meant to come until later, in her thirties, maybe, getting over a divorce from some controlling bastard. She wasn't supposed to meet The One, not now. Her twenties were for torrid affairs with colleagues, but she had no colleagues other than Martha, who worked weekends, was sixty-three and said her only true loves were HRT and her convertible Golf.

Her twenties were for crying over fuckboys in alleyways behind nightclubs, before making up in the same alleyways with slobbery kisses of beer and cigarette ash. Most girls from school who weren't on extended gap years spending their parents' money were making a fist of it with 'some guy' in a flat in Fulham and pretending it was for ever. A few were already replete with shimmering diamond engagement rings posted on social media, usually at Christmas or on a special occasion originally reserved for something else. Almost every Sorrento holiday pic, yachting weekend video, or – ultimate sin – breathless, badly filmed reportage from someone else's wedding, ended with the same hunk of sparkly rock on manicured fingernails, coy smiles and relieved eyes acting as a frame to the deceit. Most of them wouldn't make it down the aisle at whichever country pile they planned to commandeer.

Dylan was different from all these men. He wasn't suave, like other boyfriends had been; he was unrefined. She didn't mind. He was still wearing Lynx Africa under his cologne when they met. She wasn't sure which part of Africa it was trying to conjure up – although it did smell uncannily like the toilets in Johannesburg airport. She and Dylan had the real thing.

Estelle always said this origin story sounded 'a bit basic' and joked that 'as chance meetings go, "he worked in the bar directly opposite" isn't up there with *Love Actually*.' Nor was Estelle and Barnaby's story, to be fair – they'd bumped into one another at a mutual godparent's funeral, Estelle relaying the encounter to rapt friends like it were a lost Jane Austen chapter and not rather cold-blooded and depressing. Estelle had been starting out as a content creator, before she pivoted to working part-time at her mother's PR agency and writing her memoir; Barnaby had helped Estelle film a sad monologue at the graveside, seconds after the last clods of earth had been dashed onto the casket. A ring was presented two New Year's Eves ago, Estelle's vintage tea chests arrived on Barnaby's Kensington doorstep not three months later, and they were now in the embryonic stages of planning a very antiseptic, tasteful wedding, just as soon as the kombucha range from Barnaby's brewery start-up took off.

Updates on each came regularly, at the Fortnightlies – the gang's regular catchups. These were a sixth-form tradition, when they would stow regular clothes in their school bags, take a Tube a couple of stops, and try to get served alcohol in places where nobody knew them, or would look the other way. Estelle kept them going, even while much of the crew was away at university, and as they settled into their twenties and their careers – or not, in Flo's case – they'd just . . . continued. Attendance figures fluctuated, and with social media there was barely any news to share that hadn't already been blogged or posted, but Estelle never missed one. She'd pout and demand explanations on WhatsApp if anyone else did. It was easier just to go. Flo enjoyed them, really, seeing friends she'd known for ages face to face. Someone was always up to something, or doing an exciting job, or back from a lovely holiday, usually where they'd behaved terribly – she'd always feel Dylan tensing up during those stories – or had met someone interesting or, in Estelle's words, useful. Dylan and Flo didn't get out much together in the evenings – he was either working or pursestrings were tight, so he'd come along, just to spend time with Flo. Not everybody brought partners – after a couple of sessions, some would suddenly find they had 'prior engagements', the in-jokes, incessant grilling and Estelle's well-meaning and apparently ceaseless suggestions on how they could improve their life getting too much for them. That's how Flo knew Dylan was a keeper; he'd managed three years of it, although it never stopped being a struggle.

'Can't they ever go somewhere normal?' Dylan said, as they got ready for this week's, Flo cross-legged on the floor doing her make-up in the cracked full-length mirror. He sat on the bed and yanked hard at his laces. 'I think Barnaby and Estelle like having waiters to click their fingers at.'

Flo hated it whenever they did that, but they weren't used to waiting, that was all. 'Barnaby knows the guy that runs it. They're thinking of having an event there for his . . . uh.' What was it? Something you wouldn't normally drink more than a thimble of unless at gunpoint. Alcoholic soy sauce? No, that wasn't right. 'He's launching a drinking vinegar, we're . . . scoping out the venue.' She watched Dylan fret over his hair in the tiny hand mirror – also cracked, they really needed a trip to Ikea – before he came and kissed her on the cheek, his way of letting her know he was ready to go. He went through to the lounge – six paces, she counted – and sat on the sofa, its springs squeaking in recognition.

'Jonesing for free drinks, more like. All this back-scratching, and putting a good word in, scoping things out, it's not very you.'

He was still so intimidated by her friends – they were all lovely once you warmed to them, but this was turning out to be a very slow thaw.

'Estelle's very focused, driven. She's always been good at giving people a swift kick up the bum and sometimes I need that,' she said. 'And no, it isn't very me, but it's very them, and they're my friends so . . . we can't all be the same.' Flo was cool with this; she loved her friends, she didn't want to be just like them. They weren't of the same world, anyway. Flo's parents were comfortable, yes, and she'd grown up in a decent-sized house in the leafier, more desirable part of Chiswick, but they didn't have generations of cash on both sides, proper lineage. This had made her stand out at school. Other people's parents had slobbery labradors that moulted everywhere and nobody seemed to mind, the furniture in their houses was older than Stonehenge, their cutlery inherited. Flo had heard the word 'arriviste' for the first time when she was eight. She worked out later the girl who said it hadn't come up with it by herself; it had been overheard over three-course dinners, eaten off Grandma's china, across a table older than time. Estelle's father had gone to Eton. Had she not taken Flo under her wing, things could've been very different.

'Focused and driven? Interfering and controlling, you mean. I wonder what career advice I'll get tonight.'

'They mean well.' This never convinced him. 'Tell them you're through to the second round for the . . . um, the hospital drama! That'll shut them up.'

'God, let's not jinx it.'

'It's brilliant news and should be shared! But okay.' Flo did her finishing flourishes, knowing Dylan was watching – he always did. The flat was so small she could practically feel the heat of his skin against hers.

She hoped they'd lay off Dylan a little tonight. They mean

well, they mean well, they mean well. She kept repeating the mantra, fully believing it, but she realised now she shouldn't have told Estelle about Dylan's new job.

Even for Estelle and Barnaby, this was swish. Dylan's eyes bulged as he took in chandeliers and gleaming mirrored surfaces as they were escorted to their table. Dylan had waited enough tables to know that staff in places like this usually loathed their customers, so he always tried to show them he was 'normal', by being slightly overfamiliar. It never worked. In time Dylan came to enjoy the inevitable flinch as he called them 'pal' or 'lad'. He looked up. The ceiling was ridiculously ornate but the acoustics weren't great — rather than the gentle hum of chatter, he kept hearing sharp snatches of conversation from other tables. Business deals, expensive fixer-uppers, light backstabbing — it was all happening. Here be rich people. Flo didn't like it when he called her friends or family 'rich'. It had come up very early on; he was surprised by the forcefulness of her protest.

'We don't have that much money,' she'd said, clutching imaginary pearls, Dylan noticed.

'You went to private school. You had your own piano. Your mum and dad have a holiday home.'

'Yes, but only in Cornwall . . . why are you laughing?'

Now, instinctively, he reached for Flo's hand and squeezed, winking as she looked back. He'd already told Flo on the way that he wasn't drinking tonight because he wanted to get up early for yoga, then go see Priya for a pep talk. He was sure she knew the real reason, that drinks here would be expensive, or he didn't trust his tongue to be too loose around this lot, but she never let on. The usual faces awaited them; some he recognised, others . . . he wasn't sure. They all looked and sounded the same: the boys lined up in thick jumpers or tight, fitted shirts, showing off the kind of sculpted bodies that only a daily pummelling from an expensive personal trainer could provide; the girls rosy-cheeked and smiling, looking him up and down with that same curiosity they had all those years ago. Fliss and Flick and Midge and Ted and Bea and Sandro and Struan and Vérité and Vicca and Ludo and AnnaMaria and . . . whoever. Their names sounded like ironic club nights in Walthamstow. Eventually, he got to Barnaby, who pulled him close, drawling, 'Dylan, my man, good to see you.' Dylan had never been anyone's 'man' until he met Barnaby. Elijah lurked behind, cocking his pint glass in acknowledgement.

Tonight he felt relatively up and buzzing about his audition – but Dylan was always alert on these nights. Barnaby was the alpha here, no question. Unlike the other weak-chinned chums, Barnaby oozed cool. He was handsome, lithe, and perma-tanned from endless summers spent 'working remotely' from villas belonging to friends of friends of friends. Instead of concentrating on property like his 'old geezer' – he was fond of appropriating working-class vernacular, even though he'd grown up two streets from Knightsbridge – he'd helmed a series of start-ups. Team-building trampolining weekends, hiring fake paparazzi to follow you about shopping, dog roller-skates – there wasn't much he hadn't tried out of sheer boredom, blazing through family cash like diarrhoea on a campsite. He'd settled on craft beer and other fashionable drinks, making a decent go of it – not that it mattered if he didn't; there was still a healthy property portfolio in his back pocket.

Dylan hoped, early on, that Barnaby and Elijah might be his allies. He'd met plenty of posh people before – drama school had been full of them, after all – and reckoned it wouldn't be too hard to assimilate and lose himself in a world built on back-scratching and borderline-illegal tax avoidance schemes. He even tried dressing like them, but cosplaying was harder than it looked. Plain, expensive fabrics hung differently on their bodies, weaned on relaxed holidays and fed organic goodies by a series of weary au pairs. His cheap imitations made him feel a fraud. He even tried growing his hair, but it didn't fall over his face in quite the same way Barnaby's did. Bone-structure issues. Not the right shade of golden brown, either. It pained Dylan to think, as he often did, that had Barnaby showed the slightest interest in acting, he'd very likely already be an Oscar contender on looks and spunk alone. And even though they didn't come right out and say it, his face, and voice, didn't fit anyway. Barnaby, Elijah, Estelle, all of them, they had no understanding of what it might mean to come from more humble beginnings. There were always familial spare rooms to crash in, random well-connected godparents, connections to be exploited, and banks of Mum and Dad to be emptied. Once, early on, he'd made the mistake of mentioning his mum had money problems, and how he felt guilty not being able to help. They'd looked back blankly. One of them had said, 'Can't your sisters pay her mortgage for a month or two?' He had to point out his mother rented, and his sisters didn't have that kind of money. They absorbed the information like it was alien data, then moved on, uninterested in problems that one sentence of half-baked advice couldn't fix.

*

Barnaby handed Dylan the sparkling water he'd asked for, with a raised eyebrow. 'So Estelle was telling me you've got a job taking kids for a walk round the city?'

Mediocre news travelled fast. Dylan refused to be flustered by Barnaby's tactlessness. 'Not quite . . . It's an immersive experience; I play a demon gatekeeper, sharing scary stories and terrifying tales at the most haunted and gruesome parts of London.' He'd rehearsed the patter from his starter pack to perfection. 'I'm enjoying it. So far.'

'Cool.' Barnaby and Estelle spoke in unison. Barnaby nodded. 'So you're a tour guide? And you dress up?'

Dylan had managed to negotiate the uniform down from full plastic prosthetics, and dragging a foam ball and chain to something slightly more elegant – ghoul chic, he called it. He had a cape, a paler face, obligatory trickle of blood from the corner of his mouth and a gnarled walking stick which he could hold aloft for anyone trailing behind to spot easily. He was loath to play the diva, but the guy who'd vacated the position was a good foot shorter than Dylan and had no access to a washing machine. That cape had stories to tell – most of which would best be recounted around a campfire to a group of terrified scouts.

'It's not really about the costume,' said Dylan, still smiling. 'It's the experience, locations, storytelling. A good actor evokes character without props or wigs.' Dylan looked at Flo, who was beaming proudly. 'And I am good.'

Barnaby took this in, scratched his chin. 'Have you considered, and stay with me here, manifesting?'

Dylan held in a sigh so hard, his chest was going to burst. 'Manifesting?'

'Yep, me and Estelle do it all the time.' Barnaby flashed his million-dollar smile. 'You basically try to visualise what you really want. So you could . . . manifest a successful career.'

Estelle clapped her hands in delight. 'I can do you an affiliate deal on some crystals if you want. I'm sure there's one for a kind of career CPR in there somewhere.'

Barnaby laughed so wide, Dylan could see down his throat; he fought the urge to reach down it and tie a knot in Barnaby's windpipe. 'Like, I manifested the funding for Beer Babe by writing down all the things I wanted to happen, updating my mood board, and chanting. Estelle helped, the universe did the rest.'

Estelle grinned with what you might call sincerity if meeting her for the first time. 'It helps you focus, quite cleansing.'

Focused. Estelle and Barnaby loved that word, like the rest of the world was blurry and chaotic, except for them. Dylan remembered the launch of Barnaby's bizarrely sexist beer for women, in a shiny pink bottle which had half the alcohol of regular beer so they could 'keep up the pace'. There'd been as much free beer as you could drink – sadly it tasted like the backwash collected from the bottom of a can after a party – but Dylan didn't remember seeing 'the universe' there, just a load of people who looked exactly like everyone here tonight.

'I thought your dad helped with that,' said Dylan.

Estelle piped up: 'Yep, of course, but Barno's positivity made that happen.'

Dylan laughed, more from frustration than anything else. 'Barno holding out his hand for his dad's credit card made that happen!' This bounced off Estelle and Barnaby like ping pong balls; their privilege was invisible to them, and any criticism of it inaudible.

Sure enough, Estelle giggled. 'Maybe that moved things along. But seriously, Dylan, let me know about the crystals.'

Dylan breathed deeply. 'That's super kind, honestly.' He unclenched. 'But the job's great. The people are nice. Americans, mostly. They tip! Notes and everything.'

Another woman leaned over to contribute – Vérité, maybe? Meeker and slightly friendlier than the others, apparently 'very big in cupcakes'. 'Was just thinking, have you thought of settling for an advert or something? Until you catch your big break?' She smiled like a beauty pageant winner, evidently thrilled with herself.

Dylan felt his brain putrefy. An advert. Why hadn't he thought of that? How hard could it be? Christ. These people. 'Good shout.' Teeth reclenched. 'I'll look into it.'

Once the conversation moved on from picking apart Dylan's prospects, Flo felt it was safe to go to the bathroom. Estelle was waiting outside the cubicle, pretending to touch up her make-up in the mirror.

'The light in here's amazing. Shame about the hand dryers. I prefer a hand towel – at least you can hear yourself think as you dry. I'll have to tell Barno we can't have the launch here.' Her eyes met Flo's now. 'Elijah says you've turned down the hotel bar slot.'

'That's right.' Elijah telling tales. Sometimes Estelle could be quite headmistressy; she'd be a force to be reckoned with on the school run one day.

'I can see why you'd want to share as few stages with Elijah as possible, but influential people are always in there, someone might see you, offer you . . . a . . . recording contract or something.'

Just like Dylan could get an advert tomorrow, thought Flo, as she nervously ran her finger along the surface of the basin. 'It doesn't happen like that.'

'How does it happen, then? Success won't come knocking at the front door of your little flat.' Estelle applied lipstick for what must've been the twentieth time. 'You've never even invited *me* round – how is fame and fortune supposed to find it?' She stopped now, turning to face Flo. 'Dylan's job . . . I have to say something, are you okay with that?'

'Of course.'

'Is that really all he can get? I thought he was an actor.' Estelle had clearly been biting her tongue all night. Sometimes Flo could understand why Dylan wasn't a fan. 'I don't mean to be a hater, but, I could call myself a stained-glass-window restorer for cleaning the rose window above my staircase. Have you ever seen him in anything?'

Flo knew for a fact a series of underpaid, and quickly sacked, Eastern European women had cleaned the monstrous rose window in Estelle's cathedral to overpriced minimalism. 'You know I have. I go to them all. He's played a policeman in an Agatha Christie touring production! There was that little role in the West End thing that . . . closed.' Flo was accustomed to reeling off Dylan's CV to doubters. 'He was brilliant in that play at the Bush Theatre. And there was the Russian thing.'

She'd been dubious when he invited her to watch him act for the first time, in *The Seagull* at a community theatre. He was quite shy and reserved – what if he sucked? Would she have to lie, say he was great? Wouldn't it be major cringe to watch someone you fancied do a Shakespearean monologue (at that point she was unaware *The Seagull* was Chekhov)? She sat near the back, so if he was awful she could sneak out and claim an emergency. But he wasn't. Not remotely. He came alive before her eyes. His voice, face, body, all different, a blinding, brilliant light radiating from him, just for her. Any moment he wasn't speaking, she watched his lips, waiting for them to move. When he wasn't on stage, she missed him like he'd gone off to war. She ordered a copy of *The Seagull* in the interval and swore one day she'd get him to read it to her, naked.

'All I'm saying is it seems very co-dependent.' Estelle buffed her nails, enjoying acting the great sage; her Instagram captions read like they were co-penned by Nostradamus. 'The two of you holed up in romantic squalor.' Estelle saw Flo's face fall and took her friend's hand. 'I don't mean to have such sharp elbows, but what creative outlet do you have other than your little gig with Elijah? You need someone who motivates you.'

'He does! Dylan's more supportive of my music than any other boyfriend I've had!' Every guy she'd dated was jealous her attention was elsewhere, or accused her of fancying Elijah, which was ridiculous – he looked like a haunted apple. Even exes who'd liked her music had critiqued her lyrics, or tried to educate her on their favourite genres, wanting to make her into someone else. Most men looked at Flo as unfinished, someone to be moulded. Dylan was different, he respected her artistry, stood back and watched her grow. Around the third or fourth time they met, before they'd even kissed, Dylan had surprised her by coming to see her play. He enthused about her songs, quoted lines that really moved him, and even managed to be polite about Elijah's backing vocals. He'd really listened; his face shone with pride, even though they hardly knew each other.

'But those other boyfriends were stable, they could look after you, let you be a free spirit, a creative.' Free spirit. Right. Dylan hated this 'follow your dreams' ideology that people richer than Croesus liked to spout; Flo was coming round to his way of thinking.

'I don't need looking after. I like my flat.' Okay, this was a lie but she was damned if she'd let Estelle know that. 'Dylan has a huge audition, for TV, he's through to the second round . . .' She stopped herself. Too late; Estelle's ears pricked up.

'Television? Primetime? Speaking? Or dead body number three in a daytime drama?'

Flo hurriedly explained *City Royal*, that Dylan's part was a small one, but semi-regular. 'It's massively popular.'

Estelle nodded. 'Oh yes, my cleaner watches it.'

Zing. Flo smiled at two women coming into the loos. 'So you see . . . things are great.'

'Fine. I'll work on manifesting that part into existence for him.' Estelle grabbed her bag, dignified in defeat, if nothing else – probably because she knew this wasn't over. 'I worry for you.'

This side of Estelle, Flo loved – beneath her brutality, there was a huge heart. 'Please don't worry. And don't tell anyone else about the audition. Let's get back before Midge suggests Dylan "has a go" at being James Bond.'

They got a cab – Flo pretended she had a voucher to stop Dylan's usual protests – and stopped round the corner from the flat so they could get a kebab. Something highly calorific from an orange polystyrene box was the perfect palate-cleanser. Dylan got out first, walked round, and opened the door for her. Weird and old-fashioned, she knew, but she liked it. They ate in the window, Dylan squirting a mountain of ketchup over his chips, like he did over pretty much everything he ate. Flo reached over and slipped a couple of sachets in her bag.

The street outside still bustled with people dragging themselves home from the pub, stopping at the 24-hour shop for something encased in pastry, or the fruit and veg stall that seemed always open. Flo saw a man unzip his fly in a shop doorway and start to pee; she turned away. Dylan was in another world.

'You did very well tonight,' she said. Dylan smiled back and winked, but didn't say anything. 'Something big is coming your way soon.'

Dylan's smile faltered the tiniest trace; she'd given herself away there, she could tell, betrayed that tiny wobble in her confidence. Estelle always did this to her.

Dylan cupped her free hand with his. 'I know. I'm happy if you are.'

'I am,' she said, truthfully, but they were both glad when a distraction came along in the shape of a man being violently sick right outside the window. There was always somebody out there having a worse evening. 'Let's go home.'

Three.

When Dylan moved to London at eighteen to start drama school, he brought only three things: a suitcase of clothes he'd never wear again; the last £200 from his mum's savings, which he immediately spent on trainers and new clothes because even the most wholesome teenagers can't help but break their mothers' hearts; and his best friend Max. Max's parents hadn't taken the news he was gay as well as soap opera mums and dads did at that time. They tolerated it on the understanding it would go unmentioned, but Max couldn't live half a life. When Dylan asked Max to come with him, Max barely concealed his sobs as he said yes to going halves on a dream.

While Dylan was off doing what Max called 'pretending to be a tree and practising to take leading roles from more talented, gay actors', Max worked in some of London's worst bars, pubs and restaurants, toiling up the hospitality ladder until he found himself the manager of the Consulate, his basement bar kingdom in Notting Hill. Max's first hire was Dylan, and while Max refused to play favourites, Dylan's rota was generously skewed toward leaving him free for auditions, workshops, or day jobs to bolster his income.

Max was a true diamond, a staunch supporter, and huge fan of Flo, but even he had to confess their deep connection was creepy sometimes. 'You're like freaky horror-movie twins who feel pain when the other one cuts their finger over twenty miles away,' he'd said once. Dylan had tried to explain to Max that both he and Flo knew how it felt to have a natural talent and see it go nowhere and stay hidden, for their creativity to be thwarted by dull practicalities like bills and day jobs. Max had rolled his eyes so hard he'd given himself a migraine. He also had zero time for Dylan's self-pity when it came to Flo's friends.

'Not this again. If they hate you that much, tell them to fuck off,' Max said. 'Or can't Flo? I've never really understood why she doesn't fight your corner a bit more.'

'I can fight my own battles.'

'Oh yeah,' drawled Max. 'Your male pride. Always fascinating. Well, if you're too well brought up to middle-finger them, why don't you act like they're customers, turn on the charm.' Max swept his arm dramatically across the bar, looking a little tatty in places now, its early 2010s decor needing a refresh – lighting was kept dark enough to mask the wear and tear, yet bright enough to avoid someone breaking an ankle. 'In fact,' – he held up a glass to the light, scowled briefly at a smudge – 'in a way, they sound amazing. I love mega posh people who can't help but be, like, terminally rude.'

'Yeah, when you're taking their money,' said Dylan, flatly. 'I don't get paid for their Fortnightlies. Now I really need to get this job so I don't have to listen to them not-quite-say I'm a disappointment. I'd prefer it if they didn't talk to me.'

'Take it from someone who was mercilessly bullied at

school, a wall of silence hurts almost as much as a punch in the face; you wouldn't prefer it at all.'

'To make matters worse, we've got lunch at the parents' on Sunday. That's always stunning for my self-esteem.'

Mealtimes at Flo's parents' house were ceremonial. It was like they loved the idea of being 'into food', and what it said about them as people, rather than taking any joy from eating it. Flo's family always had ingredients in the cupboard – spices, pesto, oils, chillis. If they wanted, they could be halfway through making a stir fry, have a brainwave and say 'no, let's have risotto instead' and it would just . . . happen. Flo had been drinking a small glass of wine with dinner since the age of twelve. When Dylan was growing up, you got what you were given, and Tuesday night was always pie night, whether you liked it or not. Luckily, he did.

'Most bitchy people are looking for someone to scrap with, see if you match up,' said Max. 'Release your inner bitch, I can give you a crash course.'

'You've been doing that the last ten years.'

Max lightly socked his friend on the arm. 'Aw, pussycat. If it helps, I'm not disappointed in you.' Dylan smiled as he anticipated Max's imminent knockout punch. 'I always expected you to end up exactly where you are.'

'You're so wise, Maxy.' Dylan grinned at his friend. 'You love me though, don't you?'

'Only in the same way a mother has no choice but to love her very ugly, antisocial teenager.' Max batted him away and headed to his office. 'Right, paperwork awaits. Do you mind bringing a drink through?'

'Sure.' Dylan saluted at Max's departing backside and carried on setting up. He was lucky to have Max. Good friends were hard to find. Since moving to London, he'd struggled to make any outside drama school, except, before he let his membership lapse, the odd gym buddy – which Max found hilarious. 'A gym buddy is something else entirely in my world. Are you sure he's not after some extra protein?'

Dylan's phone buzzed. It was supposed to be phones off when working, but Dylan had persuaded Max he needed his on 'in case news comes about an audition'. Unfortunately this had led to a mini-mutiny, with the other bartenders claiming they too had a burgeoning acting career. Dylan squinted at the screen. Uh-oh. Lois. She was on her way.

Max hollered from his office. 'Dolly Daydream! My drink! Please?' Maybe Flo didn't have it so bad after all – at least Estelle wasn't her boss.

'I'm just gonna come right out and say it,' said Lois, as if she'd ever done any different the entire time Dylan had known her. 'You and Flo are, like, the two laziest pieces of shit I've ever seen. Y'know, when it comes to giving up, you two are fucking Olympians.' Dylan looked round to see if anybody had heard her. All heads were turned in her direction, as usual. Thank God the bar was still quite empty.

'Well . . .'

'I mean, if I can continue . . . if I may be so bold as to remind you, when me and my mom left Illinois for LA, when I got my first part on *Lucy Lemon's Tea Party Playtime*, and it was a fucking bomb, and I was out on my frilly birthday party dress ass, you think we gave up? Shipped back to Illinois to take the fucking shame and watch my poppa make little sculptures with his toe crud, the lazy sonofabitch? Hell, no, we stayed. It was shitty, boy, was it shitty.' Dylan had heard this story a hundred times but it never became less mesmerising. She'd told it, louder than this, that first day of drama school, when almost everyone else had ignored him once they'd worked out his background wasn't dynastic – he was from the wrong family of Foxes. Lois had no lineage or leverage either; all she had was good old-fashioned burning ambition and a work ethic honed working long days in the background of hundreds of kids' TV shows in Hollywood, before escaping to London to learn her craft.

'So Flo had a bad gig, who doesn't? What use is crying? She should try standing closer to the microphone too; she can't project. No news from your audition? Why you just waiting? What's Priya said about your chances?'

'She said she believes in me. And I'm not lazy, I have a new job, remember.'

Lois laughed. 'I believed in Santa and he hasn't come down my chimney in a looooong time. Don't tell me you're happy wandering London waving a stick and dressed like a Disney-fied Grim Reaper. You ain't never gonna get famous that way, unless you murder someone.'

'I don't want fame, and neither does Flo, for that matter. We want success. No shame in that.'

'You gotta measure your success somehow, and fame's a pretty good indicator.' Lois slammed back her drink and gave the come-hither for another. 'You're an enabler. You and Flo enable each other. You fuck up an audition, she can't write songs cos she's consoling you. She has a bad night, you miss out on a fucking A1 party, full of the best-connected assholes in Theatreland, and I'm stuck having my tits stared at by a guy with, and I'm being hella fucking serious here, zero chins, like nothing, it went bottom lip to collarbone – total no-fly zone in-between.' Having cut her acting teeth in the land of sculpted jawlines and naked ambition, Lois couldn't relate to the watery-faced men masquerading as hunks the UK had to offer. 'Remember us at drama school, the only ones with talent, like true talent, especially you, and those pricks couldn't handle it, and we said we'd show 'em . . . ?'

Together, they'd laugh at their classmates who insisted on calling the National Theatre 'the Nash', and share fantasies about beating them all to their dream roles.

'I remember.'

'What's your delay? You're the only guy from class with true potential, like start rehearsing an Oscar speech one day, y'know, but you're wasting it and that's a shame. Hell, that's why I dated you.'

Lois had been his first proper girlfriend – sharing a bed with Max for much of his early twenties meant Dylan's bed-post was scant of notches. After two months of exploring the sexual overspill from their emotional connection, the pair realised that, if anything, a friendship was more intimate and sustainable. That way they could support each other from the sidelines. A friendship was a greater honour than a sexual relationship, Lois always said. 'That way, you know they're hanging with you because they like you, not because they wanna jump your bones.'

Dylan reassured Flo there was nothing between him and Lois anymore. There never could've been, really – they'd clung to each other in times of need, against an unwelcoming crowd. But Flo always found Lois intimidating. This was fair; Lois had looked up the dictionary definition of 'femme fatale' and adopted it as her manifesto – the woman walked around with a cigarette holder at all times, just in case someone started watching her. Lois's rule was never to fuck actors. She broke it a lot.

'You *are* a lazy ass – like, you've had one audition and you're waiting to see how it goes, like it's the result of a CAT scan? Priya should be putting your pretty face in front of everybody, before that British beer belly of yours gets any bigger.'

'Look,' said Dylan, eager to do basically anything to stop Lois talking about his bodily imperfections in a voice loud enough to activate an Alexa three streets away. 'Tell me about this ad campaign.' Lois was soon to be unveiled as the face of a caffeine under-eye roll-on for a TV campaign and she couldn't be more pleased, adding it to the drama-school alumni WhatsApp before she'd even finished the acceptance call.

'I could be on the anti-wrinkle roller by Christmas, too. Maybe even one of the retinoid serum girls by the end of next year.'

'That sounds like a haemorrhoid cream,' said Dylan. 'You don't have any wrinkles!'

Lois swished her hair dramatically and sighed. 'That's the point, dickwipe. They won't cast someone who looks like they need ironing, will they? Anyway, back to you.' Lois's voice dropped to a more soothing level. 'I know you're scared of rejection, but promise you'll call Priya tomorrow? Assuming she's still taking your calls?'

Dylan sighed. This battering came from a place of love. He was scared. He didn't want to mess it up, be back at square one – not *even* square one; he was barely on the board. It felt nice to have someone in his corner, even if every compliment came with ten insults either side. 'Yes, she's taking my calls and, yes, I will.'

In the end, he didn't need to. Around an hour after Lois left, Priya called. It was a no from *City Royal*.

'They were so impressed, baby.' She sounded like she was telling the truth. 'But you're not right for this one. You made an impression, though.'

Dylan didn't know what to say. The thing with *nearly* getting jobs was you couldn't put it on a press release, or add it to your portfolio. He knew a guy they always called 'Last Two', because he claimed he got down to the last two for almost every famous male role you could think of. He wanted to hang up, but he thought of Lois, nagging him. 'Anything else on the horizon, Priya?' Other than sharks, he thought.

Priya sighed gently. He heard the tapping of her chewed biro on the desk. 'Your time will come, I can feel it.'

'Do you still believe in me?' Dylan was surprised to find himself choking back a tear.

Priya's throaty laugh filled his ear. 'Baby, if I didn't believe in you, this would've been a text, and in office hours. Sleep tight.'

Four.

Dylan was remarkably chirpy all morning considering they were visiting her parents for Sunday lunch. Flo's mum was not known for being chilled out at the best of times, but around Dylan, she had an officious air. Instead of her first name, Joy (the irony), she still insisted Dylan call her Mrs Battista, which was a mouthful and, Flo had to admit, with Dylan's Yorkshire twang, did sound a little like someone tugging their forelock. To Flo's delight, Dylan insisted on flattening his vowels especially for her.

'I still find it wild that you have a key, but we have to ring the bell so Mrs Danvers can come and greet us,' said Dylan as they stood waiting.

'Stop calling my mother Mrs Danvers. She'd be horrified at being compared to a servant!' Flo laughed. 'Mum doesn't like surprises. She enjoys monitoring the technique as you wipe your feet.'

Whenever they'd stayed at Dylan's mum's house together, Flo marvelled at the constant stream of visitors, barging in day or night, all there on some vague pretext. The kettle clicking on, fresh swirls of cigarette smoke, cling film being spread over and pulled off plates of beige food, the scraping of kitchen chairs on linoleum, raucous laughter or hushed tones of empathy. If she was in, Dylan's mum practically lived in the kitchen, not adjourning to the sofa until the soaps started. Flo once suggested to Dylan his mum's house should have a revolving door. He'd shrugged and said, 'She knows a lot of people, I guess. Sociable. Most people escape to London to find bustle and noise, but I never knew a minute's peace until I moved here.'

In a way, she was envious of Dylan's upbringing. It seemed much more relaxed and happy.

The door opened and Flo kissed her mother the way she liked, once on each cheek and then a bonus, always starting and ending with the left. An affectation from a year spent studying in Paris.

'Floria, darling.'

'Hello, Mum.' She saw her mother wince. Until meeting Dylan, she'd always been 'Mummy'. It felt ridiculous now.

'Dylan . . .' his name always stuck in her throat like linguine not chewed long enough, 'wonderful to see you. Come.'

Dylan smiled and sat on the love seat by the door. It wasn't for sitting or falling in love on; it was for taking your shoes off, lest you spoiled the immaculate carpet with the debris that clung to you from whichever dump you'd just come from.

While Joy did 'finishing touches to the table', Dylan and Flo had an aperitif with her father, who was his usual boisterous self, making inappropriate jokes about the week's headlines. Dylan never had to call him 'Mr Battista' – he was always 'just Charlie'. His measures were generous today, and he'd started without them.

'How's the flat?' he said. 'I lived in a dive, first couple of years at university.' He looked almost wistful. His grandparents had run a chip shop on the Byres Road in Glasgow, and even though he'd left his working-class background long behind him, he enjoyed these brief moments as a tourist. 'The key is to make sure you don't stay in them. Bed bugs aren't great at paying their share of the bills.'

Joy poked her head round the door and pulled a face like she'd caught a load of teenagers smoking in their bedroom. 'Starters are on the table.'

Flo noticed her mother watching as Dylan trapped a langoustine using a special fork that only made it harder to eat. Why did every meal together have to be a physical challenge?

'I bumped into dear Estelle in the foodhall,' said her mother. 'She looked radiant. She's done very well for herself with Barnaby.'

Flo tried not to take the bait. 'If you like that sort of thing.'

'They're such a good family.'

'Estelle once told me Barnaby's mother slaps her housekeeper.'

'You know your father is very friendly with the Downes. He could get you an internship if you just asked.'

How many times had Flo explained she didn't want to blag a high-stress career like other people from school, even her close friends? As a graduate she'd been introduced to many of her dad's rich pals – all looking for someone to harass in the stationery cupboard and pay buttons for the pleasure. It wasn't just that nepotism made her uncomfortable, she didn't want to become trapped, tangled in a security blanket. She was too scared to tell her parents outright that she really wanted a music career, but it hadn't escaped Flo's attention that the one influential person she'd never been introduced to was a record producer. That's why working at Joy's shop was perfect: enough of a leg-up from her parents to show she wasn't ungrateful or lazy, but casual enough to quit at a moment's notice, with zero guilt, should she ever get the chance to sing full-time.

Dylan crunched on his langoustine and winked. 'She's been writing more of her own stuff, you know, for the YouTube? To be honest, it's all a bit new-fangled for me, this interweb' – he nodded at Flo's dad – 'know what I mean, Charlie? But when you see the reaction she gets from people, er, tuning in, it's . . . *champion*.'

Interweb? Champion?! He was laying it on thicker than ever. Flo tried to hold herself together. 'Er, yes, I've been getting more views. Some wonderful comments from people who like my music.' Flo felt herself blushing. She hated having to justify herself. All those music lessons, the guitars, the piano; the Saturdays spent driving her to talent shows and open mic nights when she was a teenager. What did they think it had been for?

Dylan thumped the table gently. 'Call them what they are, lass.' Lass! Her mother was going to drop dead any second, she knew it. 'Them's *fans* them, love.' He turned to her parents. 'Mrs Battista, Charlie. She's doing great, magic.'

Joy swallowed her mouthful like it was arsenic and cardboard. 'Of course, Dylan, your mother and father are in the business, aren't they? I suppose you would know.'

Dylan plonked both elbows on the table, crockery and cutlery rattling in acknowledgement. 'That's right, Mrs Battista, they had a turn on the circuit for quite a few year.' A smile crept to the corner of his mouth. 'Up until the divorce, when it turned out my dad was giving other women equal billing, if you catch my drift.' He was enjoying himself way too much, but Flo silently spurred him on. 'Dad carried on the act, of course, they're still called Chase and Cheryl. Although obviously the bird . . . I'm sorry, Mrs Battista, I mean to say *young lady* he's with now, she isn't called Cheryl. Dad was too tight to change the posters, so they're stuck with it.'

Flo watched her mother's face, a picture of silent fascination, and dread. In Dylan, she saw the world she'd fought to keep Flo away from – showbusiness, seediness, depravity, sex on the sofa, mousetraps under the sink.

Dylan looked down at his plate, an absolute car crash. 'I guess I'm done.' He always finished a good five minutes before everybody else, like a starving orphan. The only thing missing was a loud belch and perhaps a doe-eyed smile as he held out his plate for more.

'I eat kind of fast,' he said. 'You had to be quick in our house, otherwise somebody would nick it off your plate.'

This was absolute bollocks, Flo knew, but was glad he'd somehow diverted her mother's attention away from setting Flo up with a miserable internship. She felt guilty though, that to take the heat off her he'd allowed himself to fall even further in her mum's estimation.

Out came the main course – a huge joint of lamb, Joy's masterpiece. Flo's heart sank, and not just because her announcement at age seventeen that she was vegan had been roundly ignored. Over the years, Flo had tried to persuade her mother that Dylan's habit of taking ketchup with pretty much every meal was not a sign of the collapse of society.

After months of hissing at each other *sotto voce* in the kitchen while Dylan and her father waited in the dining room, oblivious, Joy had finally allowed Flo to place a small silver bowl of ketchup in front of Dylan for his main course. Naturally, it had its own special spoon, no doubt sterilised after every use – seriously, where the hell did she find all this niche cutlery? Lamb days, however, were different.

Joy's lamb always came with 'the sauce', the recipe for which had been in Joy's family since the Norman Conquest and tasted like it had actually been stirred with the arrow that punctured King Harold's eye. In Joy's eyes, 'the sauce' was holy, and to take anything else with your lamb was, in turn, sacrilege. Dylan had encountered 'the sauce' a few times before, and it had always gone down like a cup of cold sick. He looked down at his plate, then up at Flo, then stared at the space where the ketchup would normally be. Flo's dad chatted amiably about another innovation in waste management, while Joy poured the sauce onto her plate, before passing the jug to Dylan without a word. Flo watched for any sign of triumph in her mother's eyes. Nothing. She'd have made an excellent poker player. Dylan took the jug and peered inside, before passing it along to Flo's dad.

'Toby Finnesbrough's back from Johannesburg,' said Joy. 'I saw his mother. That engagement didn't work out.'

Flo watched Dylan pretending to cut some lamb that she knew he wouldn't be able to chew, let alone swallow, without his ketchup. 'They never do with Toby. That's the third since we split up.'

Joy smiled like a supervillain. 'Some might say it's because he's never got over you.'

Flo kept her eyes trained on Dylan, moving food round his

plate like a toddler. 'More likely because once his girlfriends work out the passcode for his phone, they find filthy sexts from women he meets in bars, just like I did. Dylan, are you all right?'

Dylan gulped down his lamb like he was swallowing a housebrick. 'Yes, I'm fine.'

'Toby was a very nice young man; his mother says his wine business is really taking off. She's so proud of him, with good reason.'

'Oh, fuck this,' muttered Flo under her breath, reaching for her bag.

Dylan saw, eyes wide, and shook his head. 'Don't.'

'Toby was a catch, you might say. He could've married you, given you a secure future.'

'Mother. I dumped Toby five years ago. I was twenty-two. I didn't want to get married to anyone. I'm not Lizzie fucking Bennet.' Flo opened her bag, took out two sachets of ketchup from her stash and tossed them across the table at Dylan. 'There you go, monsieur.' Her mother's face was a picture; this would ruin her evening and Flo wasn't exactly sorry about that. 'And Toby's mother is delusional. He moved to Johannesburg because he'd fleeced everyone who knew him and sunk the cash into his shonky plonk company. The only thing Toby can't get over is that he never managed to get my PIN out of me.'

Dylan looked at the sachets like Flo had thrown grenades at him. 'I said it was fine.'

'Yes, but you were saying it to be polite. You don't have to be, we're family. Why shouldn't you enjoy your lamb like everyone else?'

Flo hadn't meant the 'family' mention to sound

provocative, but she could feel the electricity of her mother's outrage.

'The sauce, Floria, is also family, as I'm sure Dylan understands. We're not eating hamburgers.'

'Look, it's fine,' Dylan mumbled, sliding the sachets back toward Flo.

'No, it isn't.' Flo's heart was beginning to race. 'It's not even about the bloody ketchup, at all.' It was about Joy's every word and movement trying to say Dylan wasn't good enough for her, and it was rude and, most of all, hypocritical. When she was younger, Flo's mum told her she'd always dreamed of meeting a man who would never talk down to her from a horse, and rejected the well-bred androids with Habsburg chins that her family had set her up with. Her dad had had nothing, building up his recycling business from scratch, and making an absolute fortune with no help from any family members, or back-scratching, or networking, like Barnaby and his vanity projects.

'You know, Mum, every time I bring Dylan to this house you set a trap. Weird cutlery, food that has to be cracked open or scooped out, special sauces, steak cooked just the way he doesn't like it. Months of bickering over the ketchup until I had to beg you to let me put some on the table.'

Dylan coughed awkwardly. 'Months of bickering?'

'Yes – sorry, I didn't want you to know.'

Joy's face was stone. 'Nobody has ever complained about my cuisine before.'

Flo heard her dad sigh. He'd had a front-row seat for these showdowns for decades and they never got any easier to watch.

'Dylan doesn't complain, either. You treat him like something you've stood in, but he still comes back, still wants to be at my side. Takes all your crap, digs about our "poky East-End opium den", just for me. He doesn't try to impress you, he's just himself, every time. The first man I've brought home who wasn't a massive fake. Doesn't brown-nose you like Toby used to, or pretend to care about your shop, like Ollie did, or laugh about you behind your back like Xander.' Not strictly true, but Flo was on a roll. 'He doesn't even pretend to like your stupid sauce. He shows a strength of character you'd admire in literally anyone else, but you disrespect him again and again, like he's nothing, never achieved anything, but what have you done? Tell me that. All you did was get your rich husband to buy you a shop. Groundbreaking.'

They'd never had this argument in front of Dylan before. Alone, in the kitchen, passive-aggressively rearranging the dishwasher to their own standards, yes, plenty of times, but never like this. Dylan watched from his side of the table, looking small and lost.

'Your father wasn't rich when I met him.' Joy's talent was never looking remotely flustered under pressure, but she was cracking.

'No, but you saw the potential in Dad. Right? Y'know, one day, Dylan is going to be a huge star, I know it.' Dylan murmured something, but Flo couldn't stop herself. 'He's up for a part on one of the biggest shows on TV, *City Royal*, and his audition went amazingly. When he gets on TV, I'm going to have a crate of ketchup delivered to your front door, just so we don't go through this stupid pointless battle every time we come for dinner.'

Dylan mumbled something. It sounded like, 'Don't.'

'No, Dylan, *do*.' She turned to her mother. 'All this . . . every time. Just because he doesn't talk like us, and didn't go to a school you "know" and had never eaten olives until you literally forced him to, because you can't accept that not everyone is like you, or because the kind of work Dylan does isn't the right kind. It's pathetic.'

Dylan pushed his plate away. 'I don't need you to speak for me. I don't need you to big me up. And I wish you wouldn't carry spare sauce round with you.' He turned to Joy. 'Mrs Battista, you're entitled to your opinion of me, as low as it is. I only wish I could prove you wrong.' He looked at Flo now. 'I wanted to tell you, honestly. I was waiting for the right moment.'

Flo froze. Oh God. What was he going to say? Was he about to end it, right here, in front of everyone, like a final 'fuck you'? Why was her first thought that he'd cheated on her with Lois? 'Tell me later.'

'No, now. You're sitting there saying what a success I'm going to be, but it isn't true.' There was a sniffle. A tear? Or pepper in his eye from that sodding sauce? 'I didn't get the part on *City Royal*. It's over.'

For her part, if Joy saw this as a victory, she didn't show it. Charlie reached over and patted Dylan with one hand, knocked back his glass of wine with the other. 'Bad luck, pal, sorry to hear it.'

Flo pushed aside her plate. 'I'm . . . I'm sorry.'

'No,' sighed Dylan. 'I am.'

The clink of Joy's cutlery cut through the air. 'Floria, I just want to say . . .'

Suddenly, her father's voice: 'Right, that's enough, from

everyone.' Charlie stood slowly. 'Hand me your plates. I'm done with this lamb. Let's move on to pudding.' He picked up the sachets of ketchup and studied them closely. 'Can I keep these?'

Five.

'Went great tonight,' said Elijah through the usual mouthful of energy bar that he shoved down his throat as soon as the gig was over and they were in the dressing room. Well, dressing room might be pushing it; it was part-store room, part-airing cupboard that smelled of toilets and, inexplicably, pretzels.

Flo watched flecks of peanut shooting from Elijah's mouth to the lapels of her blazer and looked at her watch. If she left now, she could meet Dylan from the bar. He'd been so down since lunch with her parents, and he hadn't got tonight off from the bar because someone with a triple-barrelled surname was celebrating their 21st and it was all hands on deck. Dylan's seat had never felt emptier. In a bad mood for some reason, Elijah had played guitar like this thumbs had been cut off, posted to him and sewn back on, and her own performance hadn't exactly been stellar. She'd learned criticism bounced off Elijah, however, and the bar manager was a family friend, so she smiled and said, 'Lovely crowd.'

'We make a brilliant team, don't we?' Elijah took a slug from his huge, steel water bottle that he took to the gym with him. Flo had never seen him rinse it out, ever. She nodded vaguely in response; she didn't trust herself to speak. Dylan's absence tonight had inspired a new verse for a song she'd been stuck on; Elijah sapped her creativity to such a degree she was worried she'd forget it altogether if she didn't sing it into her phone right away. She was standing to grab her coat and make a sharp exit when there was a knock at the door. Narelle the barmaid stuck her head round the door. 'Someone to see you. About a gig?'

Elijah raced to the door. 'Excellent.'

Flo looked at her watch again. Dylan didn't know she was coming, so it would be no loss if she didn't make it. But still. 'Elijah, do you mind sorting it? I have to dash.'

Narelle looked like she would rather peel onions using only her acrylic nails than say what she was about to say. 'Um, well, he said, um, he asked for you, Floria. Well, he called you "the girl", so . . . I'm assuming it's you.'

Elijah looked momentarily downcast, but it wasn't unusual for people to ask to speak to Flo about arranging the gigs, especially if they were men – they'd usually try to chat her up in the process, like offering her their dog-eared business card was keying in the PIN to her heart. She could definitely skip this.

Flo shook her head. 'No. Just say I've gone. Elijah can cope.' She reached into her bag for one of their own business cards. 'I'm not spending the next half hour listening to some bloke tell me he loves my vocal range with his hand on my waist. He can either talk to Elijah or email.'

Elijah put hands on hips in mock affront. 'Come on, you're the master negotiator. Hang on, sorry, I mean mistress. Down with the patriarchy, right?'

One of these days some woman was going to hit Elijah over

the head with a frying pan; Flo hoped she'd be there to see it. No way was she pretending she was desperate for another gig with Elijah anywhere. 'Nope, sorry, I'm off to meet Dylan. He needs me.' She spritzed Coco Mademoiselle on each wrist, shook her hair out, pecked Elijah on the cheek, blew a kiss at Narelle, and slithered past to hotfoot it out the back exit. She was getting increasingly sick of dancing to Elijah's tune, let alone singing to it.

For Dylan, it had been one of those days: the kind where you burn your toast, can't find matching socks, no toothpaste in the tube. It rained during Dylan's first tour of the day, the wind so stiff it almost broke his stick in two. One teenager was sick into their bag on the Tube and a group of passing students had shouted that he was a Jack the Ripper apologist, which wasn't strictly true, as he didn't cover that area. At least, he thought, things couldn't get any worse. Fate had other plans. On his next tour, smiling beatifically alongside a small group of waiting Americans, were two very unexpected customers. Barnaby and Estelle.

Dylan prided himself on his warm welcomes – it helped with tips – but it would've taken a multimillion-pound lottery win to conjure up enough enthusiasm to appear pleased to see them. He painted on a smile. 'I don't remember saying your names three times in the mirror this morning and summoning you from the underworld, but I must have done.' As expected, the joke sailed over their heads. Flo was always telling him about Estelle's great sense of humour, but it seemed she kept it in the same vault as her empathy. They stared back, blankly. 'I didn't see your names on the list.'

'My PA booked it,' beamed Barnaby vaingloriously.

Dylan briefly imagined this poor assistant, saddled with

satisfying the whims of this dull-as-dishwater duo. Some people were born to have servants; it was a role Barnaby and Estelle relished.

'When you were talking about your new career move the other week it sounded the most delicious fun,' said Barnaby, with a crocodile grin. 'So me and Estelle thought we'd come cheer you on, bring a few peeps to swell the ranks and share the magic, yeah?' It transpired the rest of the group were families of some of Barnaby's US investors. They looked like they'd rather be anywhere else than in the London rain, following a man dressed as a vague approximation of Dracula, the Grim Reaper, and a normcore Ozzy Osbourne. Estelle addressed them like a primary-school teacher.

'This is our friend's partner, Dylan, he's an actor, and knows so much about the er . . . devilish deeds that happened in our wonderful city, so make sure you ask lots of questions and get involved, okay?' Her charges gave a low moan of agreement. She turned to Dylan and lay her gloved hand on his forearm just as it began to rain. 'We're only too happy to offer you this teeny bit of support, you know. I'll be telling them to leave reviews.'

Oh God no, the last thing he needed was a trial by misspelled online comments.

Estelle was still talking. 'You must be devastated about the audition for the hospital thingy. Flo told me how much this meant to you, how much was depending on it.'

Dylan's blood froze. Wasn't Flo supposed to have kept that to herself? He felt sick, and stupid, and exposed. Worst of all, he now had to look at Barnaby and Estelle's smug faces while he dragged a bunch of tourists around London's most haunted alleyways.

'Shall we get going?' Barnaby smiled brightly, showing off his perfect white teeth, one of many privileges he'd been born with – he'd never even worn a brace, he'd once said. 'I've been looking forward to this.'

I bet you have, thought Dylan, mentally reaching inside himself to switch off every emotion. He just had to get through the next hour.

Thanks to Estelle and Barnaby's instructions, the group had the laser-focused interrogation skills of an immigration officer, and left Dylan stuttering over everything. Unnervingly, Barnaby managed to be in his line of sight at all times, like a floater on his eyeball. At the end, Dylan was exhausted. He gracefully accepted a few tips – a father and daughter called Ken and Audra, who had him on the ropes with a series of baccalaureate-level questions about the Black Death, were the most generous, handing over a crisp fifty. Dylan felt elated as he prepared to wave them off, only for Barnaby and Estelle to stand lurking, going nowhere.

'Look, chap,' said Barnaby, in a voice that perhaps might sound comforting if your arm was trapped inside machinery and he was phoning you an ambulance, 'I've got a little *proposish* for you, bit of acting work. Thought it might be welcome at the moment.'

Dylan was genuinely taken aback. He began to have almost . . . romantic feelings for Barnaby in that moment. 'Go on.'

Estelle jumped in. 'It's a marvellous idea, you'll love it. Basically, I'm putting together some promotional webisodes for Barno's Beer Babe campaign and we're looking for a couple of guys to be in them.'

Dylan tried to keep a straight face; Estelle saying 'webisode' was one experience he'd happily never have again. 'Okay.'

Barnaby jumped in, excited. 'A few scenes, two kind of, like, lairy dudes perving on a couple of girls who match them drink for drink, eventually the babes realise the dudes aren't that bad, that they've only been acting macho to pull them. Everyone ends up drinking Beer Babe, or Beer Bro – the dudes will be, anyway.'

Babes, dudes, bros – what a chaotic blancmange of toxic masculinity Barnaby lived in. It sounded awful but adverts could be lucrative, and on the off-chance these two rich sociopaths had changed the habit of a lifetime and actually had a good idea, this could be worth a shot. Dylan broke into his best 'pick me' smile. 'This sounds . . . I mean, I appreciate the . . . shall I put you in touch with Priya to arrange terms?' Barnaby and Estelle both looked confused. 'She's my agent, you see.'

They nodded in unison. 'Gotcha, I see, yeah, sure yeah, see, thing iiiiiis . . .' Barnaby was doing that weird voice again. 'This is a no-budget situaysh, yeah? So we can't go through agents or anything because . . .'

Dylan tried not to let his face drop. 'There's no money. It's unpaid.'

Estelle nodded solemnly. 'Yep, but what's great is this will be everywhere, so people are bound to spot you and, like, wanna call you in for auditions, right?'

'Well . . .'

'Flo said you'd done things like this before, for free, is that right?'

Dylan couldn't breathe. He'd done Chekhov for free, not exactly the same thing. 'Flo said?'

'Yeah, we popped by the shop yesterday, ran it by her, she thought it was a great idea. Said you'd done a couple of weeks of physical theatre in Edinburgh for, like, experience? Or was it exposure?'

Exposure was right. On the promise of finding himself up close and personal with major casting directors he'd found himself naked but for a sock on his cock for the entire second act of a play at the Fringe, as a favour to someone from drama school who, it turned out, wanted to keep their connections to themselves. 'I've done free theatre before, yeah, but . . . usually they were . . . great parts.' He spoke slowly and deliberately, unsure of his feelings, trying not to scream. Flo had known about this yesterday. Never mentioned it in all the hours they were together last night. Had she known they would ask him this here, now, in front of a group of bored Americans, who'd all tipped him with greasy notes, like he was a backstreet pub dancer passing round a pint glass to a leering crowd?

'I can email over more deets,' said Barnaby. 'Would be great to have you on board.'

Estelle dispensed air kisses. 'It would mean a lot to Flo.'

Would it? Had Flo put them up to it?

'Elijah tells me they missed out on a potential new gig because Flo dashed off to see you – she's been worried about you.'

'Missed out how?' What was he getting the blame for now?

Estelle pulled a face as if recounting the story under pain of death. 'Well, somebody dropped by one of their gigs to offer them work and when Elijah went out to meet the person it was some woman. Reading between the lines, she didn't like the look of him and wanted to speak to Flo, but she'd already left, insisting she had to see you. The woman wouldn't leave a card. But anyway . . .' Estelle fingered his cape, her nails magically finding a hole. 'It would be fab to see you moving forward. Both of you. Unless of course . . .' Her painted nail drove through the fabric of the cape, making the hole twice its size. 'You're happier doing this?'

Dylan watched them glide away, a murmuration of arse-holes. Once out of view, he took out his phone, called his boss and said, in no uncertain terms, that he could fuck his job.

Six.

Flo was scrolling through holiday deals on her phone, sketching out an itinerary in her head: a few days in a city, maybe, before heading to the coast or some plush resort where they'd be treated like kings. She'd work something out about the cost — could she really get away with saying she'd found a special deal, or vouchers yet again? Won a competition, maybe? She heard Dylan coming up the stairs, quicker than usual, and certainly stompier. Flo sat up straight. In he came, a face not so much like thunder as ten hurricanes at once. He had, she could smell instantly, been drinking. Dylan never day-drank; he hated boozing on an empty stomach. Something was wrong. Dylan went straight to the fridge and pulled out a beer; he didn't offer her one.

'I've quit. No more ghost whispering for me.'

He sat on the armchair, its springs wheezing, and picked at a tear in the upholstery. She'd never seen him look so lost. 'Do you want to tell me what happened?'

He explained, flatly, about Estelle and Barnaby 'lording it' over him, wearing him out with questions. Shit. Estelle had said they might pop in to check out the tour, but Flo imagined they'd stay five minutes and slink off, bored. Estelle only passed history at school because her godfather was their teacher; she wasn't remotely interested in anything that happened even seconds before her conception. Everything she needed to know about the past she read off headstones in her familial graveyard. 'Sorry, I should've said. I didn't think they'd bother.'

Already done, Dylan tossed the bottle aside. She handed him another. 'They offered me a job, well, I say job, they asked me to intern on some "webisodes", playing a pervert for zero money. With your approval, apparently.'

It had sounded a nice thing to do when they'd mentioned it. Barnaby really did know everyone; it wasn't totally unbelievable that the brand could take off and Dylan be the face of it, was it?

'So what happened with your job? Why did you leave?'

Dylan groaned, already regretting his rashness, probably. Quitting was so out of character and dramatic. Dylan liked structure, a plan, to know what was coming next. Tears welled in his eyes. 'I've sacrificed my dignity plenty of times, for art, or whatever. But I've never met anyone who . . .' He clawed at his face. 'God, how am I going to pay the rent? Things were bad enough as it was.'

It was a bit late to be asking himself this question; Flo almost felt like telling him he'd been stupid, but that would make her very much her mother's daughter.

'I told you to keep the audition between us. They loved rubbing it in that I didn't get it.'

But Estelle had already known without Flo telling her. Her mother and her best friend had long ago bonded over the idea that bitching about someone behind their back was somehow an act of charity, and Joy had probably been straight onto Estelle after Dylan's outburst at the dinner table. 'Friends share stuff. I'm sorry.' She sat next to him, rubbed his hand with hers. He snatched it away.

That was the holiday done for, then, if Dylan was one job down. She turned her phone over so Dylan wouldn't see what she'd been looking up. Would sunshine and lapping waves at the shore fix this, anyway? Possibly not. She remembered the buzz of their first break together; Dylan refusing to commit to a holiday until he could pay exactly half. Flo had booked it and fudged the final cost, topping up the deficit with birthday money and a last-minute loan from her father. Dylan had been wowed by the beautiful hotel and walked round the room running his finger along everything like he'd just got out of prison.

'Free upgrade!' Flo had said, the guilt of the lie cancelled out by pleasure at seeing Dylan so happy.

Now, she reached for his hand again. 'Remember the happy place. We'll work something out.'

'I'm off for a shower,' he said. 'Get ready for the one job I still have.'

He closed the door behind him so quietly that, somehow, it felt like even more of a slap in the face than slamming it would.

The trouble with going back to the 'happy place' was that they always stopped right before it went wrong; they never talked about the last day.

That last morning, Dylan had insisted on settling the minibar tab while Flo wandered outside for a deep gulp of the air they were about to leave behind. He wasn't usually one for flexing his masculine entitlement, but his dad had a habit of leaving rooms before bills were settled, and Dylan liked to show the apple had rolled fast and far from the tree. The hotel manager was the right side of obsequious; he even had a comedy moustache Dylan couldn't take his eyes off. Dylan handed over a tip and thanked them for the upgrade. They didn't know what he was talking about. Confused there'd been a mistake, the manager brought up their booking, and the truth was revealed: there'd been no upgrade; he hadn't paid his way. He could barely look at Flo when he came outside. How could he have believed his paltry bar wages could buy them even a quarter of a paradise like this? He opened the cab door for her, then left it swinging in the gentle breeze while he got in the other side. He could hardly speak at the airport, mouth set hard as they trailed round duty free. By boarding time she'd apologised, making Dylan feel even shittier for being mad at her for doing a nice thing. He'd resolved to pay her back.

'Fifty-fifty from now on, agreed?'

'Whatever you say.'

They'd stuck to it too, or so he'd thought: a few weeks after moving into the flat he'd discovered Flo had fibbed about the rent, told him it was less than it actually was, and was making up the shortfall herself. She told him 'forget your pride' but sometimes that was all he had. He increased his share of the payment, and it was never spoken of again, but Dylan thought about it a lot.

At work, head still throbbing from his daytime drinking and the row with Flo, he asked Max if he could magic up some extra shifts from somewhere, but it was bad news. 'You know how things are. Your rota is already a love letter to favouritism. I can't give my best mate all the hours. Everyone's got bills to pay.'

After his shift at the bar, Dylan got off two Tube stops early and walked home in the rain, almost revelling in the melodrama. He'd never admit it, but he'd been hasty quitting the tour-guide job. He'd actually liked it fine; it was better than this feeling, which he hated even more. He'd never escaped worrying about money, never had more than a month or two without the threat of a nasty letter from the bank. He had nobody he could ask for help – Max had only just managed to find a new flatmate so had sunk all his money on rent. His mum didn't have anything, his sisters had families of their own. Lois, maybe? Just to help cover this month's rent. He could never take money off Flo, knowing it came from her parents, but with Lois it was different; she'd earned every penny, had everything logged on a spreadsheet. She had learned the hard way after her wicked stepfather had gambled away all her child-star earnings. Flo would tell him 'Don't worry about paying it back,' but Lois would call that debt in, and Dylan would have to endure a lecture about the importance of good accounting. Dylan needed it to feel like a business arrangement; he preferred owing money to owing favours.

All Dylan wanted was to put his hand in his pocket and find something other than problems. As much as he and Flo were in sync, she never got this aspect at all. Her background was so different, it was basically science fiction to him. Sure, she'd had worries in her life, but money wasn't one of them. Flo had never looked at something in a shop window and thought, 'if only' – she'd walk right in and get it.

He got home, soaking, to find Flo on the sofa, beaming, like a gameshow host.

'I've got an amazing idea to fix our money problems.' She looked excited, but nervous.

'*My* money problems.' Dylan didn't like the sound of this. 'I'm not taking my clothes off on video.'

Flo laughed, but it didn't reach her eyes. 'We can't really afford this flat, the landlord's a beast, it's falling apart . . . the mice are back, by the way.'

'Great, I can't even kill rodents properly.'

'Listen!' Flo looked like if she didn't spill soon, she'd explode. 'Let's move out. Stay somewhere else until we're sorted, save up, then when we're more in the black, see how things are, get somewhere else. Nicer.'

Who'd put them up for nothing? Nobody. Sofa-surfing alone was bad enough, never mind as a couple. Max had a heart of gold, but his new flatmate Gabe had arrived wielding laminated cleaning rotas and adhesive labels for his food in the fridge. It wasn't an option.

'Barnaby has just bought a rundown old pub in Hammersmith,' she said, face radiant like she was announcing she'd obtained the truth about the meaning of life. 'He's going to develop it eventually, but for now he needs someone to live there and kind of look after the place. Loads of people do it. And it's rent-free!'

His throat felt like it was closing up. The big solution was having Barnaby as a slum landlord? Was the room spinning, or was he? 'So we have to make sure nobody breaks into the place? Like security guards? So Barnaby gets us *both* to work for him for free?'

There was the flicker of an eye-roll. 'It's not like we have to wear uniforms or actually tackle burglars. We just have to be there.'

'I'm sure your parents will love me moving you into a glorified squat.'

Her hands, knitted in her lap, tightened, her knuckles going whiter. 'If we get the flat off our back, it's one less thing to worry about. If I can take just one stress away from you, it's worth it.'

He was torn: she obviously meant well but this was tone-deaf. He didn't want to upset her. Keep your voice calm and even, he told himself. 'You're taking one off, and adding ten more.'

Flo unclasped her hands and the colour finally returned. 'Oh, it's not that deep! Who cares? Why shouldn't a friend do us a favour? Same with the advert. I know loads of actors who work for free. Why can't we have a few doors open for us?'

Dylan tried to keep his voice level. 'I want to unlock doors myself, with talent, not have them held open for me.'

'I don't understand.'

He'd been afraid she was going to say that. 'Most of my life I've worried I'm not good enough. To make it from a background like mine you have to really stand out, be an exceptional talent, while mediocre people with a rich dad sail on ahead.' He saw her shudder. His tongue felt fat and bitter in his mouth. 'They get to do what they want, dabble in stuff, see if they like it, and don't have to work full-time to keep their head above water. For the system to work, it's not just about them succeeding, it has to hold others back.'

'What does this have to do with Barnaby?'

'Everything. It's the world we live in. Remember when Barnaby proudly told us he only got two A-levels but managed to get into Oxford?'

Flo's eyes dulled, as if recalling Barnaby booming this out, like a tannoy.

'He didn't even want to be a student,' said Dylan. 'His dad set up the interview through some crony and threatened to cut his allowance if he didn't go.'

'He aced the interview, though,' Flo whimpered. 'He's very charismatic. Look, arguing won't pay the rent.' Flo got that look that Dylan saw all the time in the bar when he'd ask a rich customer to keep the noise down, or hurried along someone holed up in a cubicle doing coke. Indignant. Defensive. 'I can't help it that you don't have any money. I didn't make you walk out of your job.'

'True. Fine. End of discussion.' Dylan marched through to the bedroom. It was a mess, and cold. He was furious; he needed to be somewhere else, anywhere. Flo followed.

'End of discussion? Who do you think . . . Why do you get to decide it's the end of the discussion?'

Who did he think he was, she'd been about to say. There it was. They stood in silence a few seconds, staring at each other. There was the unmistakable sound of a mouse scratching in the skirting board. 'I'm going to bed.'

Flo stayed on the couch.

Estelle poured her a large glass of wine in yet another opulent, atmosphere-free hotel bar and made a good fist of pretending she was rooting for Dylan and Flo to work things out.

'I don't think we've ever argued like that before, not since . . .'

'Oh, Greece? That bad? Yikes.' Flo shouldn't have told her about that; Estelle always cast it up whenever Flo made the mildest of complaints about Dylan. Estelle looked over at Barnaby, who was at the other end of the table holding court with three women Flo didn't know all that well. 'Barno and

I never argue, it's a waste of time. Dylan is being extremely silly and proud. But most men are.'

'That's the thing . . .' How many glasses had she drunk now? How long had she been out? She'd been too distressed to eat dinner. 'He always used to admit when he was wrong, talk about his feelings. That's what made him different.'

Estelle clicked her fingers and a waiter came running, quickly translating her crude sign language. 'I can't think of anything more unsexy than a man telling you his feelings – Barnaby goes to see a stout woman in Belgravia twice a week to get all that off his chest.'

Flo liked that Dylan was open with her, although it made for uncomfortable listening sometimes. That morning, as he'd riffled through a drawer for a clean T-shirt, he'd said he wouldn't be attending that night's Fortnightlies, or indeed any of them, ever again.

'But we always go together!' she'd protested.

'And I always leave feeling like shit.' He'd left the flat without saying goodbye.

'Is he going on about privilege again?' drawled Estelle, tasting the wine in her glass, grimacing, shaking her head and handing the bottle back to the befuddled waiter in one fluid motion. Flo had never had to think much about this kind of thing before she met Dylan. It had never come up. She didn't like feeling like she had to keep explaining herself, or making excuses for her upbringing. Flo would become embarrassed, sometimes, talking about lovely holidays she'd been on when younger, or brief flirtations with dance classes (lasted three weeks, too flat-footed) or horse riding (two sessions, the smell of the stables made her gag). Yes, she'd had lots of opportunities to try different things, but not many of them had clicked – until she found music. To hear Dylan talk, you'd think he'd spent the first ten years of his life clambering up mill chimneys and was last out of five to get in the tin bath.

Estelle snorted. 'Arguing about money is so basic. All that trickery you do with discount codes and special offers. Does he really believe that or does he just want to? I mean, poor Vérité can't ice "Happy birthday" on a cupcake without consulting a dictionary, but even she'd start to wonder why you never pay full price for anything. You're not in a girl band.' She stared off distractedly. 'Waiter! Pronto!'

Brimming with the bravado only two large glasses of rosé could give you, Flo burst through the front door, to find Dylan there already, reading.

'Where've you been?'

'Hello.' He didn't look up. 'I met Lois for a drink.'

She imagined Lois's long Los Angeles limbs draped over Dylan and tried to edge to the bathroom without touching him, lest spores of Lois clung to her. 'How was the divine Lois?' she shouted as she splashed water on her face. She swayed. You never realise how drunk you are until you're on your own in a toilet, she thought. 'Did she comfort you?' Flo sashayed back into the lounge and attempted her best American accent. 'Oh gee, Dylan honey, forget that English tramp, come live with me, eat mac and freaking cheese out of my asshole.'

Dylan laughed, not realising how angry she was. 'Um . . . no. But, look, a room's available in Lois's flat. One of the guys is going on a tour, wants to sublet, but, like, mega cheap. It's ours if we want it.'

Flo's head flooded with images. Cosy nights on the sofa with Lois. Trudging out of the bathroom every morning to find Lois waiting, looking way better on the way in than Flo ever would on the way out. Lois and her backhanded compliments, never acknowledging Flo, just speaking to the back of the room and at a point three inches above her head, like she was willing her to be taller.

She and Lois had never gelled. She was always on, everything turned up to eleven. Exclamations! At! The! Smallest! Thing! Why use three syllables when you can use twenty? Flo remembered Lois once turning to her and saying: 'I just love that "no make-up" thing you have going on. How do you make it work on stage?' When Flo replied she did wear make-up on stage, Lois had clutched her chest in mock mortification and taken a sip of her drink to prepare for her punchline.

'Do you? Well done you. I could never get away with it.' Flo's mouth had gaped in awe while Lois prattled with fake chirpiness. 'I mean, the first thing I do is make friends with the lighting tecs. What with my rough old hide.' Lois had skin like silk, her pores were invisible, she had never known blotchiness. Lois had lain her hand on Flo's. 'Well, make-up or not, you always look so fresh.' She wrinkled her nose in a way someone had obviously once told her was cute – like a piglet, Flo thought at the time.

Dylan sat next to Flo now. His face looked hopeful. 'What do you think? It would mean we're still paying our way, keeping a bit of independence.'

Independence? For him, maybe. But Flo wouldn't be able to breathe with Lois watching her every move. No way could she have sex under the same roof as Lois. She imagined Dylan getting up in the night and creeping to Lois's room – no doubt draped with red silks blasted by wind machines – where Lois waited with open arms, fucking him with her usual grace and poise, while Flo slept, unchic and oblivious, on the other side of the wall.

'Absolutely not. I won't live with Lois. She's a . . .' She stopped herself – her mother had told her that word was only suitable to say out loud if you were reading from Chaucer.

'Then what?' Dylan was pacing the room. 'This is the one situation I didn't want to be in.'

The booze took hold of Flo's tongue. 'We're in this situation because you had a bad day at work! Everyone has a bad day at work!'

'All this started way before my "bad day" at work and you know it.' He backed away, knocking his heel against the coffee table. 'Ow. Why is this flat so fucking small?!'

Flo hated this. This wasn't really them. They talked through stuff calmly, usually, kind of lazily. When they got deep, it was vague and dreamy. This seemed too gritty and real; it was like watching bad copies of themselves. She grabbed a cushion and screamed into it. 'I can't keep apologising for who I am.'

Dylan looked at her now, then round the flat, taking it all in. There was something about his face, the air around him. Flo was squinting against the ceiling light, but she still felt a dark cloud over her.

'I can't either.' Dylan knelt in front of her. 'Sometimes when everything's against you, you have to admit defeat.' Dylan took her hand. Flo wanted to snatch it away, as if to avoid the inevitable.

'I have a feeling you're going to say something I don't

like.' Flo blinked back tears. 'This is ridiculous. I don't care about . . . this stuff you think I care about. I've never asked you for anything.'

'It does matter.' Dylan lowered his head. 'And we know why you never ask for anything, don't we? Because you know I can't deliver.'

Seven.

There were no more screaming matches, no accusations, just sadness as Flo watched Dylan swing his bags and boxes into the minivan 'she'd ordered for him, with a 'discount code'; maybe Estelle was right and Dylan was stupid after all. Max had looked back up at the flat and given a wave as he'd driven Dylan away to his place, which crushed Flo all the more. This was so surreal. She walked round the flat touching the spaces where his stuff had once been. She knew this room so well; she'd often sat and stared into it, trying to think of lyrics or waiting to hear Dylan's key in the door. Every crack in the ceiling, the way the worktop had been mangled by whoever fitted it, the floor cushion they never used, only tripped over. She'd never see any of it again.

Was it really over? What did it mean, to possibly never lay eyes on Dylan again? This was the first time she'd broken up with someone she actually liked. Before, she'd let things turn sour, as men turned into lizards before her eyes; she'd been thrilled to get rid of her exes. But with Dylan, there was unfinished business, they'd been cut off in their prime. It was like a death, only Dylan was a few kilometres away in

Mile End and not in an urn on a sideboard. As she started to cry the doorbell went and she was forced to open the door with a classic break-up face: tear-strewn, looking like shit. For bonus points, it was her mother. She'd been expecting her dad or, at the very least, one of the strapping sons of his many golfing pals to help shift her stuff. Her mum gathered Flo into her arms without even looking at her surroundings. She smelled oddly comforting.

'I hope you're not here to gloat.'

'I am here to take you home.' When her mother squeezed her with genuine affection, Flo was surprised. Where it had it been the last couple of decades? Usually, if John Lewis didn't deliver it, she didn't know anything about it.

'Now you finally get to see the levels of depravity I've sunk to.' How strange to have her mother here, finally. She looked wrong, standing there out of context, like a space monster in a period drama.

Joy glanced around the room. 'It doesn't matter, you don't live here anymore.' She picked up a box, without even bothering to put on rubber gloves. 'Shall we get started?'

'Welcome home!'

Dylan took it in. The large window with no blinds – 'an aesthetic', Max had said – and the row of crooked kitchen units along one wall. Max didn't have much in the way of furniture, but at least it was his own and in good repair. Dylan saw a few decorative touches he didn't recognise that must belong to the new flatmate.

'So, pussycat, couple of ground rules.'

'Can one of them be don't call me pussycat in front of other people?'

Max laughed. 'We're just setting ourselves up for failure. Right.' He lifted the box at Dylan's feet. 'All your stuff has to be in my room – Gabe would rather you kept your personal effects out of communal areas.'

'Personal effects? Like a corpse found in the park. Great, anything else?'

'No sleeping on the sofa, which includes falling asleep on it drunk in front of the TV. Gabe doesn't want to find you slumped on it every morning like some tragic divorcé. As soon as your lids get heavy, straight to bed. My bed. Lucky old me.'

Dylan sat on the sofa and scratched himself everywhere. Moving dust had got into crevices he never knew he had. 'Gabe sounds like tonnes of fun.'

'To be honest, he's not, but he pays half the rent, and said you could stay. It took me far too long to find a flat I loved to have to look for another.' Max sat next to his old friend. 'He writes his name on his yoghurts. Probiotic. What would I want with his friendly bacteria?'

Dylan hated feeling like a burden. He promised to be super-tidy, and stay out of the way. He didn't feel much like socialising, anyway. He'd never understood what a broken heart was. He'd laughed at Max, sometimes, for being over the top when his love affairs hadn't worked out. This felt real, and incredibly harsh, like it would never be okay again.

'I'm here for you. It's gonna be peachy.' Max leaned in for a hug. 'But please go into the bathroom if you're gonna scratch yourself like that. Gabe said there was to be no overt demonstrations of heterosexuality.'

Flo had expected Estelle to crow more; winning an argument was her main source of calcium, but she was actually a tower of strength. Flo wondered if her mum and Estelle had been overtaken by parasites, but instead of suffering zombi-fication like in the movies, they'd somehow been converted into human beings with emotions and empathy – like they'd been possessed by a motivational poster. Within moments of Flo's mum pulling up in the driveway, Estelle was there, wrinkling her nose at Flo's dusty belongings, but armed with ice-cream, sweets, chocolate and a huge bag which clanked reassuringly with bottles containing one-way tickets to drunken oblivion.

'I'm here for you, gorgeous girl,' she said with a brightness Flo hadn't seen for a long time. 'I brought along the most clichéd break-up consolation props I could think of. All we need now are photos of Dylan to burn or your exes' phone numbers so we can send them a quick "how ya doin". What do you think?'

Despite herself, Flo laughed, although she couldn't help feeling like she was betraying Dylan. Hadn't Estelle and Barnaby led to this? If Dylan had kept that job . . . Either way, Estelle was in front of her and Dylan was not, and as Estelle seemed eager to fulfil the role she was born to do, nurse the victims of her own destruction, who was Flo to argue?

Those first few days were tough, though. Flo spent most of her time staring at her bedroom walls or with her head buried in the fridge looking for something to eat out of sheer boredom. Estelle came over most afternoons and Joy gave her time off the shop to avoid bumping into Dylan – something Flo hadn't even thought of. Her dad had been instructed not to mention Dylan at all, and Joy didn't bring him up, so Flo found herself in a bizarre alternative reality where it felt like the biggest break-up of her life had just . . . not happened.

Like she'd never even met him. She found herself saying, over and over, 'I'm never gonna see Dylan ever again' to try to make it real. She'd have no reason to get in touch; she loved Max but they shared no friends, really. What would it be like if she *did* bump into him, outside the bar? What if, like, in a year or two, he came into the shop to buy something? He might! How would she feel? Would he look the same? Would he still speak to her in that low, calm voice that she liked, would he fidget with the loop in his jeans? Or would he be someone else entirely? She played the scenario in her head constantly, making up snatches of dialogue, feeling the fictional anguish, and hope, and misplaced passion surge through her body. Then she realised what was happening: her brain was writing a song.

One Sunday, everybody was out, and the Fortnightlies gang were weekending at some country cottage. Flo wasn't sad to miss it. Some people channelled their pain into booze, drugs, or bucketfuls of Haribo – but Flo always reached for music in times of crisis. She needed an outlet for those mock-ups of what might've been. She tried tinkling at the piano but it was due a tuning. She picked up her guitar but the acoustics were all wrong – it felt different playing here, now, with high ceilings and amid her mother's tasteful interior design rather than the chaos and mildew and piles of recycling of the poky little flat. Before leaving for the countryside dressed like Princess Diana at the Highland games, Estelle had told Flo to throw herself into her creativity. There would be questions and pouting if she sat on her arse all weekend.

She grabbed the guitar and went to her bathroom, and sat and played in the dark a while. She started with a couple of unfinished songs but as she picked them up again she was only reminded of the last time she'd played them. She remembered Dylan's eyes watching, how he'd gently tap his thumbs on his knees in time with the music, smile creeping to the corner of his mouth as he recognised the meaning of a lyric. She gulped down tears and set her guitar to one side, trying to regulate her breathing. Instinctively, she grabbed her phone and looked up Dylan's social media. She wasn't surprised to find no updates; he didn't post much, anyway, even in 'peacetime'. Despite everything in her head telling her not to, she checked Max's too, then Lois's, just in case. Nothing. Dylan was offline. She couldn't decide which was worse, that he might be so miserable he wasn't posting or even posing for other people's photos, or that he was absolutely fine, but keeping it on the downlow.

It was too dark in here. She grabbed the guitar and went into the small guest room opposite her bedroom. It was the blankest room in the house, no personality, memories, nothing to distract her. She sat on a stool and began to play a melody totally new to her. This felt like something that had been waiting to come out. She wiped away a tear, grabbed her phone again and set it beside her, recording. She knew that this feeling could never be repeated – this was a once-in-a-lifetime moment. She took a deep breath, flexed her fingers, and began to play. The words came like they were being fed to her by some kind of celestial energy; she was lost in grief, fighting with all her might to get to the end of the song. She channelled her anger and hopelessness into the moment, and a smidge of jealousy – it still smarted that Dylan had swerved those final Fortnightlies for a drink with Lois. She'd never felt so inspired, yet so desolate and, if she were honest, eager to get this over with so she could eat. But something had taken over; she wouldn't move until she was done.

Three hours, two crying fits, and one break for instant noodles later, she had in her hands the song that would change everything.

'I don't normally approve of drinking on shift,' said Max as he cradled Dylan's chin in his hands, 'but if it'll pep you up, please go ahead.'

Dylan knew he'd been hard work the last couple of weeks; Max had been very patient. It was like someone had crept into his room at night and siphoned off everything that made him who he was. He was a vessel, a vacuum, a void – lots of things beginning with V, and none of them felt great. His tips were dwindling to nothing because he couldn't even flirt with customers – something he'd never enjoyed but approached like he would any difficult acting role. 'It's like I've had my balls cut off,' he'd said one night, causing Max's flatmate Gabe to leave the room and slam his bedroom door. 'I don't feel anything. Totally numb.'

One person not entirely sympathetic to Dylan's plight? Lois, surprise surprise. She dropped by the bar every couple of nights, in full sergeant-major mode.

'Please, you think you've got problems?' She paused for dramatic effect; this was a rhetorical question. 'The guy I'm dating is performing comedy haikus at a pop-up sake bar.' She registered Dylan's face. 'The cultural appropriation is *ironic*, apparently. I don't think he's a long lease for me, y'know? Emotionally, he's in kindergarten. He told me he snuck a can of beer into his grandfather's funeral just to feel something.'

Dylan slumped on the bar, aware of Max wincing at his unprofessionalism. 'It's hardly the same. Flo was the love of my life.'

'Who you dumped! Stand up straight, walk tall. Hell. Can we have a peek at the bright side?'

'Bright side?'

'Sure! Think how much time you'll have for self-development.' She could do with extra tuition herself – Dylan knew Lois had been stuck on week three of an online mindfulness course since last April.

'My relationship is over, Lois. I haven't retired. I still have the same amount of time, except now I'll be alone.'

'Nonsense!' Lois clapped her hands together. 'All that wallowing in that sleazy apartment, you pair. No more! You can be out, with me, meeting people, getting parts!'

'I'm not sure about the acting thing anymore.'

Lois gasped. She'd always been the best gasper at drama school. 'Shut. The. Fuck. Up. Fuck you and your lame pity party with no catering and a pay bar. You're *not* destined to work in this crummy place for evermore.'

'Oi!' Max protested from his corner.

Lois was already scrolling though her calendar. 'Okay. Wednesday, take the night off, and come to the opening of an amazing new play. It will be dripping with opportunity.' Lois raised her eyebrow. 'Of every description. Sooner you're back in the saddle and schmoozing, the better for all of us.'

'I know everything's still raw, but when you're ready to start dating again, Barnaby met two amazing chaps in Dubai who would be perfect for you.'

Flo watched Estelle absentmindedly pick up the guitar and give it an inharmonious strum, looking around at the framed prints that went out of fashion around two or three years ago, and sixth-form-era knick-knacks, a shrine to their teenage years inexplicably left intact by Flo's usually unsentimental and industrious mother.

'I mean, I know it's too early but . . . I haven't fully scoped them out yet, anyway.'

Flo smiled at the idea of Estelle inspecting these two men like prize horses. 'What are you doing? Checking Debrett's for bloodlines?'

'No, a quick rummage through their online presence, you know the kind of thing. Seeing where they ski. Speaking of which, no updates on your little channel lately. Why not?'

Flo chose to ignore the 'little' and instead focused on being grateful Estelle even looked. 'I can't stop crying long enough to play. Does that make me sound sad?' Estelle's pained smile said yes. 'I'm useless at work, I keep having to run into the back and pretend I'm making a herbal tea or going to the loo.' Martha, the assistant handpicked by her mother because she was old and unthreatening and talked like Princess Margaret, was convinced Flo was pregnant.

Estelle had been expecting at least one 'break-up stonker' on there by now, she said. Should Flo tell Estelle about the songs she'd been working on? She'd only ever played half-finished material to Dylan – to do it without him would feel wrong, like she was already over him. In a way, she was embarrassed she was even capable of writing new songs. Wouldn't it be a greater tribute to Dylan if she couldn't do anything at all: no eating, no sleeping, hair left unbrushed until it matted – like she used to handle teenage break-ups? Yet she'd managed to compose two, well two and a half, okay three, unfinished songs, and had plenty more bubbling inside her. Did this mean she'd never loved Dylan at all? Estelle was staring at her, puzzled.

'I'm waiting.'

'There's one. It's . . . I'm not sure it's right.'

'Play it.'

Flo reached for the guitar. She felt nervous, taking longer than normal to settle into position, grabbing and punching cushions, to arrange round her. Estelle stayed silent. Finally, she was ready. Could she get through this without crying? She breathed deeply, let her fingers find their starting place, closed her eyes, and played. She didn't cry, but when she finished, she noticed an expression on Estelle's face she'd never seen before. 'Are you ill?'

Estelle swallowed slowly and purposefully; a single tear rolled down her face unchecked. She didn't move. God, what was happening? Estelle never cried, she'd literally never been sad. Flo assumed her tear ducts had been decommissioned long ago. Finally: 'That was . . . I'd listen to that for ever. On an old-school record player. For all time.'

'Really?'

'Yes. The subtle references to . . . it's Dylan, right? "Bells that ring with opportunity, doors that never close, tending bars and taking cards that say nothing at all." That's the day you met, yes? The bell over the door in your mum's shop. You're so clever!'

Flo was embarrassed. 'It's not totally autobiographical. There's creative licence, you know?'

Estelle was on a roll; she was the same doing the *New York Times* crossword. 'The . . . uh, "sidelined beauty, no stars just stripes, a shot of caffeine" – that's that dreadful American ex, right?'

Flo cringed, yet she was impressed. She thought she'd been more cryptic. Did it matter? The song would never see the light of day, anyway.

Estelle leapt up, excited. 'Have you performed it live? You have to! I'll bring everyone! I'll make phone calls. You'll destroy the crowd.'

Setlist meetings with Elijah were a constant hellscape. 'It wouldn't work. There'd be nothing for Elijah to do.'

Estelle's laugh said a thousand words. 'So what's new? Do it. At least upload it to your channel so people can see this . . . wonder.'

'It isn't polished enough.'

Estelle became solemn, gripping Flo's arm tightly. 'It *is*. It's perfect. It has . . . magic. I'm deadly serious. Please.'

So, while Estelle went downstairs to pour two large cele-bratory gin and tonics, Flo set up her camera and mic in the smallest guest room, feeling leaden yet cautiously optimistic, heaved herself onto her little stool.

Estelle returned, ice in the glasses clinking in jubilation. 'Think you can do it in one take? Should I go?'

Flo shook her head. 'No, just put those bloody glasses down. Stay.'

Estelle peeked through the camera and made a tiny adjust-ment to its angle. 'Now you're centre-stage where you belong.' She sat gently on the bed. 'Just imagine I'm one of a . . . hang on, how many people can fit into the O2?'

'I'd have to google.' She knew exactly.

'Let's say twenty-five thousand. Imagine I'm just one in twenty-five thousand, and we all know the words to this song, because it's your greatest-hits tour. Okay?'

Less self-consciously than before, she began to play. It

felt different with the camera and Estelle's eyes on her. She sang the words like she was living them, trying to keep her emotions in check. She stared straight ahead, and if she felt the tingle of a tear, closed her eyes until the feeling subsided. If I can get to the end of the second chorus, she thought, feeling her voice falter. Estelle wasn't on the bed anymore, Flo noticed, she was behind the camera. Second chorus, done, but Flo could hold it no more. Every happy moment with Dylan flashed up in her mind. The first day; that first comedy accent he did at her parents'; laughing and snogging on the way home after a hilariously bad Fortnightlies; Santorini; anniversary fish and chips by the canal. A slideshow of everything she'd lost. But she also remembered those final days, Dylan so hurt, lashing out, dismissive and cruel. Lois, smiling, applying caffeine fucking roll-on to her already perfect eyes, leading Dylan by the hand round her spacious flat showing him the empty room. Max's sad little wave as he drove Dylan away. She couldn't look away anymore – as she reached the closing lines, she turned to Estelle, and found the lens, eyes wide, tears slowly making their way down her cheek. She glared right into the camera and sang the last line. 'Look what you've done to us.' One take.

Estelle watched it back. Flo couldn't. 'I zoomed in a bit toward the end. The light caught your tears perfectly.' Estelle wiped away one of her own. 'Upload. Immediately.'

'I can't. There's some lyrics I should change.' If Estelle, not the most observant person in the world, had cracked the codes, it wouldn't be too hard for others. Plus, she'd been laying it on thick for dramatic effect. Dylan was not, as the song's antagonist was, a 'lothario' or 'a snide boy, a wide boy' of any description – although some of her exes fit the bill.

Estelle looked possessed. 'There's commercial potential here. This can make you famous.'

'I don't want to be famous.'

Estelle refilled their drinks. They were stronger this time, barely any tonic. 'You keep saying that, but why else make music? Why have your channel? If one good thing can come from Dylan fucking that vulgar slut actress, it should be you at number one.'

'Please don't say that. He didn't . . . they didn't have sex.' As far as she knew, of course. Maybe they had by now. 'And don't call her a slut; I thought we didn't do that.'

'You've nothing stopping you now.' Estelle's chest was puffed with pride, like a monarch on a banknote. 'Don't you want success? You don't have to pretend you're okay with just getting by, that you're happy in a tiny flat, earning nothing. Grab this. Be someone. Be yourself.'

Flo took a large gulp of her drink. Estelle's pep talks sometimes veered into mania; Flo sometimes wondered who they were really for. 'I don't want to be *someone*. I already am someone, I'm me.'

'Fucking hell, Floria, you're being really annoying. Upload!'

So, just as she had for most of their friendship, Flo did as she was told.

The play was not amazing. It was, according to the flyer, and the reaction of stalls rows A–H, visceral. A joyless, butt-clenched ninety-seven minutes – no interval and no re-admittance if you left the auditorium, always a bad sign. Lois was a great wingman at the after-party; she introduced him to everyone, tried to drag him kicking and screaming into her conversations, but his heart wasn't in it.

'I'm going for a cigarette,' he said after an hour. Irritated by Dylan's determination to be an albatross rather than soar like an eagle, Lois let him go, even though he didn't smoke.

Dylan stood in a charmless courtyard among other, prettier, lither, younger people, suckling at their cigarettes, pausing only to bitch about anyone who wasn't there. It was always weird being around 'industry' people. At first, he'd loved these parties, seeing who was there, dissecting everything the next day. But as others' stars ascended they'd lost their charm. It was the strangest thing: he wanted to be them, envied them even, but in the same breath, didn't want to be like them at all.

Flo had been the perfect cover for opting out of these events, abandoning that crowd. It was kind of accepted, wasn't it, that couples in love locked themselves away. They were definitely in love. Flo. He couldn't stop thinking about her. He had to let her know, he just had to. He took out his phone, ready to type. He shouldn't do it. He knew that. This was fuckboy behaviour. Pathetic man-baby thrusting himself back into her life. A notification popped up, from Flo's channel. A new video. He read the title. 'The Last Hello.' His finger hovered, frightened of what he might find.

Lois appeared at his side. 'If you go in now, turn on the charm, you can reverse that damage you did the first hour you got here.' She looked at his phone. 'Don't play that.'

'Why not?'

'Might be some things you don't wanna hear. Unless she

sends you a link herself, wants you to hear it, don't. You're snooping. You have work to do.'

Dylan closed his eyes tightly against the tears. 'I can't go back in there.'

Lois sighed. 'She's moving on, creating, flexing her talent.' Lois paused, which Dylan knew would have ordinarily been filled by some kind of criticism, but she was trying to be nice. 'Good for her. Now you need to do the same. There's some dudes from *City Royal* in there. Come with me, let's show them what they missed – work a room for once in your fucking life. I know you know how.'

Dylan dabbed at his eyes with his sleeve and shivered. It was way too cold to be outside; smokers were hardcore, but he wasn't. 'I can't put on a brave face.'

Lois leaned in and cuddled him, batting away the cigarette smoke of a few reality TV stars who had no concept of personal space. 'Sure you can. You're the bravest boy I know. Remember that schools tour you did? The weird thing about the king who thinks he's an alien? Your costume was thermal underwear and Cookie Monster slippers? You styled it out every day. Brave.'

'Okay.' He kissed her cheek, and chugged back his wine. 'I'll give it my best shot.'

Lois led him, quite firmly by the wrist, through the throngs of people. She was shark-like, never stopping for a second, standing on toes and spilling drinks as she charged forward. She marched up to three men who looked like they were about to leave and launched Dylan at them.

'You guys are *City Royal*, right?' she said, her schmoozing pedigree knowing not to pause for confirmation or rejection. 'I heard you were looking for a new leading man to liven up the surgical ward and I just had to introduce you to my friend Dylan Fox – he's gonna be the name on everybody's lips very soon.'

'Why?' said one of the men, whose cheeks blushed with red wine. 'Has he killed someone?'

Lois laughed just long enough. 'Nope, but he's been killing it in an immersive theatre experience, haven't you, Dylan?' The men stepped back a little as Dylan lurched toward them. How many drinks had he had? He wasn't sure now.

'You look familiar,' said the kindest-looking of the men. 'Do I know you?'

Dylan felt the acidic churn of warm, complimentary wine in his tummy. He saw Lois out of the corner of his eye, willing him not to mess it up.

'You do,' said Dylan. 'Or at least you think you do. I tested for you. I came and I waited in line with everybody else, and I worried, and I wondered if this might be the moment someone took me seriously, someone saw what nobody else could see, and gave me a shot. I gave it everything, but it wasn't to be, so excuse me if I don't stand here and kiss your arse.'

The three men's mouths opened and closed without making a sound.

Dylan had never felt so wide, so tall, so strong. 'You see, I think you made a mistake, but I respect your decision. But I want you to know, I'll never give up, I'll never stop trying. You haven't seen the last of me, okay? You won't beat me.' Dylan staggered back slightly, kissed Lois on the cheek, and whispered, 'I'm out,' before pushing his way out to the street.

*

When he got home, an hour or so later, Max was heading to bed. Dylan collapsed on the sofa, leaned back, and closed his eyes.

'Don't fall asleep. Gabe will do his nut.'

'I'm resting my eyes,' burbled Dylan in reply. 'Go on.'

Max hovered by the door. 'You know I support you to the ends of the earth, pussycat, but four solid weeks now of moping? Nope.'

'I'm fine. Be there in a minute.' Dylan saluted with drunken enthusiasm and lay back, watching a spider skitter across the ceiling in the murky light of Max's far-too-dim lamp. 'Mood lighting,' he'd say.

Despite what Lois said, he needed to watch Flo's video. He fished out his phone and, as if Lois was still watching, pretended to innocently scroll through old photos. He then oh-so-casually checked his social media, before sneaking a glance at Flo's profiles. 'Stalker,' he said to himself, but carried on. Everyone did it, right? Totally. Eventually, he could stand no more. 'The Last Hello.' What did it mean? His breathing quickened, his finger was poised to hit play. Did he really want to hear this? He looked round the room for his headphones. Once he'd grappled with the faltering Bluetooth connection, he pressed play and steeled himself for something angry. The gentle strumming of her guitar started up, the sound that had often woken him gently in the morning and coaxed him to sleep at night. This was different, somehow. A new energy behind it. Then she began to sing. She was singing about them, about the first time they met. He remembered every second of it. 'Just you and me in our corner of the world,' she sang. He'd said that to her once. He wasn't sure how he felt about being quoted in a song. It felt . . . personal, like maybe she should've asked. He felt exposed. She looked beautiful, though, as she looked away – she could never look him in the eye when she played, unless he was in that third-row seat, of course. And there it was, mentioned: 'Third chair in the third row, bare now; where did he go?' Ouch. It was so beautiful, but like finding out someone's been talking about you when you'd assumed they didn't even know you existed. Like, finally, someone you fancied noticing you, only to overhear them saying you have a small dick.

> I can handle goodbyes,
> I know what they mean.
> They tell me you're gone, I can't follow.
> But isn't there something about promises
>   unspoken,
> Love unloved,
> Chances untaken,
> In that last 'hello'.

He noticed the camera angles changing, the close-up on her face. The tears slowly running unchallenged. She must have had someone there filming. Who? Who was her sounding board now? He felt jealous, and raw. But there was no denying the song was a work of art. The second it was over, he hit play again. Then again. And again. It wouldn't hurt, would it? To send a little text? He had to tell her how good the song was. He wouldn't say the rest, that he'd made a big mistake, that he wanted to fix everything he'd done wrong, that she'd sung right into his soul and that she'd never leave it.

No, he thought, I won't be that guy. He went to bed,

tossing and turning until Max jabbed him with his elbow. All he could think of was the last time he'd said hello to Flo. When had it been? What could he have done differently? He stared at the ceiling all night.

When Max got up, he was furious. 'All night I've had to put up with this! You're paying for my eye-bag removal when I'm forty. Aksh, make it thirty.'

Dylan closed his eyes and tried to sleep. His phone went. He grabbed it and answered without looking.

'Hello? Flo?'

'No baby, it's me!' Priya. 'Just had a lovely call from *City Royal*. Casting a new hunk. They asked for you specifically.' She sounded like she was underwater, which meant she'd probably dropped her phone last night. 'Told you it wasn't over.'

Dylan sat up in bed and looked at himself in Max's full-length mirror. 'A hunk? Am I a hunk?' He flexed a bicep. Hmmm, there was work to do. 'It was such a demoralising process last time, is there any point?'

'Dylan, if I say you're a hunk, you're a hunk.' Priya sounded stern. 'Get that face in front of their fucking clipboards. Do you know how many guys would kill to be called in like this?'

'No, but I'm sure they have a better chance than me. Phone them.'

He heard Priya scream into the sleeve of her jacket. 'Stop being such a pathetic *man*. I'm sorry about you and Flo, but don't you understand how break-ups work? A little bit of misery, then BOOM, revenge body! Revenge success! Then your ex cries themselves to sleep every night! Do you think I'd be wasting my time if I didn't think it was one hundred per cent yours?' Perhaps sensing tough love wasn't working, she switched to a more soothing tone. 'Look, Dylan, mate. Baby. You know what I say: treat every chance like the last chance.'

'Let me think about it.' He hung up before she could start screaming again. Max walked back in with two milky teas. Dylan explained.

'Even if you don't get it, you need the distraction.'

Dylan turned to face the wall and hugged the duvet round him.

Max's tone grew softer. 'What did we move to London for, huh? To make a better life, yes? To fucking live. I'd happily have you working with me for ever, but you're an actor, not a barman. Like, really not. You've still never made me a perfect mojito.'

Dylan remembered Flo's song. Promises unspoken. Chances untaken. He called Priya back. 'Okay, I'll do it.'

Eight.

'Honestly, how long will this go on?' Joy looked at her daughter, slouching at the kitchen table, feet up on the opposite chair. 'Night after night, this, staring into your computer, or your phone, waiting for something to happen. Floria!'

Joy tapped her daughter's feet gently with a slotted spoon, in an attempt to get her to take them off the chair. When it didn't work, she rapped it on her big toe.

'Ow!'

'Finally, a reaction!' Joy smiled as Flo glared back resentfully. 'You are, if I may say, behaving like a baby. Time to move on.'

Flo slumped forward and slammed her head on the table – she'd made sure there was sufficient cushioning from placemats and napkins first – and gave a low moan.

'Is that all I have to do? Move on?'

'At least when you were upstairs howling along to your guitar there was some kind of catharsis.' Joy pursed her lips at the memory. 'All that caterwauling.' Flo smiled as she remembered her mum discreetly closing the windows in case the neighbours heard.

'It's called creating art, Mother.' After the positive reaction to 'The Last Hello', she'd been really going for it with heartbreak songs, singing them with raw, unbridled emotion, not 'howling'. She now had seven new songs clocking up likes and shares on her channel – 'You Broke My Heart in Seven Places', she called the playlist. She hadn't checked the stats in days. The more views she got, the more afraid she was of the attention. Did Dylan still check her channels? Had he seen the songs? She'd aimed to write some happier songs, revive some old demos from when she and Dylan were together – but every time she sat down to film them, she was only reminded of his absence. She'd watched back a recording of a joyous track called 'Every Time Feels Like the First Time', one of her favourites, but her face looked like she was officiating at a funeral. She'd have to leave the upbeat stuff a while.

Joy was still talking. 'If guests should pop by, I wouldn't know what to say.'

Flo snorted into the placemat, trying not to laugh at how much this was annoying her mother. It was almost worth feeling miserable.

'Why not tell them the truth? That I'm your unloved, unwanted daughter still hanging around the house at twenty-seven and that I'll probably die here. Alone.' Flo heard a long breath that signified Joy was about to lose her mind when a pinging sound came from her laptop. She felt her mother tense up, atoms in the room shifting to compensate. Five . . . four . . . three . . .

'What's that incessant bleeping?'

Flo tilted her head to spy on her mother through her fringe. 'Notifications. A message. On my video channel.'

'How you can possibly say you're alone? Your computer never stops talking to you.' She sat down next to Flo. 'I've known heartbreak, you know.'

Flo wasn't sure missing the first hour of the John Lewis sale counted as heartbreak, but she appreciated the gesture. *Ping!*

'Perhaps you should read this message.'

'It's probably that guy who comments about my feet or my "lovely small boobies" under every video, Mum.' Flo idly wondered if Joy ever snooped in her messages. She had zillion-step verification on everything, anyway, after her boyfriend pre-Dylan had tried to break into her phone to delete the dick pics he'd sent – unsolicited. Flo had been annoyed at the intrusion but also found it amusing he thought she'd ever want to share them with anyone. Despite his fortunate endowment, his presentation and composition was enough to ruin his reputation altogether; maybe that's why he'd wanted them out of circulation. *Ping*, again.

'Floria. At least acknowledge it so we're spared the noise.'

'Right,' she huffed like an adolescent being told that, yes, they did have to go to school that day. The message was from someone called Lily, who managed a bar in Camden. She loved the new songs and wanted her to play at an event celebrating women in the creative industries. Heart racing, Flo called the number, expecting a very scary, power-suited type of woman to answer the phone – could you actually hear a power-suit over the phone, she wondered – but instead came the friendly, confident voice of someone who sounded pretty much her own age.

'Oh God,' Lily said once intros were out of the way. '"The Last Hello" . . . I felt that. I love how honest it is. I could feel the pain. But, like, in a good way.' Lily was after female performers of all descriptions – 'I've got this brilliant woman from Lowestoft who quicksteps with a tinfoil effigy of herself' – and there was plenty of time to network if she was interested. Flo was instantly terrified.

'I'll have to check with Elijah.'

'Is that your manager? You already signed?'

'Signed?! To a record label, you mean?' She wished. Or did she? Did Estelle have a point? Should she chase commercial success? Would she still enjoy what she did? She didn't have time for this soul-searching – Lily sounded busy. 'No, I don't have a manager. He's my . . . uh . . . partner. Musical, only. We're a duo.'

'Oh right.' Lily went quiet. 'I don't remember him in the video.'

'He didn't have anything to do with that.'

'Good. I mean . . . right. Thing is . . . this is women only. The only guys there will be serving drinks. We're celebrating women in creative industries, see. Of which you are one, right?'

She was, wasn't she? 'I'm sure Elijah won't mind.'

Lily gave a low chuckle. 'Good old Elijah. I knew he'd come through for you. I'll send you the details. Can't wait to meet you!'

Flo walked back into the kitchen in a daze. Her mother was waiting, arms folded, patience tissue-thin. 'I have a gig. All by myself . . . can I even do this?'

Instead of a half-hearted pep talk, or hissing castigation, Joy merely sighed and muttered, 'I'm opening the chablis,' before sweeping out of the room.

*

'Why are you dressed like a skater who works in a record shop on a Saturday and never washes?' Max squealed as Dylan pulled on some nondescript baggy jeans and sweater.

'What's wrong with it?'

Max wrinkled his nose. 'It's the kind of outfit you'd be found dead in. I know you and Flo are over, but could you try to get back on speaking terms with your beard trimmer? This is a big deal – at least look like you want it.'

He was nervous. Priya had got some intel from *City Royal*. They wanted this new character on-screen as soon as possible. The last hunk – the part Dylan had gone for but fallen at the final hurdle – hadn't tested well with viewers and was getting a quick off-screen death. Dylan wasn't sure he was ready for this. He needed another month or so swaddled by duvets, mooning over Flo's Instagram, Max hand-delivering milky teas. 'I don't even know who I'm up against.'

'Kermit the Frog and a sentient tub of Häagen-Dazs. Who cares? Just get the thing!' Max paused. 'I believe in you, okay?'

'Thanks, man.'

Max went to the kitchen and came back with a pair of kitchen scissors. 'But, some real talk. You look like a serial killer who ran through a branch of Gap covered in superglue. Shear that thing off your face before I do.'

Flo arrived two hours early. She stood outside, not knowing what to do. She wanted to call Dylan, tell him what was happening, make a joke about the same-seat promise. Eventually, her fingers started to go numb, so she was forced to go in. It was a huge space, wooden floors, white walls, standard London shapeshifting venue. There was the odd sexually explicit sketch on the wall, a sculpture that looked like ten car accidents happening at once, and Lily, who looked like Amy Winehouse but with shorter hair. 'Everybody says that the first time they meet me.'

The place started to fill up with lots of women, women who looked important and well turned-out but also kind of . . . normal? When Lily ushered her onto a small stage, Flo felt a lump form in her throat, but it was a relief that nobody was sitting. It distracted her from thinking about Dylan's vacant seat. She began. The lyrics were still so new, her performance still unpolished, that she couldn't yet distance herself from what she was singing – something she'd got down to a fine art having to sing Elijah's nonsense night after night. She belted away any butterflies lingering in her stomach. She could see each and every face out there, and they seemed to be loving it. Bored-looking waiters were weaving through the crowd, but not even unseasonal negronis and flat Prosecco could make the audience tear their faces away from her – especially one woman with a bright red bob, beaming widely, like she was listening to a comedy podcast on invisible headphones.

Flo finished with 'The Last Hello'. There was a deathly silence while the crowd made sure she was definitely done, before a thunderous roar of applause, shouts of encouragement and, from invisible headphones woman, a loud and clear, 'Oh fucking yes.'

Flo was getting her breath in a back room when Lily ushered in the redheaded woman, still beaming. Flo felt she was about to be canvassed by a religious cult.

'That was exceptional,' said Lily, walking into a hug. 'I knew it would be.'

The redheaded woman stepped forward, hand out-stretched. 'It certainly was.'

Lily looked from one to the other. 'Right, yes, Floria, this is my good mate Tanya, she's a manager, agent and all-round general entertainment representation legend.'

The woman winked at Lily. 'Thanks, treasure, hello, Floria, nice name, congrats on that, kinda Italian, is it? Special.' She talked at a million miles an hour; Flo felt dizzy. 'Tanya Hazell, two Ls, like Hazell Dean but you probably won't have a fucking clue who she is, which maybe you should rectify if you like eighties pop. Anyway, upshot is . . . I've been looking for you a loooong time.'

Flo gasped. 'Looking for me?'

'Saw you a couple of months ago in Putney doing a gig with some dick-faced manboy, long streak of piss, yeah, he gave me a card, which I binned immediately as he was so fucking rude. Sorry I dropped the ball on that one. Then time got away from me, one thing and another, then I saw you on YouTube because little Jesse Ribeiro, lovely little lad I do like his songs I really do – well, he gave you a share, did you see it?'

She'd heard of Jesse Ribeiro. A singer. A bit younger, just starting out, but not exactly a novice, thanks to his big brother, Sonny. Sonny Ribeiro was a hot, successful solo singer, with a raft of big hits, peaking around . . . five years ago? 'I covered a Sonny Ribeiro song on my YouTube chan-nel . . .' she said, as if offering excuses to her French teacher why she hadn't done her homework.

'Lovely. Anyway, Jesse's banging on about your song to anyone who'll listen which is . . . quite a lot of people, he's got 1.2 million followers, so, I gave Lily a bell to get you in. What you doing tomorrow?'

'I had no idea. I've been too scared to look at my stats.' Flo's head was spinning. 'Tomorrow?'

'Yeah. Comes after today if we're lucky. I happen to know Fenton Tucker has some studio time, maybe the day after as well, if you fancy it, you can have it. I mean, I'm kinda counting on it cos I FaceTimed Fenton during your performance, and his A&R guy as well and that woman who I can never remember what she does but she's always in meetings and never says nothing, all of them, and we want to see if these songs work in a studio. So we booked it. You can do that, right? Bring us your little set of . . . seven, is it? More if you've got 'em.'

Good news could sound like bad news at first. This was either the end of the world or the beginning of a new one. She managed to get some words out. 'Who's Fenton Tucker?'

Tanya threw her head back and laughed sharply, for exactly one-point-five seconds. 'Fucking gorgeous, I'll tell him you said that. Big guy at Dominion Records. Smashing, nurturing imprint that likes great big sexy hits. Jesse Ribeiro, your new best friend, is on them. Part of MRCU. You know them, right?'

She didn't, but nodded. 'Right.'

Tanya looked at Flo like an owl trying to decide whether to eat a mouse by ripping its head off or clawing its belly open. 'So if you're . . . what's the word, amenable, I'd like to represent you, what we do then is record the songs, film a take or two as well, I'll sort out a crew dead easy, three tunes will do, get the bollocks rolling, I reckon, then we get Tucker to license your existing YouTube videos as well, all counts toward the charts, and see what happens with a bit of a big label push. I wanna move on this. Triple-A are spunking millions on a female singer-songwriter but seriously she's the ugly sister to your Cinders. No offence, she is actually a very pretty girl but her songs are proper local, you're jet set, okay? This is raw talent, untouched. I even kinda like the "no make-up" thing.'

Flo was seeing, and hearing, double, too dizzy to point out she *was* wearing make-up. 'A push? What do you mean "move quickly"? Sorry I don't really . . .'

Tanya reached into her bag for a vape and took three quick successive puffs. Lily tutted. Tanya rolled her eyes. 'I know, darlin', I should be outside but I need a fag when I'm talking business.' She turned to face Flo, who desperately needed a seat, and an interpreter. 'I'm going too fast. I can get you a deal. I've already got Who-the-fuck-is-Fenton-Tucker salivating, but with the industry the way it is, things are different. The world is an applecart, you're about to upset the fucking lot, trust me. Record the three songs, get 'em on the label's channel, get Jesse Ribeiro hitting "share" faster than a woodpecker banging its cock on a sycamore, get 'em streaming, bit of a push, if they do all right with the numbers, you'll get a deal. Deal?'

A deal. A *record* deal? Flo finally took that seat. 'Do I . . . need a lawyer? Do I have to sign . . . I mean, tomorrow . . .'

Tanya nodded. 'Yeah, tomorrow's quick but there's no obligation and no cost to you because we're moving so fast. I can cut you something decent. If it doesn't work out, we go back to our lives. By which I mean I approach someone else. But believe me, Tucker needs this. In fact, you want to come meet him now?'

Flo allowed herself her first smile since meeting Tanya. 'I have a gig tonight with Elijah.'

'Make it your last one.'

'I have work tomorrow.'

'Phone in sick.' Tanya cocked her head to one side. 'We doing this, then? Be ready for the car, coming at eight.'

'Eight, tomorrow? Just like that?'

Tanya was already making her exit. 'Yep, just like that, be ready. You can start being late after we've had our first number one.'

On the way to the audition, Dylan felt in need of a talisman, and stopped at a little craft stall round the corner from the studio. He picked out a stretchy little copper wristband that reminded him of the sleeve garters his grandad used to wear, to find it was two for the price of one. When he arrived, a young man in triple denim took his name and handed him a script.

'Oh, I've already had this through, thanks. I'm doing it off-book.'

'Nope, you haven't. Last-minute change. This is the scene you're doing.'

What? But he'd spent hours over the weekend trying to channel any hunkiness he'd ever felt in his life into this scene. The character, Alfie, was a sexy himbo, basically a talking pair of Speedos. When did Dylan ever feel sexy? With Flo, mostly. He'd thought of their holiday in Greece, rivulets of sea water on their bodies, drying out in the sun, fingers wandering over bellies. His had been flatter then, he remembered with a trace of regret. Even worse, he wouldn't be rushing home to see Flo after the audition, to tell her how it went. No waking up beside her in the morning. He felt heavy from the loss.

'Dylan Fox?' He was on. He twanged the wristband, glad of the distracting sting against his skin.

The casting director and his assistants exchanged some pointed looks. He spotted the one from the theatre party straight away. 'I'm afraid . . . I didn't prepare, I didn't know about the change.'

The casting director nodded with a smile. 'I'm sure you can muddle through. So, you're a potential new doctor at *City Royal* who's just been told they haven't got the job they wanted. Whenever you're ready.'

Sounded ominous, but Dylan began to read anyway. 'You think you know me, don't you? I came and I waited in line, and I sat and I worried, and I wondered if this might be the moment someone took me seriously, someone saw what nobody else could see, and gave me a shot.'

Dylan stopped. God, this was cheesy as hell. And also . . . kind of familiar? He carried on. 'I gave it everything, but it wasn't to be. Fine. Fine. I respect your decision. But excuse me if I don't stand here and kiss your arse. I think you made a mistake, you've got this so wrong. And I want you to know, I'll never give up, I'll never stop trying. You haven't seen the last of me and you won't beat me. You understand? Never!'

His heart sank. So this was their game: humiliate him, teach him a lesson. Dylan tossed the sheet to the floor. 'I'm sorry, I was drunk, but . . . this is what I said to you at the theatre, isn't it?'

The casting director chuckled. 'Well, I had it zhuzhed up a bit, but it was quite dramatic on its own, to be honest. There's still some more to read. Do go on.'

Dylan sheepishly picked up the script. He didn't recognise this bit. 'Trust me, you don't know what you've thrown away with this one. You'll never meet someone so commit-ted, someone who's worked so freaking hard to get where he is, had every door slammed in his face and never lost his spirit. He'll give it his all, every day. There isn't one scene this guy's gonna do that won't knock it out the park, okay? He may be drunk tonight, but tomorrow he'll be sober, and talented as hell, and working for someone else unless you make your move.' Dylan stopped again. 'Hang on, did I say all this?'

'No, but your firecracker American cheerleader did, after you stropped off.'

Dylan hung his head. He couldn't tell whether he owed Lois his life, or an argument. 'Sorry.'

'Don't be embarrassed. She helped get you back through this door. Now we've done the histrionics, tell me how you got into acting, Dylan. Why are you doing this?'

He'd always had a lie prepared, something palatable, about his craft, and destiny. Once, he'd even invented being inspired by a famous grandparent, just so he could fit in. Now, he decided to be honest, and as unsentimental as possible. 'Drama clashed with geography on the timetable, and I was no good at geography. Turned out I liked it. So I joined a theatre group when I was fourteen, because I fancied Chloe Pickles. Turned out I was good at it.' He was a natural, according to the group leader, a fragrant woman called Lesley who had over seventy-six scarves. 'I couldn't sleep thinking about it, dreaming about the next time I could be on stage. Turned out I didn't want to do anything else.'

'And Chloe Pickles?'

'I don't know what happened to her.'

'That's showbiz.' The casting director smiled. 'To be honest,' he said, in a rasping voice that sounded like Max doing one of his caricatures, 'you'd be wasted on Alfie – nice guy but "nipples of the week" territory, which is crucial to the show but . . . not right for you.'

Was this a hint Dylan needed to put in a few more hours down the gym? 'So we're thinking . . . There might be another option for you. Heath, a new doctor, brooding, inner turmoil, a secret that's destroying him.'

'Heath?'

'Yes.' The casting director looked at his assistants and rolled his eyes. 'Dr Heathcliff. We're not big on subtlety here, Mr Fox.'

'Are you saying . . .'

'Heath has been on the cards for months, but we can't find the right guy. He's our next huge storyline and we want it on-screen soon. We're doing bisexuality, but sympathetically. And . . . okay, slightly gratuitously but not just in a "tired old nipples of the week" way.'

This guy really loved saying 'nipples of the week'; Dylan looked down at his own chest.

'Even drunk, even without your friend's incredible testimonial, you impressed me,' he said. 'Although you do owe that girl a bottle of champagne. What say you? You okay with kissing boys? Assuming you don't already.'

Dylan wanted to weep. Before he could stop himself, he blurted out: 'My best friend is gay!' They stifled their laughter.

The casting director clapped his hands joyously. 'Then, sweetheart, welcome to *City Royal* and welcome to Heath. Buckle up, this is gonna be huuuuuge. Just one thing . . .'

Dylan held his breath.

'Can you grow a beard? More light growth, Brad Pitt after a five-night bender, say, rather than Father Christmas. OK?'

Shaking so hard he could hardly hold his phone, Dylan

stopped for breath before going into the Tube station. He looked at his watch. What time was he supposed to be at work? He called Max.

'You're not in tonight. You're off. Last Thursday of the month. You usually book it off in advance, remember?'

Of course. Flo's regular gig. Same-seat promise. But not tonight. Never again. Unless . . .

'I've some absolutely *incred* new songs we should try.'

Flo looked up from doing her make-up to see Elijah staring back eagerly. Feeding back on Elijah's songwriting was always slightly awkward because he needed instant approval – like a dog needs a biscuit for giving you its paw – even if the song required loads of work. Which they always did. All Elijah cared about was the reaction, the sugar rush of validation. Flo painted on a bright smile, like she was serving a rude customer in the shop – she'd had a lot of practice. 'What are they about?'

'You, in a way.' This didn't sound good. 'Inspired by . . . what happened.'

Flo's smile didn't slip, her cheeks began to throb. Oh no. This was going to be 'root canal surgery without anaesthetic and Simply Red's greatest hits playing while it happens' levels of painful. 'What?'

Elijah grinned widely. On past experience, this face meant there'd be even more mangled metaphors than usual. 'You and Dylan. People love a good break-up song, don't they?'

Good ones, yes, thought Flo. 'I have a few of my own, actually. Seeing as, you know, it did actually happen to *me*.'

'Brilliant,' said Elijah, not listening. 'I've something really empowering, that can touch the audience. There's so much raw feeling to be uncovered.'

Clichés about 'touching the audience' aside, this energy was new. Elijah had never seemed so inspired. His songwriting wasn't always terrible – sexist tropes and fetishisation of women's bodies notwithstanding – but it was done with minimum effort. Everything he submitted had the air of something he'd thought up while waiting for his Coke Zero to thunk to the bottom of the vending machine. Flo was feeling charitable, still buzzing from her afternoon with Lily and Tanya, being among people who appreciated her music. She'd seen the effect 'The Last Hello' had on the audience; she wanted that feeling again.

'How about . . . we do one each?'

'Tonight?'

'Yeah. You do your break-up song, and I'll do one I've been working on.'

Elijah looked at his watch. 'We don't have time to learn them, the one I wrote is for a woman to sing.'

Learning one of her tunes had never troubled Elijah before; most of the time he did it his way, whether she liked it or not. He was really trying to show her something. Didn't everyone deserve a chance? 'You sing it. What does gender matter? Dismantle that shit. It's a song. Heartache is heartache.'

Elijah looked a bizarre mixture of sheepish yet unable to contain his excitement. 'It's called "Stiletto".'

Flo smiled. Of course it was. 'I'm a fast learner. I'll play you mine and then you can play . . . um . . . "Stiletto" for me and we'll do whichever we prefer. Democracy.' Democracy her fucking arse – the only way Elijah's song would be played on that stage would be if Flo dropped dead ten seconds before going on.

'I'll go first,' beamed Elijah, very *un*democratically. He picked up his guitar and closed his eyes. Flo swept her make-up bag to one side and leaned back against the dressing table, awaiting what could be Elijah's first flirtation with brilliance. Then he started playing.

Hmm. Not the tearful break-up ballad Flo had expected. Instead, Elijah's song was an embittered, angry call to arms for wronged women everywhere – but a comic book, schlocky novella version of wronged women, who seemed to be wearing skin-tight office wear when discovering their lovers' indiscretions. The song, which Elijah had the grace to sing without making eye contact, decreed that women should 'reclaim their sexy miniskirts and push those titties high'. *Titties*. Christ. Next, he encouraged the made-up, ultra-cool, kickass girls in his song to 'take that stiletto' – he actually pronounced 'that' as 'dat' and Flo reeled in horror at how problematic this was – and 'stab him in the eye'.

Elijah's hard sell of the benefits of murdering an ex ended with the refrain 'never mind the bad guys, the mad guys, the actors who hunt ya / just stick to the good guys, with blue eyes, in front of ya.' He finally looked right at her.

Flo sat open-mouthed for a few seconds, before taking her guitar and playing him 'The Last Hello', not looking at Elijah at all while she sang. Once done, she saw he was ashen-faced. Fuck, this song really did have something, didn't it? Everyone she played it to seemed to lose their minds. Maybe she *should* be more confident.

'I think mine has perhaps a less obviously patriarchal message . . .' he began. Flo said nothing, a small, light cough the only sign that she had no intention of responding or giving any feedback. Elijah slumped back in his seat, defeated, all mansplaining energy depleted. 'Maybe yours is more polished. Okay, you win.'

Glancing at her watch, she scooted into the bar area to grab a drink. Narelle was setting up the rowed seating.

'Third row, third in from right as usual?' said Narelle, hovering with a RESERVED sign.

Flo didn't want to explain. Didn't want to make it real. 'It's cool. No need tonight.' She scurried back to the dressing room before Narelle started asking questions.

Onstage, Flo's voice was shaky, even on songs she'd sung a zillion times, anxious at what was coming up. She'd look, occasionally, at the promise seat. A punter was using it for their coat, the space in the crowd acting as a metaphor for the hole in her life that wouldn't close. They performed 'The Last Hello' at the end. Some of the audience had already left, others were looking for their coats, or wondering if they had time for another drink. Elijah had agreed not to play while she sang 'The Last Hello' but instead tapped along lightly on the back of his own guitar. As she began singing, she felt nerves get the better of her; the crowd looked bored, like they'd rather be having a bikini wax or washing their car. She tried to look beyond, right through them, to the back of the pub, and the regular seating where boozers crowded round tables, oblivious. In one corner, an unmistakable silhouette: Dylan.

No way. She hadn't expected to be so floored by the sight of his face – his fucking gorgeous handsome face. Her heart creaked in recognition, like the timbers of an old ship remembering their time in the forest. It was like her voice box, her stomach, her pipes, every part of her body, recognised him, and her nerves disintegrated, and her voice soared, the last note piercing the air. The applause was so loud, the cheers genuine but disorientating. Flo smiled and bowed and looked to the back for Dylan again, but he was gone. She hurried off-stage, pushed the fire exit open and ran out into the cold night, the wind whipping up around her as her eyes searched the dark for Dylan.

'I didn't want to put you off.' He was standing behind her. 'But a promise is a promise.'

She turned to face him. He was holding out a rather bedraggled bunch of flowers. She was thrilled to see a reduced sticker on the cellophane. The old days reached out to her through a chink in time. How long had it been? A month? How could he look so different already? Why was he here? What did she want him to be here for? She wanted to touch his face – could she still do that? Was it allowed? She stepped toward him, slowly, like he was a timebomb. She felt sick, but held it together. 'Hello.'

Dylan lay his hand gently on her shoulder. She felt a charge through her. 'You smashed it. You blew me away.'

She didn't know what to say that wouldn't overcomplicate the moment. 'I'm glad you came.'

'So am I. Take these.' The flowers felt like deadweights in her hand now she realised they were being offered as a goodbye. 'Go back in, your audience awaits. Enjoy it.' He leaned in and kissed her on the forehead. 'Night, superstar.' He began to walk away.

'Wait!' she shouted after him. He stopped. 'Two minutes. I'm getting my stuff. You can't just give me flowers and leave; I'm not a cenotaph! Buy me a drink and tell me how brilliant I was again. Okay?'

'Okay.'

Dylan realised they'd been to this pub before. Back on one of their earliest dates, their first away from the Consulate. A food mix-up meant Dylan had sat and watched Flo eat – his main course arrived as she ate her last bite. Now, they caught up, trading facts and figures like news reporters, talking about everything but what they actually wanted to talk about.

His auditions, her gig, the studio time. Max's growing impatience with everything Dylan said and did, Flo's mother being her usual robotic self. When she got to the part about Elijah and his 'Stiletto', the pair of them were in tears laughing.

'An eventful month,' said Dylan. 'Tomorrow, the studio . . . the big one. I'm so proud. Is this the moment you finally get rid of Elijah?'

Flo blushed in guilt. 'Sounds awful, but . . . I hope so. Even if nothing happens at the studio tomorrow or I don't like the setup, whatever, it's time to go it alone.'

'You're getting good at that.' He regretted saying it immediately; he hadn't meant to sound embittered. He realised that, without thinking, they were now holding hands across the table.

Flo slowly moved her hand away. 'Can we cut the shit? You miss me, and I miss you. Isn't it obvious? You've heard the song. I sound like I've buried twenty husbands. You do miss me, don't you?'

Dylan nodded. Flo tried to hide her exasperation. 'We broke up for the wrong reasons. People interfering. Me being a jealous cow over Lois. I regret that.'

'It wasn't just that.' Dylan didn't want to lay the blame elsewhere. 'There were other issues. My . . .' Come on, he thought, you can say it, admit to your stupid pride. 'The way I like to do things, take care of myself.' Wimp, he thought.

'Oh yes!' She laughed. 'But aren't we better off working

through stuff together rather than walking away?' A barman called last orders. 'Everything that's happened the last few weeks, all I've wanted to do is tell you. I can't think of anything else.'

Dylan went to get more drinks. Plonking them on the table, he said, plainly: 'Same. I can't think of anybody else.'

'Then, again, cut the shit. Let's get back together.'

All Dylan wanted to do was say yes, so his days could mean something again. 'What about your mum? Estelle? All I ever seemed to hear was how bad we were for each other. That I was holding you back. Lois was the same. How can we work through stuff in all that noise?'

Flo sighed deeply and downed her drink. 'How about a spot of method acting?'

'What do you mean?'

'Not tell them.' Flo was grinning like a gameshow host. Dylan could almost see lightbulbs flashing above her head. 'Yes! Pretend we're still broken up, to everyone.'

A smile crept across Dylan's face. 'All they ever say is we're getting in each other's way. But if we keep it low a few weeks . . . I'll be on TV, you'll have your record deal.'

Flo showed a flash of worry. 'Hopefully I will. But, yeah, all we do is carry on thriving and then say "I told you so", when it turns out we've been together all along. Right?'

'It might be hard to hide how happy I am to be with you again.'

'Am I really gonna have to remind the actor how to act? Just fake it. Comfort eating, staying in bed, blasting out depressing ballads, generally being the biggest downer the word has ever seen. To be honest, it'll be business as usual for me.'

'And how long do we do this for?'

Flo looked excited. She knew she had him now. 'We could pencil in a little reconciliation for . . . say, the start of the summer? It would be magical! What do you think?'

Dylan chuckled. 'It's gonna be hard not to tell the world. I suppose it keeps people off our backs, lets us just . . . *be*, no interruptions or opinions.' The more Dylan thought about it, the more appealing it was. More space, working through things in private, focusing on themselves.

Flo kissed his hand. 'I honestly, honestly think the stuff that's been annoying us will fall away if we keep it to ourselves.'

'I can't even tell Max? And you can't blab to Estelle?'

'Nope. Admit it, it sounds exciting. Sneaking around? Like being in the French resistance, or a spy or something?'

Dylan looked into Flo's eyes. It was so good to see her again. 'A lot of them ended up getting shot by firing squad so not the best comparison.' But there was something romantic about it. 'Here, take this.' He slipped the little copper wrist-band over her hand.

'What's this? Are we part of a cult?'

Dylan smiled shyly. 'I picked it up earlier. I've got another. Two for the price of one. I *knew* I was meant to buy it; I've been lucky since the second I put it on. It's brought me back to you.' Its twin was still in his pocket; he popped it on now. 'Maybe we could think of each other, of us, while we're wearing it. You don't have to, though.'

Flo snapped it lightly against her wrist. 'No, I like it. Our little secret. Less melodramatic than half a locket.'

They hugged and each wristband promptly got caught in the hair of the other. 'Fucking ouch!' yelped Dylan.

Flo winked. 'No cosying up to other girls, or that's what you'll get. And so will they.'

They were the last ones in the pub. The night was over. All he wanted was to take her home, show her how much he'd missed her, then eat a fourteen-inch pizza, naked, like they used to. But Flo had a big day tomorrow and Dylan needed to get his head round this.

They waited outside for Flo's cab. They stood apart from one another, like they'd had an awkward first date; he'd already forgotten how to be around her. He was sure it wouldn't take long to get reacquainted.

'I won't text you in the morning, I don't want to put you off. I'll be thinking of you. I'll be there in spirit.'

'Of course you will. All the songs are about you.'

Shit, he'd never mentioned the songs, asked her about the lyrics. Too late now. 'Are we sure about this?' said Dylan.

'You'll already be on TV playing one part. What's another? I'm sure.'

'I love you.' He leaned forward and gave her the kiss they'd both been waiting for. It was like ten Christmas Days. 'As long as it's a limited run. Just a few weeks.'

'Early summer, latest.'

'Then I'm ready to go onstage.'

PART TWO.

part two

Nine.

'Cautiously optimistic' is how Dylan described his feelings about his first few days on the show to his mother. Everyone he met, he liked. He was still pinching himself every time he walked into the studio and, taking Lois's advice, had made instant friends with hair and make-up. 'They're the difference between looking like a heart-throb and a heart attack,' she'd warned.

When he sat in her chair for the first time, head of hair and make-up Della had told him she was glad to finally get her hands on a naturally handsome face, which made him blush.

As a 'brooding' soul – their words – Heath was something of a mystery and hadn't had many big scenes with major characters. His first appearance on camera was lying under a pile of bricks. This was apparently the result of a helicopter landing on the hospital just as Heath was walking through the doors for his first shift – a scene not untypical on *City Royal* – but his main storyline was a romance with a sweet nurse called Holly, played by an equally sweet actor called Georgia. Her hospital nemesis was the brilliant superbitch surgeon Alessandra Malone, whom viewers would expect to be intent on stealing Heath for herself. The twist? The one to watch out for was Alessandra's brother, Mario, who was in the process of being recast because the previous actor turned out to have homophobic tweets from 2011 in his portfolio. Mario, with his new face, would catch Heath's eye and, in characteristic spite, Alessandra would encourage the union to get at Holly. Reading the storylines made Dylan's head spin. He hadn't yet met Ciara McLean, who played villainous Alessandra, but being a voracious magazine and gossip site reader, Flo had the insider info already.

'She's shagged every single man on that show,' Flo claimed one afternoon as they FaceTimed. Dylan was peeling off the scrubs he'd bought online when he'd discovered he couldn't smuggle out his costume, much to Flo's disappointment. 'The Last Hello' was climbing the charts, and Flo was haring up and down the country doing personal appearances and radio shows, so a quick half an hour getting each other off through a screen was the best they could hope for. They still managed to speak every day. On more wholesome nights, they'd play their good old Top Five game. If they weren't in the mood for chatting, they'd leave their phones on and watch a movie together. It was still quite romantic.

'Ciara McLean is supposed to be the nastiest bitch,' continued Flo, clearly enjoying herself. 'Anyone she hasn't shagged, she's dashed vodka in their face, I read. Including that one who plays Holly, Georgia Thingy.'

Dylan caught Flo's eye as he untied his trousers. 'She's been off for a few weeks, so I haven't met her. Not sure I want to. Apparently she doesn't hang out with everyone else.'

'She *is* very beautiful, though,' Flo mused. 'Maybe that's why she's so mean.'

Dylan manoeuvred the trousers down his legs slowly. It was quite hard to do this gracefully while trying to keep his eyes on the screen. 'Well, you're beautiful and the opposite of mean.' He saw Flo give a shudder, like she was shaking away a bad thought. He chuckled. 'Flo.'

'Yes?' She dropped her gaze.

Dylan wished he could walk his fingers up Flo's naked back. She liked that. 'Please tell me you're not . . . uh, worried about some woman I haven't even met.'

Her face was very red. 'I think she looks like Lois, don't you?'

So that was it. 'I'm immune to Loises,' said Dylan in as soothing a voice as he could muster. 'I'm with you, anyway. I've never been unfaithful.'

Flo bit her lip. 'But you're outwardly single and I know you . . . haven't had lots of experience with . . . uh . . . anyone, I mean women, so maybe you will . . . uh.'

Dylan laughed. 'Seize the opportunity and become a sex machine overnight? Doesn't seem likely, look at me, I'm doing a striptease with my socks on.' He whirled his underwear round his head and saw Flo's face relax. 'Now . . . are you ready to go under?'

A few weeks ago, when something amazing happened it would have Flo hyperventilating and diving for her phone to message everyone she'd ever met. Now, she now took time to enjoy the moment, safe in the knowledge that, sooner or later, it would be topped by something even more fantastical. Today, however, was big. Flo stood against the white backdrop as the camera flashed, the hunk of metal starting to feel clammy in her hands. A video camera was being set up in front of her – the tripod kept collapsing but she'd learned not to laugh at technical hitches, as time was money and she had precious little of either. She was about to film her reaction to what still seemed like a dream. The guy setting up the video camera – Bobby (she was trying to remember everyone's names) – took the award from her and shined it with his cuff.

'Fingerprints,' he said, grinning. 'We get hundreds of comments online if there's even one little smudge.'

He hopped back to the camera, did a final check, and somewhere in the room, someone did a countdown from five. Flo's eyes darted quickly to find Tanya in the room and when they did, Tanya winked and nodded. The light on the camera brightened. Showtime.

Flo smiled and let out an involuntary squeal, staring into the camera like it was her lover's eyes. She imagined Dylan's face and took a deep breath.

'Hello!' she gushed. 'Oh my goodness! I just want to say . . . you've made my dreams come true.' She looked adoringly down at the award, before remembering it needed to be prominent in the shot, and raised it to kiss. 'Errrr . . . This means so much to me. Thank you, from the bottom of my . . . my broken heart' – that bit had been Dylan's idea, she struggled to keep a straight face – 'for making "The Last Hello" an actual, proper, chart-freaking-topping number-one single.'

The light snapped off, signifying the recording was over, but for Flo, the room was still filled with brilliant light. A tear fell down her face.

'Ooh,' cooed Tanya as she wrapped a protective arm around Flo. 'Shame we didn't get that on camera. They love to see you cry, don't they, sadistic buggers.'

Flo leaned her head on Tanya's shoulder. 'They identify with it, I think. Vulnerability . . . it's . . .'

'It's working.' Tanya absentmindedly blew a kiss to the departing cameraman. 'Thanks, Bobby. Right . . . next.'

It was the performance on the radio that had sent her viral. She'd done 'The Last Hello' and a cover of 'Fast Car', which Jesse Ribeiro had just had a hit with – a nod to his part in her success, Tanya said. Soon social media was aflame, abuzz, a-everything, her views were through the roof. With everything happening so quickly, there wasn't much time to style her or give her a specific image, which Flo found a bit disappointing, but Tanya told her was a blessing in disguise.

'Lucky for you, starting out at twenty-seven, not seventeen,' Tanya had said. 'If it were up to them, you'd have gone full Princess Leia golden bikini.' Flo hadn't understood the reference; she'd had to google. 'You're real. A bit of girl-next-door, mixed with . . . keeping-up-with-the-Joneses glamour. Everyone wants to be your mate but ain't quite got the guts to ask you out for a drink.'

'I don't mind a little bit of . . . gold bikini? Maybe just the top half, with a . . . shirt over it?' But it was a no. Her boobs were staying resolutely out of sight.

Flo's main selling point was her voice, though her face was important. Tanya said all she needed was a make-up artist she could trust for the inevitable close-ups of raw emotion. She now never arrived anywhere without false lashes thicker than draught excluders and immaculate eyes and lips.

Estelle had screamed in delight when she first saw Flo in her popstar getup. 'You look like a drag queen whose glamorous ballgowns got ruined in a fire so you've had to borrow clothes from . . . I don't know, an MP, maybe. But I love it!'

When the popstar embellishments were swept away with a wet wipe, Flo looked like . . . her own plainer, younger sister. This had the fortunate or unfortunate side-effect – Flo couldn't decide which yet – of never being recognised anywhere she went. They knew her song, they knew her voice, but that was it. They probably didn't even know her name – Tanya had advised her only to use her first name. 'Floria is a good six letters, ends with an A so nice and feminine, looks sweet on single covers and posters. Girly, but approachable.' Battista was, apparently, too 'foreign'. 'Current climate, y'know,' Tanya had said. 'Sounds a bit like "bastard" as well. I wouldn't want to chuck it to the tabloids to play with, y'know?'

Soon, 'The Last Hello' was all over the radio and, after she sang on a late-night chat show, charted in the Top 40. And now . . . number one. Her phone started buzzing with messages.

Estelle: This is EPIC. Am buying red carpet on eBay as we speak. This was very likely to be the truth.

Barnaby: I'm so happy for you. I didn't even realise the charts were still a thing! Well, at least he messaged.

Serena: You've always been my number one, and now the WORLD can see it.

Serena was, of course, the name Dylan's number was stored under on her phone, in case Joy went snooping. They'd worked out a code for getting through to each other when prying eyes were nearby. They called it their 'basic bitch intro'. One of them would text: Hey hunni, how u doin? Heard the latest? xox

If there was no answer, they'd leave it. Any reply meant the coast was clear.

There was no congratulatory message from Elijah, of course. A bridge she'd have to cross sooner or later, but as Estelle had said, 'A deal for the pair of you was never on the table. Elijah won't starve.'

Once her next interview was over, Flo flopped into the car, the make-up artist leaning over to add finishing touches.

'How long we in the car for?'

Tanya didn't raise her eyes from her phone. 'About forty-five. We've got a phoner in twenty. Can you talk in a moving car? It's not gonna make you yak up your breakfast, is it?'

'No, it's fine.' Flo reached for her own phone and put on her headphones, staring into the screen.

The make-up artist leaned over. 'What you watching?'

Flo didn't look up. 'Special *City Royal* and *Emergency* cross-over episode tonight.'

'I didn't know you liked soaps,' said Tanya. 'All those surgical scenes, that melodrama. Grosses me out. Do you always watch it?'

'Not always,' said Flo quietly. 'Just want to see tonight's.' Her eyes stayed glued to her screen as the titles ended and a camera panned over what looked like a disaster scene. She scrunched her eyes up slightly as she surveyed the devastation. In there somewhere, under a tonne of foam bricks, was the love of her life, making his screen debut.

Dylan had promised his mother he'd come back to Yorkshire for his first on-screen appearance, so he and Max made a weekend of it.

'Your last weekend of freedom before housewives, and

householders, are throwing their knickers at you,' Max laughed as the pair of them mainlined cans of lager on the train, neither prepared to admit how scary this was.

His mum started crying as soon as she opened the front door, bursting with pride. The good version of pride, Dylan thought, not my warped hang-up about splitting the bill in Pizza Express. He'd tried to watch Flo's number-one video sneakily on the journey up, but Max kept slapping his phone out of his hand and telling him he was an unsociable bitch.

Dylan was sick with nerves as he waited for *City Royal* to start. Not just for himself, but everyone watching, everyone who'd believed in him. Even Lois had stayed in to see it, she said, to make sure he'd been worth her outburst and inevitable blacklisting from that casting director's future projects. Please just let me be good, he prayed to a higher power he had no interest in any other time. He'd intended to sit in another room, but his mum led him to the sofa and sat rigid with anticipation, clasping his hand. And there he was, better-looking than he'd ever thought possible – in his head, he thanked Della's magic touch. For a second, he dared to believe he deserved it. He looked at his mum, her eyes streaming, and Max, his boy, there for him since the off, and couldn't help but spill his inner monologue. 'I did that for you,' he said, which set his mum off even more and had Max pile on top of both of them. Dylan thought of Flo. This moment had been close to perfection, but he wished she'd been there to share it. He'd have to get used to that feeling.

Flo sat in the park, waiting. Her first full day off in weeks, and she'd hidden it from everyone. Her friends, especially Estelle, were feeling neglected.

'When do we get to spend a proper night with you?' Estelle had moaned as a zonked Flo had cried off the Fortnightlies. 'You're not too famous for your coven, are you?'

But even now, with a number one under her belt, Flo didn't feel famous at all. She didn't get mobbed at radio stations or TV shows – even the paparazzi were quite polite. It was like they confirmed Flo's biggest fear – that this was temporary, a blip, and she'd soon be back unboxing amethyst face-rollers at her mum's shop. She wasn't a star in the making; this was her fifteen minutes. Any story about her she read painted her as lonely and some made her sound like a victim, thanks to this faceless 'lothario' ex. Flo's official line in interviews was 'it was over a long time ago', and it felt that way at times – she couldn't even connect that awful break-up with where she and Dylan were now. Despite spending so little time together, she'd never felt closer to him.

But today, on the way here, a little taste of honey. She was recognised in public for the first time ever, on the Tube. Two girls spent ten minutes nudging each other and whispering. Then, once it was clear Flo was getting off and about to sail out of their lives for ever, they pounced and asked for a selfie. Today of all days, thought Flo, as she smiled shyly, not sure whether she should've loved this as much as she did.

She sat and watched people pass by, oblivious to the woman who'd spent her fourth week at number one sitting right there, in the most expensive summer dress she'd ever bought. Despite her mother's claims the music business was tawdry and disgusting, populated solely by swivel-eyed coke addicts who'd pressure her daughter into sex in exchange for a record deal, she knew her parents were proud.

An old man hobbled into view, scratching his beard and

looking puzzled, evidently searching for somewhere to sit. His eyes still had a hint of their youthful sparkle, but were almost lost in the crags and creases of old age; beneath a straggly beard, his tongue poked out, red and panting in the heat. Flo had always been brought up to be kind and patient with her elders, which she largely stuck to – besides her mum – so she ignored the wart on the end of his nose, and that his eyebrows hadn't been trimmed since England last won the World Cup, and shifted up to accommodate him. Yet another blissfully happy couple strolled by.

'Thanks, petal.' The man's voice was strained and weary, like it had taken Herculean effort to speak. Once seated, he stared ahead. 'Beautiful day.'

'It is.'

The old man sniffled and leaned in closer to Flo. She didn't flinch. 'Trees are in bloom. Quite lusty.'

Flo stared at more passers-by. 'Yes.'

As the strangers disappeared from view, the old man shuffled up. Flo checked to see if anyone was around. Very calmly, she replied: 'There's a beautiful cluster of trees down there.' She pointed vaguely.

The old man chuckled. 'I see.' His voice was more animated now, no longer straining. 'Wanna take a walk there and fuck my brains out?'

Flo turned to the old man and burst out laughing. 'Dylan! For fuck's sake, stay in character!'

Dylan's joyful laugh contrasted with the tired, worn face in front of her. His eyes gleamed. 'I'm managing to keep my hands off you, which is very out of character.'

This wasn't their first secret liaison. There'd been furtive fumbling in the long grass on Parliament Hill once, and a chaste, romantic afternoon with nothing but fingers entwined, in the corner of a pub garden where nobody would ever know them. Even if Flo's face wasn't familiar, her song was everywhere, and Dylan's face was beamed into millions of homes every week, so they'd had to get inventive. A night away in Brighton had been a disaster – they'd gone in disguise, booked two rooms in the crummiest hotel they could find and pretended to be colleagues on a business trip. They found themselves among a convention of Tina Turner fans who sang the wrong words to 'The Best', so far out of tune they'd need a map to find their way back to the melody, way into the early hours. They daren't even leave the room to escape the racket – as soon as they'd arrived a woman in full Tina *Beyond Thunderdome* drag had pointed at Dylan and said, 'Ooh, aren't you on the telly?'

They were reduced to sneaking to Flo's when the Battistas were out, or Max's when he was at work, or . . . ridiculous scenes like this in the hope of some time alone. A regular date was nigh impossible.

'I didn't realise you were going to look so hideous! That beard, my God. It's so real. Who did it?'

'Hair and make-up. Told 'em I was surprising a friend. I need it back in the box by seven. So? About these trees.'

Flo stood and began to walk away. 'Come on then, Grandad, and keep your hands on the walking stick until we're out of sight.'

Dylan followed at a snail's pace, like every second was torture, but knowing it would be worth it once they were alone.

Dylan's first flushes of fame had been rather different. With a soap opera – sorry, continuing drama – it was instant.

He'd already been on the cover of *Soap Suds* as part of an ensemble and a solo cover was imminent. According to Max, no fewer than seven Facebook groups were dedicated to discussing the mysterious and brooding Dr Heathcliff. So far, 'mysterious and brooding' seemed to translate to having hardly any lines, skulking about interrupting other characters doing something more interesting, or striding purposefully out of rooms. He hadn't had a 'nee-naw' yet, their name for when the last scene of the episode ended on your face, before the theme tune started up with its signature wail of an old-school ambulance – that was a sign you'd really arrived. He was desperate to get rid of the beard, though – fake and real.

'It was really ticklish,' laughed Flo as she adjusted herself in the little rowing boat they'd hired on the lake. 'It must be driving you mad.'

'At least this comes off. My real one is a nightmare. I can't touch it, only hair and make-up can trim it, for "continuity". I'm really hoping they write in a way to get it singed off.'

'Maybe when he comes out he can go clean-shaven.'

'That's ages away.' Dr Heathcliff's bisexuality reveal to viewers was *City Royal*'s Christmas cliffhanger, and even after that, it was set to be a potboiler for many months.

Flo dragged her hand in the water. Ducks looked on, hoping she would drop some food. 'It must be nice knowing what's ahead of you. I don't know what's coming next.' Another single was on the cards definitely, and probably an EP by the end of the year. But a full album? Nobody seemed to be saying anything. Maybe it wouldn't happen at all. A couple more YouTube stars were already blowing up, with labels eager to replicate Flo's literal overnight success. Once you'd had a taste of it, it was too easy to feel on the back foot – even if you were at number one.

Dylan leaned forward, his fluid movements at odds with his old-guy drag. 'I know what's coming. Superstardom. Isn't this so fucking brilliant? So mad? All falling into place. Soon we'll be . . .' He stopped himself from mentioning it, telling everyone they were back together. Flo had a lot riding on her image as a scorned songbird. He tried not to think of the song's lyrics too much. Flo had assured him the parts about 'lotharios' and 'snide boy, wide boys' had referred to previous useless exes, not him, and the rest of the song, the happy parts, were reminiscences of her time with him. Maybe she was sparing his feelings, or regretting her post-break-up candour. Lois was utterly oblivious to any mention of her, thankfully. 'How are you managing to keep up the broken-hearted act?' Dylan imagined Estelle and Vérité and Midge and Pidge or whatever, and the rest of them queuing up with voodoo dolls for Flo to stab to shreds.

Flo laughed. 'I've been trying not to overdo it, but if I'm in the mood for comfort food or chicken nuggets, I might pinch myself to get a tear. It's the only way I can stop Estelle slagging me off for not ordering a salad.'

'Speaking of slagging off . . . I bet Estelle's having the time of her life.'

Flo looked into the distance and shivered. 'I thought we promised not to talk about that.'

'Sorry.'

'Actually, no, not too much gloating. She can see it upsets me. She's not a monster.'

Dylan decided to keep quiet.

'And you? Managing to keep up your extra acting job?'

Max had threatened to kill Dylan only that morning if he didn't 'snap out of it'. 'All that success, on literal televisions with an actual acting job and you still look like you've had a bad wank in the rain in Blackpool. Can't you try to enjoy it?'

'I'm managing,' Dylan grunted as he grabbed the oar. 'You'll have to help me with this. I'm supposed to be ninety.' They began to row, but out of sync, so the boat started turning in circles. 'It'll be brilliant when we can stop pretending, won't it?'

Flo smiled. 'Yeah. It will. More brilliant than it already is. Once I know about the album . . . we can really show them how brilliant we are.'

'Can't wait.' Dylan scratched his fake beard distractedly. He had to stay focused. Not much longer now.

As they got off the boat, they saw a group of tourists looking over warily. Some were pointing.

'Fans of yours?' said Dylan, realising he should've stooped while disembarking rather than hopping out like a gazelle. He clutched at his stick extra hard now.

'Two celeb spots in one day! Maybe they think you're my dad.'

One tourist peeled away from the group. Flo quickly practised her best 'yes of course you can have a selfie' face, secretly thrilled to get another go so soon. Shame the tourist's orange gilet would clash with her dress.

'It *is* you, isn't it?'

Flo stepped forward like she was accepting a prize. 'Yes.'

But the tourist brushed past her and headed for Dylan. 'Murdering bastard!' she said, producing a water bottle and dousing Dylan with its contents.

'Wh-what?'

'You should be locked up. What are you even doing here in the open air?!' The tourist chucked the empty bottle at Dylan and it bounced off, falling to the ground with a pathetic clatter. 'Rot in hell!' She spat at his feet – Flo noticed now how ugly Dylan's old man shoes were, fastened with velcro. Had he taken them off while they fucked? Yuck. Once done, the tourist walked back to her group, hollering 'Gerald Caldwell! Murderer!' over her shoulder as she went.

'What just happened?' Dylan's breathing was panicked. His prosthetics were deteriorating rapidly as the sweat poured. 'Is my acting that terrible?'

'Ah, right.' Floria tapped into her phone and showed Dylan her screen. 'Gerald Caldwell, demonic doctor, killed ten of his patients.' Flo scrolled. 'He actually died of a heart attack in prison in 2017 so it's no wonder she was surprised to see you. The resemblance is uncanny.'

Dylan's eyes flicked from the phone to the rapidly departing crowd of orange gilets. 'Wow,' he muttered. 'Fame really is for ever, isn't it?' They both looked at each other, the weight of that truth hanging over them for the first time, like a raincloud.

Ten.

Dylan read the headline at the top of page seven again.

FLORIA'S SECRET SNIDE BOY IS CITY ROYAL HUNK

What a world, to be called a hunk and snide all in one sentence. What would his mum say when she saw this? All his life he'd tried to keep his nose clean, never bring bother to her door like the other boys on the estate, but here he was, exposed as the subject of Flo's not very complimentary number one. He'd originally told his mother the song 'probably wasn't autobiographical' – this fell apart now a so-called 'close pal of the couple' had mentioned Dylan's 'destructive obsession with a glamorous ex'.

It was a fairly extensive character assassination, and to avoid repeating themselves, they'd given him a new slew of nicknames: not only was he a 'love rat who used his dead-end bar job to pick up women' he was also a 'loser lothario who spent his days loafing around while Floria worked all hours in her mother's shop, or singing at sleazy bars to make ends meet'. They also called him a 'secretive thesp' which made him laugh out loud. Dylan assured his sisters, hysterical in group chat, that their childhood cats had a greater breadth of sexual experience than he did and tried not to feel too repulsed by his dad's leering phone call, every chuckle an accusation and a validation.

'I never knew you had it in you, son.'

'I don't.'

'Sounds like it's been in everyone else though.'

Flo was inconsolable over the phone, desperately sorry, unable to think who would've sold such a lie. Even though Dylan felt sick and kind of violated, not to mention worried the *City Royal* bosses would be furious, he was, dare he admit, impressed the paper had thought him worthy enough to mention. As low as some of the blows were, it was all so ludicrous, he couldn't even find it in himself to be mad.

'There's no point trying to work out who it was. What would we do about it?' Dylan had flicked through enough of his mum's Jackie Collins novels to know there was always someone with a grudge in the background, desperate for publicity. But he didn't want to make Flo paranoid, especially as he couldn't console her in person.

'I'd know who to trust,' sniffed Flo, her anguish heavy. 'Obviously we have to issue a strong denial.'

'Do we?'

Priya had thought differently. No denials, she'd said. 'Baby, once you say you didn't do something, any time you stay silent, they'll think you *did* do it. Say nothing now, they'll expect nothing in the future. Keep people guessing. People will look at you different after this – and not necessarily in a bad way.'

Flo was gobsmacked. 'So we do nothing at all?'

Dylan didn't like to think of her upset. This was his opportunity to be that man he'd wanted to be, unbothered by anything, proud in the best way. Stoic. 'Forget about it. Priya's on it.'

'By the way,' said Flo with a trace of a giggle. '*Grazia* has done a post on Instagram about you. Five slides! You should see the comments.'

'Do I want to know?' He definitely did.

'Women, going ga-ga, mainly, one of them said she wished she could be "that cheap little bracelet on your wrist", or "OMG I love Dylan Fox's cute little copper mangle.'

'What the hell is a mangle?!'

'A man-bangle, I think. The *Guardian* did a thing on masculine jewellery too, using you as inspiration. So . . . as bad as this tabloid thing is, it's got you noticed.'

Dylan's hand went up to the St Christopher round his neck. He felt weirdly dirty. He wasn't sure this was how he wanted to be noticed. 'Gotta go, Priya's on the other line.'

'Baby, baby, baby, all is good with the exec producer, okay? *Soap Suds* is giving you that solo cover and apparently a broadsheet's coming in to do a piece on *City Royal*'s so-called rejuvenation. Press office has been trying to make it happen for months and suddenly – boom! – it's on. Think we can guess why.'

Sure, this was great for the show, but what about his reputation?

Priya spoke very slowly, like she was talking to a child. 'Lean into this as much as you can. You're playing a sexually . . . adventurous character on the cusp of a hot and heavy love-rat story of your own. Embrace it.'

'Do I really want to be known as the guy who broke Floria's heart?'

'For now, why wouldn't you, baby? That's exactly what you did, didn't you? For better or worse.'

Dylan twanged the copper bracelet against his wrist, reminding himself of the role they were both to play. No slip-ups, no breaking character. 'Yeah,' he said, resignedly, 'I guess I did.'

Dylan's first scene with Ciara McLean was the following day. She barely acknowledged him when she arrived; they did a couple of run-throughs, then went for the take. Dylan was nervous, but as Flo always told him, 'Call it excitement and you'll feel better.' In their first scene, Heath was supposed to warn off the evil Alessandra on behalf of saintly Holly, so Dylan had to get up close and be as menacing as possible – no mean feat when the actor the tabloids had nicknamed the Tigress was staring back at you.

Once they heard 'cut', they went back into position for the next take. Ciara was examining her nails with deep fascination. Dylan stuck out his hand. Ciara's eyes tracked slowly from it, up to his face. Lean into it, Priya had said – now was his chance.

'Hello,' said Dylan as evenly as he could, trying to grin and hoping she couldn't hear his knees knocking, 'I'm the love rat, loser lothario, or snide boy. Take your pick.'

Ciara nodded curtly, a smile crawling to the corners of her mouth as she shook his hand. 'Tigress, pleased to meet you. Rats, tigers . . . there's a whole zoo here.'

Dylan laughed. Ciara moved a step closer. 'I heard that song. The one about you.'

Dylan felt himself going red. Nope, no blushing. No true lothario wide boy, snide whatever would blush.

'Quite an honour, shame you had to behave so . . . dishonourably to be in it. Assuming it's true of course, not that I ever would.'

Dylan was about to stutter a denial, or an apology; he wasn't sure what. But Ciara's face reset and she stepped back into position.

'Second take. Action!'

The morning was exciting, although Ciara swept off without another word, but now Dylan had to hang around for a quick scene with Georgia, playing his angelic girlfriend. How luxurious to feel a tiny bit bored, in his dream-come-true job. He tried to stay out of the way until he was called, crew scurrying around him, lights flicking on and off, someone in the distance shouting for wardrobe. He saw a young woman waving at him. He'd seen her hanging around; she was the journalist doing the feature for the broadsheet. He smiled back, which she took as her cue to approach.

'You don't seem as monstrous as I've heard,' she said, after introducing herself. No denials, Dylan remembered, lean into the lothario. He looked at his watch. 'I don't change into a werewolf until midnight,' he said, pausing for the journalist's inevitable laughter. People always laughed at his jokes now, no matter how awful they were. 'Anyway, as you know, there are always at least two sides to every story.'

The journalist laughed politely again. 'Maybe I can help you tell one.' Dylan was sure she batted her eyes then; he'd never seen anyone do it in the flesh before. 'I can see why Floria is gutted to lose you, though, I hope you don't mind me saying.'

Of course he fucking didn't. He tried to suppress his grin. Maybe the lothario lifestyle wasn't so bad after all.

'I have a few questions . . . for the profile? Stop me if they're too painful, I understand.'

'I thought it wasn't about me?'

'Oh no, it isn't, and I probably won't use it, but you're a rising star. A couple of quotes will help put you on the map, get you into the homes of some readers who don't know you.'

Dylan liked the idea of being discussed over breakfast in the kitchens of well-heeled readers. It would be nice for his mum to see him in a quality paper with no screaming head-lines above his face. The idea of infiltrating the Battistas' silent breakfasts was quite appealing, too. 'Okay, shoot.'

How long were he and Flo together, how did they meet, when did they break up, what was it all about? Dylan didn't answer the last question. He didn't want to lie, *or* tell the truth. 'Floria sings that better than I could tell it.' Mysterious. Maybe playing Dr Heathcliff was rubbing off.

The journo smiled patiently. 'I have to say I'm puzzled why a . . . a well-rounded guy like you, a man of the world, would be with a girl like Floria.'

'A girl like Floria?' Dylan tried to ignore the *Jaws* theme music gradually getting louder in his head.

'She's a bit mumsy, isn't she? Kind of sweet and . . . not innocent, but demure, maybe? From the very proper side of the tracks while you are . . .' Was she going to go there? Was she going to cast up his background? Apparently not. 'Is that accurate? What I'm saying is . . . were you her first boyfriend?'

Dylan suppressed a laugh. The journo was completely misunderstanding their dynamic. Maybe if he had been 'well-rounded', things would've been easier. The secret to a good lie was to weave the truth throughout.

'No. I wasn't her first boyfriend, far from it. She kissed a lot of frogs before she . . .' This sounded shit, but Flo had said that once. Scores of boys before him who never hit the mark, that she'd never loved. Was it too personal to reveal? Too late now. If Flo could quote him in a song, why couldn't he quote her? 'That's what she told me, anyway.'

'I see. First love, beautiful. I guess you taught her how to love, then, brought her out of her shell? After so many disasters? That passionate awakening she'd been waiting for. She must've been so fragile.'

This was starting to sound like Dylan was some kind of swashbuckling walking Viagra erection and Floria a hapless, overpowered virgin. This felt weird. There was 'leaning in', and there was lying.

'She didn't need me to bring her out of her shell . . .' he paused, thinking of their last assignation, clawing at each other in the woods, her hands pressing hard onto his chest as they both came. 'We couldn't get enough of each other. Wherever we went. Anywhere.'

'Anywhere?'

He should have stopped, but he wanted to big Flo up, make her sound less pathetic than the journalist was suggesting. Flo wasn't the fragile girl-next-door, or cold and unfeeling; she was a magnificent, passionate woman. 'She taught me a hell of a lot. The woods, little hotels, we . . .' He trailed off, his words sounding incriminating. Was it so bad? The reporter was from a broadsheet, after all, and the piece wasn't about him, anyway. 'Can we talk about the show now?'

But then his call came and he had to say goodbye. The journalist raised her coffee cup in farewell, like she was toasting a victory with champagne. Although he was sure he'd done nothing wrong, he was unsettled. It took him eighteen times to say 'tracheotomy' without stuttering.

Tanya popped her head round the dressing-room door as Flo sat reading a piece in *Music Week* about her forthcoming EP.

'Not sure about them calling me the "queen of heartbreak", Tan.' She tugged at her little wristband, which she'd taken to hiding under her sleeve – if she could – since it had suddenly became not just a symbol of their love but 'the Dylan Fox mangle'.

Tanya peered over Flo's shoulder. 'You've earned that title. Took Madonna about a decade to be called a queen.'

'Makes me sound so miserable. I'm not, am I?' Despite the headlines, she had to act cheery around her new colleagues, in case her 'wronged ex' persona made her look 'difficult'. Women celebrities couldn't afford that label, Tanya said. Flo could now serve up a genuine-looking smile in record time; she hadn't frowned in weeks.

'Course not.' Tanya coughed. Something was coming; it was the same cough she'd used when the 'Snide Boy revealed' story had broken. 'Just thought you should know, babes, nothing to worry about but we are where we are so I have to tell you but again do not panic.'

Flo was getting better at taking in Tanya's Tasmanian devil-speed sentences, but still. 'Okay. I mean, I *think* okay, I didn't catch some of that.'

Tanya pulled up a chair and brushed a wisp of hair out of Flo's eye, like her mum used to do. 'Right fine so basically the horrible evil ex wide boy-bracelet-bothering type has told a tabloid you're a whore, by which I mean a woman who enjoys sex and will never fuck him again. Probably in retaliation to the "Snide Boy" thing at the weekend. His team must think we're behind that.'

Whore? His *team*? Did Dylan have a team? She'd met Priya once – she was lovely and funny, but slick she was not; she'd had pesto rosso down the front of her top. Flo had spoken to Dylan on the phone less than twenty-four hours ago. They'd discussed their top five toasted sandwiches. (The humble ham and cheese a winner in each case.) He'd never mentioned any of this. Was it a hoax? Flo tried to speak but only a croak came out.

'Precisely. Anyway, there's fuck-all else happening right now, allegedly, so this is getting a box on the front page and a double-pager inside on your journey to fame so far. Couple of quotes from . . . Dylan, is it? Then a line or two from some stained-tracksuit piece of shit, another ex, who's wisely kept anonymous. I bet you don't even remember him. Not all bad, though: there's a line-by-line analysis of "The Last Hello" lyrics, lots of talk of the next single and the new buzz track – gotta think of the numbers, and it introduces you to a new audience. Anyway, I've said no comment.'

Flo was on a one-minute delay. 'A . . . whore?' Dylan would never call her that. He wasn't that kind of man. He never talked about his sexual exploits; it had taken three months of dating him before he revealed, yes, he'd once taken a finger up the bum and, yes, if she didn't mind, he'd be up for it again.

'I haven't seen the wording but kind of . . .' Tanya braced herself like she was about to recite a poem. 'Sort of that you love shagging in the woods? And had twenty boyfriends, some of whom are probs being emptied out of the garbage piles they reside in as we speak, for their commentary. OK? Aw, look, don't cry. It's standard stuff.'

'I'm not crying.' Her eyes were watering, but it was shock, like she'd been punched in the stomach. She refused to believe he'd said this. This must've been how Dylan felt when he'd read the stuff about him. Or when he listened to the lyrics of 'The Last Hello'. God. What had she done? 'They're not digging up Dylan's past, are they?'

Tanya laughed. 'Course not. First of all he's a bloke so unless he's been taking a length off another bloke nobody cares, and second of all, which past shag will they dig up and interview? His right hand?'

'You said there was . . . an anonymous ex?'

'Doesn't sound like he thinks of you very fondly these days, whoever he is. Any idea?'

Flo looked into the mirror, face blank and tired. Suddenly the dressing room seemed very bright, floodlit almost. 'I didn't realise I'd have enemies.'

'Look . . . I don't know how to put this, but . . .' Flo wasn't facing her, but she heard a deep swoosh of Tanya's vape and realised some extreme home truths were coming. 'When you're a woman in the public eye, they'll always find something. You could be a good girl who volunteers at a homeless shelter, says her nightly prayers, and goes to bed before *Newsnight* every single day, and they'd still get something on you.' As if suddenly aware this may be too hard to face for a woman still finding her feet, Tanya pulled up a chair, and brought her face close to Flo's. Flo could smell the sweet pong of Tan's cherry vanilla vape; it was strangely comforting. 'Don't worry. The trick is, yeah, work it to your advantage. This ex being a soap star won't do you any harm. It's even better. Fans love an origin story, love to protect their fave from bitter rivals. You know what "shipping" is, right?'

'When fans want two people to get together . . .' Hang on, was this the light at the end of the tunnel Flo was waiting for? Could this bring her and Dylan back together? Would the fans demand a reconciliation?

'Fans wanna root for you, they want you to feel what they've felt. They've all had some shitty ex badmouthing them, or cheating, or . . . you know, refusing to get out of their face so they can move on.' Tanya took a huge chug on her vape. Flo could barely see her through the cloud of pungent steam. 'When relationships end, it's like a death. Through you, they can grieve. Your singing, your lyrics, everything about you . . . it's medicine, Flo, get it? You're a therapist, magician, doctor, and entertainer all in one. Your suffering, it's like a mirror.'

Flo sat back in her chair. This was deep. 'So what about the "shipping"? Does this mean . . .' She hardly dare say it, this could change everything. 'Does this mean they want to see me and Dylan together again? Do they, uh, ship us?'

Tanya pulled the kind of face a baby might pull when biting into a lemon for the first time. 'God, no! Don't worry – they don't want that for you, they're not sadists. Dylan's the bad boy you're trying to get over. He's the muse, not the solution. Nah, we gotta find someone for them to get excited about, someone new. You know what that means.'

'Do I?'

Tanya stood up. 'Rebound! A date to dip your toe back in, before realising you ain't quite over Dylan yet, then writing a few more songs about that. Perfect.'

Flo slumped forward. It sounded like everything – including how she was supposed to feel at any given time – was all mapped out.

Tanya looked at the clock. 'Right. Get that mascara back on the lashes where it belongs. Them's your last tears over that prick, OK? Until we shoot another video.'

Eleven.

Dylan definitely wasn't imagining it. There was a chill in the air. The ladies on reception, usually so sweet when he swiped in, smiled curtly, no 'good morning'; Vince the security guard definitely tutted instead of his usual nod. He was expecting some fallout from the story, but it wasn't just him – the journalist had spoken to other boyfriends too, who'd said much worse things, and anyone could see he'd been ambushed, surely. He'd managed to smooth things over with Flo at three in the morning, finding himself talking about context and leading questions like a barrister, and explaining how he was trying to stop her sounding so frigid.

'I guess . . .' he'd clutched at any old straw, 'it's very . . . authentic. We definitely look broken-up now.'

Flo gave a long, desperate sigh. She was lying down, he could tell; she always breathed differently when she was lying flat next to him, or around him. 'I know we're pretending to be exes, but we don't need to slag each other off. They've had to take all my social-media passwords off me because of this. Can we agree to stick to "no comment" from now?'

'Absolutely. Floria who? Right?'

Dylan heard Flo draw the covers in tight around her. 'Don't forget me altogether, though.'

'Never.'

Now, as he popped his head round the door of hair and make-up, Dylan felt more frost. Flo's new single was blaring out of the battered speaker. Before, even though the hair and make-up team were fans, they hadn't played Flo's music in his presence. Out of 'respect', they'd said. Now, the gloves were off. His favourite make-up artist, Della, couldn't look him in the eye.

'Aw, c'mon, I was misquoted. The journalist said it was about the show, not me. I thought she was decent, I didn't know she was moonlighting for a tabloid.'

Della busied herself in her huge box of tricks, pretending to look for something. Not a sledgehammer, he hoped. 'So you didn't cheat on her?'

What should he say here? He was supposed to be leaning in, but . . . somehow it was different with people he knew and cared about. Della was one of his closest pals on set and, crucially, she had the power to make him look ugly on television. But, if he denied it, wouldn't that make Flo's song a lie?

'It wasn't like that. I didn't cheat, I promise.'

'You promise? That's what they all say.' Della began wielding her brush.

'Do you mean . . . you don't believe me?'

'She wasn't singing about you for nothing . . . and what you said in that interview . . . you didn't say that? It was made up?'

'I didn't cheat on her. Please.'

Della's touch was slightly more forceful than usual. 'It's none of my business anyway, but I've had enough men in this chair to know that when they say "it wasn't like that" it usually is.'

This was how it was going to be, wasn't it? Dylan stared at his reflection in horror. He was the same guy, with a more even complexion, but they saw him completely differently now. He'd never win. This wasn't about leaning in anymore, it had been decided for him. Maybe Priya was right when she said 'No denials' – this one wasn't getting him anywhere.

He caught Della's eye. Her face was closed. 'I didn't mean to be a bad boy,' he said, hoping a version of the truth might melt her heart. 'I don't expect you to forgive me but . . . I promise. I've learned my lesson.'

Della grunted and rolled her eyes, but she was gentler with him then, and when he left to go on set, he saw a hint of a smile.

In the canteen, he saw Ciara alone, reading, a half-eaten salad in front of her. Nobody else met his eye, so he plonked his tray on Ciara's table with more force than he'd intended. Its plasticky clack echoed off the walls. Ciara didn't move.

'Hey.' Dylan looked at his lunch. Baked potato and two ketchup sachets. Again. He'd given up chips. Flo was always telling him his dietary habits were like a seventy-five-year-old in hospital having their gallstones out. Ciara carried on reading. 'You angry with me as well?'

Ciara slowly raised her head; she really wanted to make him wait. Dylan gulped.

'Why? What have you done?'

'Uh . . . The interview.' God, she was terrifying! 'It was totally . . . uh . . .'

'Out of context?' Ciara raised an eyebrow.

'Yeah.'

'Interesting.' Ciara shut her book with a snap, eyes trained on Dylan, poised and grateful like a cat on a silk cushion, but with claws on alert, ready to pounce. He knew better than to actually call her cat-like out loud though; only days earlier Ciara had told him it was a lazy and sexist way to describe a woman. 'Cats kill mice and birds, and poo in a box of gravel,' she'd said. 'Just because some women have a slinky walk or overdo the eye surgery doesn't mean the rest of us are in any way feline.' Now, she drummed her fingers on the table, searching for the right thing to say. Or the wrong thing – she didn't seem too concerned with Dylan's feelings.

'Life hack, bucko: don't do press about exes. Exes don't have "context".'

Dylan felt twelve years old. 'She asked.'

Ciara muttered a profanity under her breath. 'They always ask. It's their job. You didn't have to tell.'

'I didn't mean . . .'

Ciara's eyes flashed, a sign he should remain silent. 'D'you know how many times someone I hardly remember meeting has called me a slut in the papers, or on some blog or podcast, wherever they can find someone who'll listen?'

Dylan looked down at his potato. No steam coming off it now. Cold. 'No.'

'Neither do I,' drawled Ciara, 'but it's too many. Trust me, it hurts every single time.'

'I'm sorry.'

'I'd say apologise to her, not me, but perhaps you're better off leaving her alone. But, seriously, think. I know you're new to all this' – Ciara gestured round the canteen like it was a car showroom – 'but you're not stupid, you have a phone, look at the world. Women have enough shit going on – all women, not just actors – without slut-shaming.'

Dylan felt like a piece of shit. Three women he respected giving him a dressing down on the same day? And he hadn't even called his mum yet.

Ciara arranged her cutlery and napkin neatly on her tray. 'I don't know you, I realise that, but we'll be working together a lot.'

'I know, I've been looking for—'

'Wait.' Ciara's voice was sharp. 'You've been . . . what's the word? Entrusted with a huge storyline that could change lives.'

Was that true? It was just another infidelity story with a hint of bisexuality thrown in to pull in viewers, right? Whose life would it change, other than his?

'You have a responsibility to vulnerable people. Our viewers count on us.' She glared at him. She *was* cat-like, fuck it. 'If it's just a job, and you're only here for a year, so you can get a slot on a big-money reality show, or do touring productions of low-grade jukebox musicals, then fine.' Ouch! 'But I expected more, better. We could've been friends. You're a talented guy. Just this once I hoped a new cast member wouldn't turn out to be a dickhead. Was I wrong?'

Dylan put his hand to his mouth. 'No! I promise.' Another promise!

'Prove it.' Ciara stood, hoisting her tray to her chest. 'See you down there.' She marched away. As she left, Dylan saw everyone was watching and, worst of all, Ciara appeared to have spoken for all of them. Nobody seemed to believe his version of events; he was now the bad boy. What was it his mum used to say? 'Might as well be hung for a sheep as a lamb.' Forget leaning in, if he was going to get through this, he had to dive in.

Flo winced as her mother clanged shut the dishwasher door with considerable force, Joy's favourite way to show anger – their annual glassware bill was the GDP of a small country. This was Flo's first proper night at home since the story had broken and Joy wasn't coping. Flo wanted to do something really ordinary like sort through the laundry or do a cross-word; she could do without the two-pronged wrath of her parents. She explained Dylan's words had 'probably' been twisted, but she couldn't confirm, of course, or it would reveal that she'd spoken to him. Her dad maintained that he'd 'hang the wee bastard by his balls'. Usually her mother cringed when Dad went full Glaswegian, but on this occasion, she remained doom-faced and agreed, albeit with less emotive language, that castration was the best punishment.

'It's so unseemly. Imagine speaking to a newspaper, a tabloid at that.'

'I imagine he has to, because of his job. *City Royal* is a . . . it's a continuing drama that millions watch. I suppose at least half as many want to know about the people who star in it. Ciara McLean is mobbed every time she's on a night out.' Flo felt herself bristle as she mentioned Ciara's name.

'Well, you don't speak to the tabloid press.' Joy was prac-tically holding her nose having to say the word.

'I have a team around me, protecting me. They do it.' That word again, 'team'. She never imagined herself the centre of any team, not since Estelle dropped her from netball squad in lower sixth for what she called 'the coordination of ten plates of salad being thrown in the air at once'.

Flo watched her mother a moment. Was Joy playing double agent? Could she have sold the first story? No, hang on, she was being ridiculous; she was letting paranoia cloud her mind. Her mother? Go to the press? And let everyone know what a disappointment her daughter was? Hell, no. Joy would rather confess to a sideline in drug trafficking than let her neighbours think she'd stooped to talking to a journalist. But someone had done it; Tanya was always warning her about friends turning into snakes. Annoyingly, Dylan didn't seem to mind being revealed as the inspiration for her break-up songs. If anything, it gave him an ego boost. He'd started signing off texts sometimes with Snide Boy. x even though Snide Boy wasn't supposed to be him! He'd referred to himself as a 'bad boy' more than once, too. She was glad, in a way; his lack of confidence and terminal imposter syndrome had been doing him no favours. But she couldn't help regretting that Dylan's blossoming had come at the expense of her broken heart – they'd been apart for real when she'd written the songs, after all.

'Mum, can we move on? I want to forget about it.'

Joy looked down her nose through her specs – another favourite intimidation move, worked a treat when she wanted her husband to shut up at a dinner party. 'How can you move on when all you're singing about is Dylan?'

'It's my career.'

Joy recoiled. 'Of course. Maybe it's time to find something new to say. He's a disgrace.'

Singing about Dylan wasn't the problem. At worst, her mother had worried Dylan wasn't good enough for her, and while Flo had hoped his newfound fame and stability would be the rehabilitation he needed to be welcomed into the family, all he'd done was prove Joy right.

I can do this, thought Flo, all we have to do is keep out of the headlines.

Now Flo wasn't as regular a guest at the Fortnightlies, when she did attend, she felt out of place. Maybe it was because Dylan wasn't around to take the edge off. She'd always found his presence reassuring, knowing they could signal each other and leave whenever they wanted – Dylan didn't mind doing exaggerated yawns and saying he had to go home early. Now she had no excuse. She was behind on gossip, such as it was, and looking at her friends again after being away from them for a few weeks, she saw them through the eyes of someone on the periphery. She began to remember why Dylan had found it overpowering.

'I promise I won't go on about this,' lied Estelle. 'But this newspaper stuff is horrifically bad form. How could he?'

'Estelle is right, sweets,' said Barnaby, patronisingly. It made the hairs on the back of Flo's neck stand rigid. 'Nobody who cared for you would do this. I didn't see the paper, of course, I don't take it – but one of my executive assistants read it out to me over Skype.'

How charming. Flo tried to explain about context but it was lost on Barnaby, who shrugged and wandered off to talk to Tobes and Felix.

'You know this brings it all back how Dylan never supported you,' exclaimed Estelle. She was knocking it back a bit tonight, Flo noticed. She almost pitied Barnaby: a hungover Estelle was a force to be reckoned with.

Flo tried deflecting. 'Does Barnaby support you?'

Estelle's mouth gaped in response. 'Oh gosh, totally. He does most of my networking, even when I'm not there.' Estelle hiccuped, very unlike her. 'I've had countless lovely girls get in touch saying they knew Barnaby, asking me to collaborate.'

'What kind of girls?'

'PRs, influencers. That's how my agent found me. She met Barnaby at . . . something.'

'Dylan couldn't exactly do my networking, whatever that is. Talking to random women, by the sound of it. He worked in a bar.'

'Hmmm, yes, the bar. So, please, tell me why he never once got you a gig in that very bar? It's a no-brainer?'

Flo had never thought of that.

Estelle's piercing blue eyes cut through the air like lasers. Some nights, Estelle didn't exhale carbon dioxide, she breathed out truth serum – she was almost impossible to lie to. 'Have you had any contact? At all?'

Partial truths sounded more believable than flat-out denial. 'He messaged congratulations when I went to number one,' she replied, as evenly as possible. 'The first time,' she added. 'Crushed', a buzz track and not even an official single, was just enjoying a surprise first week at the top. A little twist of the knife there – they were still schoolgirls at heart and a number one certainly beat a sixth-form netball captaincy.

'That's it?'

The air thrummed with Estelle's suspicion. 'That's it.'

Estelle sipped slowly. 'Let's hope we never see his face again!'

They clinked glasses but the sound sent a chill through Flo.

'He's on TV every Thursday, so we probably will see his face,' said a small voice further down the table. Little Vérité. 'I quite like *City Royal*. I like the operations. They tore out someone's colon last week.'

Estelle regarded Vérité like she was a tourist asking for directions. 'Maybe we should arrange for someone to rip out Dylan's colon!' She rested a hand on Flo's. 'It's kind of better he's out of the picture. I like it when it's just us.'

Just us. But that wasn't true. Plenty of other partners had been accepted into the fold over the years. Why was Dylan so different? And why did Estelle call the shots anyway?

Tanya always told her that her fame would change her friends, but they hadn't changed at all. Nothing had. Flo seemed no closer to convincing them she was better off with Dylan by her side.

Twelve.

Dylan looked at his watch, feeling tense, excited, terrified and about a thousand other emotions at once. He walked round Gabe's bedroom slowly, memorising the placement of the few ornaments and adornments. Dylan always wondered what went on behind this eternally closed bedroom door. Not much, as it turned out. Gabe lived minimally – his room was a cell. After smoothing down the freshly changed bed-sheets for the millionth time, he pinged the side of the ice bucket that was standing, waiting, on Gabe's bedside table. Everything was ready. Then the buzzer shrieked, echoing louder than ever off the kitchen walls. She was here. Finally.

She'd lost weight, Dylan noticed, and looked tired round the eyes. Whenever he saw her on social media, or TV, she was fully made up, or lit like an Old Master in the national gallery, but now, in real daylight, a few feet away, he could see the toll this was taking. He wondered if he looked any differ-ent. If he did, Flo didn't say anything; she stood meekly in the kitchen, like a vampire waiting to be invited over the thresh-old. She was still wearing her bracelet. It had been too long.

They kissed. 'You taste toothpastey,' said Flo.

'Sorry.'

'No, I like it.' She watched in delight as Dylan ran his tongue over his teeth. What the hell was that taste? 'I had a bag of salt and vinegar on the way over.'

They both laughed. Flo peeked into Gabe's room, like it was shark-infested waters. 'I'm scared. Surely we're not supposed to be in there?'

'He's away the whole weekend. New job. I didn't ask what, he doesn't like it when I address him directly.' Dylan reckoned if they timed it right, they could stay a full night and nobody would ever know. Max was working and wouldn't be back until late, before flopping right into bed. They could sneak out for breakfast before he got up and return, if they wanted, once he'd gone to work again – he always went in earlier than usual on a Saturday.

'Won't Max wonder where you are?'

'He'll think I've stayed out somewhere.' Dylan felt the room temperature dip a degree or two.

'Do you do that a lot?'

She was trying to work out if he was seeing other women. Dislike of Lois aside, had she always been this suspicious? Or was she leaning into her role as wronged ex? 'On late shoots, there's a budget hotel near the studio.'

'Oh.' Flo took one step into the bedroom.

'I'd get my own place but . . .' They exchanged glances. 'I'm hoping my next place will be *our* place.'

'It will.' Flo strolled into the room and Dylan followed, hugging her from behind as she reached round and grabbed his bottom.

'Holy balls – have you been doing squats?'

Dylan chuckled. 'I've a bare-arse scene coming. Every

male character under forty-five has a towel slip in the first six months, it's practically in your contract. I'm ready.' That wasn't all he'd been warned about. While the bosses at *City Royal* were sympathetic to his recent brush with the press, he'd been instructed not to utter a syllable to the media unless someone from the press team was by his side or listening in. Dylan was glad, really. The last thing he needed was to screw everything up and find himself back behind the bar at the Consulate.

Flo looked round the room. 'It's so . . . macrobiotic. So pristine. We can't shag here, surely? You'll never get his sheets dry in time.'

Dylan sauntered to the bed and folded back the duvet with a flourish. 'Waaaaay ahead of you. I bought these sheets specially, and the duvet cover. Pillowcases too. His are folded nice and neat waiting to go back on once we're . . . uh . . . done. If you see what I mean. He's always away on Tuesdays too, if you fancy sneaking over. Nice to have our own space.'

Flo peered round the room, unsure. 'It's not ours, though. What if I break something?'

Dylan flopped back onto the bed and laughed. 'I was kind of hoping you would break something. Me. In literal two. Please, for the love of God, come and take my clothes off.'

This was how it went for the next few weeks – Tuesdays and Fridays, they'd take over Gabe's room, before meticulously rearranging it the next morning. Max didn't have a clue. It was just them, revelling in their own delicious bubble. They still tried doing 'normal things' out and about, in disguise, but now the weather was warmer, woolly hats looked more conspicuous, wigs were uncomfortable, and sunglasses were great outside, but got more attention if worn indoors. Not only was Dylan on TV once a week, but his star was rising: his bangle had its own parody Twitter account, for a start. Flo's face was appearing on posters, and she was doing more TV, too – it would only get harder to stay incognito. There'd been a couple of hairy moments – a casual café date turned into a major escape mission when a new friend of Flo's – Lily – had walked in. Dylan just managed to sneak off to the loo to hide, frantically texting Flo for the all-clear. Sadly Lily hadn't been taking away her giant iced coffee and had spotted Flo. Once people started banging on the toilet door, Dylan had had to admit defeat, shove on his Ray-Bans, rearrange his fringe and make a sharp exit. Through the very tiny window. He even lost a shoe on the way out. It was almost worth it to see Flo's shocked face as he limped past the front of the café and gave her a sly wave.

Another time, Dylan had hidden in Flo's room while she went down for the lunch her mother had unexpectedly brought home, worrying that every gurgle of his empty stomach would give him away. If anyone had hyper-sensitive hearing, it would be Joy. It didn't help that Flo had casually said, seconds before she slipped downstairs to eat her artichoke salad, that her parents were quite keen on disembowelling him should they ever lay eyes on Dylan again.

Sneaking around was fun, but they'd run out of places to meet that wouldn't lead to recognition by their adoring public or, if caught *in flagrante*, arrest. So they enjoyed this brilliantly boring and functional time, sitting and talking nonsense, just being a couple. They exchanged the latest scandals from their respective corners of the entertainment industry. It was still amazing to them how cavalier people were with their own secrets; camaraderie opened mouths faster than free champagne did. They covered who'd screwed who, much-loved celebrities who'd turned out to be dragons, and their shared loathing for one gossip columnist in particular – Michael Richards, whom everyone called Mick Dick, for reasons that became obvious within seconds of meeting him. Tellingly, they'd each heard slightly different versions of at least half the talking points. The time together now was so fleeting, so precious, that it seemed the problems they used to have had happened to someone else. It was amazing how not having to talk about money, endure dinner with her parents, or Estelle's leading questions, made everything feel lighter. For the first time in their relationship – and for the first time in Dylan's life, Flo realised now – the lack of cash wasn't grumbling away in the background like a low-level migraine. Maybe one day Dylan would stop flinching when Estelle and Barnaby were mentioned, or a passing comment about Lois wouldn't elicit a strange sharp tang at the back of her mouth. Baby steps.

They'd occasionally talk about what life would be like when they were back together. Flo felt like she was stalling every time, but Dylan said he could wait. After all, Flo had more people to convince, plus what Tanya was calling 'the narrative'.

When Flo was disappointed to learn her EP would contain no upbeat songs, Tanya promised her a potential song on a comedy soundtrack. 'But until then, we want stormclouds, drunk texts, floods of mascara down your face, red wine hangovers, chucking ornaments into an open fire, the pits of despair and only your voice to carry you through it. That's the narrative.'

It almost became a joke – Dylan would laugh and say, as he slipped off his underwear, 'This isn't keeping to the narrative, Floria.' One day, however, the narrative would have to change.

One warm evening, they sat eating takeaway pizza by the open window – 'Don't want Gabe to smell pepperoni fumes when he comes back,' was Flo's reasoning – and watched London begin to busy itself for a Friday night.

'Would you go back?' said Dylan through a mouthful of his Hawaiian. 'If you could. Back to how we were? It's not even that long ago.'

Flo looked down at her manicure; she certainly wouldn't go back to her old nails. 'I miss being with you. I hadn't realised how much of our spare time was spent together until you weren't there.' Not that she had much spare time now.

'But, like, our old life? That shitty flat.'

Flo winced as a piece of pineapple fell from Dylan's gaping mouth. Who ate pineapple on a pizza, anyway? Had he always eaten pineapple on a pizza? She couldn't remember. She didn't miss the flat. She'd liked the romance of it, at the time, but she was glad that when they were properly back together she wouldn't have to compromise so much on comfort. 'I like now that it's just you and me. Although, speaking of you and me . . .'

Dylan paused mid-chomp. She knew from the look on his face that he had pregnancy panic. 'Right?'

'I might be going away for a while. Well, I will be. On tour! Well, a mini-tour. Hopefully. Tanya's in talks with Jesse Ribeiro's people. Weird, isn't it, people being in talks? About me?'

There was a possibility of a few dates across Europe, then

the UK, with Jesse Ribeiro – both as a nod to how Flo went viral in the first place, and the fact neither were big enough to fill arenas alone.

'Jesse? The guy who made your video go viral back in the day?' Dylan paused, in acknowledgement, perhaps, that 'the day' he was talking about was only a few months ago. 'Hang on. Is he good-looking?'

He was. But Flo was no fool. 'In photos, everyone is. Haven't met him yet. I guess if you're seventeen he's probably all you'd want.'

'What if you're twenty-seven?'

Flo threw her head back and dangled pepperoni pizza into it like she had crocodile jaws. 'He's very clean-cut. His brother, mind you . . .'

'What about him?'

'You've heard of him. Sonny Ribeiro. Got really far on *Star Searchers* years ago . . . in fact, did he win? Anyway, he's a fox.'

'Of course I have. A fox? I thought I was the only Fox in your life.'

It amused Flo to see Dylan play jealous boyfriend – his acting on *City Royal* was certainly much subtler. 'Nothing compared to you . . . Doctor,' she cooed, knowing it would make him come running.

Later, they counted down their top five people they'd hate to be stuck in a lift with – Flo had to bite her tongue not to put Lois at number one – and finished their bottle of champagne. Flo noticed he was drinking a little faster than usual.

'I'm a bit nervous,' he confessed. 'I've just got my script through for my first scene with Mario.'

'Ooooh. The gay snog guy! Is *he* a fox?'

Dylan waggled his eyebrows. 'Not my type.'

'You should ask Max for tips, to be extra authentic.' Flo laughed. 'Want me to run a few lines with you?'

Dylan scurried off to find his script while Flo gently eased the cork out of the next bottle, terrified it would explode and somehow leave indelible black ink all over Gabe's pristine walls. Dylan re-entered looking agitated.

'Can't find it.'

'What?'

Dylan shot her a quick, impatient look. 'Script.' His tone was clipped, dismissive; he didn't like asking for help, or appearing disorganised.

Flo stood up, regardless, ready to play peacemaker. 'Did you look in the waste-paper basket?'

Dylan pressed his fingers to his temples. 'The . . .? Why would it be in the bin?'

'Sometimes it's an autopilot thing. I've done it loads. Jewellery, sometimes.'

Dylan stalked out to the kitchen. Flo heard rustling. He was having no luck. 'Try Max's room,' she called. He thundered over the floorboards, then returned looking ashen.

'Nope. Shit. I really wanted to be on top of this.'

Flo looked under the bed. 'Not here. Can you get someone to email you one?'

'Who?'

'I dunno. Production. Another cast member?' Flo distinctly heard Dylan stamp his foot. She stopped searching and looked across at him. 'What?' He looked distraught.

'I can't let them know I can't be trusted with a script. They're top secret, personal. Watermarked and everything. I have to be reliable, on it.'

Flo walked out to the lounge and began peeking under

magazines and unopened post on the coffee table. 'I'm sure it happens all the time.'

'Only to people who don't take it seriously or think it's just a job, and something else will come along, so they can toss their script into the *waste-paper basket*.' Their dust atoms swirled in the sunlight. 'Why do you say that, anyway?'

Flo stopped her riffling. She'd done nothing wrong. She tried to keep calm. 'Say what?'

'Waste-paper basket.' That tone.

'That's what it's called.'

'It's a bin, isn't it?'

Why was he doing this now? 'Po-tay-to, po-tar-to. We've always called it a waste-paper basket. A bin is like . . . outside. A dustbin.'

Dylan's face was pinched and miserable. A face reserved for second-prize announcements or unfavourable gonorrhoea diagnoses. 'All bins are just a bin. Is it an affectation because the idea of saying "bin" is horrifying to you?'

Flo stood up straight to face Dylan. His tone was quite spiteful. 'An affectation? Like that accent you do when you phone your mum or dad?'

'What do you mean "that accent"? It's my accent!'

'You don't talk like that to me. Your vowels are way flatter when you talk to a northerner. You and Max in full flow is like a scene from *Coronation Street*.'

'That's Lancashire, not Yorkshire.' Dylan sniffed. 'I'm an actor. We assimilate.'

Flo laughed sharply, like a bark. 'You what?'

Dylan's voice was smaller now, less confident. He was in retreat. 'We assimilate. Adapt our voices and . . . actions to those around us.'

Flo exhaled deeply. 'So when I call a waste-paper basket by its name, it's an affectation, but when you do it, you're an actor? Sounds like you're assimilating into being a dickhead.'

Dylan raised his hands in astonishment. 'Why are you attacking me?'

'I'm not. You're pissed off you can't find your script and lashing out.' Flo rushed back to Gabe's bedroom and began gathering her discarded clothing.

'Where are you going?'

'Home. Away. This argument is a strain on my voice.' She sat on the bed and tugged socks onto her feet in fury.

'We're supposed to spend the night together. The whole night.'

Flo stood up and looked for her jeans. 'Umm, whatever could you do instead? Why not phone your dad and say "bath" to each other over and over? You'd like that.' Flo made for the exit but Dylan barred her way.

'Please.'

Flo pushed past. 'By the way, your script's on the coffee table underneath a copy of *Soap Suds* with you on the cover. You're welcome.'

She slammed the door.

Seconds later, Dylan ran out to the shared landing of the apartment block. He was now wearing underwear. He seemed relieved to find Flo still standing there, so that was something.

'I'm sorry. I get like this sometimes, the job makes me crazy. I'm so scared someone's gonna tell me it's been a mistake. It means so much. But you mean more. Please, please, please don't go. I'll beg.' He began to kneel.

'Y'know, I understand. I feel like this sometimes, too.'

Flo crouched to meet his eye. 'But please, please, please stop having a go at me for . . . being a bit different. I thought we were over all that.'

Dylan hugged her. 'I'm sorry, I am.' There was a hint of a smile. 'You can't help being posh.'

'Dylan!' Her scream echoed off the walls. There was a creak; a neighbour's door opened. They saw a suspicious eye peek out.

'Please, can we go back in? I'm standing here in my underwear.'

Flo looked down. He was even more toned than he used to be. 'Your pants are back to front, too.'

'Oh God. Please. I'm a twat. I know. An assimilating twat.'

'Okay, but only because I couldn't find my knickers.' Flo walked slowly back into the flat. 'And you're a *dickhead*, remember. An assimilating dickhead. I love you.'

Thirteen.

Flo clenched her buttocks tight and gripped the seat beneath her for dear life as Tanya's monstrous utility vehicle mounted the pavement to avoid hitting a pigeon. 'Always gotta be careful in case reincarnation is a thing,' Tanya explained. 'So . . . it's time you met Jesse Ribeiro. He's really looking forward to it. Word is, he likes you.'

Suddenly, she was back at school having her pigtails pulled by a boy whose hands were 25 per cent bogies. 'The word? Likes me? Whose word? Likes me how?'

'His word. Told me himself,' Tanya trilled. 'I'm inches away from poaching him from his manager, who's a sexist old pig. Anyway, back on our timeline . . . it got me thinking about our narrative.'

Yay, the narrative. What fun to be treated like a character in a shoot 'em up game.

'I know you want to pivot to up-tempo and I'm here for it in a way so . . . what if we start sending you two on a few dates? See how the chemistry pans out. Nothing major, no falling in love or nothing, just a few little nights in chi-chi restaurants, standing looking sexy on a cheeky red carpet or two, maybe send you jet-skiing for a couple of days? Do you know how to jet-ski without ruining a blow-dry? Paps love jet-ski shots. He looks like an angel. You might even fancy him. Very good for the tour, too.'

Flo's blood ran cold imagining telling Dylan of this plan. A plan *within* a plan, going on dates with a guy with whom she was about to spend weeks on tour. And what about poor Jesse? Did he know what he was letting himself in for? Did he know her manager was pimping her out? She pictured Jesse Ribeiro's inevitable clumsy pass, after a day of frolicking in the surf, having to let him down gently or, worse . . . what? Kiss him? Pretend it was real? That didn't seem fair on anyone. She ran this over in her head and tried to think of a way she wouldn't look like a bad person.

'I'm not sure about jumping into a showmance. What is this? Nineteen forties Hollywood? Yes he looks like an angel, but I don't fancy him. He's too clean-cut. How old is he? Sixteen?'

'Showmance!' Tanya laughed. 'How do you know you don't fancy him? You've never met him. Told ya, he's a babe. He's twenty-four, by the way. He uses excellent moisturiser.'

Wasn't this taking her further and further away from her actual aim, the big reunion with Dylan? She'd seen enough love triangles play out in the media to know the woman always got the blame. It would quickly turn her from relatable heartbreak victim to villain, and then who'd cry listening to her break-up songs?

Tanya swerved as she waved away Flo's concerns like she was sending an overcooked steak back to the kitchen. 'Stop fretting. You managed to get an entire album out of that scraggy-bearded TV doctor who wears a shitty charm bracelet and looks like he couldn't fuck his way out of a paper bag. Who knows what a night or two with Jesse will do for your creativity?' Tanya zoomed through a red light and grabbed her triple-shot strongest-blend Colombian from its holder. 'I'm not here to make you do anything you don't wanna do. But being seen together is good publicity, gets cameras snapping. If we don't explicitly confirm or deny you're together, it can't hurt, can it?' She rested her hand on Flo's. 'Coupla dinners? The Yukis?' Tanya clocked Flo's puzzled face. 'Come on, love. Yukis – UK TV Awards, you know those, right? You watch telly?' Flo nodded uncertainly. 'One tiny peck on the cheek on the red carpet? For me?'

One little dinner was no big deal, right? And a red-carpet event, well, anyone could go to those; it didn't mean they were lovers, just two mates all dressed up. Dylan knew about publicity; he said he'd go to the opening of an envelope if it helped raise his profile. And he meant it; he was off to cut a ribbon on a taco stand in Camden Market later.

'You don't even have to hold hands. I can get you any dress you want. You look like a Valentino girl to me. Am I right?'

'Givenchy, actually,' purred Flo. 'Can you do that?'

Tanya smiled and took a hard vape. 'I can do anything. Someone'll be in touch about a fitting tomorrow.'

'Fine. When are we meeting, then?'

Tanya swerved again. 'Oh, I should've said. Now. We'll be there in about ten minutes. You might wanna do a bit of googling, all right?'

Shit!

Flo drank in Jesse's life story like a vampire. His dad was Portuguese and his mum was from Angola, and he'd grown up not that far from where she had, although they'd had very different childhoods. Jesse was born to be in the public eye – in fact, he practically was. He was only a kid when his older brother Sonny got his big break on TV talent show *Star Searchers*, thrusting the family into the spotlight. Flo pored over years' worth of photos of Jesse turning from gawky teen hiding behind his mum while his brother performed, into an artist in his own right. Jesse was currently the star of a very popular meme, because in a recent interview he'd been eating a rapidly melting ice-cream and licked some off his forearm, which had caused a sensation.

Through a series of anodyne social-media posts about as revealing as a balaclava, Flo watched Jesse break the hearts of teenagers up and down the country by either not noticing them at all or, even worse, *actually* noticing them and saying hi. It seemed that to actually get his attention, then lose it in the space of a one-word reply on social media, rendered these poor youngsters inconsolable. 'Talk to me again, KING,' they'd cry, into the ether.

'So nice to finally meet you.' Jesse's voice was soft, with a hint of shyness, but sincere. 'I love your music. "The Last Hello" totally floored me.' He jerked his head toward the speaker and Flo followed its direction. 'The Last Hello' was playing, she hadn't realised.

He smelled clean and expensive, but so did almost every other popstar Flo met. She wanted to sniff her own hand right after shaking his – she was absolutely sure it would smell herby and fresh. His face was . . . well, without sounding too clinical, symmetrical. Properly. His skin was smooth and bright, not a single bump, blemish or nick, no trace even of a childhood scar, and was responding well to the terrible lighting they were standing under in one of the record company's least salubrious meeting rooms. White walls replete with gold discs, chrome chairs, a Flipchart easel in one corner, crudely torn, pages blank. He flashed her a grin which, she couldn't help noticing, seemed a little half-hearted. His teeth were very straight, and white. Not off-the-peg porcelain white, but 'well cared for after eighteen months in braces with some whitening solution every night' kind of white. The body was good, if you liked that sort of thing. In proportion, tight, firm, hairless as far as she could tell. He was wearing a v-neck but there was no evidence of the smattering of chest hair peeping up that Dylan had, that she always found so endearing. Everything was streamlined, a body designed by committee and . . . it worked. Even though an assistant was noisily arranging a drinks trolley in one corner of the room, Flo could hear fans outside cheering his name. Now she was part of the Jesse Ribeiro experience.

'Thank you for . . . sharing it. The song, I mean, on social media.' Should she curtsy? Was there a hierarchy? She had the most number-one singles now, but a few clicks on his phone screen had basically made her career – there was nobody out there screaming *her* name. She counted the number of people in his team that he had with him today. Three. Hmmm. She only had Tanya with her. Becca from the record label was supposed to be coming, but was stuck on a bus, in traffic.

They adjourned to some uncomfortable seating and exchanged first-date pleasantries – backgrounds, musical heroes, Netflix binge favourites. He reminded her of someone. He was attractive, Tanya was right, but whether it was loyalty to Dylan or immunity to Jesse's pheromones, she didn't fancy him. If he really was interested in that way, he wasn't showing it, either. She'd been around long enough to know when a man wanted to be more than friends. Even Dylan, whose flirtation and pick-up techniques made a trainee priest seem forward, managed to show his intentions. It was in the eyes. Even if the mouth couldn't speak and the body language was indecipherable, the eyes didn't lie. Flo had never fetishised eyes – every man she'd dated had had them, yes, but whatever – but as she looked into Jesse's now, all she could think of was Dylan. The hunger, the hope, the rawness of attraction wasn't there. Jesse could turn it on when he wanted: there were plenty of photos of him gyrating on stage, posing for smouldering selfies – nothing shirtless as far as she could see, so she guessed he had a third nipple, a concave chest or shared Dylan's ridiculous hang-up, that one pectoral muscle was slightly bigger than the other. But one-on-one, in this admittedly atmos-free room, there was nothing, only a nice young man your grandmother would love, so long as she wasn't racist. He really did remind her of someone else.

'I'm looking forward to the Yukis,' he was saying, as Flo zoned back in. She'd had a Diet Coke placed in her hand – as always a fruit bowl was nearby. Who ate this fruit? Who paid for it? Where did it come from? Where did it go? 'I don't do many red carpets; I hate being interrogated.'

Flo smiled. He was sweet. 'I've not done many, either. They always ask really silly questions, don't they? Stuff nobody could possibly be interested in.'

'Yeah, silly questions.' He trailed off, reaching out for a memory. She resolved to google him again once this was over: what red-carpet questions could reduce Jesse Ribeiro to looking like a wounded puppy? 'It'll be great to go with someone!' He brightened. 'I'm usually on my own, or trailing behind my brother, getting in the way.'

'Me too, except the brother part,' said Flo, thinking of all the times walking into events that she'd waited for Dylan's guiding hand on the small of her back. It used to infuriate her, but she now missed getting angry about it. 'Your patriarchal, possessive claw', she'd called it once, making Dylan's eyes roll right back into his head.

What was the right thing to do here? Stand Jesse up? Make it clear she was unavailable? What if he told Tanya, and the deceit came crashing down around her? As far as she could see, she had two priorities: have hits, and get Dylan back into the fold. If it meant leaving behind her throne as queen of heartbreak and turning to a new, optimistic future – one that included going public about Dylan – Flo was more than happy to have this angel on her arm, so long as he kept his hands where she could see them. Mind you, she was willing to bet Jesse Ribeiro never touched a woman without written permission. If ever.

Max looked round the restaurant awkwardly. 'When you said you were taking me out for dinner, I didn't realise it was gonna be so . . . white tie.' He smiled as the waiter brought the wine and sat patiently through the whole 'swirl it round the glass, taste it, tell the waiter it's great, wait again as he pours out two glasses' rigmarole before casting his eye over the pale, perfumed clientele again. 'Well, white everything.'

Dylan held his glass aloft. 'Thought we should celebrate.' They touched glasses at an angle that made more of a clang than a clink. Dylan could have sworn the polite background buzz of chatter dipped in recognition. He'd always wanted to walk into the room and have the music stop playing, so this was the next best thing. 'You deserve a night where someone else is serving drinks for a change.'

'Celebrate you finally driving Gabe up the wall and out of my flat? It's a bit like throwing a divorce party.'

Even though Dylan forensically scrubbed the entire room after Flo's visits and placed everything exactly where it had been, a stray pair of boxers had somehow found their way behind Gabe's headboard. Dylan had started to weave a tale about fancying a night in a bed without Max for a change, but only seconds later, an enraged Gabe had also fished out a very small pair of knickers that definitely couldn't be explained away as Dylan's. It had taken Gabe forty-seven minutes to pack his belongings and a further fifteen to tell Max what a crap flatmate he was, followed by mere seconds relaying to Dylan exactly what he thought of *him*, before he stormed out. Out of guilt, duty, and concern for Max's health once he saw the vein throbbing in his friend's neck, Dylan had agreed to take the room and cover the rent in the short-term.

'I suppose you're still not going to tell me who owned the scants? You never go anywhere to pick anyone up. Is it Ciara McLean? I'm jealous, she's an absolute queen. Or maybe the mousy girl who plays Holly?'

'Georgia. No, neither of those.'

'Oh God, not Lois?'

Was it easier to pretend it was? Dylan put his finger to his lips. 'I don't kiss and tell, and this is not a very upmarket conversation when we're eating so fancy.'

In all honesty, the restaurant was a bit too fancy. Flo had recommended it as the perfect place to take someone when you had bad news to share, because if they needed to cry, everybody would be too polite to mention it, and the lighting in the toilets was very forgiving.

Once the main courses were underway, Dylan was ready to make his move. 'The new guy starts soon, the guy I'm supposed to be madly in love with. So I need your help.' Max stopped, fork halfway to mouth, and made a gagging sound. Dylan glanced about to see if anybody had noticed. 'Don't look so frightened. All I want you to do is tell me what it's like to kiss a boy.'

Max's mouth engulfed the forkful of steak and he chewed a while, long after the meat had disintegrated. 'I don't get it. Why's it different to any other pretend kiss? Just do what you always do.'

Dylan shrugged. 'It's a guy, isn't it? But not just that. I want to tap into the feelings of a gay guy.'

'I thought the character was bi.'

'He is. Same thing, isn't it? From a snogging approach?'

Max sighed. Dylan knew that look: would his days of trying to educate straights never be over? 'Not necessarily. What do you mean "tap into feelings"? You're not in a café asking for the Wi-Fi code.'

Dylan tried to explain that he wanted to convey a sense of longing. Asking Max might have been a mistake – he seemed offended.

'First of all,' Max said, putting down his fork, 'the kiss is like any other. It's just a man. Prepare for stubble. You've always said you find kissing a female actor unsexy. This is the same. There's no formula. You don't get a boner snogging on stage, do you?'

'Okay.'

'But . . .' Max looked into the distance, eyes tracking over the diners around him, as if switching them off one by one, like a series of lamps. 'There's stuff that comes with it. Baggage. Not for everyone, but me . . . yes.'

This was more like it. Mindset. History. The lot. 'I need to know the pain and anguish Heath will be . . . uh . . . channelling. He's wrestling with his sexuality. It's consumed him.'

'Channelling. God.' Max laughed sharply. 'You don't wrestle with your sexuality, it's not a tiger. It didn't consume me. I lived alongside it, waiting for it to get bigger than me, so I'd have to talk about it. That's the thing with gay kids, or bi ones, or trans kids too, I guess. It doesn't eat us alive. We don't exist in permanent anguish.'

Dylan began to wish he'd taken notes. 'What do you mean?'

'This happened right before your eyes, when we were growing up. Did you never clock it?' Max rested his hands on his chin. He seemed older, wearier than ever before. 'Gay kids . . . we go to school, queue for lunch, listen to the teacher, do our homework. We get the bus, watch telly, we enjoy it. We laugh. Yeah, there's sleepless nights, but not every night. Life goes on, we pine a bit, worry a bit, and we bury it.' He sat up straight, almost looking right through Dylan. 'It's not a secret, or shameful, it's . . . a thing you can't acknowledge, or explain, because once you do there's no going back. Before you dare to put a name to what you are, you can't imagine what life would be like if everyone knew. You think it can never happen. Coming out is what you long for but, at the same time, what you're scared of most.'

'Mate.'

'I'm not done. You asked. Listen.'

Dylan bowed his head in apology. 'Shoot. *Please*. This is . . . you're amazing, you know.'

Max ignored the compliment. 'The crushes are the hardest. When you're young, and gay, so much time is just . . . looking, and never finding. I've spent half my life looking across rooms at men who don't know I'm alive or, worse, actually *do* know I'm alive, but don't care. Hoping they'll notice me, that they might feel the same, break the spell, get it out in the open. These feelings starve you, and they feed you, and they don't care about you. But they give you hope.'

'Mate. Maxy. Wow.'

'That day I told my mum and dad, you remember. They said they hated the sin, not the sinner. As if that made it better. I said there's no such thing as sin – just things you won't do, that I will.'

'I remember, Maxy.'

Max's eyes began to well up. He was so still, so straight, so calm and quiet, it was unnerving, yet Dylan didn't want him to stop; he was staring something so powerful right in the face. 'So when I kiss a man, that's who I'm thinking about. The boy who I was, who I thought I'd always be. What he wanted, what he was frightened of, all that future ahead of him that he thought he'd never get to experience. Every time a guy kisses me, he's setting that boy free.'

Dylan realised his jaw had dropped.

Max snapped out of his trance and looked down at his plate. 'Will that do you? I'm full. Can we have more wine?' He looked up again, smiling, back to his normal self, his tears already dried to the merest trace of salt on his cheek. 'Or is that all I get now that I've put out?'

Dylan ordered two glasses of champagne. Max looked bemused. 'Actually, I have something else to ask you.'

'Are you going to make an honest woman of me?' He cackled, managing to turn a few heads.

'I want you to be my date.' Max looked blank. 'For the Yukis. You know the Yukis, right?'

'Yes! How the hell did you blag tickets! I didn't realise you were that famous!'

'Um . . . it's not being announced until tomorrow morning but . . . I'm nominated. Best newcomer.'

Max screamed. 'Are you fucking serious?' Even more confused faces turned their attention to their table.

'Deadly. Funnily enough everyone is totally fine with me at work again. I'm sure it's a coincidence. We've got a record five nominations this year.'

Traditionally, the newcomer award was a public vote, with the shortlist announced only days before the ceremony. When word got out Dylan's name was on it, he was lifted on colleagues' shoulders like a war hero. The whole crew had conga'd round the studio – except Ciara, who'd watched impassively from the sidelines.

'So will you come, be my good-luck charm?'

Max was trying desperately to hold it together. 'Yes, yes, yes. God. Wow. The boy has done it. I . . . I need the loo.' He strutted across the dining room like he had three Russian dictionaries balancing on his head. Dylan watched him go and felt a red-hot glow from his toes, which rocketed straight to his face when he saw, being shown to a table, Barnaby. He was with a group of guys he didn't recognise – although, they could've been regular Fortnightlies attendees; Dylan had blanked out a lot – and a tall, beautiful blond woman who looked like Estelle, but was very much not Estelle, draped all over Barnaby like a velcro poncho. Yep, they were more than friends – Dylan even saw their tongues flick at one another, like lizards having a go at a Cornetto.

This was his big chance. Finally, he could have the satisfaction of watching Barnaby choke while introducing Dylan as a huge soap star to his weak-chinned coterie. He'd die at being caught out with his bit on the side, too; Flo would definitely have mentioned it if Barnaby and Estelle had split. Dylan made his way over, trying to be sleek and assured, but bumping into numerous chairs. One guy at Barnaby's table saw him approach but said nothing. Barnaby had his back to him and was, Dylan could see, edging his hand quite far up the young woman's thigh. Dylan coughed to attract his attention. Nothing.

'Barnaby.' Again, nothing. '*Barno.*'

Barnaby turned round, pupils popping for a millisecond. 'Yeah?'

Dylan could feel his cheeks rouging up; he also spotted Max returning from the loo. 'Fancy seeing you here.'

Barnaby's eyes narrowed. 'Oh hi Darryl,' he said, in a graceless monotone. 'You good?'

Dylan's mouth was dry. 'Dylan.' He quickly sluiced saliva over his teeth to stop his lips sticking to them. 'What a surprise!'

Barnaby wasn't remotely cowed. He didn't introduce him to his friends, who all stared back, without a hint of curiosity. There was no response, just Barnaby expressionless, eyes scrunched like he was staring straight at an eclipse.

'I'm . . . having dinner with a friend,' said Dylan, shimmying out of the way as a waiter edged past. The next table was looking now. 'Celebrate my Yukis nomination. It's on Tuesday.'

Barnaby nodded like he was half-listening to the radio, as if he had this kind of conversation every day. 'Yeah, not sure I'm gonna go this year. Bit busy.'

Dylan was aware of a presence beside him. The waiter was trying to take Barnaby's drink order.

Barnaby pulled a face at the waiter. 'Sorry, yeah, can I get a . . .' He then stopped to look at Dylan as if he'd not expected him still to be there. 'Take care of yourself, my guy.'

Dylan trudged back to his table, cheeks and heart and brain aflame. Everything pulsing. Barnaby hadn't cared, wasn't bothered about being caught out, wasn't impressed or intimidated by Dylan's fame, was unmoved by Dylan being at the Yukis – wasn't even sure he was going himself! Dylan sat down.

Max smiled. 'Who was that handsome bastard?'

Dylan guessed he'd always known. It didn't matter how successful he was, or how confident, or how much he thought he had the upper hand – he'd never match Barnaby for ease and confidence. They'd never accept Dylan, because to them he was nobody. No TV role, or Yuki nomination was ever going to change that.

Fourteen.

Estelle sat on the bed, surveying the hotel room while Flo was being fastened into her dress. A hair stylist and make-up artist fluttered round her, making finishing touches: incessantly teasing strands of hair down and tucking them back behind Flo's ear again. It was one of Flo's pet hates, but unlike when her mother did it, now when she was prodded and pulled and poked by strangers, Flo couldn't pull away, or tell them to stop. They knew what they were doing, Tanya said; all Flo had to do was relax and enjoy it. She couldn't, though; it didn't feel natural to have servants. It always felt like these people – who were always very kind and lovely – should be off somewhere else, dressing and titivating someone actually famous, who was worth the trouble.

'I think it's fine,' said Flo, bobbing and weaving to look in the full-length mirror. Tanya had booked a hotel barely five minutes' walk from the Palladium, but Flo would, like everyone else, arrive at the Yukis in a huge car, which was probably already waiting outside. Jesse was two rooms down, but would wait for her in the bar. Even though she wasn't attracted to him at all, she was hoping he'd gasp in delight when the lift doors opened. 'What do you think? All good?'

'Lovely shade of green,' Estelle replied, distractedly, walking a full circuit around Flo. A perfect match for your face, Flo thought, stifling a giggle. Estelle probably wouldn't find that funny. 'Nice to see you in colour. Suits you.' Estelle hugged her lightly, barely touching so as not to disrupt the dress/hair/make-up/scent/anything else. Dressed like this, Flo felt one sneeze away from disaster.

'Dylan's going to be there, isn't he?'

Flo held her head high, trying to look staunch yet a little fragile. Play the game. 'He's nominated, so I suppose so. I'll have Jesse to protect me.' Although they'd toyed with meeting up in secret, Flo and Dylan had decided to avoid each other completely at the ceremony – no headlines were good headlines.

'Typical, you can't even enjoy a wonderful evening with a handsome man without the spectre of your . . . of that man.' The beautifiers began to tidy away their kit. Estelle rested her hands on Flo's shoulders. 'Look how far you've come. You look very Hollywood . . . but in a good way.'

It was true. Flo could barely open her eyes for lashes and eyeliner and eyeshadow and God knows what else, and her face felt like it was peering out from under a duvet, but she did look incredibly glamorous. Light years away from her days behind the counter in yoga daywear or slouching in huge jumpers – although she'd *always* worn colour. Estelle was misremembering, maybe drabbing down Flo's pre-success life for effect.

'Elijah showed up to Fortnightlies last night,' said Estelle, in a tone that suggested this was not a random anecdote. 'The new duo hasn't worked out.' According to Estelle, things had gone awry when Elijah realised his new singing partner had a better set of pipes than he did – 'again' – and some very strong views on his songwriting, plus the clincher: a girlfriend.

Poor Elijah, thought Flo. Absence, and the knowledge that part of her life was absolutely over, prised open a chink in her armour, and nostalgia seeped in. Flo couldn't get out of her head that if his songs hadn't been so terrible in the first place, maybe she wouldn't have looked as good, or be here now.

'I'm putting my touring band together. One of my usual guitarists can't do it. Should I ask Elijah?' While Flo wasn't big on the ins and outs of karmic energy, giving Elijah a spot on the tour would assuage her guilt– though, to be completely honest, she'd lost more sleep over missing episodes of her favourite game show.

'What a terrific idea!' Estelle's enthusiasm for Elijah was uncharacteristic. Had she set her up? Had Flo mentioned needing a guitarist before? She couldn't remember. 'He can keep an eye on you. And I won't have to look at his miserable face at the Fortnightlies, attempting to engage us in a convo about melodies. Of which, I gather, he knows zero.'

There was a knock at the door. Estelle answered, returning with a beautiful, delicate-looking rose in the faintest purple. 'Not sure what you're supposed to do with it. Wear it like a corsage like it's a school social? It won't go with your dress.'

Flo felt a rush of excitement. Dylan, it had to be. Hence the lack of note.

Estelle twirled the rose round in her fingers; it visibly wilted at her touch. 'The creep at the door said it was from Mr Ribeiro. That's nice, isn't it?'

'Oh. I mean, yes, it is. Lovely.'

The colour drained from her face, but thanks to her make-up, you couldn't tell. Was it so bad, going on a semi-fake date with a near-stranger? They'd gone on a few outings over the last couple of weeks to try to get acquainted. He was incredibly sweet and polite, but guarded, and at times seemed terrified of her. One evening, Flo had told a filthy joke and Jesse had forgotten himself for a moment and laughed uproariously, before covering his mouth with his hand and regaining his composure, like he was ashamed of having fun. He talked a lot about loving Flo's album, how he'd just learned to drive, how he was looking forward to the tour, how they should collaborate soon; in fact, he barely stopped talking. But, aside from a few mentions of how close he was to his older brother Sonny and some highlights from his rise to fame, which sounded lifted from a press release, he gave nothing personal away. His patter seemed rehearsed, like he was holding back. Maybe he thought the same; there was so much in her life that she couldn't share. Her official line on Dylan was: 'It didn't quite end like was reported but I want to move on. I wish him well.' It came so easily now, like it was true.

'Ready?' said Estelle, with a bright smile that Flo quickly tried to match.

'Red-carpet ready.'

Dylan gawped out of his window as his car drew up near the Palladium. Huge screens flashed up the nominees in all categories. He sat a moment waiting for his face to appear. It didn't.

Max nudged him. 'Come on. We've gotta get out.'

They walked slowly up the red carpet – not by choice; it was pretty crowded. Journalists, reporters, fans, influencers and God knows who else were shouting out names – nobody shouting for him as far as he could hear – and cameras flashed. No sign of Flo or Jesse. Probably a good thing. A microphone found its way under Dylan's nose, a camera leered at him.

'Dylan Fox from *City Royal*, right?'

'Right.' Dylan remembered where he was. 'I mean, yes, that's me! Hello . . . erm . . . hello.' Who was this reporter? He looked like he lived underground, like a mole, or a potato. He was sweating, even though it wasn't that warm. 'How are you?' He gestured at Max. 'This is my friend . . .'

The reporter glanced at Max for a microsecond before turning back to Dylan. 'Yeah, cool. I'm Michael Richards from *Snap!* as you *no doub*t know. We're live right now on Celebrity Network Extra TV.'

'Of course. Hi, *Michael*.' Mick Dick, showbiz columnist on daytime TV, in a leading tabloid, and one of the sleaziest gossip sites. He'd been behind that initial 'Snide Boy' exposé, but this was neither the time nor the place for revenge. Dylan was a professional, and on camera. He was here to work, and to win.

Mick Dick flashed his bright white teeth. They were small, like Tic-Tacs, his gums swollen and purple. 'How are you enjoying playing Heath? He's certainly an *interesting* character.'

Dylan ignored that Mick Dick's voice was like hearing vomit dribble down a drain. For once, he could speak honestly. 'It's my dream job. Heath is a brilliant role. He's got many layers, there are some huge things coming up.'

Mick Dick beamed. 'Yes, I heard about that. A *real* treat

for viewers.' How did someone who looked and sounded so insincere manage to go this long without being taken out by pest control, wondered Dylan. 'One more question!' Dylan braced himself to be asked if he was looking forward to kissing his male co-star or something about LGBTQ rights. He'd accepted this, rehearsed his answers; he'd be fine.

Mick Dick's eyes widened – difficult, as they were small and characterless like a hen's – as he prepared to unload the juicy tidbit he was choking on. 'I see your ex is dating Jesse Ribeiro.'

Dylan's mind worked overtime; he decided to keep smiling and let Mick Dick get wherever he was going as quickly as possible. 'Hmmm.'

'Yes,' Mick Dick said now, perspiration rapidly misting over his Botoxed forehead. 'Those two lovebirds were right here a few minutes ago, gaaaazing into each other's eyes. I'm loving Floria's revenge body, and Jesse Ribeiro is gorgeous. Looks like the queen of heartbreak's found a new king! How's that feel?'

Max squeezed his arm. 'We better get to our seats.'

Mick Dick was poised, salivating. Dylan shrugged. 'I hope she gets a nice song out of it.' Shit, why did he say that? 'Have a wonderful evening.' Dylan walked away, Max flashing Mick Dick a sarcastic smile and following. 'Maxy, how much would it cost you to flirt with that guy and get him not to print that?'

Max shivered. 'You can't afford it. Now smile, pussycat. There are cameras everywhere.'

Walking the red carpet in her incredible dress, Flo felt like she was sailing, but she couldn't get Dylan out of her mind. Jesse Ribeiro said all the right things and smiled in the right places. He was the perfect gentleman but . . . he didn't place a protective hand on the small of her back once. Gauchely, they'd arrived bang on time, which meant there was a minor traffic jam of people ahead of them. They were under instructions not to talk to anyone, just smile and turn toward photographers when asked, like mannequins.

Then, a voice she knew: 'Holy fuck. Flo!'

She turned to see Lois, looking resplendent in a dress a few shades greener than her own, polished and lithe like sexy spaghetti, grinning and holding an electronic clipboard. 'What are you—' She checked herself. 'Lois! You look . . . really nice. I didn't expect to see you here.'

Lois's grin didn't falter but you didn't need a dictionary to translate it. 'You look ravishing. Givenchy, right? A popular choice. Yeah, anyway, so unlike you superstars here . . .' she gave Jesse a cursory glance up and down, as if looking for something, 'I'm actually working.'

Lois was typically the last person Flo would want to see on a red carpet, but right now she felt majestic, and was actually glad Lois had spotted who her dress was by. Determined to avoid a catfight, Flo said only, 'Oh?'

Lois's job was to guide attendees toward the step-and-repeat, the bit of the red carpet where you posed in front of a background emblazoned with the Yuki logo and those of various sponsors, just like a proper celebrity, and then shoo them off again so they could be guided elsewhere, by another immaculately made-up model.

Flo hated herself for biting, but couldn't resist. 'Wouldn't you rather be here as a guest? Picking up an award, maybe?'

Lois laughed. 'You fucking kidding me? Cramming this beautiful dress into one of those tiny wooden seats and listening to people thank their agents and the wives they're cheating on? No way.' She put her arm out to stop a relatively famous actress pushing ahead. 'Hold on, lady, this isn't a free-for-all.' And back to Flo. 'Rude! Yeah, so I get to be out here sipping champagne and seeing who's where and who with, and once it's over, I can just walk into any party. My next ten jobs could be right here for the taking.' She looked behind her. 'Okay, you're on. Y'all have a great night.' Another glance at Jesse, her expression unreadable. 'I'll say hi to Dylan for you, huh?'

Flo was too winded to speak. She tried not to blink as the cameras flashed like fireworks, then they took their seats. Lois was right about the dress; what looked like a masterpiece on the way in was now a bundle of shimmering laundry with her fighting for breath beneath it. It didn't help that Flo felt very light-headed; she'd eaten as little as possible since the final fitting. Such a cliché. Flo tried to subtly look round the auditorium to spot Dylan. Maybe it was best she didn't. She wouldn't know how to act if she saw him when other people were around – it had been just the two of them for so long.

Flo and Jesse sat in amiable silence as a few minor awards were announced. Some of her dress was draped across his knee; Jesse didn't object. It was like she wasn't there.

'Are you having a nice time?' She wanted to check he was still breathing.

'Uh. Yes, thank you.' So polite! He'd obviously been miles away.

'What you thinking?'

Jesse smiled, full Hollywood beam, not reaching his big, sad, brown eyes. 'Nothing. Nothing at all.'

She didn't believe that for a second. There was way more to

Jesse than personable airhead; there was a smart guy behind those pristine looks and clean-cut smile. You didn't win the devotion of teenagers of numerous countries in the world – or boardrooms full of industry suits – by being a monosyllabic dullard, famous sibling or not. The third glass of wine she'd downed before entering the auditorium finally reached her tongue – she was beginning to regret being so grabby whenever she saw a silver tray. 'You're very pretty, Jesse Ribeiro. A bit like a painting, and I mean a nice painting, not a Picasso where the eyes are all down one side of the face or up your arse or something.'

Jesse looked terrified. 'I don't know much about art.'

'Why haven't you been snapped up yet?' Jesse looked like he'd rather talk about imminent nuclear Armageddon. 'Don't tell me, you haven't met the right girl.' God, she was like Dylan's aunties that first time she'd met them, complimenting and teasing her at the same time, forever topping up her glass to make more secrets spill out.

Jesse laughed, but it was hollow. 'No.'

Flo laughed too, to put him at ease, but pitched it wrong and it sounded more of a cackle. Heads three rows in front swivelled to investigate. She was on the verge of coming right out with it and asking if he fancied her, even though she wasn't sure what she'd do with the information. She watched Jesse's face flush. Was he just shy? Did he think she was out of his league? She wondered where Dylan was. Was he having fun with Max somewhere? She smiled at the thought of them having a lads' evening, even though she'd said she wouldn't mind if he brought a woman on a date. He'd been quite understanding about Jesse – it wouldn't have killed him to have been a little jealous, now she came to think of it. Ugh, enough.

'I'm gonna go find us a drink. Whaddya want?'

'Just a water, thanks.'

'Water's for chucking on fires, Jesse.' Flo rolled her eyes. 'Fine.' She hurriedly gathered up the dress she'd stepped into so tenderly hours before, and tiptoed exaggeratedly up the aisle, thrusting open a door and gasping in the comparatively fresh air of the deserted bar. There was nobody about, really; a few servers setting up for the after-party, for the press and the competition winners. She had a pass, of course, to at least three better ones; she tried not to be too excited but it was still a thrill. Flo made a beeline for a stack of glasses of indeterminate wine when she saw, across the bar, Dylan, sloping into the men's bathroom. She hurried over, checking left and right, trying not to topple over on her heels, and peeped round the door. Miraculously, not a soul. Dylan never could pee at a urinal; he always got stagefright. Ironic, given he never suffered it on stage or indeed during any kind of performance. Flo crept in – she could say she was lost if asked, who cared – and peeked under cubicle doors. Nope. Nope. Nope. Bingo. A pair of very shiny shoes, size nine. Monsieur Dylan Fox himself. She tapped on the door.

'Sorry, it's taken.'

Flo stifled a laugh and tapped again. She could practically hear Dylan's stomach lurching, wondering how to refuse his first invitation to do a spot of cottaging.

'Errrr, taken.'

And again. Tap, tap, tap.

'Look, Max . . .'

Flo laughed sharply then covered her mouth. 'Let me in . . . hunniiiiiii.' A zip was hurriedly refastened, shirt tucked in, then Dylan's face appeared at the open door. Flo barged in. 'What are you doing in here? Why'd you think I was Max?'

Dylan put a finger to his lips. 'Max has been threatening to get coke all evening. I thought maybe he'd managed it and was about to banjax my career. As for what I was doing, I'm crapping myself with nerves! What else? What are you doing in here?'

Flo did an exaggerated mime of a firework exploding. She really should've eaten more; she was hammered. 'Surprise, bitch!'

'How's it going with your rebound boyfriend?' Dylan's whisper was frantic. '*Lovebirds*, Mick Dick said. You're supposed to be pretending!' Oh he was jealous. Thank God!

There was a noise outside. They stood, breathless, as someone emptied their bladder and emitted noxious, noisy gases into the atmosphere, whistling the theme tune to *City Royal*. Once their footsteps subsided – they did not wash their hands – Flo giggled again.

'Jesse? He's not interested in me! I think he'd rather be at home writing in his gratitude journal.'

'You shouldn't be here! We'll get into trouble.'

Flo laughed. Dylan hated breaking rules of any kind – he'd said once it was something to do with him and Max getting stopped by the police all the time as teenagers for 'no reason'. Flo had never met a boundary she didn't like to push. She placed Dylan's hand in the small of her back. Ah, that was better. 'Make it worth the risk then.'

'What?!'

'Come on, best newcomer nominee, time to impress the jury.'

*

As Dylan zipped up, Flo checked her reflection in her compact. 'I look like . . . like I just got fucked in a toilet, really.'

Dylan kissed her, heat off their faces sparking between them. 'You look amazing.'

'By the way, those underpants . . .'

'What?'

'They're silky, like lingerie.'

Dylan felt himself go red. 'The designer sent them. They go with the tux. Can you believe that? Knickers to match a suit?'

Flo wiped sweat off her brow. 'Yes, I can. I'm wired into a piece of fabric that costs more than a sports car.' She looked at him now with mischief. 'Do you have to send them back?'

'The undies? Of course not!'

'Can I have them?'

'What, now?'

Flo put her thumb through Dylan's belt loop and brought him close. 'I wanna pop them in my handbag. Kind of sexy. Nobody will know.'

Beyond some mild spanking, a desert island fantasy, and wearing nothing but a tie sometimes during sex, Flo had never shown an interest in kinks. Where had this come from? 'You want to put my pants, that I've had on all night, in this roasting hot theatre, in your handbag and carry them around?'

'I'd find it a bit thrilling. Wouldn't you like it if I sent you my knickers in the post?'

Dylan was excited by this new rampant side to Flo's personality, but rather wished it hadn't shown itself when they were standing in a toilet. 'I need to wear them, I don't like everything . . . swinging freely.'

Flo laughed. 'Swinging? Your bollocks aren't that big.'

'Imagine if you didn't wear a bra. It's like that. Too much

movement. I can let you have a sock or something? They match, too.'

Flo frowned. 'You know nothing about women. I'd love to never wear a bra again. I hate them.'

'Really?'

'Yes, so can I have the pants or not?'

'Not. Look, you'd better go.'

'Fine.' Flo was gathering herself together when they heard the unmistakable voice of Max, outside, asking someone if they'd seen Dylan.

Panic gripped Dylan's throat. 'What do we do?'

He wished Flo was as sober as he was. She chewed on her fingernail, feigning deep thought. 'Um, I'll say I was desperate for a pee, or I'm a stupid bimbo and, gee, is this not the way to the press room, or whatever. Damsel complex, works every time.'

'Max knows you're not stupid.' Shit, shit, shit. 'We'll have to come clean.'

Flo thwacked him with her clutch. 'No! I'm supposed to be falling in love with Jesse right now. Look, let's pretend we saw each other, popped in here for a private chat, and now we're arguing. Right?'

'Arguing about what?' Dylan was whispering so hard, his throat was sore.

'Um . . . well, how about you're not that happy to have a song written about you, for a start?'

Dylan stuck his head over the cubicle wall. He could hear Max out there babbling at someone. 'So I've started the row? First I'm snide, now I'm dragging you into some toilets to shout at you?'

'Quiet!' Flo hissed. She was rapidly sobering up. 'Okay,

it can be my fault. Just go. And . . . look . . . don't spare my feelings.'

What was she talking about? 'I'm not going to hurt you.'

'If this is gonna work, it has to look real. Max knows you better than anyone. Now let's go. You first. Say something as you leave, something like you don't want to speak to me, okay?'

'Okay.' He kissed her. He didn't want to do this, but he had to do it for her. 'Love you.'

'Me too, hope you win.'

Flo breathed deeply as Dylan left. The cue she was waiting for didn't come. Forgotten his bloody lines already. He must've run straight into Max, who sounded frantic.

'God, look at the state of you. Are you all right? Where the fuck have you been? Your category is up next. And what the fuck's happened, you look like you've just done a thousand squats.'

Time for her big entrance, she guessed. She saw Max trying to get some sense out of Dylan, who was asking Max what a heart attack actually felt like. She puffed out her chest. 'Don't you walk away from me.'

Max's face was actually brilliant – such shock and awe. She wanted everyone to look at her like that when she entered a room. 'Flo!'

Thankfully, Dylan remembered his part. Trembling, he spun round to face her. 'I've nothing else to say to you. I'm done.'

Max's eyes ricocheted between the pair of them, like match point at a Wimbledon final. 'Have you two been in there together? F . . . fighting?'

Well, almost, thought Flo. Dylan's eyes flashed to the corner of the room, and Flo turned to see Mick Dick stomping across the plush carpeting toward them.

'Well, I've got plenty to say to you.'

Dylan's face changed before her eyes; he became the Dylan she'd seen on stage. Swagger. Nonchalance. Balls. He curled his mouth into a snarl; it was quite hot. 'Why don't you put it all in yet another song? Talk to me through the radio.'

'At least then I won't have to look at your smarmy face.'

Max was agog. 'What the fuck's going on, guys? There's no need for this. We're all grown-ups.'

Flo saw Mick Dick tapping furiously on his phone. This wasn't about fooling Max anymore, was it? The room was being readied for the interval, there were a few more people around than before. Waiters were pretending to clean mirrors or pour drinks – one was even pouring imaginary champagne from an empty bottle. Their public awaited.

Dylan stood up straight, with a dismissive leer. 'Shouldn't you be getting back to your date instead of obsessing over me?'

As if by magic, Jesse appeared now, sipping the water Flo had never brought him. 'Floria, are you okay? When you didn't come back, I . . .'

Flo grabbed Jesse's arm. 'I'm with Jesse now, Dylan, and he's sweet and kind, and I've never been happier.' Jesse looked surprised by this development. She could see Dylan trying not to laugh, channelling his energy into looking furious, like he was imagining all the casting directors who'd said no.

'When you fuck it up, I'm sure I'll hear all about it in your next song!'

Oh, very good! He always said he was bad at improv but he was nailing this. Max was still taking it all in. 'Like, I really wanna stay and watch but my bladder's so full Tom Daley could swan dive into it. We have to stay classy, and we have to get back to our seats.'

Dylan started back toward the auditorium. The usually inscrutable stewards looked startled but heaved open the heavy doors as he approached. 'Goodbye, Flo, my award's up next. This is over.'

Flo was thinking of one final comeback when she spotted Lois, gliding like she was on casters, photobombing two Oscar winners, a glass of champagne in her manicured hand, a smile on her face that suggested she'd matched all six numbers in the lottery. God, was there no escape? The pretend bile in her throat suddenly felt very real. 'Oh that's right, your award, for your part that your ex had to beg for?'

Dylan slipped out of character. 'What?'

'Yeah, you're always banging on about how you didn't go to the right school, and how you want to earn all your parts, and boohoo what a fucking struggle, but in the end, it took Lois flashing her cleavage and doing her shopping-channel act to get you on *City Royal*. You got that part the old-fashioned way, and everybody knows it.' Whoa, where did that come from? And why did she feel so . . . energised by it?

Mick Dick, from his vantage point near a large tray of canapés, was loving this; he was practically touching himself. Dylan looked stunned. He stormed off toward the auditorium. The stewards held the door open awkwardly, waiting. Flo followed, grabbed his shoulder; she felt possessed by a demon.

Max put himself between them. 'Stop this, it's tacky. This isn't you. You guys aren't like this.'

The stewards tried to shut the doors but the three of them were in the way. Jesse chewed his nails. Some people in the bar were filming them on their phones. Lois, she saw now, was looking right at them, glass paused halfway to her lips.

Dylan seemed to find some anger within. It didn't suit him, made him larger, more imposing. 'Bullshit. You wouldn't even have a career without me.' Flo saw the heat rising in him. Had she gone too far? 'Writing break-up songs, telling lies about me, all from your childhood bedroom. Nice. Good luck finding another idiot to fuck you in it.'

'Guys . . .' said Max.

'Look, please . . .' Jesse now. 'You need to listen.'

Flo could see the headlines now. She felt an overwhelming urge to wound him; it was like the hurt from breaking up had bubbled back up to the surface. She knew it wasn't real, but she had a story she needed to tell. This one was for the fans. They would demand justice. She grabbed the glass of water from Jesse's hand and dashed it in Dylan's face. 'I hate you. I never loved you.'

Dylan gasped, no response at hand. His face was drained of colour; he looked like he'd just been shot. There was loud music, the lights beamed right into their eyes and made them blink. Max was cheering for some reason. She saw Dylan turn slowly away from her, toward the stage, to find everyone in the auditorium looking at him. On their feet. Applauding.

'Go on,' Max was saying, shoving Dylan toward the dazzling lights. 'Get up there. They said your name. You won.'

Fifteen.

The rest of the night was a blur. Dylan couldn't even remember what he'd said in his speech, his post-show interviews, anything. After the photo call, he'd wandered round one of the parties looking for Max. He accepted congratulatory hugs, handshakes and kisses on the cheek in a daze – all he could think about was Flo's face during that argument. Don't spare her feelings, she'd said; he hadn't realised she would relish not sparing his either. He lasted twenty minutes before climbing into a cab home, wishing the award in his hand was a kebab, or Flo – in that order, he'd skipped dinner. This was not how he'd imagined fame would feel.

As he pulled up at his door, Dylan spotted a shadowy figure in a tracksuit clutching a pizza box. Flo, of course, stripped of her extravagant gown but with full Hollywood face of make-up intact. 'I just babbled some goodbyes at Jesse, went back to the hotel to take off the monster dress, and came over. Is that okay?' They stood staring at each other for a moment. Barely two hours earlier, they'd been snarling at one another like attack dogs; the water Flo had chucked at him had long dried, but the splash felt tattooed on his skin. Those last few hurled insults lingered around them like fumes. Dylan breathed deeply, relieved to taste only crisp, clean night air, and broke the silence with a chuckle.

'Not gonna lie, this is a sexy look. I hope there's real pizza in there.'

'Sorry, it's a prop. I fished it out of the waste-paper . . . the bin. Can we phone one in?'

Inside, he opened wine. 'We're still together, then, even though you never loved me?'

'Of course!' She grimaced. 'Did we go too far? I couldn't think of anything to say. I was going to shout out that your dick was small or something but it didn't seem right.'

'Because it's not true? Right?' Sometimes he worried about this.

'No!' Just for good measure, Flo grabbed it through his trousers. 'It's truly lovely. But I saw Lois and . . . I don't know . . .' They'd agreed no more jealousy, but he knew Lois still made her twitch. 'Did you know she was going to be there?'

Dylan handed Flo a glass. 'I kind of assume she's going to be everywhere, it's easier that way. I didn't enjoy that exercise, by the way. I don't want to have to talk to you like that. It's not worth it if we have to do that.'

'I didn't mean it, I'm sorry. I thought it might make a better story, throw people off the scent, make it all go away. We'll never need to do it again, I promise.'

Dylan had seen how excited Mick Dick was by it all, everyone's faces as they stared. It was like they were feeding off it. He knew an audience hungry for more when he saw one. 'I'm not sure it's your promise to make. I think we might have attracted a bigger swarm.'

'I quite liked your line about getting fucked in my child-hood bedroom, though. Can I have it for a song?'

When they first woke the next morning, everything was back to normal. They could be anyone, anywhere. It felt like they had everything they needed, right there – which wasn't very much. Since moving into Gabe's old room, Dylan hadn't had much time to make it his own. His card-board boxes, which had sat in the corner of Max's room for months, had teleported into Gabe's room pretty much still packed up, save for where Dylan had torn one open in frus-tration trying to find something. Half the hairdryer flex still trailed in one box; he hadn't even bothered to fully unpack it before blasting his hair. Whereas before this transient state had felt like the tragic side of bachelorhood, that he was now too busy to do anything about it made him strangely proud, like some kind of honourable nomad. Flo had made a couple of comments, like, 'If you leave that pile of stuff any longer it'll become sentient and sell our sex tape to the papers', but largely she was unbothered.

Dylan stretched and picked up his phone. Time to turn it back on. Flo snuggled into his chest. 'This is lovely. Do we have to admit there's an outside world?'

They were, predictably, all over the showbiz gossip sites.

'Your mum and dad are gonna love this,' said Dylan, read-ing Mick Dick's very gingered-up account of their role-play in one of the tabloids. 'He's suggested hashtags to show who you support, Team Dylan or Team Floria. What the hell? I don't like the idea of us being pitted against each other.'

Flo sighed. 'Hmmm, you'll probably come out of that better. Nobody can ever spell my name. I guess I'll stay off the internet for a while – Dylanettes can be pretty harsh. At least they mention the tour, and the EP! And I'm number one on iTunes again. Tanya will love it.'

'It's Foxettes, I think.' Dylan reached for Flo's hand. 'Was a bit scary, though, saying those things. Didn't feel good.'

Flo kissed his fingertips. 'It's just playing. The pictures are amazing!' Flo showed Dylan a slideshow, taken by Mick Dick. 'Lots of finger-jabbing. I didn't know I could get my mouth that wide.'

'No comment,' said Dylan with a wry smile as he shoved the papers off the bed. 'I need to get going. Lois is coming into the studio today.'

'She really does get everywhere.'

'Now, now. She's been nagging for a tour for weeks. I arranged for today because I'm stupid, I didn't think I'd actually win. Aaaaand, it's my new gay lover's first day on set.'

'Big day for you.'

'Which will be topped off by a bollocking for getting on the gossip pages.' He'd had several missed calls from Priya already. A shaft of sunlight caught Dylan's gleaming award, plonked in pride of place atop an ironing pile. 'I suppose it's worth it, right?'

'It honestly is. If I can keep this going until after the tour, then . . .'

'After?' But the tour was on until December, so that meant no public announcement about their relationship until when? After Christmas? Dylan knew he had to be patient, but the goal slipping further away from him made his heart sink. He wanted to be in a regular relationship, having arguments in Ikea like everyone else.

'It needs to be very "me and Jesse" for the tour so the

earliest spot in the narrative for big news is afterwards. Do you see?'

Dylan nodded, trying to hide his disappointment. *Very me and Jesse.* Lovely. The fucking narrative.

Flo began to grab her clothes. 'I'd better get back to my hotel before they come for the dress. To think I waited years to wear a Givenchy dress and I just left it in a heap on the floor.'

Dylan crept out and put his ear to Max's bedroom door. He swung it open. The bed wasn't slept in. 'He never came back.'

Flo tiptoed through. 'What was he doing when you left?'

'I didn't see him. I texted but he blanked me. I thought he'd snuck into an after-party.'

Flo grabbed her temples, hangover kicking in. 'Man, I have so much apologising to do. I need to go see poor Jesse. Mum and Dad. Estelle's been messaging through the night.'

Dylan held her close. 'We certainly look like very convincing exes. You and Jesse got in the papers, your queen of heartbreak crown is intact.'

'Watch it, Snide Boy.' She peeked at his watch. 'Have we got time for . . .?'

They made time.

Lois stirred her tea and tapped the spoon on her mug three times, then the newspaper in front of her. Dylan watched droplets of tea stain his face, the paper darkening outward until it consumed Flo's forehead and began to dry out as it edged toward a shocked-looking Jesse. Quite the tableau. Dylan wanted to say something about how broad his shoulders looked, but it probably wasn't the time.

'This is too much!' Lois glanced round the *City Royal*

canteen. It was busy, but nobody looked up. Low ceilings, the clank of breakfast plates, and the cheery shouts of the dinner ladies denied Lois the usual acoustics she needed to command an audience. 'I never thought I'd see you and your own little Princess Diana reduced to tabloid trash! Such unflattering shots too, were they taken on a courgette?'

'Nobody's safe from Mick Dick's telescopic phone.' Dylan pushed the paper aside. Underneath was the latest issue of *Soap Suds*. Dylan was on the cover, again, with a couple of co-stars peeking from behind his shoulders – yes, definitely broader than ever. He felt a tiny flash of pride. 'I look good in this one, though.'

Lois picked the magazine up like she was fishing hair out of a plughole. 'I can't believe you've beaten me to a magazine cover how many times over? Even if it is only *Soap Suds*.'

'Literally one of the most popular mags in the country, with a loyal and engaged readership, thanks.'

'Look, no, honey, listen, I'm happy for you.' Dylan stared back at her, incredulous. 'I *am*! Honestly! And good to see you finally getting your say after the way Flo used you.'

Had Flo used him? Or was Lois just being mean? He was afraid to ask. To hear Flo talking this morning, she had more riding on this fake break-up than he did. What was actually in it for him?

'You should be doing merch. Is Priya on it?'

'Merch?'

Lois tutted loudly and grabbed the bracelet on his wrist. 'My agent would've had these mangles in production weeks ago, and I won't rest until I get a Team Dylan T-shirt.'

'Don't go there.' Dylan pulled the bangle gently. 'I like that this is the only one.'

Lois looked round the canteen again. 'Who's that, over there, talking to Ciara McLean?'

'Oh, so you know who *she* is, then?' Dylan turned to follow Lois's gaze. It was the new guy. Montagu Stephens. New casting announcements always made him uneasy. He'd never forgotten that he'd climbed over a few corpses to get his own role. 'That's my future on-screen lover. Storyline kicks off properly soon. They're going for a slow burn. We don't actually, uh, hump until Christmas Day.'

Lois cringed. 'Hump. Cute.' On hearing they hadn't yet met, Lois decided to play hostess, hollering across the room. 'Hey! Monty! Come over and meet your new man!'

Dylan wanted the ground to split open and drag him beyond, but when it didn't, he smiled widely and stood as Montagu approached. Ciara retreated to another seat nearby; she didn't look over.

There were awkward introductions. 'It's Montagu,' he clarified after Lois called him Monty another three times. Luckily, Lois had never met a silence she couldn't immediately fill.

'So, whatcha been in? Where have I seen you?'

'Do you go to the theatre?' His voice was deep and mildly disdainful.

'Yeah, once or twice.' Lois rolled her eyes. Dylan had seen her do this before – always to dazzling effect – when reeling in a new man. 'Lemme guess, *Jack and the Beansprout*.'

'*Beanstalk*.' Montagu gave a tight smile.

'Sure.'

'Anyway, no, I've been at the . . . actually, how rude of me, I haven't asked about you at all.' Good deflection, thought Dylan. Lois wouldn't pass this up. He watched as Lois gave

Montagu a rundown of every speaking role she'd had since uttering her first word.

In his headshots Montagu looked approachable and handsome, but in real life, his good looks were cruel, almost ugly. He was wearing a T-shirt that said LOOKING FOR TROUBLE. By the twisted, sneering expression on his face, he'd already found it, and it had been carrying a cricket bat, yet Lois was acting like Michelangelo's David had nipped down from his plinth for a quick skinny latte with her. Montagu had the kind of suntan that could come only from spending your entire summer either on a building site in direct sun, or yacht-hopping in the south of France with rich, triple-barrelled Europeans. Given his hands had likely never tackled anything more strenuous than a half-hearted wank to *Wonder Woman*, Dylan assumed Montagu was, therefore, posh. Dylan had met a million Montagus at drama school; despite looking about as natural on stage as a haunted bedside table, most of them had a superiority complex that could be seen from space. Montagu was a Barnaby-and-Estelle hybrid created in a meth lab, had spent three summers in Biarritz, and was now ready to cash in his entitlement. At least he was chewing gum, so any kisses would be minty. Dylan couldn't think how they'd convince viewers they were destined to be together; this was going to be the performance of his life.

Montagu took Lois's social handles and promised her a DM later in the week, apologising that he had to go to make-up. Lois watched him go with a bemused smile.

'I thought you weren't sleeping with actors anymore?' said Dylan. 'How are you still awake? Every word was like a tranquilliser dart.'

Lois hushed him. 'Are you crazy? He's a back-up plus one

for when you get too famous or wanna take your gay best friend to all the good parties.' Lois suddenly sat up straight, as if a teacher had caught her passing a note. Ciara McLean herself was approaching.

'Hope I'm not disturbing,' said Ciara, sitting next to Lois without waiting for an answer. Dylan loved how she did that; an audience with Ciara was not an offer anyone refused. Dylan was surprised to see Lois starstruck. He never thought he'd see the day.

'I wanted to apologise,' said Ciara, smiling warmly. Wow, this was the biggest acknowledgement he'd had in weeks.

'What for?' He caught Lois's eye. She was practically salivating. 'Do you want to talk privately?'

Lois tried to kick him under the table but missed, her foot chiming against the metal table leg. Her face!

'I want to say it here, in front of your . . . friend.' She knotted her fingers in serious contemplation. 'I was very hard on you after that story about your ex. Sometimes I forget you're new to this. I should've given you the benefit of the doubt. Moreover, it was none of my business.'

This was new. 'Don't give it a minute's thought.'

'I read what happened last night. I've been there.' Dylan instinctively bowed his head. She was talking like it was the worst thing ever, best not to show that it was all a joke. 'If you need to talk about anything, if you're not coping . . . I'm here, okay?'

Dylan's heart raced. Lois was dumbstruck. But Ciara wasn't done. 'I also wanted to say . . . how proud I am. You deserved to win.' Dylan was starting to feel quite overwhelmed and unsettled by this sincerity; at least when she was gliding past him in the corridor, he knew where he stood.

'Anyway, that's all.' Ciara stood up. 'I'm going for a drink with Della and the make-up girls tonight if you want to come?'

He could barely speak. He squeaked out a 'terrific', as she walked away.

Lois waited until Ciara was out of even her earshot before she spoke. 'Pull the limo the fuck over. She's into you!'

'Don't be silly.'

'She is! I have eyes! So does she, and they were glued to you! I love it.' Lois looked down at her nails, like she was sharpening them with her eyes. 'Okay, I'm ready for my tour. That's if you can stand up, of course. Or is that a gun in your pocket?'

Flo rang the buzzer and waited. Jesse's distorted voice crackled over the intercom. 'Come up!'

She rode in the lift – no mirrors, sacrilegious – before padding along the deep-carpeted hallway to the apartment. Before her knuckles made contact, the door was whipped open and Jesse stood before her, bathed in brilliant white light.

'Fucking hell, it's bright,' exclaimed Flo as she walked through the flat, her shoes clip-clopping on the white-tiled floor, which joined up somewhere with the white walls, themselves coming to abrupt ends and giving way to wall upon wall of windows facing out onto . . . well, not much really. Just more of the same. 'It must be like living in a fish tank.'

'I've not been here long. Just getting used to it. There's more natural light than I was expecting.'

'Do you not get how windows work?' Although Flo didn't

know Jesse well, she hoped this light-hearted back and forth would loosen him up.

Jesse laughed. 'My mum usually opens and closes curtains for me, and turns lights on and off – I've never had to think about it before.'

'Lucky! Both her, for finally getting rid of you, and you, for this amazing . . . operating theatre you've moved into.'

Jesse placed a glass in Flo's hand. Flo glared down at the fizzy water wishing it had a lemon and two measures of vodka floating in it. 'Listen, I need to say sorry straight away for abandoning you last night. I hope I didn't ruin your evening.'

Jesse looked uncomfortable. He turned to gaze out of the window, not that he had much option; everything was a window. 'You didn't.'

It didn't feel fair to drag him into her dramas, tour or no tour. Time to have the talk, say the unsayable. Cards on the table. 'I need to be really clear about something.' Flo steeled herself. 'I like you, and I know we were kind of thrown together, and I enjoy hanging out with you.' He turned back, squinting. Don't stop, she told herself. 'But, last night . . . what I said about being "with you", I was . . . lashing out.' She was flailing. Come, friendly bombs and fall on Floria.

Jesse seemed to look right through her. 'Look . . .'

She had to continue. 'Tanya said you had, uh, intentions, but I don't get that vibe between us. And fake relationships are a bad idea, aren't they?' She paused, anticipating a lightning strike from the god of irony. Jesse's face changed. He didn't look upset, or insulted, but he didn't say anything either.

They sat in silence for . . . what? Decades? Flo was sure she'd leave the flat to find hover cars had been invented. Then, Jesse sat down. 'Floria . . .'

Please don't say you do actually have feelings for me, she thought, please please please.

'I'm gay.'

'I'm sorry, Jesse, I'm not ready for anything serious yet . . .' She stopped to let her brain catch up with his words. 'Oh!' Of course he was. Obviously. Where had her head been the last couple of weeks? 'You are! I mean, you are?! Excellent!' He looked puzzled. 'I had you down as bi-curious at least.' Flo cringed; Max would've eviscerated her for that.

Jesse forced out a smile. 'Definitely gay.' He explained, without much emotion, that he was happy, but not fully out. It made it difficult to meet people. Interviews were tough: he never lied about his sexuality, just never confirmed it. This came with its own pitfalls – from accusations of 'queer-baiting' from gay fans who thought he was straight, to nasty slurs from straight fans who thought he was probably gay. He didn't want to mislead anyone, but if people drew their own conclusions about his relationship with Flo, it took the pressure off.

Flo reached out and held his hand.

'I suppose I'm frightened. Scared they won't love me anymore.'

Flo felt like someone was singing a song about her for a change. 'I know how you feel. I mean, I'm not gay, obviously, but . . .' She was making a mess of this. 'I know how hard it is to always be the person your fans think they know. That seeing the real you might mean it all ending tomorrow.'

Jesse looked more like a child than ever in this vast, sterile room. 'But . . . you're so real. I could never show my emotions like you do. It must have been like sitting next to a robot last night. You really gave it to Dylan, and he deserved it. You were angry and powerful. I wanna do what you do, express myself through my music, my sexuality, my desires, be upfront. No compromises. That's why I love what you do. Listening to you is like reading a diary.'

If only you knew, sweetheart, she thought. 'Believe me, I wake up every day scared it's all a dream.' She was trying to reassure Jesse, but it was true. She'd been an overnight success; she could easily be an overnight failure. Things moved fast: more than once she'd overheard someone talking about 'the next Floria' or 'we need another "Last Hello"'. Sleeping in her old bedroom, welded to her old life, probably didn't help – something she needed to remedy soon.

'I like you, I'm glad I told you,' said Jesse, looking relieved. 'My brother says I need to find the right time to tell the world.'

The famous Sonny Ribeiro – he should know; he'd been doing this a lot longer than them, and probably had a wise word or two about what happened when the hits stopped coming as thick and fast, too.

'I'm not hiding. I want to really commit to it, you know? I don't just want to say, "Hey, I'm gay, but it's no big deal" and pretend it never happened and go on as before.'

Flo felt a mixture of admiration and fear on Jesse's behalf. 'So what's stopping you?'

'I wanna go all in, but maybe I'm not ready for the conversation that comes with it. I know what'll happen: some fans will think they're not my target audience anymore, some will say I've been deceiving them. I see stuff. I know who I am, and I'm proud of who I am, I wanna stand on stage, sing about my relationships, and not have everything in code. I wanna dance close to a guy and for it to mean everything and nothing at the same time. But . . . I'm scared. If I come out, is it gonna be the only story they let me tell? You understand, right?'

Did she ever, albeit on a slightly less life-altering scale. Flo hugged him. 'I'm honoured you felt you could share that with me,' she said, her eyes glistening. 'I'll do whatever I can. Pretending to fancy you will be no hardship if that's what you need.' He was beautiful, after all, and if she was going to be fake-single, she might as well have a fake-fling with Jesse to go alongside. 'Seriously, name it.'

Jesse smiled warmly. 'You could start with . . . telling me more about Max.'

No. Fucking. Way. She should've known. That's who Jesse reminded her of! Max! Flo held out her glass. 'Please, please put vodka in this. Then tell me everything.'

Dylan tiptoed overdramatically into the flat. He stumbled as he reached for the light to find Max on the sofa, hands in lap, holding a glass of wine, looking very serious.

'Why do you have whipped cream on your face?'

He looked mad. Aw, no, not a telling-off, not now. Dylan wouldn't be able to keep a straight face. 'Been out,' he said, trying desperately not to slur. 'Della put some on my nipples and licked it off. It was funny.' There'd been a few camera flashes, too – Dylan should probably text Flo before he went to bed. 'Where did you stay last night?'

Max had a strange look in his eye. 'Remember that singer guy Flo was with? Jesse?'

Dylan felt his stomach churn. He'd forgotten about their little display. Maybe this was why Max was looking so moody – Dylan and Flo had left the pair of them to the mercy of the press. 'I'm sorry about that, it was . . . a lot, I know.'

'Do you believe in love at first sight?'

Dylan retraced the day he met Flo. It was all so clear: opening the door, the little bell tinkling in warning, the other assistant – Martha? – moving out of the way to reveal Flo, behind the counter.

'I was with him.'

'What?' Dylan tried to process where Max was going with this. 'At a party?' Had Max heard something about Flo? Had Flo slept with Jesse and Max had found out? He couldn't give the game away by looking too stressed.

'No. I was *with* him, with him. He's gay.'

'You boned?' Dylan flopped onto the sofa, his throat already scratchy for want of liquid. This was a new twist. This didn't bode well for the narrative. 'Like, a one-night thing, or a see-you-again thing?'

'See me again.' Max's voice was flat, a technique Dylan recognised as Max's way of trying not to show he was too happy or too sad. Which was it? 'I can't tell anyone. Not for a while, maybe not ever. Ridiculous, right? Who'd put themselves through that?'

'Why can't you? Nobody cares if someone's gay, do they?'

'I don't expect you to get it.'

Dylan looked into his best friend's eyes, red and drawn from his confessional. He had to let Max know he wasn't alone. He could trust him. 'Not sure if this is the right time but . . . maybe I do get where you're coming from.'

Max eyed his best friend over his wine glass. 'Why do I get the feeling that as usual, you're about to steal my thunder?'

Dylan's words sounded ridiculous, yet somehow

wholesome, almost twee. 'Flo and me . . . we've actually been together all this time.'

Max had never been one for understatement. He threw himself to the ground, hugging Dylan's shins and begging him to 'beam me up to my home planet'. Dylan was used to these dramatic displays, so gave him a moment to collect himself, his heart racing. Once Max had worn himself out, he climbed back onto the sofa, his mouth opened so wide Dylan feared falling in.

'I can't decide if this is the most romantic thing I've heard or the most stupid. So you never broke up?'

'No, we did.'

'So . . . you broke up, got back together, and now she's pretending to see Jesse, who is gay, yay for me, amazing, all because of . . . what? The tour or something? And you're going along with it all because . . . what's in it for you?'

The more Dylan tried to explain his and Flo's bizarre scheme, the less he understood it himself.

Max put his face up close to Dylan's until their eyeballs were almost touching. 'You really love her, don't you? I think I only just realised how much. You're playing a dangerous game, sneaking about, fucking with the press.'

'I know. Can you keep it to yourself?'

'I spent most of my life pretending I didn't know stuff that was staring me in the face. Worry about yourself; every actor needs to come off-stage at some point.' Max winked and hugged his friend close. 'I'll take it to the grave that your non-stop fuckery is absolutely certain to land me in.'

sixteen.

'You told Max?! Why?' Uh-oh. Dylan had wanted this last date before Flo left to spend weeks cooped up on a tour bus to be chilled and romantic, but he couldn't hold onto the secret anymore.

Flo scratched irritably at the blond, bobbed wig she was wearing. 'I feel like I have a cat on my head, I hate it.' She was in one of his favourite disguises: her 'personal trainer' look. The cycling shorts got him every time. The wig went flying across the room.

'It felt like the right thing to do. We're like brothers, you know that.'

'We agreed nobody should know. Stay in character at all times.'

'The rules change sometimes, don't they?' It sounded like a dig; Dylan regretted it. 'It's cool, he's not gonna say anything, he's got a secret of his own.'

'Oh right.'

Oh right?! Was that it? Dylan knew Flo too well to believe she didn't want the details. She thrived on gossip – her blood type was OMG-negative. 'How long have you known?'

She tried looking innocent, but there was a reason he was the actor and she was the singer. She cracked. 'Jesse's really into him, it's gorgeous to see. Please tell me Max feels the same.'

'Oh, he does!' Dylan whooped loudly. A neighbourhood dog barked in response. 'Wow! Something good has come of this nonsense!'

Flo nudged Dylan hard. 'Oi! Plenty of good's already come from it! We're together!' A cloud crossed her face. 'Can he keep a secret? Will he tell Jesse?'

'Wait, you didn't tell Jesse about us?' Dylan couldn't work out why he felt offended. Was she ashamed of him? He could feel a deathless spiral of overthinking coming on.

'I don't know him that well. We're colleagues, really, so . . .'

'He's trusted you with his secret . . .'

'I know, but . . . it's better if he doesn't know. What if he blurts it out in front of my manager, or something?'

It didn't seem fair Jesse wasn't in on it, but Dylan guessed it made sense; Max wasn't in touch with anyone who 'mattered'.

'Fair enough. Pizza?'

After they ate, they sat a while, scrolling through their phones, piping up every now and again when something interesting caught their eye, neither wanting to admit they were worried about not seeing each other for a couple of months.

'You're in Mick Dick's column, did you see?' said Flo. 'Just a small box, you're wearing that aubergine emoji T-shirt.'

Dylan didn't look up. He was typing animatedly on his phone, engrossed. 'Oh yeah?'

Flo tossed her phone to one side. She watched him for a couple of minutes, seeing his body tense up, brow knotted, teeth clenched. 'You stuck on your sudoku, or what?' she asked, finally.

'Huh?' He didn't look up. Again. 'Social media,' he murmured. 'Arseholes.'

'Yeah.' Flo sighed. 'What now? Has your bangle been cancelled?'

Dylan grunted with irritation. 'Just some dickheads being dickheads.'

'Please tell me you're not checking the hashtags.'

Dylan grunted again. 'Not exactly.'

'Oh whoa. You're not actually replying, are you?' Nobody did that! 'If they don't like you, fuck 'em. Plenty of people do, award-winning Dylan Fox.'

'It's not me.'

Flo felt a muscle twitch. Ah, he'd discovered her haters. She would much rather not know. 'I've stopped looking, I've had to try to stop caring. My team does my socials.'

'What, you don't look at all? I find that hard to believe.'

She grabbed his phone. 'Do you really? I suppose you're looking at #TeamDylan, right? Seen some choice comments about how you should've wrapped your St Christopher round my neck before you dumped me, have you? Tip of the iceberg. Do you ever check out #TeamFloria? My advice is don't. You wouldn't last ten seconds.'

'I know they say things about me, actually.' Dylan sat up straight. 'Why are they like this? What have *you* ever done?'

'A woman doesn't have to do anything to get a pasting! Exist. It's automatic. Butting in, explaining stuff you already know, repeating jokes back to you, every fucking thing analysed so your words don't make sense anymore.' Dylan looked like he was trying to understand but it didn't seem to be going in. How could he? She'd now accepted this world was closed off to her for ever: no more posting a few holiday snaps or tweeting out some random opinion. Every scrap of content was a loaded gun. Even though she never sought it out, she still saw it; people always ended up showing her. The Russian roulette of how many comments she could stomach before closing the page, like facing her old school bullies all over again. Back then, Estelle shielded her, always fought Flo's corner; now she had to pay people to have her back.

Dylan placed his hand on Flo's, but she whipped it away without thinking. 'I don't see why I can't stick up for you.'

He obviously meant well, but meaning well was not the same as doing good. 'First of all, we're supposed to be enemies, but you're fighting a forest fire with a water pistol. People who love you have been programmed, by us, to hate me. Don't interfere with the narrative – this will play out on its own, whatever we do.'

Narrative. Oops. She knew he hated that word. Dylan sat back on the bed and closed his eyes. 'You're right. I know it's hard. I'm sorry.'

As Flo kissed him, she looked at his phone and saw the tweet he'd been so mad about. Ciara McLean, Dylan's co-star was, according to this anonymous troll, 'a grotesque slag but still ten times the woman Whoria could ever hope to be'. Fuck the internet, thought Flo, and all who swim in its sewage.

Dylan listened to traffic outside while Flo gently snored. Their last night together and he'd been acting like some dumb man on the internet. He did understand, though, in a way. Nobody was outright abusive to him, but he felt icky over how people talked about him online. Objectification puzzled him – it felt nice, validating, but dirty, and it all mounted up. Whenever he posted a selfie, at least three people would comment 'BOOM, I'M PREGNANT' underneath – sometimes even men. One magazine called his St Christopher 'that delectable "touch of council estate" that makes Dylan Fox our favourite bit of rough'. The parody social-media account for his bangle posted working-class clichés in clumsy Yorkshire phonetics. He didn't understand why it made him feel so cheap. Max was largely unsympathetic – they'd been out for a burger when Dylan had happened upon an article about who had the best body in *City Royal*. He'd pushed his plate of fries aside. Max had rolled his eyes.

'The pressure is real,' Dylan had complained, deepening his voice to avoid sounding whiny. 'The constant threat of not being hot enough anymore.'

Max looked Dylan up and down. 'At least you don't have far to fall.'

Once out of the shower, Flo dug out Dylan's one mirror – she always said that, for an actor, he was reassuringly reluctant to preen – and set about doing her make-up. Dylan sat on the bed and watched, just like he had in the old place. He enjoyed observing her rituals, it made him feel close to her. So much he wanted to say. He desperately wanted his last few normal moments to be perfect, but the grief of being apart had arrived early. It was like hovering over a hospital bed, waiting for someone to die, misery only on hold. He took a deep breath. 'The plan. Us. This . . . How much longer?'

Flo, still with her back to him, locked eyes with his via the mirror. 'When the time's right.'

'How do we know when that is?' She sighed, like he was a small child bothering their dad during the ten o'clock news. 'You said after the tour, but what's the difference if we do it now? People won't return their tickets. We're strong now, stronger than ever, nothing Estelle or Barnaby could say would get in our way.' That was a point – a secret he was still sitting on, Barnaby in the restaurant with what Mick Dick would probably call 'a mystery blonde'. When would be a good time to spill that?

'I want this as much as you do. But it's not just about Estelle, or my mum, or your . . . Lois. Not now.' Flo shifted a little.

Dylan got off the bed to sit behind her, rested his chin on her shoulder. 'Then what is it about?'

'It would be confusing for the fans. The tour . . . They expect me to sing about heartbreak night after night, how I'm hoping things will turn around. I'm a work in progress. The audience is there to fix me. It has to be authentic. How would it look if I'm suddenly back with the guy who broke my heart? I'd look weak.' Flo stared into the mirror, like a million thoughts were raging in her head. 'Tanya explains this better than I do.'

Weak. Nice. Dylan collected last night's dirty glasses off the table. 'Shall we get Tanya on the blower to explain it to me?'

'Getting back together now wouldn't be realistic.'

'Realistic?! We're pretending, remember? Being together would be the most realistic thing we've done in months!'

Flo chewed the inside of her lip. 'It should feel natural,

gradual, not like a big trick we've been playing on everyone, y'know? I don't want it to look like we've been taking the piss. We have to introduce ourselves back into the relationship slowly.'

'You sound like a press release.'

Flo looked like she'd rather count grains of rice than have this conversation; she began busying herself with her make-up again. 'I thought you were enjoying your status as a heart-throb.' She smiled mischievously. 'I've seen those photos of you and that girl who likes licking cream off your nipples.'

'Della is a lesbian. She's more interested in the cream than anything I can offer. And it's no different from you parading up red carpets with Jesse.'

She smiled in satisfaction. 'That's business. I don't mind. Carry on playing the lad, or coming to Ciara McLean's rescue on Twitter.' She'd seen it, then; he'd wondered. 'You have my blessing.'

Strange she was offering her blessing, but never asked for his when she was singing about what a bastard he was, mascara going full Niagara down her cheeks – she'd confessed to wearing a special kind that showed up better on a screen but didn't look over the top. Dylan pulled at his bangle nervously; he noticed Flo doing the same.

'You owe it to your Dylanistas to get over me as publicly as you can, think about it,' Flo said, laughing now, the mood lightening but getting further away from Dylan's original question.

'It's Foxettes, as well you know.' That was another thing eating at Dylan: Flo's fans' trust and songs' popularity hinged on him being the bad guy, that he'd cheated, and broken her heart. Flo had never confirmed this, but she hadn't denied it either.

Dylan looked defeat in the face and decided to blink first. 'Okay. Slowly, slowly. We'll stick to the plan.'

'It's for the best, honest.' She blew him a kiss. 'Right. I've got a couple of hours before I meet Estelle. Breakfast?'

'Ah, yeah, your big send-off before the tour.' Dylan was disappointed; he'd assumed they'd spend her last night together.

'It's a double celebration, actually. Estelle's got a deal for her memoir. I forgot to say.'

She hadn't forgotten to say, she'd just chosen not to say, because she knew how Dylan would react. Estelle, falling on her feet yet again. What could she possibly put in a memoir? How could she even sit and write a book? She probably dictated it to one of her minions.

'I'd say pass on my congratulations, but we're not supposed to be in touch.'

'I know you have your issues with her, but for any relationship to work, you need friends on board. Estelle is like my Max. She's known me for ever. She doesn't just know where the bodies are buried, she helped dig the graves.'

'Then I'll try my best not to end up six feet under.'

'I am sorry I can't stay. In a normal world, I'd be staying in for a romantic goodbye with my boyfriend,' said Flo, burying her head in his chest. 'But in our weird world, I don't actually have a boyfriend, do I?'

'I guess.'

'Estelle has been such a cheerleader, I have to be there for her. Whatever you think of Estelle and Barnaby, they show up for their friends. They're loyal.'

Dylan felt a flash of spitefulness and jealousy. Loyal? Ha! He sipped his coffee, savouring what he was about to say. 'Barnaby wasn't looking too loyal last time I saw him . . . did I mention I bumped into him just before the Yukis?'

Seventeen.

Flo was kind of looking forward to her first 'what goes on tour, stays on tour' scandal but the fantasy didn't live up to reality – her tour was a hedonism-free zone, devoid of glamour. Every backstage area smelled slightly of cooking, her dressing rooms were shabby and badly lit, sometimes just a curtained-off corner with little privacy, and no matter the venue, there'd always be one random crew member standing around eating a baked potato out of a cardboard box. Always.

She'd imagined long nights quaffing champagne with hunky lighting technicians and hilarious sycophants, but her carefully curated image as friendly neighbourhood siren translated to the crew as 'likes to be in bed before midnight'. She and Jesse always had a quick beer with them after the show – Jesse never finished his – but before even the first catering services sandwich had curled up at the edges, she'd be manoeuvred to the hotel or tour bus, whereupon the true after-party would begin without her. Or so she imagined. It didn't help that Jesse was wholesome to the bone. One of his biggest hits was 'Picnic by the River', a lovely tune, but one that sold a lie of vague juvenile romance that could never be achieved in real life — there was no mention of annoying people playing frisbee nearby, floating sewage, or wasp attacks, Flo noted. Not much bite to be had. Flo herself wasn't particularly rock and roll either; her songs could give a sunflower seasonal affective disorder. Not for the first time, she regretted her lack of edge, and wondered how far her brand of heartbreak could take her.

Imposter syndrome never left her, but she tried not to complain too much. There was always someone reminding you that, as shitty as life could be, others would kill to be where you were. Some probably had. Flo was grateful, truly. Doors had never opened for her so fast: whatever she wanted, she got — she fantasised about testing the limits of this, but hadn't dared yet. People kept telling her, over and over, that she was brilliant, that this tiny piece of art she'd made was special — it was a constant head rush. It was obvious why people got addicted to fame. But there was that persistent doubt eating away, that this magic could only last as long as she played her role as the wronged woman, the queen of heartbreak. Once she and Dylan went public, that side of her would be gone, and she'd have to come up with something else — she wasn't entirely sure she had much else to give. She and Dylan had never been better; all she wanted to do was write about her joy. Tanya always told Flo she should believe her own hype, but warned the road to hell was littered with singers like her — women especially — who'd peaked too early. If Flo wanted to get a full album out of this, maybe even two, she'd have to keep up the act.

She thought having Elijah on board might've been a comfort, a familiar face from the real world, but he didn't want to hang out with her either, happier to act like she was the uncool boss lady. She'd heard he was doing a decent job and that he was a 'good guy', but he'd been nowhere near as grateful for the opportunity as she'd hoped. Flo tried to look on the bright side: at least he was boring someone else with his self-penned sexist anthems. Now he had no choice but to play her songs.

Because finding alone-time to talk to Dylan was difficult, Flo spoke to Estelle a lot. Estelle's advice for tour-bus blues was 'Oh just write a song and have another lovely little hit to take your mind off things', which wasn't hugely useful. Flo was still reeling from Dylan's revelation that Barnaby actually was a real-life love rat. He'd been there, at that last brunch, so she hadn't said anything, just eyed him coolly over her mimosa. She felt she should say something, but she couldn't just do it over a call; it had to be in person. Estelle had demanded full backstage access to her upcoming London show, so maybe they could get some time together then. She felt protective over her old friend; very occasionally the way Estelle had acted around Dylan made sense to her now.

But until then, Flo was stuck on mainland Europe with a gay man who took a glass of milk to bed and people who were paid to be nice to her. The old adage 'careful what you wish for' rang hollow and true.

Then, like a favourite song coming on the radio, everything changed.

Flo was examining her face close up, seeking reassurance from her make-up girl Nina that, no, her pores were not bigger than Lake Michigan, when a deep voice came through the curtain that acted as her dressing room door.

'Hey, uh, Floria? It's Sonny Ribeiro.'

Flo froze. Sonny Ribeiro. A curtain away. Jesse's big brother was what pop stardom was all about – four number-one singles, and enough platinum discs to comfortably wallpaper a roomy downstairs lavatory. She hadn't known he was coming! Jesse had asked him to tour with them but he had declined due to 'prior commitments' – a code for finalising his divorce.

'I wanted to say hello,' he said, still through the curtain.

'Hello,' she trilled, like a child answering the phone when their parents aren't at home.

Flo stared at the make-up team. Nina exaggerated curtain-pulling movements and mouthed, 'Ask him in, for fuck's sake!'

'Um . . . sure! Come in.'

After a few agonising milliseconds of curtain wrestling, Sonny Ribeiro was standing in front of her. Everyone was shorter than they looked on TV – Jesse had stood on a box in the promo photos for the tour programme – but Sonny had stature.

Flo froze like she'd been caught sneaking ice-cream out of the freezer by her mother. She extended her hand, but he came in for a hug. Their cheeks barely touched, but Flo felt the heat. He smelled lovely, just as Jesse had that first day. She felt weird and gooey. She was fangirling, majorly; Dylan would die laughing when she told him. Sonny was saying he loved her music, what a natural, talented performer she was, and how 'The Last Hello' had such depth and meaning, that it felt like the soundtrack to his own life. She was trying to drink it in, but this was so surreal; this patter must be from a 'how to meet Floria' starter pack somewhere because *everybody* said it to her, he couldn't possibly mean it. She really needed to go to the bathroom and, looking at the clock, had to start getting her make-up on.

He'd stopped speaking. She should say something. 'I've been a fan of yours since Text Usherette!' she squealed, hoping to get extra points for remembering his first ever band, back when he was in his teens. 'I was so sad when you came second in *Star Searchers*, I wanted you to win.'

If he was embarrassed she remembered him from the days before he'd had his teeth done, he didn't show it. 'Thank you. Back then only white guys won, you see, I never stood a chance.'

She felt her face burn as she searched for a response that wouldn't make her sound like an idiot. Sonny didn't seem that surprised by this reaction. She racked her brains for trivia. 'I used to cover your songs on my YouTube,' she said, unable to stop herself, desperate to claw back some professionalism. 'I loved your last album.' Her mind was a total blank and she couldn't remember a single track – she hoped there wasn't a test.

Sonny let her finish, bemused. He licked his lips lightly, to let her know he was ready to speak. 'I wanted to wish you a fantastic show. I'm looking forward to seeing you, uh, close up. Jesse can't stop raving about you; I'll be duetting with him on a couple of songs at every show, so I'll be around for a while.'

'Oh, thank you,' gushed Flo, feeling silly now, aware everyone was watching. 'Um, I'm super pumped to see you and Jesse sing together.' Super? *Pumped*? When did she ever say that?

'He's a better singer than me, don't you think?' There was a glint in Sonny's eye but Flo wasn't sure how to proceed.

Was Jesse a better singer? He had range, power, and . . . oh God, what should she say? Sonny spotted her discomfort and seemed to find it amusing, so offered her the get-out clause her stunned silence was grasping for. 'You've thought about that a tad too long,' he joked. 'You can say yes. I taught him everything. I want him to be better than me.'

'You can always tell when someone's had a good teacher,' croaked Flo, twirling her hair round her finger and hating herself for it; she felt like a competition winner.

'Who was yours? Is there a big brother or a talented mum or dad cheering you on?'

Flo smiled but felt a tinge of sadness. She'd offered her parents tickets to one of her London gigs, but her dad hated being around young people at the best of times, and her mother claimed it would be 'too noisy'. 'We prefer watching you on television,' Joy said, as if Flo was on their screens every minute of the day and not just the musical guest on the odd chat show or a thirty-second interview on breakfast TV. Her parents were only in their fifties but acted like they had priority boarding for the pearly gates. What did it take to make them happy? She'd assumed breaking up with Dylan and getting actual number-one singles would make them proud of her talent, but nothing seemed to have changed. Maybe she was the problem.

'No,' said Flo. 'Nobody musical in my family.'

Sonny laughed. 'Even better. You're the one the descendants have to beat. Perfect!'

She could listen to his clichés all day. So handsome. An assistant called to him beyond the curtain. He said his goodbyes, grappling once more with the dusty fabric on the way out.

*

Flo watched Jesse and Sonny on stage together that night, envious of their bond. She didn't know what it was like to have siblings; Estelle, also an only child, had been a surrogate. What must it have been like to grow up with someone who shared your DNA, created by the same people as you, but was still their own person? Someone to have your back, tell you that you were great, or squabble with over the TV remote control, or sweets, or portions at mealtimes. Maybe she owed her talent to her solitude. She'd sat in her room playing guitar day and night – if her parents were out – love songs and tributes to half-formed ghosts. She watched how Jesse and Sonny moved together, how instinctive they were. It was slick, but not from hours and hours of rehearsal; this came naturally. Jesse was, obviously, very good-looking, fresh-faced and charming, but his elder brother had something that eluded Jesse: he was actually sexy. It wasn't his looks, or his body – although everything was in order there – it was his whole aura. And Flo didn't even believe in auras. It was how he moved, and spoke, how he treated the crew. The air around him was charmed by his presence.

Nina stood alongside her, almost salivating. 'Look at his arms, the way his bum pops out. Super firm. I could rest my brushes on it. You seen his Instagram?'

Flo was starting to feel very warm. 'Not recently.'

Nina chuckled. 'He's got his bum out in it. I've never seen such a perfect arse.'

Right on cue, Sonny turned his back to her and she saw for herself what the fuss was about. She took it in, the way he stood so confidently, like he owned the stage, a knowing look that went right to the back of the theatre, holding each and every one of them under his spell. When they finished, he reached out and touched Jesse tenderly on the cheek and Flo was almost embarrassed to admit to herself that she wished that cheek had been hers.

Nina blocked her view and tutted. 'God, you're not half sweaty, come through for a touch-up.'

Once the show was over, the atmosphere in the hotel bar was different, somehow. Sonny was relaxed and upbeat, and the crew delighted in his salacious stories and tales of terrible encounters with other famous people – it still amazed Flo how willing celebrities were to stab one another in the back. When Jesse did his traditional theatrical yawn and made his excuses, Flo made to leave too, but Sonny and the crew begged her to stay, Sonny threatening to lead a chant if she dared leave.

'The trick,' he said in her ear, once she'd sat down again, 'is to leave when they're having a good time, so they remember you were there for the fun.'

'I thought they wanted me out of the way.'

Sonny laughed. 'No, they want to hang with you. You're a star. But you're also the boss – they need their downtime, to slag you off.' He winked. 'Well, maybe not slag you off, just gossip about you a bit. Have two or three drinks, laugh at their jokes, then skip off to bed or . . . somewhere else.'

Under normal circumstances, she'd pinch herself that Sonny Ribeiro was giving her tips on how to socialise, but in her job, normal was a fluid concept. She was already too inebriated to even feel a pinch, anyway – thank goodness there was no show tomorrow.

'I must say, Floria,' said Sonny, toying with his empty

glass, 'you're not the queen of heartbreak I was expecting — you're full of life, and joy.'

Amid the smoothness, Flo felt a flash of paranoia. Had Max blabbed to Jesse who had, in turn, told Sonny? No, she was being ridiculous. 'I can't be heartbroken all the time. I've got shows to do.'

'Those songs . . .' Sonny signalled to the bartender and nodded to Flo to see if she wanted a drink. She shook her head, with a trace of regret. 'They come from a dark place.' He took his refilled tumbler. 'That ex of yours must be some piece of work.'

'It's complicated.' Boy, was it.

'Love of your life, am I right?'

Flo's eyes began to sting. Tired, obviously. 'He was.'

'Definitely *was*?'

Flo felt sharper than ever; he did know something. 'What do you mean?'

'It can be hard to let go. I see it in you. Not quite over it, maybe.'

Flo looked at the clock. It was way too late for a drunken counselling session with a new divorcé, even a hugely famous one. 'I'm over it.' She decided to shift focus. 'Are you?'

Sonny laughed and downed his drink. 'Working on it. G'night, Floria. Time for my exit.'

Flo didn't exhale until she heard the ping of the opening lift doors, before they closed again and took him to his floor. She knew exactly what she'd be dreaming of later.

Flo grew to enjoy her little chats with Sonny; he had heaps of stories and tonnes of advice. If she had a problem, he always knew the answer, but he'd wait for her to ask his opinion, he didn't just volunteer it. Most of all, he was fun. Sonny's presence made everything feel less like work, and more like a family holiday, but with people she actually liked. Flo was starting to enjoy herself. Having a roomful of people sing back the lyric you first composed in your bedroom while feeling like absolute shit . . . it never got old. Flo would finish her section with, what else, 'The Last Hello' and some nights she could barely hear herself sing, as the crowd hollered it to the sky, like tuneful wolves baying at the moon.

The crew were more relaxed now, too; they loved hanging out together. Sonny would organise day trips – touristy villages, gorgeous parks, or random country inns. Once they found a theme park, where they'd jumped the queues, much to Flo's embarrassment but the park managers' insistence; Dylan would've started an all-out class war if he'd been there. Sonny whooped and screamed alongside her, not minding when she was paralysed by fear and digging her bloodless fingers into his arms which, she noticed, were very firm. Jesse didn't always come along – he said he preferred to rest his voice, but Flo guessed he was knocking one out with Max on a video call. She toyed with the idea of bringing Jesse's sexuality up with Sonny, but reasoned it was better to keep conversation focused on the two of them.

Sometimes photographers got a tip-off that Sonny was out and about, but he was always gracious, even if they were rude and intrusive. 'The trick is . . .' he said, he always seemed to be telling her about a 'trick', she noticed, like a wise owl. 'Use social media to let people know what you're up to, then you've got control.'

'I let my team do it.'

Sonny nodded. 'I get it. Official stuff is important. But if you share a few behind the scenes, it makes the sneaky pap shots less valuable. You control the narrative then, see?'

The narrative! She immediately thought of Dylan, and his place in her narrative, one she was definitely not controlling. They'd promised to have a goodnight call every day if they could, but sometimes she finished too late, or he was night-filming. Messaging each other wasn't the same.

'Let's take a couple of selfies, show the world we're having a blast, that they should come see us on tour.'

Flo and Sonny huddled together and posed, and she posted them immediately, as if any delay would mean that it wasn't real, that she was dreaming.

On the last night, before they returned to the UK, Sonny came to Flo's dressing room. It wasn't unusual for him to pop by and wish her a good show. Tonight she was feeling especially excited, so was delighted to see him.

'Hey, Sonny Bunny,' she beamed as she did some final checks. She'd called him that ironically at first – he was very much not a cute little 'bunny' of any description – but now, like most in-jokes, it had stuck. He didn't seem to mind.

'Look, I was thinking . . . it might be cool if I joined you on stage for a duet, too. Make it extra special.'

'Mmmm?' Flo couldn't speak; Nina was busy slicking on twenty coats of lip gloss.

He smiled widely. God, he was so good-looking. 'The crowd would love it, give the evening a twist. Keep things exciting.'

Flo felt her fingers tingle, like her blood was crystallising. He'd obviously had the idea this would, somehow, be doing her a favour. He was waiting for a reaction. 'A twist?'

Sonny smiled again, wider. 'You know I'm a huge fan of "The Last Hello" . . . what if I did a little ad lib, maybe even half a verse, from the guy's point of view.'

Flo felt butterflies, creeping dread. When she'd first met Sonny, all she'd wanted to do was say yes to anything he asked. She'd thought he understood her, that he'd been to that place the song came from, what it meant to her fans, but now, she wasn't so sure. 'What guy?'

'The ex! Would be quite something, wouldn't it? Give us a little headline when we land in the UK.'

This didn't feel organic, or fun; it was cynical, a business move. Had Tanya had put him up to it? Sonny always said he respected her as a performer; maybe he was coming at it from a fan's point of view, and didn't know this was the last thing she wanted. She weighed it up, as Sonny looked back with an eager, hopeful expression she was reluctant to wipe away. Might it be . . . an honour? Wouldn't it be fantastic to be close to Sonny onstage, see him singing her own song – or a bastardised version of it – back to her? His eyes on hers, his hand resting on her cheek, her hand on his . . . well, she wasn't sure. On his bum? Maybe it wasn't a big deal. So what if he sang a verse from 'the guy', defending himself, maybe disputing her version of the facts . . . hang on, no, absolutely not. This was her song.

Flo took a couple of breaths, gathered herself, and, not quite believing what she was about to do, placed her hand gently on Sonny's beautiful, toned arm. 'Sonny Bunny . . . that's so kind and . . . I know anyone with a brain would jump at the chance to share your stage.' Sonny's face began to curl up like the pages of an old newspaper, anticipating the rejection.

'But?'

'I can't share my songs, not these songs. They can't be changed to fit you, because they're mine, from that moment. It would be like . . .' Flo looked round to see her team gawping in horror, incredulous she was turning down Sonny motherfucking Ribeiro. 'It'd be like showing you my diary and asking you to add notes. I can't. "The Last Hello" isn't a duet, and the guy . . .' She looked down at her feet, feeling petty, aware this might end her career. 'He doesn't get his own verse.' She thought of Dylan; he'd never complained about the lyrics once, only told her how good the song was. She felt a surge of guilt she'd have to deal with later, but turned her mind back to Sonny. 'If he wants to reply, he should . . .'

Sonny patted Flo's hand. 'Go write his own fucking song? Am I right?'

Flo managed a weak smile, her hands trembled. 'Something like that.'

'No problem,' said Sonny, giving a small salute and strutting out of the dressing room.

Kyle, her hair stylist, gasped. 'Your chaotic energy is . . . amazing. I love it.'

What if this chaos had cost her a friend?

After the show, they celebrated as normal, drinking through the rider. Flo stuck to water, but Jesse managed a few drinks. He couldn't wait to get home to Max; they were clearly mad about each other. Sonny bailed before Flo had a chance to talk to him; he was flying to the UK early for a prearranged visit with his son.

Jesse caught Flo watching Sonny go to bed, briefly dipping

his head to her as he left the room. 'Sonny told me about his idea.'

Finally, Flo let her guard down. 'What the fuck have I done? Have I upset him?! His face . . .'

Jesse laughed and popped an unprecedented fourth beer. 'Don't sweat it. He'll respect you for it.'

'What?!'

'I'm serious. Anyone else would've handed the song over, totally compromised their . . . what Sonny likes to call his artistic integrity, for the sake of a headline. Sonny knows he's a big deal, even if he doesn't act like it. You showed him you're different.'

'So why isn't he talking to me? I thought I'd offended him!'

'He's embarrassed that he tried to muscle into your moment. Your star-making moment, he said to me.'

Flo was gobsmacked.

'You've humbled my brother,' laughed Jesse. 'Enjoy it, I've never managed it.' Jesse saw the relief in Flo's face. 'Seriously, he likes a challenge, likes it when . . .'

'When what?'

'When he's made to work for it. He really rates you.'

'He rates me?!'

'Yep. That duet will happen one day, but on your terms.'

They clinked glasses. Sonny Ribeiro rated her! Finally, this plan was getting her somewhere. When Jesse wasn't looking, she raised her glass again and gave a silent thank you to Dylan, wherever he might be.

Eighteen.

'Look at this one more time and tell me I'm imagining things. Go on.' Dylan held his phone up to Max's face. 'Don't pull that face. Look!'

Max pushed the phone away and went back to buttering his toast. 'You're being weird about this. She's on tour with the guy; what's she supposed to do? Ignore him?'

'She's on tour with Jesse. Sonny's the special guest.'

Max shoved past Dylan, perched on the sofa, and shovelled a slice of toast into his mouth. 'It's way too early in the morning to be accessory to your social-media stalking. I know you two are play-acting being broken up, but this . . . obsessive behaviour is a bit method.'

Max was right. Kind of. Not entirely. He hardly got the chance to speak to Flo – she never had a spare moment, so how else could he keep up with her? Dylan had hoped Sonny Ribeiro would turn out to be one of those guys who only looked good in photo shoots, but if Flo's videos were anything to go by – and Jesse's, and Elijah's, not that he was stalking their accounts – Sonny was as handsome behind the scenes in a grubby old T-shirt and tracksuit bottoms. He was a proper man. In touch with his feelings, Dylan could tell from his lyrics, which he'd also been obsessing over, but a bloke all the same. Strong arms, gravelly voice, he played guitar, brilliant dancer! Sonny was the full package. Dylan struggled with the cha-cha slide; he couldn't compete.

'You don't have to compete,' Max told him. 'It's you she's with.'

'Look how happy they are together. They were up until three a.m. yesterday!'

'We've been up past three twice this week.'

'That's different!'

Max had taken to sticking his fingers in his ears when Dylan went on about this, but Dylan wasn't imagining things. She, Jesse and Sonny – of course! – had even started doing 'Top Fives'; that used to be *their* thing. Despite telling Dylan she hated being away from him, she was tired, and all she wanted to do was go back to normal, Flo seemed re-energised, a new woman. Endless pics and videos, the three of them exploring unfamiliar cities, places he would probably never go. Hopping in and out of cabs, pulling funny faces, shopping, misbehaving in restaurants, eating candy floss. She was a kid again. Dylan found it endearing at first. At first. Christmas was getting closer but their supposed 'reunion' seemed to be getting further away.

When Dylan casually-but-not-very-casually mentioned to Flo that she seemed to be posting a lot of personal stuff he was disheartened to hear the excitement in her voice.

'Sonny's idea. Someone's been leaking stories to Mick Dick or telling paps where we'll be.' Dylan wasn't sure how posting your every breath helped matters. 'It spoils their story,' Flo explained with a hint of impatience. 'If we post everything ourselves, all they can do is report it, they don't get a scoop. Following us about isn't worth the hassle. Get it?'

Oh, he got it. Clever Sonny, the fucker.

'But enough about that!' said Flo, excitement rising. 'London's calling! You need to tell me how many tickets you want!'

'Are you sure you want me to come? Won't it look weird if I'm there, the ex to end all exes, stalking your show to listen to myself getting slagged off.'

'No! You're a celebrity, where else would you be?'

Which bit was funnier? That he was a 'celebrity' or Flo's assumption that nobody in their right mind would miss her and Jesse's show. He peered into the lens. 'Is this a publicity stunt?'

'No, honestly. Bring loads of people, make a night of it. I'll have a bundle sent to you.' She looked behind her, like there'd been a knock at the door, though there clearly hadn't. 'Gotta go.'

Bring loads of people, she'd said. Why not, eh? It might get him even more brownie points with his castmates. Della was totally up for it, of course – she'd never stayed in more than once a month since her eighteenth birthday.

Montagu had firmly declined. 'I'm not into chicks' music.'

Dylan was unsure whether to ask Ciara, but she was delighted. 'I've never wanted to say in case you had a meltdown,' she confessed when accepting her ticket, 'but I do love those songs.'

'I don't mind!' It felt good not to lie. 'She's very talented.'

'Do you speak?' Ciara asked. It was unusual for her to ask personal questions. He assumed she got information on people by hiring private investigators to hack their phones or something – she seemed way too grand for mere chit-chat.

'No.' Switching back to lying so fast was deflating. 'I dropped her a text when she went to number one. She got the label to send me tickets. I'm proud of her.'

Mischief flashed across Ciara's face. 'She has you to thank, though. You were perfect source material. Where would she be without you?'

Max was sent some tickets for the gig too, by a 'mystery benefactor' who was, obviously, Jesse. He refused to say exactly how deep their feelings were, but Dylan noted Max's phone was no longer pinging with any other offers.

So it went on, with Dylan watching, yet again, the video of Flo and Sonny taking it in turns to fellate an ice lolly, or the one where they covered themselves in candy floss. Did Ciara have a point? Was Flo's success all down to him?

'Not again,' said Max, one night after work. 'You know they can see who's viewed their videos? Your username will show up. On Flo's, on Elijah's, on Jesse's. On *Sonny's*.'

Dylan looked up from the phone. 'I'm not that stupid.'

'Aren't you?'

Dylan shook his head. 'No, but you are.' Max served him a suspicious eyebrow. 'I'm logged in as you. You've used the same password for everything since we were fifteen.'

Max threw a cushion. 'I'll be changing that for both our sakes. If you really wanna do something about this, stop pining and serving "restraining order" energy, and start playing your part.'

'What do you mean?'

'You've got carte blanche to act like a single man. You told me . . . Flo gave you her blessing. Go out on the town, party.

Stop moping and scrolling like a teenager who's all wanked out. It's not a good look, it's not healthy. Flo's having a ball. Why aren't you?'

'Like an act of revenge? "Anything you can do" kinda thing?'

Max's head dropped to his hands. 'No, not "revenge", but because you deserve to enjoy your success.'

'All while staying faithful, of course.'

'Of course. Honestly. Imagine being a famous actor and needing to be bullied into having a good time. There's no hope for you, pussycat, truly.'

Nineteen.

Flo was nervous, but determined not to show it. The whole point, as Tanya always told her, was to make everyone feel like she was singing to them, and only them.

'Like the first time I saw you, in Camden,' Tanya said, often, after a couple of drinks. 'It's that magic. You don't see it every day.'

This was her biggest venue yet, the crowd full of strangers. She'd toyed with the idea of putting Dylan in his usual seat, but thought it might look weird and attract the wrong kind of attention. She could see the seat now, from where she stood, waiting to go on – somebody she didn't know was in it, eating a large hot dog like they were being filmed for a sex tape. Dylan was out there somewhere, on one of the VIP balconies, in the same room as her for the first time in weeks with 'a few mates from *City Royal*'. Flo wondered if the gang included Ciara McLean, and whether she had a right to be jealous, especially after she and Sonny had posted a video, about an hour ago, re-enacting the climactic scene from *Dirty Dancing*. Mind you, Dylan's social-media strategy was taking a turn too, with a distinct increase in shirtless photos. It had started with head and shoulders, cut off at the nipple for decency, but the other day, both had been on display, tiny and pink and sitting almost uncomfortably on his pumped-up chest, a bright white towel round his waist. What had happened to her shy guy, oblivious to his own hotness? How long before the towel dropped?

'It's what people do! Likes and shares are good for the show,' he'd claimed. 'I've had to work on the body. It doesn't mean anything.' Adding to her nerves was the presence of her parents, chaperoned by Estelle, who'd refused to accept that Mr and Mrs Battista wouldn't be there for her big moment.

'I promised a car to and from, and some amazing titanium ear plugs for Joy in case she goes full church elder,' warned Estelle on the phone. 'I told her, quite plainly I must say, that it was the biggest night of your life. All the music lessons, and day trips to talent shows and weird open mic events when we were teenagers – time for them to see what it was all for.'

Flo had almost forgotten how long they'd been friends, how much they'd been through together. Flo had written off her mother as a downer for so long that she'd overlooked how big a part her parents had played in her musical curiosity. They hadn't encouraged her, as such, or been pushy stage parents, but they'd let it happen, only pushing back later, when it became clear it wasn't just a hobby. What had gone wrong? She'd never worked it out.

'Thank you, Estelle. I'm so happy.'

'Don't mention it! We're so excited! Well, I am. I can't speak for Ma Battista. I daren't.'

Flo had felt a rush of affection for her old friend, and was reminded how persuasive and, yes, kind Estelle could be when she dropped her overbearing act. It bugged her she'd never extended that kindness to Dylan, though – that would need to be addressed sooner or later. Sooner, as it turned out.

Dylan took a swig from his beer and swished the dregs round the bottom of the bottle knowing, now, that someone would be watching him do this and would slip another into his hand without even asking. Nobody in a VIP area ever had to catch a waiter's eye. Despite himself, he was having fun and he wanted the world to know. Dylan had been accepting more invitations to go out, which had the not entirely unwelcome side-effect of being photographed on the arm of more than one of his gorgeous castmates. All platonic – as soon as the bulbs stopped flashing, they'd spring apart. He looked over at Ciara and smiled as he caught her eye. She was being interrogated by Lois, who had somehow managed to wheedle a plus one from somewhere, and had turned up wearing a 'Team Dylan' T-shirt. Dylan had been horrified.

'Oh chill out, you drip, you should be glad of the support,' Lois had said through laughter. 'They've got "Team Floria" ones for sale by the hot-dog stand.'

Tonight, a lot of people would be watching him – it was only fair he gave them a show of his own. He could already see people down in the stalls who'd spotted he was here and were sneakily taking photos on their phones. For their benefit, he stared ahead as if brooding on something, but inside he was nervous and excited, for himself, for Flo. He'd tried to arrange some flowers to be sent to the arena under a fake name, but the florist had hung up when he'd said, 'Can the bouquet look like it's been run over by a petrol tanker?'

The house lights dipped, then went off entirely for about ten seconds, before the stage was bathed in dazzling light.

In the middle stood Flo, in a dress that cost more than a year's rent on their grim flat. Dylan closed his eyes as she started to sing. He was back there, back in the backstreet pubs, faceless hotel restaurants, the dive bars. Different seat, but the same promise. It always used to feel like they were the only people in the room, but tonight something didn't sound right. He opened his eyes and saw she wasn't even facing in his direction, and as wonderful as she sounded, she sounded different. She wasn't singing only to him anymore; she belonged to everyone else now. Even though he knew he didn't need to, Dylan clicked his fingers to get the waiter's attention.

When Flo had been in the audience at gigs and the artist had said 'I love you' to the baying hordes, she'd rolled her eyes, but now she got it. In those moments, making those connections, she did love them. She wanted to stand and stare at them for ever, hear them shout her name, sing the songs back to her. She was beginning to understand why people fell so hard for fame – it was like being in love with ten million people at the same time. Now she couldn't wait to see her friends' faces. After a quick change and a hair and make-up refresh, Flo found Estelle backstage with the usual entourage. She was organising drinks for everyone, including Flo's parents, who seemed exposed and vulnerable amid the velour sofas and hotel-chic flower arrangements of the green room. After a drink or two, her dad would be out of his shell and pogoing to whatever was blaring from the speakers; when she looked at her mum, she felt a strange protective urge. It unsettled her.

Everyone was garbling about her performance, although

much of the praise seemed to be directed at Sonny, who wasn't wearing a shirt under his jacket.

'My eyes were firmly on you,' said Estelle, grabbing her for a hug. 'I don't like to see men banging on about their feelings.' Lucky really, thought Flo – Barnaby rarely showed any kind of emotion unless he dented one of his cars. Did he ever tell Estelle he loved her? Where was he tonight? 'You were fantastic. I'm bursting with pride.'

As she was ready to move on to talk to her mum and dad, she saw her make-up girl Nina helping them back on with coats taken off barely five minutes ago. This had the mark of Joy's anti-fun patrol all over it. Two minutes of Dad enjoying himself and she'd be mentally sat-naving the journey home, whisking him away in a cab. Joy, for her part, looked semi-apologetic. 'We had a lovely time, but your father's tired.'

'He doesn't look tired.' He actually did, but Flo's default was to disagree with her mother.

'Long day, sweetheart.' Her dad lay an arm on Flo's shoulder. 'I don't mind.'

Flo tried to suppress her rising anger. 'I *do*. When's this ever gonna happen again? Me, on tour. In London. Opening night. Stay. One more?'

Joy's face hardened. 'No. We're set. You'll have a much better time once we've popped off.' Was she talking about leaving or dying? Flo felt a pang of guilt and bit her lip in shame. 'Estelle and your friends have been very kind, but I'm sure they want to enjoy themselves.'

Flo decided not to fight them. 'Okay. I'm glad you came.'

'You were fucking incredible,' laughed her dad, his true self peeping out in a last burst of energy. 'Young Jesse, very handsome lad.' Flo thought it better to nod in agreement than start that whole debate.

'Yes, very spirited,' came her mother's insight, presumably a reference to Jesse's impressive hip-swivelling.

Once they were gone, though the room was full of people, Flo felt strangely alone, and irritable. She crossed back over to join Estelle, Bea, Vérité, Binky, Midge and the others who'd kind of melded into one. Jesse, Nina and Sonny had also joined the circle. One of the girls was saying they'd seen Ciara McLean in the VIP toilets. Jesse and Flo exchanged a quick, panicked glance, though neither was quite sure why.

'Do you think she was here with Dylan? I saw another *City Royal* actress waiting outside for her.' Vérité was still an avid viewer, then.

'I don't know.' Although now Flo definitely did.

Estelle's face turned to stone. She held out her glass and someone refilled it, Flo saw from the corner of her eye. A very Estelle move. 'At least he can't get backstage. What was he even doing here?'

Sonny piped up. 'I've a few things to say to that dude. I'm sure we all have.'

Flo turned to Sonny now. 'You don't even know him.'

'Sure, but I know the songs, I know the pain.' For fuck's sake.

'I sent him some tickets,' said Flo in the tiniest of voices.

Estelle gasped. 'You didn't! Why?'

Flo grabbed a drink. 'He inspired the song that made me a . . .' She still couldn't say 'star', didn't think she'd earned it. 'It got me to number one. I thought it would be a kind of olive branch. No hard feelings.'

'No hard feelings? He dumped you!'

'It wasn't quite like that.'

Estelle chugged back her wine. 'I applaud you for being so mature, gorgeous girl, but that man made you miserable. He shouldn't be allowed to forget it.'

There was a distinct sense of mercury moving downward. 'I wouldn't say miserable . . .'

Estelle pulled a face. 'You've never been able to fool me.' Sensing this heading somewhere ugly, Jesse excused himself. Estelle didn't even notice, her eyes locked on Flo's. 'He had bad energy. You can't pretend he didn't. I was there, remember.'

Bad energy? Now would be a good time to forget it, maybe. Gloss over it. Say, 'Oh never mind' and propose a toast to bad ex-boyfriends. But one day, Dylan and Flo would be together again, going public, and it had to be a fresh start. No more wars between friends and lovers that, when Flo thought about it, nobody seemed to have a reason for fighting. Time to have it out, then. This was her territory, her night.

'Maybe some of that energy was to do with you?' Flo found herself saying. 'You and Barnaby could be quite patronising, sometimes.'

'Patronising? Me?' Estelle's face went full Edvard Munch. 'When was I patronising? I always took an interest in . . . his little projects. Why, on this huge night, are you wasting your time talking about Dylan, who is, as far as I can see, no longer architecturally significant?' She turned to the group, looking for back-up. 'Honestly, this guy. Dylan was ridiculously over-sensitive, wasn't he, Bea?' Bea nodded. 'Not a single joke he could take, right, Vérité?' Vérité shuffled awkwardly.

Flo wouldn't be beaten, she'd come this far. 'I don't think that's fair, you made him feel like an outsider.'

Estelle reached out her glass again, bowing in thanks as it was filled this time. 'I took my cues from you, sweets. Things you said, how you acted around him, that poky flat that made you so miserable, that he made you live in.'

'You never visited the flat.'

'I don't have the right jabs to drive that far east. Look, Dylan might've inspired the song, but would you be performing in arenas if you were with him? I doubt it. You were pretending to be someone else, faking it, suppressing your true self. And Dylan was so sarcastic and caustic. It was rubbing off on you, making you cynical, embarrassed by yourself. You used to be my sweet girl.'

Sonny removed himself from the circle and went to join his brother. God, why couldn't men handle confrontation? Flo moved slowly to the nearest seat she could find. The idea that Estelle had been making Dylan's life a misery out of some misguided loyalty to her made her feel gross.

If there was one thing Estelle hated more than being accused of doing something wrong, it was being accused of doing it maliciously. 'Dylan thought he was better than us, different from us, like his life had meaning and we were just shallow idiots. Always moaning about having no connections. For someone so disadvantaged by being working class, he seems to be doing okay. Weren't his parents in showbusiness?'

'They were club singers in the eighties and nineties. Not exactly Beyoncé and Jay-Z.'

'Right. So they'll have contacts. Gave him the confidence to go to drama school. He wasn't hatched out of an egg and left to fend for himself. He had advantages, he chose not to see them.'

'He grew up in a council house!'

'Lots of people do. Barnaby has a couple of council flats in his portfolio.' Estelle smoothed out her ponytail. Its shine was almost offensive. 'Westminster, obviously. Barno says they're surprisingly roomy.'

Barnaby! Flo said what she knew she shouldn't say. 'And where's Barnaby tonight?' The crease between Estelle's eyebrows deepened ever so slightly. 'Out visiting one of the other women in his portfolio?'

'Ah.' The room was silent, save for the gurgle of wine being poured into Estelle's glass.

'Dylan may have been many things, but he was faithful.' Flo tried to get her breath. She was sweating as Estelle's eyes bored into hers. 'I'm sorry you had to find out like this . . .'

Vérité interjected now. 'I think that's enough, darlings. We've had too much booze and we're getting silly.'

Estelle put up her hand to silence Vérité. 'Oh, you thought I didn't know?' The room was a sea of blank faces, all desperate to see what happened next. 'Think you're being clever, do you? I know Barnaby has other . . . interests. They're insignificant to me, I don't give them a moment's thought.' If she was wounded, she didn't show it.

'But, how . . . ?' Flo felt like an absolute turd. 'Look, I didn't mean it . . . I don't know what I'm saying.' She burst into tears.

Midge turned to Nina. 'Last day of term was always like this. Too much excitement, one of us always ended up crying.'

Estelle sat alongside Flo. 'Floria, you knew exactly what you were saying and . . . I don't blame you at all. I was lashing out with some uncomfortable home truths, you lashed out straight back. Fair's fair.' The rest of the room, assured nobody was about to be murdered, backed away from the epicentre and settled back into a light hum of conversation. 'I know you don't want to hurt me.' Her voice was so calm and gentle, like she was putting Flo to bed. She stroked her hand. 'Anything Barnaby has or hasn't done is small beans. What hurts is that you knew, and chose to tell me during an argument.'

'I shouldn't have blurted it out like that, I didn't want to keep it from you.' Flo badly needed a tissue for her nose. 'I didn't know what else to do.'

Estelle produced a handkerchief and pressed it to Flo's nostrils quite firmly. 'I understand. I pushed you.'

Flo looked at her friend through streaming eyes. Estelle was composed and impenetrable as ever. 'I can't believe you're taking this so well.'

'Nothing to take. I'm just glad our fight is over.' Estelle smiled. 'Our friendship is much more important to me than any man, you know?'

'Same for me.' In that moment, Flo realised there was every chance this was true.

The cab slowed to a stop. Ciara craned to see where they were. 'Oh! This is me!'

Dylan and Max peered out at Ciara's apartment block. Pretty plush. Those rumours about her huge divorce settlement must've been true.

Ciara caught their eye and read them like they were magazines. 'Oh, boys, don't believe everything you read, but if you can, divorce someone richer than you, unlike me. This flat was all I managed to hold onto. Luckily, I have a brilliant agent and love a lucrative voiceover.' She sized them up like they were the last two croissants in the bakery. 'Tonight was a lot of fun. I don't go out much, I'm not into being . . . the centre of attention, believe it or not.' She turned to Max. 'You're a delight. I'll be coming to the Consulate for that free cocktail you promised.'

Dylan could feel Max's knee trembling. Max always went to pieces when he met his heroes, especially if they were amazing women. 'Any time, my queen.'

Ciara turned to Dylan. 'You can come, too. You did great tonight. Can't have been easy watching your ex singing about you.'

Dylan shrugged. He couldn't wait to tell Flo that Ciara was a big fan. 'I'm flattered really.'

'Before I go, I must confess . . . I bought a Team Floria T-shirt. It's for my niece, honest.'

For fuck's sake. He was definitely going to ask Lois to get him a Team Dylan T-shirt printed. 'It's fine.'

'Good sport. Thank you, gentlemen.' Ciara winked and clambered out, every step to her front door betraying how much wine they'd thrown back. She waved from the doorway and let herself in.

As the car pulled away, Max crumpled back in his seat. 'Wow. I can die happy now.'

Dylan socked Max on the arm. 'I never knew you were such a fanboy.'

Max poked Dylan back. 'You never listen to a word I say. She's amazing.'

'I didn't think famous people fazed you these days, now you're shagging a popstar.'

Max leaned into Dylan as the car took a sharp corner, his face stern – that drunken, proud, borderline angry face he did when Dylan upset him.

'Don't call it shagging,' Max's voice was sharp. 'Don't make it cheap. I don't care that he's a popstar. I wish he wasn't.'

'Sorry, I didn't mean it. It's not, um, serious, is it?'

Max's face turned glum; the streetlights flashed over his eyes, but there was no life to them. 'How serious do I look? How do you think it feels not being allowed to go see him backstage?'

'I can sympathise there,' said Dylan, bringing Max closer. 'Same for me, innit?'

Max buried his face in Dylan's coat, sniffling. 'Not sure it is.'

Dylan sensed this was about to get deep, so got his phone out. 'Right, let's get to the important stuff.' He felt Max's body relax. 'Socials!'

Dylan and Max had gone on full social-media assault. Pre-drinks! Dinner! The arrival! Selfies galore! Ciara took a while to thaw but relaxed once she realised Max was a talented photographer. Soon she was pouting along and laughing, forgetting herself. There was the show, then the after-drinks – they'd swerved the official after-party on the advice of Ciara who said exes should always be enjoyed from a distance. Then came an hour of frenetic dancing in a club so tiny and seedy there was sweat running down the walls – well, they hoped it was sweat. The icing on the cake? Posting a game of Top Fives with Ciara in the cab on the way home. That would get people talking. It might even make Flo a teeny bit jealous, make her realise this thing went both ways. Not that he was aiming for that, of course.

Max read his mind. 'Checking to see if Flo's seen your shameless showing off?'

Dylan nudged Max sharply. 'It's like you said . . . I'm letting everyone know I'm single and having a good time. Looks convincing, right?'

Max conceded it did. 'How does it feel?'

'Good! Like I'm my old self again.'

Max grimaced. 'Ugh, which old self? Please spare us the late teens; I don't want to do the hair-straightener years again. Have you heard from Flo? How did it go? Has she posted anything? Jesse's phone's off.'

Dylan tap-tap-tapped and searched for Flo's account. 'Oh.'

'What?'

'There are no posts.'

'She's had a busy night.'

Dylan frowned and brought his phone closer to his face like it would make the photos suddenly appear. 'No, like, there are no posts at all. Has she deleted everything?'

'Who are you logged in as?'

'Thanks to your security crackdown, I'm logged in as myself.'

'Gizzit.' Max peered at the screen. 'Ah, right.'

'What?'

'There are posts, but you can't see them. She's blocked you.'

Twenty.

It was just as she remembered it. Almost exactly a year since she'd been here; it was like she'd only stepped away for a moment. The Christmas lights were typically low-key: multi-coloured bulbs around the top of the roof and round the front door, some flashing, but not all; warm white lights frenetic in every window. And, as last year, two reindeer made entirely of fairy lights, which had initially stood proudly in the front garden but had been rearranged – no doubt by the naughty children next door – into what Mick Dick's column would call 'a sex act'. The only thing missing from Rudolph and Prancer's workplace romance was Santa himself – Dylan's mum said his face creeped her out, so sleighs were banned from her festive display.

Flo tugged at her bangle for luck – she wasn't wearing it much these days, but today felt appropriate – took a deep breath, and rang the doorbell, which played 'Jingle Bells'. Brilliant. Business as usual. There was the familiar clatter of the inside door opening and Dylan's mum's shadow through the opaque window of the porch. For only the second time ever, Flo felt nervous at seeing her. The first time Dylan had brought her home, she'd stepped meekly into the living room, while around ten of Dylan's relatives sat or stood, cradling mugs of tea, obviously warned to be on best behaviour. She'd clocked their reactions the first time she spoke, as the difference in vowels registered, her accent foreign and awkward so far from home. They'd exchanged quick glances, but not unkindly. Once the first cup of tea was out of the way, one of Dylan's cousins was asked to bring wine and beer from the kitchen, and any tension fell away as Flo chatted to Dylan's mum, and his sisters, and aunties. She hadn't met people like these before. They listened, interjecting every now and again with a flash of wisdom or gentle teasing – usually ribbing each other, not Flo – but making sure Flo was in on the joke, explaining why something was funny, going deep into the etymology of nicknames. It was so different from her family's attitude to Dylan or, indeed, anything. Flo still remembered the light draining from Dylan's eyes that first time he'd met the Battistas.

The door opened and Dylan's mum stared at Flo, in shock, before smiling widely and pulling her in for a warm hug.

'Hello, Cheryl.'

'Flo, I don't believe it! What you doing here? It's . . . bloody hell, it's like Madonna turning up at my door! Have you met Madonna yet, by the way?' Was it possible Cheryl asked questions even quicker than Tanya? Flo was ushered into the living room – this year's Christmas tree was even bigger than usual. 'I tried to hold out,' said Dylan's mum, as they gazed at the tree, drooping ever so slightly, 'but December the first, it was up. I don't feel Christmassy without it.'

Flo noted a few additions to the wall and crowded mantelpiece. A couple of Dylan's soap magazine covers. A signed

City Royal publicity shot, Dylan in full medical garb. A framed photo of Dylan in a shoot for a men's magazine, in a beautiful suit. His hair looked different. She didn't remember him telling her about that one. On one shelf, still, a picture of Dylan and Flo. She remembered it being taken, what they'd whispered to one another as they waited for Max to stop pissing about lining up the shot.

Cheryl saw her looking. 'I hope you don't mind me keeping that up, what with you and Dylan not being together.'

It took Flo all her power not to reveal everything. 'Gosh, course not! It's your house. It's a nice photo.'

'Such a good one, I always said Maxy should do it for a living. You look very happy.'

Dylan really looked like his mum, she noticed now. It made her miss him more. More than anything, she wanted to tell Cheryl they were still together, let her share the joy. Well, okay, joy might be an overstatement, same for the 'together' part. Since she'd blocked Dylan on social media, she hadn't heard a peep. He hadn't even asked for an explanation. Sulking, probably. For all his brash swagger online, he was still sensitive; perhaps Estelle had had a point. Flo had been on the verge of messaging him a few times, to tell him she couldn't spend her life obsessing over his posts – her last sight before she blocked him was a video of him tunelessly reciting the Macarena while Ciara McLean looked on like she was watching Frank Sinatra back from the dead, and it had sent her over the edge. No more comments about her and Sonny 'looking very cosy' or Dylan getting defensive if she mentioned he was showing a lot of skin. She had to focus, and so did he – his big love scene was coming up. The longer they left it, the harder it was to break the silence.

Cheryl poured the tea; she'd always been so lovely to Flo. She got the feeling Cheryl was glad Flo was different, not from the same background, had her own interests. Or, maybe Cheryl was just glad someone had taken him off her hands.

Cheryl chatted about her eldest daughter's impending wedding which, Flo now realised, she wouldn't be attending, because, officially, she and Dylan were over. 'I'll send you some photos if you like,' said Cheryl wistfully. 'But seriously, what the hell are you doing here?'

Flo was doing a show in Leeds that night – the tour was drawing to a close. 'It would've been rude to not come see you!'

'You always were very considerate.'

That wasn't the only reason. She couldn't explain it even to herself, but she wanted to get a sense of Dylan again, the Dylan from before, away from the narrative, and the new lives they'd made for themselves, away from the Dylan that Estelle had so precisely deconstructed. Being here again made the gap between then and now seem even wider. 'Must be weird, having a superstar son.'

'Oh, it's lovely. He's so good to me.' Flo knew Dylan had taken his mother to the food hall in Marks and Spencer, loading the trolley with all kinds of luxurious things. His mum was grateful, if bewildered. As the champagne, cream cakes, and smoked salmon were packed away, she said, 'There's no point me getting used to this; I'll be back in PriceDrop Paradise next week.' Dylan's heart had broken into a million pieces.

Cheryl turned the TV down; clearly she was about to say something important. 'I shouldn't be breaking confidences and what-have-you, not that he's said much, but . . . he misses you.'

Flo wasn't sure what to say. None of this was real. It was like Cheryl was talking about two soap characters.

'If I mention you, he changes the subject. It's like he can't talk about you, it hurts him so much. He won't tell me what happened, even after those horrible stories in the papers. He was so upset.'

Flo had always thought Dylan found the 'Snide Boy' stuff hilarious, a sign he was properly undercover. She knew he hated lying to his mother, which would explain why he never talked about Flo. Lying was his father's speciality and Dylan knew that reading about his alleged infidelities in the paper would bring it all back to his mum. Flo felt a pang of guilt. She should've cut Dylan more slack when those stories broke. She didn't care about upsetting Joy – she managed that with barely any effort – but it must've been tough for Dylan, especially as none of it was true. She had to make it right, without giving the game away. Cheryl deserved her blue-eyed boy.

'I want you to know, Dylan didn't cheat and never would. The papers made it up.'

Cheryl's relief was palpable. 'Good. I never doubted him.'

She totally had. Flo saw her opportunity for a window into Dylan's soul through the other woman who knew him best. 'I always wondered why he never had a serious girlfriend before me.'

Cheryl dunked her biscuit. Once withdrawn, the soggy part trembled precariously over the cup. 'At one stage I thought he'd take holy orders – or was maybe having a thing with Maxy or something . . . which would be fine, but, no, he was shy, I suppose. Quite reserved when he's not performing, isn't he?'

Flo didn't have time to unpick the problematic notion

that a single man with a gay best friend would automatically be presumed to be having sex with them. 'Came out of his shell at drama school, though, right?' Flo couldn't help but think of Lois.

Cheryl nodded. 'Yes, but he found it hard. Most of them were very well-to-do, nobody from . . .' she looked round her living room, 'anywhere like this. He nearly dropped out a few times.'

Dylan had said often how insufferable his classmates had been, but never that they nearly drove him to give up. Cheryl was still spilling. 'He can be hard to get on with. Eager to please, gives himself hell when he comes up short. I'm talking out of turn, but he hates not to be liked. If we ever argued he'd be back in an hour saying sorry, even if he wasn't in the wrong.'

Flo remembered how dejected Dylan was when the *City Royal* cast blanked him, how cut up he was about upsetting Della from make-up and . . . yes, that one. Ciara.

'You won't tell Dylan I came, will you?'

'No! I'm glad you did, though. Nice to see you. I'm so proud of you. The girls bought me these amazing head-phones—,' Cheryl reached down the side of the sofa and produced a massive pair of headphones, bigger than Flo used in the studio. 'I can listen to your songs and then, if Dylan rings, he won't hear your voice blasting out!'

They collapsed into laughter. Flo's phone rang. The signal was weak and she could see she'd been out of range for a while – notifications and messages began pinging through, too many to read.

'Hello?'

'Floria, it's Sonny. We've been trying to get hold of you.'

'Why? What's up? Show is still on, isn't it?'

'Where are you? I've got a car sorted. I'll pick you up.'

Shit. What was going on? Sonny couldn't find her at Dylan's mother's. 'No need. I'll meet you back at the venue.'

'There's no time.' His voice was clear now, assertive. This was important. 'I'm taking you back to London. Your dad's in hospital. Sounds like he's had a heart attack.'

The twenty minutes before the car arrived were a blur. Dylan's mum made her some sandwiches, mixed her a large vodka and tonic in an old water bottle, and gave her a box of tissues. Flo clambered into the car as Cheryl stood waving her off, looking small and worried. Once inside, Flo dissolved into tears and Sonny drew her in tightly, almost until she couldn't breathe. She was grateful for the distraction – she wanted to blank everything out. Sonny had the scent of home about him, a similar woody, tobacco smell to her dad, especially if he'd been in the back garden smoking. Sonny's voice was soothing, authoritative. Everything would be all right, nothing to worry about, they'd be there soon. These off-the-peg reassurances would seem empty any other time, but now Flo needed to believe them. Any questions she asked – the tour, the audience, what happened now – were batted away, somebody else's problem. Sonny was a forcefield. In a way, Flo was almost sad her sobs had to subside, that panic was receding, and she was returning to a relatively normal state, because he loosened his embrace, and allowed her to sit up, catching the last of her tears with his thumb. She felt a weird flash of anarchy, that nothing else mattered; if this was the apocalypse she'd go down fighting. She had the urge to tear his shirt open and touch his bare chest. It was brief, but it shocked her. Sonny seemed to register the change in temperature.

'You okay? Never be afraid to show your emotions, not to me.'

As the car zoomed down the motorway, driven by someone she'd never seen before in her life, Flo looked out at the road signs whizzing by. On long journeys as a child, especially when driving to Scotland to see Granny Battista, she'd absorb these strange place names, imagining short blasts of lives other than hers flashing by in the blink of an eye. While her dad would bellow at the top of his voice singing along with Bruce Springsteen or Fleetwood Mac or Deacon Blue, Flo would compose songs of her own about these magical places. Remembering her dad so happy and relaxed broke her a little. The last time she'd seen him, he'd looked fragile and weary; she'd bawled at him for daring to go home early. What Estelle had said was true: he'd driven her to all those shows, gone over her lyrics with her. 'Just give it plenty of Stevie Nicks, angel,' he'd say, 'but without the coke and stuff, obviously?' Her funny, mouthy dad; what state would he be in when she got there? How could she face her mother?

Her memory drifted off to her tiny old flat, Dylan's socks on the radiator, the smell of cooking, the clank of central heating starting up and conking out minutes later. Who had she been back then – what did it even mean now? She was desperate to call Dylan, but he might be filming, and wouldn't it be weird to re-establish contact with a catastrophe? What would be the opener? 'Yes, sorry, I blocked you, but can we park that, my dad's about to die and I don't know what to do.' Should she tell him she didn't want to be alone, that they should forget the silly fake break-up and ask him to meet her at the hospital? That this didn't really matter anymore? But she wasn't alone, Sonny was with her, and she didn't want to send him away. There was so much to say that, in the end, she decided to say none of it.

When they arrived at the hospital, Sonny led Flo by the hand through its confusing corridors, spending a good five minutes bewildered by hostile hospital signage, before they happened upon Joy, helplessly prodding at a vending machine. Flo was expecting her mother to look bitter and judgemental – angry, maybe, that Flo had been away enjoying the trappings of stardom while her father was clutching his chest. Instead, it was like that night backstage: Joy looked small, vulnerable, winded. Her face was pale, hands shaking. This was not the ferocious Joy she'd argued about boys and underage drinking with in her teens. Even more uncharacter- istically, Joy seemed delighted to see her. When they hugged, it seemed Flo could feel every single one of her mother's bones through the trademark cashmere. Sonny grabbed them drinks from a nearby coffee shop – huge, sweet lattes they'd never be able to finish – then excused himself, saying he'd be back soon, and to call if they needed him.

Alone, in lunar-bright lighting, surrounded by unnerving white noise, Joy recounted what had happened like it was an out-of-body experience. He'd complained of chest pain and collapsed on the stairs, before tumbling back down them.

'Just a couple, not the full flight. He broke that vase. You know the one. I don't mind; I never liked it.'

Joy could barely tell the rest. Ambulances, paramedics, sirens, corridors, rushing, breathless conversations and explanations. People trying to calm her but making it worse. These things happened to other people, not them.

'I just wanted you here,' said Joy, in a small voice. 'They said to wait in that room.' Joy nodded down the corridor to the kind of room you'd only hear bad news in: glass walls, pastel-coloured interior partially hidden by strategically drawn Venetian blinds. 'It felt too far away. Reminded me of a chapel of rest. So I'm sitting here.'

Wordlessly, Flo went to the small room and retrieved three scatter cushions, making her mother stand to put one under her on the uncomfortable seat, before putting another behind her back, then taking the last one for herself. The strange tenderness of the moment hung in the air; Flo felt like a proper grown-up for the first time. Flo attempted small talk, telling her mother about the tour. As usual, Joy seemed uninterested. Fair enough under the circumstances, but still. It stung. She checked her phone in case Dylan had gained the superpower of telepathy. Nothing. Her head was swimming.

'I read your interview in *Guardian Weekend* earlier,' said Joy.

What was her mother doing reading the *Guardian*? 'Oh yeah?'

'I was surprised to read you'd never had a music lesson. I very distinctly remember paying for them. And buying the instruments.'

Flo had forgotten about that. Another of Tanya's 'narrative' ideas, to make her look 'more authentic' and stop people accusing her of having a leg-up. As if the music industry wasn't dripping with nepotism.

Joy actually looked hurt. 'I was at the recitals, shows, we got that piano and had it tuned every year, even though the man who came to tune it was a disgusting sexist, telling dirty jokes about the patterns on the tiles in my hallway.'

'That was a publicity thing. I'm not supposed to look like

I've been trying too hard. Being discovered makes a better story. I have to twist the truth sometimes.' Flo felt a teensy bit bad; she should've warned her parents about that. Had her dad seen it? Was Joy blaming her? 'That's what I've had to do to succeed. I know you haven't always been on board with my music career, but you see now it's worth it, right?'

'Lying, though, in a magazine. Black and white. What if someone checked?'

Oh so that was it. 'Don't tell me you're still worried about what the neighbours might say?'

'Is that what you think? That I care about appearances over your happiness?'

Was it? Flo wasn't quite sure what she thought of her mother. She was so used to the general awkwardness she'd never analysed her. Looking too hard into your parents' psyches never seemed a good idea – there was no possible way to find anything you'd like.

'I thought you'd be pleased, that you'd want more for me than . . .'

'Than what? Just being a housewife, with a little shop that her husband bought her because she was bored?'

Ah, that. She remembered saying that now, at that final dinner with Dylan. Her mum must've been holding onto that one. In the absence of a defence, Flo chose silence.

Joy took a deep breath and knotted her fingers together, not quite in prayer, but like she was summoning the strength to speak. 'I wasn't bored, actually. I always wanted my own shop – it was a thank-you from your father.'

'Thank you for what?'

Joy gave Flo the side-eye. That had hurt, Flo could tell. 'For everything I'd done for him. For working and bringing money in while he did God knows how many business courses, for putting my own needs last while he got the business started, for running his home and raising his daughter while he pulled fourteen-, sixteen-hour days, for listening to his crackpot ideas, for entertaining guests night after night, for never making him think about anything that wasn't the business, or his favourite hobbies, for looking after the admin, and . . . probably, for not leaving him when so many wives would have done. For being patient when he drank too much. For sacrificing everything I used to be so we could be who we are. He said he owed me, and once you were older, when things calmed down, he lent me the money for the shop.'

'Lent you?'

'I insisted.'

Shit, thought Flo, I'm that bitch daughter I'm always reading about in airport novels. 'I didn't know.'

There was a noise from one of the side-rooms and Joy started, listening out in case it was anything to do with her husband. Satisfied it wasn't, she shook her head. 'I wasn't cut out for the shop. So many big ideas, plans. Everything fell flat, I couldn't get rid of product. I did what I had to do. Selling the same thing over and over, becoming a clone of all those other shops like mine, next door, two streets away, wherever.'

'Why didn't you quit?'

A tear escaped and landed on Flo's hand. 'It meant so much to your dad that he could finally help me with something that was just for me. My mother taught me that keeping your man happy was paramount. I didn't listen to her very often, but I believed she was right about that. I suppose that was my problem with you. I worried that once you achieved your dreams . . . then what? You'd be like me.'

'I love my job!'

'Do you? Night after night singing about misery? Never at home? Looking so tired and drawn? Newspapers analysing every atom of your relationships – first with Dylan, and now this new gentleman – ignoring that you're a person with feelings? It's so tawdry.'

New gentleman? Did she mean Sonny, or Jesse? Who was she accused of shagging this week? Flo couldn't keep up.

Joy carried on. 'I dreaded this. I was glad you showed musical promise, honestly, I was! I thought it would be a nice hobby, a talent to entertain your children. I never had any to speak of. Then I saw how good you were. I didn't want your passion to become a chore, for you to be trapped by it. Do you see?'

In a way, Flo understood. Sometimes she did feel trapped, and wondered whether she would have tried so hard to break through if she'd known what fame was going to be like, but she was glad to have the option. As Tanya told her one night, 'I firmly believe it's the duty of all children to live as breathtakingly glamorous a life as possible, in their parents' honour.'

'What about Dylan? What was wrong with him? You should understand better than anyone. Your family were so pissed off when you met Dad. Why give Dylan such a hard time?'

'They were, yes, but your dad had vision; Dylan had dreams. Dreams shatter. It wasn't personal. I wanted you to have everything on your own terms.'

'You should've given him a chance. The ketchup thing, I mean, Christ. Who cares?'

'I know. I don't even think I actually like that lamb sauce.'

Joy smoothed down the sleeves of her cardigan. 'My mother told me that daughters are fated to repeat their mothers' mistakes. I was so caught up trying to stop you repeating mine, I ended up repeating hers.'

Flo felt a lump in her throat. 'Dad, me . . . we weren't a mistake, were we?'

'Maternal feelings,' Joy sighed. 'It's not the same for everyone. It's not all hugs and kisses and baby-talk. I show mine through worry. No, of course you weren't a mistake.'

'I'm sorry, Mum, about what I said. The shop, everything you've done. It was hurtful, I didn't mean it.'

Joy placed her hand over Flo's. She didn't say anything, but an understanding had been reached. Sometimes promises didn't need to be said out loud – things were going to be different.

Twenty-One.

It was going badly, there was no fudging it. Dylan hadn't been looking forward to this bedroom scene, but he approached it like a professional. It was simple: Heath and Mario, talking, shirtless, in bed, after their first time having sex. A post-orgasmic debrief. Easy. The only difference was that, instead of cradling a woman's head on his chest, it would be a man's. No problem! The trouble wasn't the gender of the head, however, but the shoulders it rested on. Montagu. He was being a prize prick.

'This scene is very submissive,' said Montagu, script still in hand. Dylan had already learned his lines. 'It plays into stereotypes. Mario's a red-blooded male who just happens to be gay.' Those last five words were a red flag, Max always said; nobody just happens to be gay. 'Why is Mario lying on Heath? Heath is the closet case – he should have his head on my . . . I mean, *Mario's* chest.'

Dylan flicked his eyes over Montagu's chest. He didn't fancy being anywhere near it. It was toned, naturally. Tattooed in places, too, which surprised Dylan at first. They weren't ornate or artistic; they looked like stick-and-pokes scratched on at parties. Inane scribblings of the drunken rich, not the careful and considered scrolls and swirls of men he'd known growing up back home. He noticed a few fainter tattoos near Montagu's near-perfect navel, and understood. They'd been inked with the confidence of someone who knew they could afford to get them lasered off whenever they liked. Nothing painful was ever permanent if you were privileged.

Members of the crew huddled in corners; there were trips to the series producer's office. Dylan sat waiting for someone to satisfy this moron's ego. They were running over. Dylan pulled his robe tighter – only boxers underneath, he was freezing, but had to be ready to jump into bed at any minute. Ciara's character was set to discover them *in flagrante* – or as close as pre-watershed broadcast would allow – and take the storyline to the next stage, which by the sound of it would be interminable months of whispering in corridors. She wandered over to Dylan, brandishing a spare coffee.

'This guy, eh?'

Dylan took the cup. 'Thank you. Yeah, this guy. Heath has bad taste in men.'

'You know he's up there asking for clarification on who's penetrated who.'

'You're kidding!' Dylan gasped as Ciara shook her head. Then: 'Hang on, who has?'

Ciara shook her head even harder. 'Fucking hell. Men. I'm sure you both get a go at the doughnut, darling, don't worry. Oh, watch out.'

Montagu glided back onto the set.

'Well?' said Dylan brightly, anxious to avoid a scene so they could just . . . finish this scene. 'Whose breast is best?'

Montagu scowled. 'As before. Mario's head on yours. But

you have to take off your horrible cheap friendship bracelet. It gets caught in my hair.' Dylan looked at his wrist. Montagu had always been jealous of the attention his 'mangle' got. What a world. 'And don't kiss the top of my head. I've spoken to upstairs, and my agent, and we agree. The kiss is infantilising.'

'Are you serious?'

'Yes. It suggests an imbalance of power. It's a hygiene issue. Heath kisses Holly in the scene before and it's mentioned she has a cold sore.'

'I can't give you a cold sore through your hair. They've been licking every single part of one another prior to this scene anyway. Mario will have cold sores everywhere.'

Somewhere, a member of the production team groaned. Montagu looked aghast. 'Should I speak to Darren about this?'

The director charged into the middle of them. 'Look, no kissing on the head, okay, fine, fuck the cold sores. Get back into fucking bed; I've got book club at nine thirty.'

Once it was over, he and Ciara shared a cab into town. 'Fancy a drink? We can go to my club.' Dylan didn't need to be asked twice. It was exciting to follow Ciara through the door that had magically opened as they approached. The walls were covered with paintings, big, small, hung randomly, not lined up. He imagined his mother seeing them and asking the waiters why nothing matched. The place was lit like the ghost train at Whitby, with candles flickering on each table and high on ornate mantelpieces. Ciara and Dylan attracted a few double-takes as they were shown to a cosy corner table, leather armchairs overflowing with cushions. Dylan could see over Ciara's shoulder to a terrace, where thin people in nice clothes stood smoking. It was special, but he didn't feel out of place. He had a right to be here.

'Cocktails, I think,' said Ciara, smiling.

They got through the first quickly, a second was ordered. Ciara went to powder her nose and Dylan got his phone out, realising it had been switched off all day. Missed call from Flo. It was the first time he'd heard from her in about two weeks. He hadn't known what to say after she blocked him, he assumed it was related to 'the narrative' but he couldn't hear that again without exploding with rage and he didn't want to argue. He didn't block her back, though, in case she changed her mind. Should he call? Maybe she'd called to wish him luck for his big scene. She couldn't stay mad at him for ever.

Ciara returned, sitting on the low chair as gracefully as she could. 'It's like sitting on a futon. My spine will hate me for this tomorrow.' Dylan's face must've betrayed his anxieties, because Ciara took one look at him and asked. 'Who died?'

Dylan reached for the nearest plausible lie. 'Oh, it's just . . . Montagu and I have no chemistry. He's making this all about him.'

Ciara hummed, like she'd heard this before, from Montagu perhaps, Dylan thought. Did she bring him here? They were on-screen siblings after all. 'There's no such thing as "chemistry". It's just acting, good or bad.' Her mouth curled up in amusement. 'It's his acting that's bad, by the way, not yours. I'm not saying that to impress you, either. Acting with Montagu is like trying to react to a pedal bin.'

Dylan blushed.

'Don't worry about Montagu, he's a paranoid, posh, homophobic wanker. I've been on the show a long time, he's "one year and out" if ever I saw one.'

One year and out – the ultimate nightmare for anyone cast

as a soap regular. Big fanfares when you joined, promises your character would 'ruffle feathers' or 'set hearts fluttering', but if the audience didn't take to you, or you pissed off the producers, or had the acting ability of a removal van, you were out, contract not renewed, a year to the day after it started. As much as Dylan hated Montagu, their storylines were interwoven; if Montagu jumped ship, he'd drag Dylan overboard. He dreaded having to schmooze with Lois again, being ignored by fit, rich smokers on terraces like the ones he could see now, or saying three lines a night to a half-empty dress circle for buttons. He couldn't voice these fears to Ciara; she'd think him a big baby. He needed to speak to Flo. He sensed Ciara wasn't ready to draw the night to a close; she seemed to be reading his mind.

'Tell me about Floria. It must be tough seeing her, hearing her everywhere.'

Dylan deflected this in the worst way. 'No tougher than you working alongside any . . . well, fellow actor you've . . . uh . . .?'

Ciara registered the slight but remained calm. 'I know it's common lore that I've worked my way through every cast member but . . . oh, what do I care? I don't waste time trying to change people's minds about me.'

'Sorry.' He meant it. That was a dick move; Flo would've kicked him if she'd been there. 'I suppose I don't want to talk about Flo or the past. Do you mind?'

Ciara nodded. 'Actually I do.' She paused to give Dylan time to look surprised. 'It's the weirdest thing. I've never met a man who didn't like a good bitch about his ex. You'd have more reason than most.'

Dylan stayed still, like he was being stalked by a predator.

The room felt quieter somehow, even though it was packed with people. 'So?'

'You never slag her off. Never say you miss her, or reminisce. Even at the show, no stories about her, nothing. It's like she's been wiped from your mind.'

Again, all Dylan could say was: 'So?'

Ciara shrugged. 'So nothing. It's weird. Either you're a perfect gentleman, or a robot, or . . .'

Dylan swallowed hard. 'Or?'

'Or you're hiding something. Feelings you've not dealt with, maybe. Shame you couldn't work things out. She seems nice. So do you.'

Dylan thanked the waiter who placed the new round of drinks on the table. How stupid of him! In trying not to give the game away, he'd forgotten the golden rule of having an ex – you actually talked about them. Everyone did. But he hadn't, to anyone. His mum, his friends. Only Max, really, but that didn't count, because he knew everything. Time to start, he guessed. He began to talk – if he were honest, quite one-sidedly – about Flo, and her friends, especially Estelle and Barnaby, and her mother. Everything that had driven them apart, casually leaving out that most of these issues had been resolved and they were back together. Maybe 'resolved' was the wrong word? Saying it out loud made him realise how different their worlds had been.

'So this is why you and Montagu don't gel. You've got a few class insecurities,' said Ciara, looking round the room as if expecting Montagu to appear. 'He'd get on well with your ex's little sidekicks. You shouldn't let them get to you. Most people spend their early thirties shedding the mates they make in their teens and twenties. She'll get rid eventually.'

Dylan sipped his drink carefully; his and Flo's thirties were a good few years away. Two tables over, a woman loudly complained about the wine, before boasting that she was being flown somewhere first-class by a record company. It could almost have been Estelle herself. 'You never talk about your own background. Why not?'

'You really wanna hear it?' Ciara sniffed daintily. 'Here's the condensed version: I grew up in a tiny flat above a pizzeria with my mum and my sister. I did odd jobs for neighbours to pay for drama club and a generous Irish granny gave me every spare penny.' Ciara noticed Dylan's shock. 'I have a horrible feeling you're going to say something about authenticity.'

'I'd never have guessed. You sound quite posh. I've always thought of you as graceful, elegant, untouchable.' He was a bit drunk already.

'What? You can't picture me crushing a beer can on my forehead? You'll have to take my word for it, then.' Ciara drained her glass and waved at the waiter, who was at her side like lightning. 'You can learn grace and elegance anywhere; they don't just belong to royalty or horse-faced heirs. As I said, I've stopped trying to change people's minds. And I never listen to men telling me who they think I am.'

'Sorry.' Dylan lowered his head in contrition. 'You should talk about it more.' He thought of Flo's infamous narrative. 'It's a great success story.'

Ciara flinched like a ghoul had jumped out at her. 'I'm not a story, I'm a person. Why would I talk about it? To get typecast as a downtrodden tart in a cop show opening the door to the bailiffs, or a dead sex worker? I wanted to be Alexis Carrington from *Dynasty*. Do you know who that is?' Dylan nodded even though Ciara wasn't looking; she was contemplating her history, located a few degrees above his left shoulder and, from what he could tell from her expression, a dark place. 'We've all read those profiles in the Sunday supplements with actors whose parents just happened to work in film, or were successful lawyers or doctors. I cottoned on quick that my "story" would be the only interesting thing about me. I'm not ashamed of it, and I didn't hide it . . . but I ignored it, never complained about what was staring me in the face – that acting is a rich person's hobby. Now I'm successful enough to make a difference, I'm reconciling with my past.'

Dylan was dumbstruck. He'd assumed, from her nerve and poise, and the respect she commanded on set, that she'd exploited her connections, was wielding the power of a wealthy background. It was one of the reasons he was confused by feeling so drawn to her. Knowing that, in a way, she was like him didn't make him feel less confused, unfortunately.

'You get this. I know you do. I've seen this bollocks about your copper bangle, and the chain.'

Dylan's famous jewellery – the parody Instagram accounts had almost as many followers as his official account. He knew what Ciara meant, what they said about him.

'It's weird,' he muttered, mouth furry with booze. 'I read this stuff about how sexy my chain is, what my *mangle* – to give it its official internet name – means. How they'd love someone like Heath to give them a bed bath. But these people, the ones saying it and writing it . . . they wouldn't have looked twice at someone like me before, they'd cross the street.'

'It's a fetish! It's why middle-class people are desperate

to tell you they're middle class even though they went to private school. "It wasn't a very famous one!" they say! Wankers!' They both laughed loudly. They were drunk. It felt good to be drunk with someone normal. He didn't have to pretend.

'Why'd you think they're so obsessed by who I sleep with, why it always feels so nasty?' She looked into her empty glass, the candle casting a melancholic shadow on her. 'They know where I come from, but they know I don't care anymore. Instead they paint me as some tragic whore searching for affection at the end of my co-stars' prostates. All those pregnancy rumours, so they can do "poor Ciara" the week after to remind everyone I'm barren and alone.' She dabbed at her eye with her finger.

'I know it's a million times worse for women,' said Dylan, remembering Flo had rightly savaged him for engaging with trolls on social media. 'I always get this vibe on set, or in interviews. They try to work out how I came from nowhere, find the catch. Who do I know? Who did I fuck? Or who wants to fuck me?' He'd infiltrated a little club and, as Montagu's outburst had shown, they didn't like it. In a way, that's what going out with Flo had been like – had he been her 'bit of rough' after all?

'I hear you. Don't just sit complaining, though. Do something about it.'

Dylan felt mildly offended. 'What do you mean?'

'Change it. Make it better for someone else. Sponsor an after-school drama club, or mentor someone. Otherwise you're just pulling the ladder up after you.'

It had never even occurred to him he could do that. He should do that!

'Be proud of where you're from, make it normal for people like you to want to act.'

'I am. I will. Thank you.' Dylan sighed and settled into a drunken, lopsided smile. 'You know, Miss McLean, wherever you're from, you're still out of everybody's league.'

Ciara leaned back and smiled thinly. 'Not everybody's, I hope.' Time slowed to a stop, words formed in Dylan's mouth. Sensing a good time to make a temporary exit while the atmosphere recalibrated, Ciara whispered, 'Loo break.' While she was gone, Dylan broke protocol and called Flo with no preceding warning text. Her phone was off. The waiter asked Dylan if he wanted another round. After looking at his phone a few seconds, and firing off a quick Everything okay? to Flo, Dylan looked up, and smiled broadly. 'Yes.'

'What the hell is pericarditis? Is he going to die?' Flo had taken the doctors' silence for a lack of knowledge, but then she saw that familiar look in their eyes, the one she saw in shop assistants or cabbies – recognition dawning. They were fans.

'It's an inflammation of the fibrous sac around the heart. The symptoms can be scarily like what you might expect a heart attack to be, but your father will be fine. Out of here tomorrow, hopefully. Do you want to see him?'

Joy and Flo crept into the side room. Charlie was falling asleep. Flo tried to look beyond monitors and tubes, and also how hairy her father's shoulders were; she felt a flash-sideways to how this could have been. She held his hand.

'I'm fucking knackered,' he managed to croak. 'Not dying is harder than it looks.'

When they went back into the corridor, they were

surprised to find Sonny waiting. There were definitely more nursing staff than usual hanging around, nudging one another. He'd come, he said, to see if they needed anything. When he learned Flo's dad was going to be okay, he offered to take them to dinner, to his club.

'That's very kind, Mr Ribeiro,' said Joy, in her best charity fundraiser voice, 'but I'll stay here.'

Flo was dying to escape, eat some nice food and – more importantly – throw herself face-first into a glass of wine, but fresh starts had to begin somewhere; she knew she should stay with her mum. 'Me too.'

Joy turned to her. 'No. Not all our evenings need be ruined. After Mr Ribeiro was so gracious to give up his time for us, you should take *him* for dinner.'

Sonny suppressed a laugh. Flo shrugged. 'I don't mess with Mummy when she goes authoritarian. If you're sure?'

Once outside, Flo took a huge lungful of air, and with it, the relief she'd craved over the last three hours. She only stopped crying when the car stopped outside a large black door and Sonny said, 'We're here.'

Sonny took care of everything. He ordered brandy for the shock, a cocktail he thought she'd like for an aperitif, and recommended three things from the menu for her to try.

'You know the menu like the back of your hand,' said Flo. She'd actually been here a few times before with Estelle, but she could tell Sonny was trying to impress her so she looked around as if taking it in for the first time. Not that she could see much, it was darker than her parents' cellar. 'How much time do you spend here?'

'A couple of days a week, but . . .' the big brown eyes met

hers, 'usually on my own. Unless I bring my son. He likes the milkshakes.'

'You must miss him. Not living with you, I mean.' Sonny's face fell. She apologised for getting too personal, but he waved it away.

'I only have myself to blame. I could've made it work, but . . . things happen.'

Flo wasn't sure whether this was male bravado or flippancy. She knew from his songs he was a sentimental soul, unless age and experience had made him bitter. It happened to the best and the worst of them, Flo had been told.

'My boy's better off now me and his mum are living apart. We're happier. It trickles down. Anyway, you understand – look at how much you've grown since your break-up.'

Flo blushed; she wasn't sure why. It excited her and unnerved her in equal measure that Sonny not only noticed a change in her, but was observing her in the first place. How could he see a difference? He hadn't known Flo before, and the break-up wasn't real anyway – any 'growth' was a result of something else. Had she grown? She thought of Dylan. She wished she'd sent a message now. Would he notice a missed call? Maybe it was best he hadn't called back; she'd only have to explain where she was. And with whom. Maybe, she thought now, unsure where the idea would take her, it was knowing Sonny that had changed her. 'You act like you've known me years.'

Sonny swirled his drink round his glass. 'I get the feeling you're the kind of person who might not have . . . I don't want to make assumptions about you.'

Now she had to hear this. 'Go on.'

'From seeing you with your friends.' Sonny noticed Flo

cringing at the memory of what had happened with Estelle that night. 'Don't be embarrassed, you shouldn't be. That looked like one of the few times you've stood up for yourself. The last few months must've been exhausting. I've been there, remember, that "hot new thing".'

'It's been a wild time.'

'It'll get wilder.' Sonny's eyes bored right into her. 'There's something real about you. Authentic. On stage, you don't hold back: your heart, pain, joy, all there to see. Nothing fake about you.'

Christ, if only he knew.

'Maybe you're hiding part of yourself away,' said Sonny, leaning so far forward, Flo could've touched the tip of his nose with her tongue. It felt like he could say anything, and whatever he said would change not just the course of the night, but her entire life. Her head swam with possibilities. 'Will you ever open up?'

How the hell did you answer a question like that? What did it even mean? Open what?

Luckily, Sonny was happy to continue playing armchair analyst. 'Dylan, for example,' he said now, as Flo's stomach churned in spasm. 'He's good-looking, on the rise. Do you wish you'd stayed together?'

Flo's skin prickled at Sonny's intense stare and frank questioning. She glanced away quickly, catching sight of Ciara McLean throwing her head back in laughter, her bony back and tiny bum strutting out of sight, holding the arm of a man Flo couldn't see but knew, instinctively, just from the elbow, could be only one man. *Hers*. Dylan.

'Wish I'd stayed with him?' said Flo. 'No. No, I don't.'

Twenty-Two.

The first time they spoke again, they were like two teenagers. Not the soppy kind, but awkward ones on the sidelines at parties, or whose parents force them to stutter out apologies to neighbours for playing music too loud. It was so polite. Video calls were excellent at stripping personality out of a conversation; Dylan was glad that one day, when they went public, he'd be leaving them behind.

'It makes me feel sick I couldn't be there with you.' Imagining Flo alone in the hospital while he was drinking cocktails with Ciara McLean kept him awake on more than one night. Flo didn't seem to mind, though; she said she understood.

'I'm sorry I blocked you. It seemed like the right thing to do. I see now it was a bit over the top.'

Dylan shrugged. 'It's fine. Adds to the narrative, even.' A bit of her own terminology to make her feel comfortable. 'Thanks for the birthday card, by the way.' He reached and flipped the card over in his hand. It was fairly impersonal, sent, ironically, by a personalised card printing service. The message inside was spelled out in fake computerised scrawl rather than Flo's usual flourishes. And signed from 'Me'.

'I wanted it to be ambiguous. So nobody would know who it was from.'

Dylan laughed. 'I had trouble working it out myself. It reminded me of when the local Conservative club sent me an eighteenth birthday card. It was addressed to Miss Dylon Fix. And a year early.'

'My handwriting is very distinctive.'

Dylan remembered when this cloak-and-dagger stuff was exciting, before it became the norm. 'It's the thought that counts.'

Flo held up her wrist and pinged her bracelet. 'I'll twang my mangle on the hour every hour so I'm thinking of you all day.'

They collapsed into laughter. 'Next time I see you, I'll be twanging more than your mangle.'

Jesse flashed his most wholesome smile as he handed over the hugest bunch of flowers Flo had ever seen. She was so used to Dylan's withered blooms that they came as quite a shock. 'Don't worry, these are for you, not your dad. How is he doing?'

Flo's dad was doing great, back to his old self – bar the usual five glasses of whisky or whatever – and was good-naturedly complaining about being bossed around by Joy, although he secretly enjoyed being pampered. Flo had for-gotten how good her mum could be in a crisis.

'I was thinking,' said Jesse, sniffing at the mulled wine he'd just been handed and placing it on the table next to him untouched. Flo was always handing him booze he'd never drink. 'Well, Max and I were thinking, why don't we get away for a few days in the New Year? One of Sonny's mates has got a place in Marrakech that I can use anytime.'

'Good idea, you should.' Flo remembered that holiday she'd been about to book when she and Dylan broke up. It seemed like centuries ago. 'But . . . what if people see you flying together?' It was quite depressing how she could easily second-guess the tabloids now.

'We're flying at different times. He gets there two days after me. I leave two days before him.'

'I can't decide whether it's genius or ridiculously convoluted. Doesn't Sonny know about Max?' She was surprised to see Jesse vigorously shake his head.

'Sonny always says I should put my career first, never get too personal. I don't like keeping stuff from him, but I like his lectures even less.'

More bloody secrets, thought Flo. But fine. 'What are you going to do on your own for two days before Max turns up? And what will Max do for two days by himself after you've gone?' Her phone buzzed. She'd forgotten to turn it face-down and a message from 'Serena' popped up that looked quite . . . graphic. It was a while since she and Dylan had seen one another. She hurriedly flipped the phone.

'You can reply if you like,' said Jesse. 'I don't mind.' He sipped his mulled wine. Jesse? Alcohol? This was new.

'No, it's okay.' Flo traced her fingers along her bracelet. 'So? Two days? You'll be lonely, won't you? And Max will be even lonelier – he can't even go to the toilet by himself.'

Jesse laughed. 'I know. But I won't be lonely, you'll be there. At least I hope you will.'

'Me?'

'And at the other end, Max will have Dylan, if all goes to plan.'

'Dylan?!'

Jesse leaned over and tapped Flo's mangle. 'This is nice. Where'd you get it?'

Flo almost felt herself slip into a sinkhole; her vision went blurry as if she'd stood up too quickly, even though she was still very much clamped to her mother's upholstery. 'How long have you known?'

'Ever since I saw you pinging this little sucker against your arm on tour. I thought it was like a religious thing, at first, like self-flagellation or whatever, and then I saw Dylan has one too. He was wearing it at our London show; he was in all the papers the next day.'

Shit. Fuck. Bollocks. And yet . . . relief. The sky hadn't caved in. Flo had long felt guilty about keeping this from Jesse, and thought he'd be mad, but instead he seemed to find her discomfort extremely amusing. 'And Max?'

'Obviously he caved as soon as I put it to him; he'd be a really shit spy.'

'I know he didn't want to lie to you. Neither did I.'

That wholesome smile again. What a sweetheart he was. 'I believe you. But, if you're feeling shitty about it, make it up to me by coming to Morocco.' The plan, such as it was, would see Flo and Jesse staying at Sonny's friend's riad, and then, once Dylan and Max flew out and moved into a nearby-ish, but not so near that it was obvious, riad, Dylan and Jesse would do a quick swap for a few days.

'All this for a few days alone together?'

Jesse's smile faded. 'It's harder to pull off than you think.

I just want to know what it's like to be a normal couple, on holiday, for once. This way, we both get a secret romantic holiday.'

'Normal?' There was something else, she could feel it. 'But why do you need me there?'

'Okay, those first couple of days . . . I'm doing a big cover photo shoot, unlike anything I've done before. Pushing boundaries. The kind of thing I've always said no to, but this time I can't. It's the next step. I need someone there I can trust, and . . . when the crew leaves, they can tell the gossip sites that I was there with you. Just in case I'm . . .'

'Not ready to push those boundaries too far? You don't want to wander too far from the closet yet? I understand.' What could she say? A chance to help her friend stay under-cover and be with Dylan – what could possibly be standing in her way? Or, more to the point, who? She pushed that question far out of her mind.

'But how am I going to convince Dylan?' Jesse touched Flo's bracelet again and gave it a quick tug; she recoiled as it whipped against her skin. 'Ouch.'

'Sorry, I wasn't expecting something copper to be stretchy,' he said. 'Don't worry about Dylan. Max is asking him right now.' Flo's phone buzzed again. 'In fact, that's probably him. You'll say yes, won't you? For me? Please?'

Not for the first time, Flo understood why Jesse Ribeiro made young girls' (and boys') hearts melt. 'For you? Literally anything.'

The wait was almost over. In a special episode on Christmas Day, viewers would see Heath and Mario kiss for the first time, hiding behind a nativity scene. Dylan was called in to the producers. As always, he assumed it was a meeting telling him thank you very much but his contract was over. Instead, they wanted to wish him a lovely holiday.

'Good idea to go off-grid while the fallout settles.' It had never occurred to Dylan there might be any 'fallout'. He hadn't been worried before, now he was. 'Sit by a pool with a friend and . . . stay out of the papers. Think secluded, private, not a lads' piss-up, if you can.'

'It was like being talked down to by a headmaster,' said Dylan as he and Flo had a secret video call. 'Anyway, when do I get my present?' Dylan smiled wolfishly. 'Unless you've got a little something for me now beneath those buttons?'

Flo drew the duvet in closer round her head to muffle her voice. 'Dylan, I'm not unbuttoning anything. Not on Christmas Eve. My mum's got fifteen people down there working their way through fizz and canapés. I don't want anyone staggering in because they can't find the loo and finding me with my baubles on display.'

'Shame. I don't mean to keep you from Mrs Danvers' caviar blinis. Are you looking forward to Morocco? Max is going out of his mind with excitement. Tanya's definitely cleared it, yeah?'

'She has.' Flo laughed. 'She said to me that my January diary is a graveyard – charming – so why flog it to death and give myself wrinkles I'll have to pay to get Botoxed away? She told me to take the girls on holiday, spend one week shagging and the second week writing songs about it, so long as I don't get chlamydia or come back married.'

Dylan tried to imagine Flo's 'girls' on holiday, giving hell to waiters in phrase-book Arabic. 'We don't need to come back married but . . . maybe this can be the build-up to supposedly getting back together? Running into one another in Morocco.'

'Bit far-fetched.'

Dylan bit his tongue. 'No more far-fetched than literally everything else that's happened this year! It'll be perfect.'

She managed a smile. 'I can smell the suntan lotion already.'

'A few days where nobody knows us, lounging by a pool, no dashing off home in disguise. Bliss.' The screen began to pixelate.

'Shit, my mother's coming up the stairs!' Flo's whisper became panicked. 'Break a leg for Christmas Day. I'll be watching.'

Dylan blew a kiss. 'Just remember, when I was snogging his face off, I was thinking of you. Except your beard is bushier.'

Doctor Heathcliff's Christmas Day kiss with Mario was a massive hit in most circles, with a rapturous response from LGBTQ people on social media, but there was a huge number of complaints, too. Some were unsparing and brutal. Dylan's eldest sister read out some tweets. They'd laughed at first, but after a while, spotting the look on Max's face, she'd stopped. This was no joke.

Max repeated a few, like they were forever engraved on his mind. '"Nasty faggots. It's three kings at Christmas not two queens. Bring back crucifixion. Blaspheming bummers on holiest day of the year." Nothing's changed, has it? When you get down to it?'

Dylan brought Max in for a hug. 'It will. I'll make sure of it.'

Twenty-Three.

Flo and Dylan hit the souks on the first day, fairly confident nobody would recognise them. Just in case, Flo went in full headscarf and huge fifties' sunglasses, while Dylan sported his invisibility-inducing baseball cap. It was quite sobering for Dylan to realise most of his attractiveness rested on his hair – he said he was going to research the likelihood of genetic baldness when he got home.

Flo liked being lost in the middle of alleyways stretching back for what felt like miles, getting narrower as they wound off into the distance, fascinating treasures as far as the eye could see. They could be anyone. Just two people in love, wondering whether they could fit a giant tagine into their hand luggage. Flo got some silk trousers she knew she'd never wear at home, but had to have. This led to a mildly embarrassing yet hilarious discovery that Dylan had never haggled before and was willing to hand over the equivalent of his entire savings account to pay for them. Flo took charge, and Dylan was eager to learn as always, although perhaps a bit too eager – he went way too low at the next stall and almost insulted the man trying to sell him a beautiful leather satchel. When the deal was done, he modelled it proudly. He looked adorable.

'Adding a manbag to your mangle?' said Flo mischievously.

'It could be a thing. I'd call it a matchel, obviously,' said Dylan cheerfully, perusing the rest of the stall's wares. 'And I could add that shawl . . .'

'A mawl, right?' Flo laughed.

'Exactly.'

They held hands, stopped for mint tea, and wandered, enjoying the adventure. Something they hadn't done in so long. They were both relieved they hadn't forgotten how to just be.

Over lunch, Flo presented Dylan with a paper bag. Dylan took it and rubbed his fingers over it to guess what was inside. 'I didn't see you buy this.' He opened it and took out two thick copper bangles; each had a tiny jewel on it – probably glass, of course. 'These are lovely.'

'Thought it was time the mangle had an upgrade.' Flo slipped one on her wrist. 'What do you think?'

Dylan put his on and held it up to the light. 'I love it. I'll save it for best. But you know . . .' He pulled a face like a mechanic telling you you needed a whole new engine. 'The fans will lose their minds trying to get their own. Marrakech, watch out.'

On the second day, the weather was a little nothing-y. Flo was adamant they eat lunch on a perfect roof terrace, but this time, with a goal in mind, the wandering was less fun – the longer it took, the more it felt like failure. To hurry her along, Dylan kept suggesting places that weren't quite right. She remembered him in Greece, happy to go along with whatever; he was now obviously more used to calling the shots, but she didn't give in. They settled on a terrace not even ten minutes from Flo's riad, a fact she could tell Dylan was choking on, but suppressing to keep the peace. They felt less like romantic escapees and more a married couple limbering up for a minor row. Just hungry, Flo told herself.

Dylan seemed much more relaxed once they'd sat down – trying out and rejecting two tables before settling, like Goldilocks, and after a few minutes' perusing the menu in contented silence, he beckoned the waiter over. Flo knew Dylan wouldn't have a clue what to order, as usual, so was about to choose as safe a selection of food as she could, when Dylan piped up. 'Could you just tell me a little more about this, please?'

Flo swallowed her words as she watched the two of them debate the menu, Dylan nodding and making tiny exclamations of uncertainty or, more often than she was expecting, delight at the waiter's suggestions. Her stomach rumbled as Dylan respectfully repeated the waiter's pronunciations back to him. Occasionally, Dylan glanced over at Flo, saying, 'That sound good to you?' and she'd nod back, dumbfounded. Once this consultation was done, Dylan made his choices and sat back, satisfied. Then, a brief look of concern. 'God, sorry, Flo, I'm not much of a gentleman, am I? I should've let you go first. Is there anything you want to add?'

Flo's eyes tracked the menu. 'Seems you've got it all under control.'

He sensed her surprise. 'I've had to get used to ordering for myself.'

'I'm sure I caught a few snatches of actual culinary knowledge there. Did you really ask about food with low acidity?'

Did he blush slightly? 'Just a thing . . . looking after my stomach, y'know? I suppose it was time I got less lazy.' The waiter brought drinks. Why was there a little bit of her that rather hoped he couldn't function when she wasn't around? She knew Dylan was a very attentive student but who was teaching him? She liked the idea of a slightly more sophisticated Dylan, but if anyone was to smooth out his rough edges, it should be her.

It felt like time to address the elephant in the room: how people might react once they were out in the open again. Friends, parents, colleagues and – of course – the people they'd never factored in when cooking up this whole thing: the 'public'.

'I worry sometimes that people will think I've deceived them. I've known Estelle a long time and I know she can be . . . cutting, but friendships between women are important.' Flo paused as Dylan's eyebrows rocketed to the clouds. 'Right, okay, more than cutting. She was an absolute rock when we broke up, she really encouraged me.'

Dylan ignored this glowing testimonial. 'If it comes off as organic,' said Dylan, 'like we met up and realised there was still something there, it'll be fine.'

'What about Lois, what will she say? Your workmates? Ciara McLean?'

'Lois will find it hilarious. The crew will gossip for a while. As for Ciara . . .'

Flo hadn't mentioned that she'd seen him with Ciara the night her father was taken ill. He'd later told her himself that he was there, when they'd finally spoken again, so there didn't seem any point telling him she'd been there with Sonny. It was totally innocent, anyway.

'Ciara will be delighted to meet you. She's a huge fan.'

'Speaking of fans . . . what about the Dylanizers?'

He gagged slightly on his wine. 'Foxettes! You do that on purpose! Hopefully they'll see it for the happy ending it is. What about Team Floria?'

Flo worried about this way more than was healthy, but for now, to avoid spoiling the mood, she shrugged and said, 'As long as the album is great, they won't care. Maybe they'll be happy for me. It will . . . it's gonna get a lot of headlines.'

'Hang on,' said Dylan. 'Never mind our thousands of fans. What about your *mother*?'

'Bloody hell. Let's cross that bridge when we come to it.'

The food began to arrive, waiters laying down plates and dishes with calm efficiency. It looked delicious, if a little overwhelming. Flo swore she could see Dylan's eyes pop slightly. As they started to dig in, something Estelle had said at the London show, about Dylan's parents, kept whirring in the back of Flo's mind. 'My mother's never supported me, anyway, so I'm not expecting this to be any different.' She cringed in anticipation at the clumsy segue she was about to attempt. 'Not like your mum and dad, they've always supported you, haven't they?' Eek. That was almost as bad as her trying to change gears in her dad's car. Luckily Dylan was too busy examining a large prawn to notice.

'I guess. Not always, though. Not in the early days.'

'Really? They must've spent years trying to help you make it, taking you round the clubs and stuff and introducing you to . . . I don't know, talent scouts?'

Dylan looked like he'd been told a joke but was still decoding the punchline. 'I've told you this before, haven't I? They weren't that encouraging. They took me round the clubs, though, yeah. I could beat grown men at pool by the time I was seven.' He forked something in a dish and pulled a face.

'Oh come on, they must've helped you out somehow.'

Dylan carefully removed some gristle from his mouth. 'They thought I was stupid to go into acting. Didn't understand it. It embarrassed them. They wanted me to get a proper job.'

'I refuse to believe your lovely mum wasn't cheering you on.'

Dylan pushed one plate aside and tried another. 'My mum is lovely, yeah, but . . . it's not what people like us did. Performing to them means belting out seven cover versions in some clapped-out club where the carpets are ninety per cent chewing gum and cigarette ends. All it did was turn me into a precocious little pool shark who was determined not to be a pub singer. I love my mum and dad but . . . they couldn't see it. At all. If it hadn't been for my drama teacher, Lesley, I'd never have done it.' He laid down cutlery. 'Look, I can't do this.'

'What?' Had she gone too far? Been too obvious? Had she sounded too much like Estelle's ventriloquist dummy? She had to stop letting people get in her head so much.

Dylan looked down at the floor. 'I . . . I'm really not that keen on any of this.' He pawed at one plate pathetically. 'I think I'm finished.'

Flo felt a wave of relief. Her old Dylan, back. 'We can just order some fries, you know, nobody's going to judge.'

'Are you sure? But what about . . .'

Reading his thoughts, Flo slid her hand into her bag and took out three sachets of ketchup, laying them on the table.

She tapped the wine bottle in front of them. 'In case of emergency,' she said, 'fill glass.'

Dylan laughed loud into the brightening sky. 'You know me too well, and I love it. And you.'

On their third day together it was hot enough to laze by the rooftop pool in swimming gear. So they wouldn't be disturbed by staff, Flo fetched their food and drinks herself. 'It's nice not to have anyone run around after me.'

They popped open the duty-free gin she'd bought on the way over and drank it neat from heavy tumblers, in the pool, taking a corner each and gazing out at the city before them, feeling hedonistic, but content.

'I still can't believe Barnaby has been cheating on Estelle,' drawled Flo, booze slackening her tongue. 'She's got everything, she's perfect. She could have anyone. Why does she put up with it?'

Dylan didn't want to dwell on this; it was hard to talk about Estelle as a sympathetic character. 'Men like Barnaby always do. It's a sport.'

'You'd never do that to me, would you?'

Dylan answered honestly. 'No.' His dad had been a philanderer; he'd seen how much it had hurt his mum. It wasn't just that; he couldn't live with the guilt of breaking someone's heart. While they were drunk enough to share anxieties like it was over-the-fence gossip, Dylan took advantage.

'Do you ever worry about when we're a proper couple again? Just not what people will say or whatever, but what we'll do when it's not a secret? We won't be going back to how we were, will we?' He heard a slight ripple of water, like Flo was squirming at the thought of it.

'No shitty flat,' she said. 'No cheap takeaways, or playing pool in the Duchess.'

Dylan leaned back and let his eyelids tingle in the sun's glare. 'We'll still do that, but in a nicer flat, or pubs with decent toilets. We're the same people. Same flesh and bones. That's all that matters.'

'I do worry about it being taken away from me,' said Flo. 'Like it never happened, none of it.'

The heat and blue beauty of the sky filled Dylan with the confidence he'd been searching for all his life. He didn't like thinking of their reunion in terms of the problems it created, not anymore. 'I shouldn't have asked. Let's not get worked up worrying how bad it might be. Let's just . . . let it happen. We're still us. Nobody can take it away from us.'

'No, I'm glad you asked. I think about it loads. Sometimes when I can't sleep I lie awake on my phone looking at photos to remind me of stuff . . . it feels like decades ago. Like, getting my first number-one award, then performing on tour.'

'Not looking at pictures of me, then?'

Flo threw an ice-cube. 'Maybe.'

'I sometimes worry that I'm so bad at all this,' said Dylan, the heat and gin making him confessional. Therapists should hold sessions in rooftop pools, he thought – nothing seemed too private under a blue sky, with nipples submerged. 'Interviews. Like bad small talk at a crap party. All people ever want to know is your personal stuff. What you have for breakfast. Music you like. Who you're fucking.' He looked over to see if she was looking back. She was. 'They miss the whole point. I'm being someone else, a character. But they never want to know more about them, just me. How does knowing what my childhood was like help people enjoy the show more?'

Flo splashed water on her face. 'It's the same with me. There's like two questions about the music and then twenty on what happened when you met some famous person at a party that you can't even remember because you were only there five minutes.'

'Maybe I'm not a good enough actor. I've made Heath so boring that they don't want to know any more about him. They won't they let me hide behind him.' Dylan's head felt cloudy. He needed to start adding tonic to this gin. 'The way I see it, me and Heath are two cakes in the bakery . . .'

'This analogy is already shockingly bad.'

'Shut up, I'm a bit drunk. We're cakes, right? The customer says, "Ooh I'd like a cake, please . . ."'

'Why do they say, "ooh" like that? Did they stub their toe on the way in?' Flo was beginning to convulse with laughter.

Dylan swallowed his own chuckles. 'I'm being profound about my craft, please! Anyway, bakery guy, well, the baker, I suppose, hands the customer the Heath cake, but they want the me cake, the Dylan one, and they're disappointed. Oh I give up, I'm talking rubbish.'

'You are. I get it, though. We have one of those jobs where we're always on, like we belong to anyone who recognises us.'

'I don't belong to anyone . . . except you.' The gin was making him cheesy and sentimental; the slight slur of his speech giving it an air of sincerity. It went over Flo's head anyway.

They looked at one another, bodies twinkling as the droplets of water on their skin caught the sun. The moment for unloading had passed, they embraced holiday mode again.

Dylan paddled to Flo's corner and kissed her, stroking her back before sliding his hand down to rest at the top of her bikini briefs. She kissed him back, but as he moved his hand, to his surprise, she seemed to shrink away.

'What's wrong?'

'Nothing, it's perfect.'

Dylan lowered himself slightly so their eyes were level. His breathing was getting heavier. His hand stayed where it was. 'I know.'

Flo smiled. 'What I mean is . . . oh this will sound silly.'

Dylan played with the waistline of the bikini. 'I bet it won't. Go on.'

Flo looked nervous. She stared at his body as if seeing it for the first time, gave a sharp intake of breath – that gym membership was reaping dividends – and bit her lip. 'Have you noticed, while we've been . . . on this, like, hiatus, or whatever . . .'

'Our fake-up break-up? Or do you mean the holiday?'

'The break-up, yeah. Well, whenever we've grabbed some time together, it's been . . .'

'It's been hot.' Dylan lowered his voice. This usually got a response. But . . . did he imagine that? Did she twitch with irritation?

'It has. Every day, almost every night we've spent together, we've had sex.'

'Isn't that what we've always done?'

He got the distinct impression Flo was wishing she'd not said anything. He smiled in encouragement. 'Normal couples don't do it every day. Know what I mean? Some days, before, we . . . cuddled, happy to be around each other. Do you get me?'

He did and he didn't. 'Uh huh.'

'The last few months have been like having an affair,

fucking whenever we get the chance. I want the chance not to, for one night.'

'Have you gone off me?' He'd become so used to having sex when they were together, not to mention his inexplicable rebranding as some kind of sex object, that he worried this was a sign the spell was wearing off. 'Is this because I said I was like a cake?'

'No! I want one ordinary night, us together.'

'Just one? You still want to have sex at some point?'

Flo laughed and grabbed him through his swimming shorts. 'Yes, sex pig. Promise! Tomorrow, back on it. I want to imagine what it'd be like if we were here weeks and weeks, regular people, together.'

'I'd still want to do it every night.' Dylan winked, which got him the outcome he deserved – a five-second dunking. When he came up for air, they kissed and he was all the happier knowing he'd get to lie next to her, even if they didn't touch at all.

Rap rap rap. Such a polite little knock. Was it inside his head or for real? They came in threes. Dylan opened one eye and experienced that unique disorientation after a holiday nap. A room familiar, but not permanent. A one-night stand, kind of, with furniture he'd never come into contact with again after today. He was about to shout 'Who is it?' when he saw Flo sitting bolt upright, finger clamped to lips, eyes bulging in terror. Who could be at the door? Finger still to mouth, Flo ushered Dylan out of bed, wincing whenever he made the slightest noise. She steered him to the bathroom. He made for the light switch, but Flo shook her head furiously, pointing from the light to the shuttered window onto the terrace.

She crouched to the floor and he dropped to his haunches. She mimed – quite aggressively he thought – 'stay there' and closed the bathroom door, leaving him in murky half-light. He sat, sulkily, on the cold marble floor, his testicles shrinking back in protest. He craned his neck to catch the sound of Flo hastily reaching for pyjamas and dressing gown. She opened the door. Mumbling from outside. 'What a lovely surprise!' The only exclamation he could hear, then it was back to mumbling, for ages. This was their last day together and he had precisely zero suntan; he wanted to make up for lost time, in more ways than one. He looked down at himself and shivered; dangly flesh on marble floor was not his finest look. Finally, Flo reappeared, shell-shocked.

'What the fuck?' whispered Dylan.

Flo's eyes darted about the bathroom, as if searching for a fire exit or escape hatch. 'I don't know what to say. It's Sonny. He's come to join us for a couple of days.'

Dylan felt like the floor was disappearing from under him. He stood up. 'Sonny? Join us?'

'Well . . .' Flo wrung her hands desperately. 'Join me, and Jesse.' Flo paced the room, trying to work out what to say next.

'Where is Jesse?'

'I don't know!'

Flo left the bathroom and began walking round her bedroom. 'We have to find a way to get you out without him seeing.'

Did they, though? Was this a sign? Maybe it was time to come clean, let another Ribeiro in on the secret. The suggestion didn't go down well.

Flo rolled her eyes. 'You've been on a soap too long. Too

many people know about this already. We're not doing a big reveal. I'll distract him. You get disguised up and sneak out.'

'But I won't see you before you leave the country!'

Flo hugged him. It felt motherly, like she was sending him away to boarding school. 'I'll call. We can do a fake moustache hook-up on Parliament Hill or something.'

Dylan looked around him. 'My bag. It's . . . all my stuff is by the pool. I don't have any clothes in here. We got changed by the pool, I went to get the gin, and the chargers, remember . . .'

Flo's eyes nearly leapt out of her head. 'What?! Sonny is by the pool!'

There was a knock at the door. Sonny's voice. 'You ready for a dip?'

They stood breathing in each other's panic.

Flo kissed Dylan lightly on the cheek. 'Just wear something of mine. If you climb out the back window, we can't see you from the pool. Okay?'

Okay?!? How was this okay? Wear something of hers? She had ten sundresses, each with a different pattern on, and that was it, as far as he could see. Her eyes pleaded. He couldn't let her down.

'Okay.'

Once she'd gone, Dylan scrabbled round for the least attention-grabbing outfit he could find, settling on some floaty trousers and a tasselled sweatshirt with GIRL BOSS emblazoned on the front. A gift from Estelle, for sure. His baseball cap was at the end of the bed. He heard distant laughter – Flo's familiar chuckle briefly harmonising with another, deeper, stranger, heartier one. He half wanted to march up and confront them but . . . it was either do it naked or dressed like an influencer doing an apology video. The trousers, it turned out, were very sheer and looked indecent in the most sensitive of places – he definitely needed underwear. He had no qualms about wearing Flo's knickers if they were in bed, but leaving the house in them without her knowledge felt like it breached the lines of perversion. Suddenly, a key in the door. Shit! Help! He froze, feeling the strange exhilaration and disappointment of a man who hadn't quite got away with murder.

In walked Jesse. He stood for a moment, his eyes slowly taking in Dylan's ridiculous get-up. 'We meet at last.' Dylan's hands instinctively went to his groin, as if Jesse was about to take a penalty. 'Max said you were different. You sure are.' Dylan started to laugh in relief, but Jesse hushed him. 'I'm on a rescue mission. He tossed Dylan's duffle bag over to him. 'Found this by the pool. Yours, right? I managed to sneak it down.'

'How did you . . . Does Flo know you're here?'

'There's no time to explain.' Jesse paused, pleased with himself. 'I've always wanted to say that. Anyway, get dressed, I know a back way. I'm even better at secrets than you are.'

'Can you keep another one? Please don't tell Max about these trousers? Please.'

Jesse looked him up and down; Dylan recognised Max's influence in his facial expressions. He knew the answer already. 'No.'

Twenty-Four.

Sonny knew Marrakech well. Was there anything he couldn't do? As he guided Flo and Jesse round the city, taking them to his favourite spots, it was like the crowd parted just for him. Sonny's ease and charm was electrifying: he worked a room, got them the best table, and made instant friends with the waiting staff. Jesse didn't seem remotely fazed – years of witnessing it first-hand, perhaps – but Flo was fascinated watching Sonny play the role of a lifetime, joking with the waiter, asking about the menu with confidence and gusto, so different from Dylan's polite and slightly nervous questions the day before. Sonny knew the quickest way to get someone onside was to show your curiosity about them and their world. Samples of dishes they hadn't ordered arrived, waiters were laughing and joking as they flame-grilled at the table, and specially mixed mocktails started lining up. Flo loved that the tabletop was already at capacity but more kept coming, Sonny throwing his head back in carefree laughter at the happy preposterousness of it all.

It couldn't have been more different from dining with

Dylan, who usually preferred 'no faff, you know?' Sometimes Flo liked ceremony. It was nice, occasionally, to make a big deal, for everything to be a performance. Dylan always scoffed at Joy's rules about cutlery and what to drink with certain meals, but what Dylan saw as decadence, Flo found comforting. There was something exciting, still, about knowing something would be done properly. God, she sounded like Estelle, but it distracted her from worrying about what Sonny was doing there, and whether he'd seen Dylan. She and Jesse hadn't had a second alone together to debrief since that morning, but if Jesse was as shocked as she was by Sonny's arrival, he didn't show it. If anything, he seemed to find it amusing. Mid-conversation with Sonny, she would catch Jesse watching them with a wry smile, or looking at her like she had spinach in her teeth or he'd seen her sneaking a cigarette behind the bike sheds and was holding in the secret. Maybe he wanted Sonny to find out about Max, or perhaps he'd had more practice hiding his true feelings than Flo had. Anyway, it was time to live more in the moment, forget everything else.

'This has been incredible, but shall we ... get a little drink?'

Sonny smoothed out his napkin and looked at his brother, who was texting – exchanging filthy messages with Max, probably. 'I know just the place.'

It was the same roof terrace Dylan and Flo had eaten lunch at days earlier. Now, at night, it was transformed, with flame-lit torches, music pumping from speakers and an array of good-looking socialites, svelte as chopsticks and babbling at one another as they sipped wine.

They found a corner and gazed out at the city, which

stretched ahead like a luminous carpet, the contrast with the blackness of the sky making Flo's eyes swim. She looked out across the Medina, walls pink and glowing in the street-lights, trying to pinpoint the souks she'd visited with Dylan, trying to get her mind back there, remembering how they'd laughed. Drivers tooted their horns and hollered at one another, but not impatiently like back in London. Flo still found noises and snatches of conversation more exciting if she didn't know the language. She remembered the happy place, and Dylan's look of awe as he took in their hotel room. She realised Sonny was talking to her – even Jesse had torn himself away from his phone. 'What did you say?'

'I said I'll never, as long as I live, get sick of being high up, and looking out over a city,' said Sonny. 'No matter who you are, the views stay the same, however successful you become.'

Jesse laughed. 'Yeah, but the richer you are, the higher up you are. No penthouses in the basement.'

Sonny shot him a castigating look. Brothers! 'A cleaner sweeping the top floor of the Gherkin can still pause to enjoy the view.' Jesse looked cowed, and Sonny looked into the dark again, raising his glass to his lips. Flo couldn't tear her eyes away from the muscular flex of his arm.

'Your mum was a cleaner, wasn't she?' Of all the things she'd read on Wikipedia about Sonny and Jesse, *this* was what she remembered.

Jesse and Sonny exchanged a look she couldn't decode. 'Mum's got a business degree,' said Jesse. 'She was a cleaner before . . .'

'Before I did *Star Searchers*,' said Sonny with a flat smile. 'But she always had a business degree. She had different jobs.

She doesn't clean anymore.' Sonny poured drinks, as if to disperse the bad energy. 'How's the songwriting? You got inspired?'

This was the exact moment Flo remembered the supposed point of her trip. She'd done nothing, not a scrap of a melody, or tortured metaphor. 'So-so.'

'I wouldn't say that,' said Jesse, whose eyes went wide, lips curling into a forced smile, his glazed panic palpable even in the half-light. She realised they were supposed to act like they'd spent the entire time together. Telepathy would've been great about now, but it was pretty clear Jesse was still not ready for his brother to know about Max. 'You've been thrashing away at a couple of surefire bangers, don't be modest.'

Sonny mumbled appreciatively. 'Anything you can share? Would love to hear the genius at work.'

Flo was glad to rely on something she always said in interviews, that she never played anyone a song until it was totally finished. The exception had been Dylan, of course, but he was out of the picture – in this particular universe, at least.

Finally, Sonny excused himself to go to the loo. Jesse and Flo huddled together like conspirators.

'Did you know Sonny was coming?'

'No! He messaged me from Arrivals. He's always been impulsive. It can be a nightmare. That's why I dashed back – I helped Dylan get out, didn't he tell you? I saw his dick and everything. I feel like shaking your hand.'

'No, I haven't heard a peep from him since this morning.' She was glad, in a way; he'd looked furious last time she saw him. 'What do you mean you saw his . . . actually, never mind. So what the hell is Sonny doing here?'

Jesse rolled his eyes. 'He's not here for me. This is all for your benefit. It's his thing.'

'Nothing is going to happen. I'm with Dylan. I know your brother just got his heart broken . . .'

'I'm not worried about Sonny. He's always been good at looking after his own interests. But as for you . . .'

'What?'

'Look. Sonny's very charming, but his agenda is a mystery even to me sometimes.' Jesse necked his drink as he saw his brother returning. 'If he offers to play a song for you, do not pass go, head straight to bed and think about your boyfriend.'

'I've been working on something,' said Sonny as he sat back down. 'It's nearly there. Fancy giving me your opinion?'

Flo looked at Jesse, then at Sonny, and found herself saying: 'Sure. If you think it might help.'

Jesse shook his head, half in disappointment, half in amusement. 'Just don't keep me awake all night mewling break-up songs at each other,' he said. Such a Max line! Flo almost laughed. 'I'm off on a solo shopping expedition first thing, get something for Mum.' Bloody liar.

Sonny touched Flo's hand. 'Great. Can't wait to hear what you think.'

What the hell was she thinking?

Back at the riad, Sonny grabbed his guitar and sat by the pool, checking his phone.

Flo shakily poured him a drink from her duty-free gin. 'Everything all right?'

He nodded. 'Goodnight text from Tiago.'

'Tiago?' Who was that? Another brother? She mentally scrolled through the first page of Google for 'Sonny Ribeiro'.

Sonny peered over his glass at Flo. 'My son.'

Flo realised she hadn't even asked his name. Tanya had warned her that becoming self-involved was as common a side-effect of fame as a sneeze was to hay fever. She was about to mutter an apology when Sonny strummed his guitar a couple of times. Showtime.

He had a false start, humming the tune to himself to find his place. 'I'm never great on something new.' He began. Flo realised she hadn't asked the title; someone playing their song to you was like being introduced to their spouse at a party – you should always ask their name. Tiago, Tiago, Tiago, she said to herself. That should stretch to sons, too.

She listened. The lyrics were . . . fairly simplistic, there wasn't a lot of symbolism to unpick. The first verse was about a woman whom Sonny was very into, but there was a definite undertone it was about to go wrong. 'Just to watch you across a crowded room/Your face, your voice, your body – boom!/ Pity me for believing a star could shine so bright on me.' Your body, boom, hmmm. Joni Mitchell wasn't likely to be quaking in her boots tonight, thought Flo, but he sang it well. Sonny kept looking up as he sang; to avoid his gaze, Flo closed her eyes – a casual observer might be fooled she was lost in the music, the melody was washing over her. The chorus was a bunch of bad metaphors for a woman's crotch, before the second verse came in. 'Candy floss and fairgrounds, a hard joy I couldn't hide/But I was the rollercoaster that you took for a ride/Your eyes say you want me but you never let me in.'

A rollercoaster what? And . . . was the first line about getting an erection in a fairground? This was . . . Flo couldn't believe this was the same man whose songs had soundtracked a million wedding nights. The song went on and on, about this woman being a tease, a mystery, telling everyone about her heartbreak yet breaking hearts herself. Flo sat up straight in preparation for the big crescendo, dreading where this abomination was going to end.

'Oh Scarlett, I know I was nothing to you/Oh Scarlett, you played me like a fool/Oh Scarlett, I travelled the world like you asked me to/What's a sucker like me supposed to do in the shadow of a loser no good for you . . . oh Scarlett.'

Hang on. Candy floss? Fairgrounds? Travelled the world? Shadow of a loser? Flo's stomach lurched, she reached for her drink. It was empty. Sonny was smiling at her, stoking his guitar like it was a cat. 'What do you think?'

What could she say? Not only was this song the biggest heap of balls she'd ever heard in her life, the ballad equivalent of the Crazy Frog ringtone she'd loved when she was about ten, but it seemed to be about . . . her? Right? It was called Scarlett. Her actual middle name! Who else knew? It wasn't even on the internet. So she did what generations of women had done before her when presented with something substandard by a man they inexplicably wanted to impress: she went across to Sonny and kissed him gently on the lips, said it was lovely, and waited until she was by herself before vomiting up every clichéd line that godawful song had just fed her.

'Mick Dick, that gross fucking slug. I'm gonna kill him.'

For a change, Lois's voice was actually pretty calming — well, as calming as you can be when you're calling someone at seven a.m. to tell them there are creepy paparazzi shots of them all over *Snap!* magazine. 'Honey, don't panic about this, okay? Obviously the photos look, okay, I'm gonna say incriminating, but this is totally fixable. Just get Priya to do a quick statement and put this to bed.'

Dylan scrolled through the photos, trying to work out where the photographer had been hiding. It looked bad; they were all over each other.

'A statement? Right. Then it'll be fine?'

'Sure . . .' cooed Lois. 'It's just you, hanging out with a CPF.'

'CPF? This is no time for weird valley girl code!'

'Jesus, calm down. What I mean is you two never made any secret that you're super-close. You've been seen together and behaved . . . almost as affectionately before. There's no proof you were . . . uh, stoned, you seem drunk to me, really.'

What had they been thinking? Right out in public, in the park, draped over one another? Max caught Dylan's eye and mouthed, 'Sorry' before heading into his room to get the last of his things. Dylan looked at the top photo again, imagining how big it would look on a computer screen, or a billboard, or projected into the sky. It wasn't even the usual blurry creep-shot, either. It was crystalline; you could see every line and freckle, Dylan's eyes sharper than ever, and wrinkled in pleasure.

That brief peck on the lips frozen in time for ever and transformed into something salacious, Dylan's 'mangle' shining like neon on his wrist, his other hand lost somewhere in the locked embrace.

It had seemed a good idea at the time. The day before Morocco, the pair of them were already in holiday mode; it felt like the old days, before things mattered. One of Max's new barmen had given him some weed – 'Seriously,' Max had said, 'he's a sweet boy but if he talked any slower, he'd stop.'

Feeling nostalgic for simpler times, they'd smoked a few joints, wrapped up warm, and gone for a walk so they could laugh and point at stupid things, say hello to dogs in the park, buy piles of chocolate and never get past the first bite. Just the usual dumb shit they'd done since they were teenagers. They were touchy-feely, yes, but they loved each other, there was no need to hide it. It was never an issue because Dylan was always comfortable enough in his own sexuality, and Max was resolute that a) he found Dylan about as attractive as three weeks of norovirus and b) gay men didn't fancy all straight men, thank you very much. They'd held hands and had shoulder-rides at a festival, slept in the same sleeping bag on freezing cold floors, and, yes, gave each other a peck on the lips to show they had no time for masculine bullshit – and not a single minute of it was remotely homoerotic. But now, looking at *Snap!*'s hallowed pages, with a stranger's eyes, Dylan had to admit it seemed a tad overfamiliar.

'Read what it says again,' said Dylan. The copy around the photos was Mick Dick's usual heady mix of casual homophobia and salacious speculation, drizzled with his trademark venom.

'The way Mick Dick writes gives me a migraine, but okay. You ready?' Lois coughed like she was about to give the performance of a lifetime, Evita's final radio address or something. She perfectly mimicked Mick Dick's horrible faux transatlantic drawl – he was actually from Sydenham.

'"Casual observers might be forgiven for thinking they were being treated to a live show of yoyo-dater Dr Heathcliff's pendulum passions, but this guy-on-guy smooching isn't a location shoot for *City Royal*. They say life imitates art and it looks like Dylan Fox has been getting over his ex,

Queen of Heartbreak and 'The Last Hello' hitmaker Floria, and heading in a *very* different direction. Seems the fantastic Mr Fox is snide-curious, taking his cue from his moody, switch-hitting on-screen alter-ego Dr Heathcliff. Yup! He's gone method! No word on the identity of this mystery fella twanging Fox's famous mangle – *yet* – but the lucky, lickin' lad is first in the queue for a very special examination. Not just his life in Heath's hands.'"

Dylan felt like he was going to heave. 'Seriously, this man is a cunt, Lois, he can't even write. What's switch-hitting? Pendulum passions? It's like reading the contents of a baby's nappy.'

'He's vomit dribbling down a wall,' said Lois, with disgust. 'Screw him. Now scoot, call Priya for a bit of damage limitation, so she can smooth it over with the producers.'

'Smooth it over?' Rising panic, tingling fingers, a cold sweat – Dylan really could do without this.

'Getting wasted and fondling some dude in a park is kinda not the sophisticated image your character is known for,' drawled Lois nonchalantly, like she was ordering a takeaway and trying to decide whether to have duck or prawn gyoza. 'And looking again, in some photos you look like you've taken a heap of glue. Happy to help. Have a safe flight, honey, can't wait to see your tan lines.' She hung up before he had a chance to reply; Priya called a split-second later, exuding serenity.

'Take a deep breath, baby.'

'What am I gonna say in this statement, then?' Dylan looked over at Max, who was wheeling his suitcase out of his room.

'It's simple.' Priya's voice was soothing and masterful.

He'd witnessed emergency calls coming through to her from other clients before – bigger ones, with more to lose. He never dreamed he'd be on the other end of one of those calls, let alone however many it had been now. Three? Four? All with Mick Dick at the heart of them. It was starting to feel personal, this one the cheapest shot of all.

'Here's what I'll say.' Priya read out the statement she'd prepared, stating firmly that Dylan was definitely not gay, certainly not bisexual, and nothing improper was going on. They were two lads, old friends, having a laugh. A final reiteration that he was straight, a request to respect his friend's privacy, and that was that.

He read each line back. 'Sounds good. Thanks. Bastards.'

'Don't sweat it, baby,' cooed Priya. 'There are worse things to accuse you of.'

'Car's here,' Max called from the courtyard, before quickly trundling his case toward the street.

On the way to the airport, they didn't speak. Dylan fielded messages from his mother and sisters, and rejected three calls from his father which would be nothing but raucous laughter. He texted Flo a link to the story and a reminder they had a date in the great outdoors pencilled in soon. That last day she'd been here, with Sonny, they'd maintained radio silence in case Sonny got suspicious. He'd not heard much since she got back, only that she'd landed and was going straight into the studio to do album stuff. Oh, and that he'd torn a hole in the arse of her trousers when he'd tried them on, followed by a pig-snout emoji. Dylan had a strange urge to text Ciara. He knew she'd totally get this. She couldn't be photographed with her neighbour's labradoodle without the papers insinuating she'd shagged it. He looked up to see Max peeking at his screen.

'Getting your story straight? Straight being the operative word.'

Dylan was about to ask what he meant, but they arrived at the airport. Max had the door open and his trainers on the tarmac almost before the taxi stopped moving.

Queuing for baggage drop, going through security, and wandering through duty free, Max didn't say a word. This was very unlike him; Max never stopped talking, he was usually a one-man radio breakfast show. Now, zipped. They'd be here a while, too; Max was pathologically frightened of missing flights and had been known to suggest setting off to the airport the night before and sleeping in the long-stay car park.

Somehow, without speaking, they settled on a snack bar, and sat on uncomfortable steel chairs. Dylan bought two sandwiches and a couple of Cokes, setting one in front of Max. The boy had manners, he couldn't help but say thank you, but then nothing. Max stared out impassively at the hustle, bustle and squawking progeny as it trooped past their table like a dishevelled military parade.

Dylan couldn't stand it anymore. 'Max.' Nothing. '*Max.*' Silence. 'Maxy.' He ignored him. 'Maxibellissimo. Come on. What is it?'

Finally, Max turned, as slowly as he could. 'I overheard your "no homo" statement before. Nice.'

Dylan shrugged and tore at the paper bag of his sandwich. 'Damage control, that's all.'

'Damage. I see.' Max's eyes dipped. 'What's damaging about being gay, or bisexual, Dylan?'

'Urgh, stop saying my name like I'm in trouble at school. Being gay is not bad, but I'm not gay, I had to put them right.'

'Did you? I thought you liked dirty little secrets.'

Dylan sighed. What was this even about? If this was what being in love did to Max, maybe he was better off perpetually single. 'You know better than most how important it is to be open and honest about sexuality, Max. It helps prevent stigma.'

'Stigma! You sound like a leaflet in a doctor's waiting room.' Max pushed his sandwich aside, cracked the can open, menacingly. 'How many gay or bi kids do you reckon will be inspired by your statement, one that sounds like a lawsuit because you're so offended someone thinks you sleep with men?'

'What do you mean?'

Max looked round to check nobody could hear, not that anyone knew who they were anyway. 'You've sat back and let accusations of cheating and womanising wash over you for the best part of a year. All of a sudden, someone hints you might sleep with men, and you've got a denial out faster than I can piss.'

Did he have a point? It wasn't the same, was it? Dylan mulled his options and chose deflection. 'You're not beyond a few little lies about who you're banging.'

'Banging. Lovely.' Max looked straight ahead. 'What are you actually faking being single for?'

'You know what for.'

'I know what you *say* it's for. Your career. Or Flo's. Very romantic. But what are the stakes if your secret gets out, Dylan? What do you really lose? If anything, you'll be even more popular, all over the papers for a good reason for once.'

Dylan laughed. 'Yeah, cos being "all over the papers" has

been a top ride for me so far! It could ruin us. Flo especially. Her fans and that . . .'

'Don't be so stupid,' Max spat. 'Everyone loves a love story, overcoming the odds, getting back together, love never dies, heartbreaks can mend, blah blah blah. You've read the books, you've seen the rom-coms. One day you'll even be in one.'

Dylan had never had to say it out loud before. What *was* this all for? He knew about the 'narrative' and all that crap, but what did it actually mean? Max was kind of right, wasn't he? Nobody was gonna die, after all. He reached for other positives.

'Maybe that's not all it is. There's the sneaking around part. Just like you. Don't tell me that doesn't excite you.'

'Don't make this about me.' Dylan noticed Max had crushed his can almost flat. 'Sneaking around doesn't excite me. It terrifies me, I'm constantly scared I'll give the game away, or that I'm too gay, or that I'll turn people against Jesse, make life difficult for the man I love.'

Dylan smiled widely and nudged Max. 'Ooh. Love? You caught feelings there?'

Max didn't smile back. 'I sneak around because my man isn't ready. He knows who he is, and what he is, but he can't face everything that comes with it. It's not just about me and him, is it? How can he be sure he's backing the right horse, that I'm worth the risk? He can't.' Max's voice cracked; Dylan felt his heart might, too. 'This actually could cost him his career. In his world, it's about your sexual availability. It's valuable. Sure, some fans would support him, maybe a lot of fans, but . . . there's no way of knowing.'

'It's different now,' said Dylan. 'Nobody cares about that.'

Dylan reached and touched Max's shoulder.

Max glanced at Dylan's hand, but didn't shake it off. 'Don't they? Remember I haven't spoken to anyone in my family except my baby sister for over three years? Look at the reaction whenever anyone famous comes out. Online comments. People talk about the "lying" or "deceit", come on, you've seen it. When you're out, prejudice doesn't disappear in a puff of smoke – don't even fucking think of making a joke about "puff", by the way. I've watched it play out all my life. What people say at parties when they think I can't hear, shouting, "Faggot" at me in the street.' Max sat, fists clenched, and swallowed hard. 'It's the way you came down so hard with that denial, freaking out because you had your arm round me.'

Dylan's most treasured relationship began to crumble before his eyes. His best friend, his boy, how could he make him see if he couldn't explain it himself? 'I wasn't getting at you!'

'You made me feel cheap. You've got a gay best friend but you know nothing about the gay world, unless it suits you, when you want to know what it feels like to kiss a man, for research. I'm kind of sad for young bi people with you as a role model. Imagine what a bi actor could've done with that role, how inspiring they would've been?'

Dylan was horrified. 'That's not my fault! They just hire the best person for the job. It was a fair audition.'

'Was it? What if the casting guy was gay and fancied you? Or what if the straight producers were weird about casting someone who's actually LGBTQ? You love bitching about Flo's friends and how they take opportunities that belong to other people, but didn't you do exactly the same thing?'

No! This couldn't be true! How could Max say such things?

'Nobody else they'd seen was right, they told me that. I got that part fair and square. End of!'

'End of,' Max repeated, slowly standing up, gathering his things. 'Ah, a straight white man has spoken. My apologies.' He walked away.

Twenty-Five.

Flo's head was a mess after Morocco. She even resorted to sitting and writing a list of her feelings, to try to make sense of them.

1. It was flattering, beyond flattering, that Sonny had written a song about her, but: 1a) what did this actually mean? And 1b) should she be furious that the song was kind of . . . not good? Sonny's back catalogue was an array of proper heart-melting tributes to gorgeous women; this song about her was like toilet-cubicle graffiti. So was she a crap muse?

2. Then there was her reaction: the kiss on the lips. She'd felt drawn to him, yes, but also kind of obliged to show appreciation. At least, 2a) there had been no tongue, and 2b) she had gone to bed – alone!!! – straight after. However, 2c) she hadn't been able to stop thinking about it since, and 2d) even though she was annoyed she'd inspired a song so cringe-inducing, she didn't want it to start a row.

The one she really got stuck on:

3. What now?

She decided the best bet was to play dumb. She'd pretend

she had absolutely no idea that she was the inspiration for the song, never mention it other than to say it was 'lovely' through gritted teeth, and politely avoid Sonny for a while so she could cool off. As ever, fate had other plans.

In what Tanya was calling his 'lo-fi comeback', Sonny took a leaf out of Flo's book and uploaded a recording of 'Scarlett' online. Flo expected it to be dead on arrival, but, it seemed, more music fans had mittens for ears than Flo realised, because it took off quickly, mimicking her own success, in a way. Flo was surprised by her envy. Not of the song – despite a couple of rewrites, it was still atrocious – but of how easily Sonny had found success again. She'd kind of liked it when she was the overnight success everyone was talking about, but now here was a man doing it, and an already established one at that. The stakes had been so much higher for her, it was a genuine 'moment', she'd thought, so to see it exploited, and exposed as just another gimmick, was so disheartening. Plus, her songs had been good, very good. At least her album was on the way, and it was wonderful, even if she did sound like she was on the cliff's edge for much of it – only one upbeat song, at the end, like someone handing you a fizzy cocktail and a multicoloured tissue after you'd spent an hour crying. She couldn't wait until smiling in public became part of the narrative. This should've been the happiest time of her life: she was nominated for two gongs at the British Music Awards, Best Female Artist, and Best Song. However, there was a 'but' – there was always a 'but' these days.

Tanya wanted Flo and Sonny to duet on a special version of 'Scarlett' at the ceremony. There was something off about this, like it was a joke at Flo's expense. She remembered turning Sonny down on tour, and Jesse telling her she'd do a duet one day on her own terms, but this wasn't that day. She had three suggestions for an alternative verse turned down, her changes accepted only when they served the myth that the titular Scarlett was some untouchable, manic pixie dream girl – which Flo most certainly was not. She liked to think her own complications made her interesting to every- one – not just men. She tried to emotionally distance herself from it as much as possible. The song might be named after her, and some of the lyrics felt freakishly close to home, but this was very much a man's idea of a woman – even in her own verse. Sonny didn't seem to mind what she sang, but there were hours of murmuring behind the scenes, people disappearing into corners and coming back with stern faces. In the interest of not becoming that difficult woman she was always told nobody wanted to work with, she went along with it – on the condition she could finish the song with a chorus of 'The Last Hello'. Might as well remind people of a much superior track, she thought, bitchily, relieved she still had the capacity for mean thoughts after nearly a year of looking grateful behind her too-heavy fake lashes. It made perfect 'business sense', they said – Flo could feel artistic integrity leaking out of her like an envelope filled with rice pudding. Their unique, one-performance-only version of the song would be released online once the ceremony was over and, according to the excitable buzz emanating from numerous teams swirling round them, it had chart-topping potential. If it made it, it would be a third for Flo, and a sixth for Sonny – his first in seven years. In a way, despite the song being about as pleasant a listen as ten cats doing the running man on hot coals, Flo really wanted to bring this home for Sonny, after everything he'd done for her. That said, the theme of this year's awards – 'Equality. Diversity. Community.' – felt especially ironic. She was a passenger in this ride, not a driver.

Desperate to control at least one part of her life, and tired of living at home, Flo moved into a new flat in an ugly but stylish, sprawling development that looked like a pile of egg boxes, near the river. It happened fast; she'd spent about three minutes listening to the letting agent talk about lamp circuits and renewable energy towel rails before she blurted out 'Yes!' and agreed to take possession immediately – no need for references or credit checks when your face was on a big poster right opposite the agency. She thought Dylan was pleased that they'd have somewhere new to meet alone, but he was annoyed.

'I thought we were doing it together.' He'd sounded like a child who hadn't got what they wanted for Christmas. Flo had gritted her teeth before replying.

'You can move in! It's only a six-month lease. I can't have two number-one singles and live in my teenage bedroom. It's weird.'

He brightened a little, but she still felt a pang of guilt that she had kind of broken a promise.

On her first visit the day before the awards, Joy circled the flat like Margaret Thatcher visiting a colliery, face like a collapsed lung, dying to say how vulgar it was. It had colour, unlike Jesse's sterile clump of adjoined cells a few blocks along, yet this did not escape Joy's forked tongue.

'A red wall? Accents! How late nineties,' Joy delighted in saying. 'We had one. I was painting over it before the bells for 2000 finished chiming.' Despite the distinct detente between them since Charlie's illness, the air still zinged with tension. In a funny way, that's how Flo preferred it; she let it wash over her.

Jesse was much more enthusiastic when he came round, gasping in delight at every nook and cranny, before handing over a delightful white . . . ornament, maybe? It would go on a shelf she hadn't even put up yet.

'I'm surprised you could find this in your igloo. Have you painted anything a colour yet?' Flo poured two large glasses of red, before remembering Jesse was on a post-holiday detox. 'Shame to waste,' she said, keeping the two glasses for herself and handing Jesse an orange juice. 'Can you even drink anything that's not clear? Aren't you frightened of staining something?'

Jesse laughed. 'Please shut up.' It was incredible how much confidence he'd gained compared to that sweet but frightened guy she'd met a few months earlier. Max had done him the world of good, and she hoped she'd played her part in it all too; this guy was a friend for life, she could feel it. 'I have something to tell you.' He looked nervous, but happy – so . . . not terminally ill.

Flo's eyes flashed. 'You're not gay! You're in love with me, too!'

Jesse smiled but narrowed his eyes at the 'too'. Flo clamped her hand over her mouth, trying to shove whatever she meant back into it.

'I don't want to hide. Those photos of Dylan and Max got me thinking. I don't want Max to be some sleazy story.'

Flo glugged at her wine. 'Oh God, are you . . . are you coming out? Like, as a couple? Wow, Jesse. This is a big step.'

'But the right one. Isn't it?'

'Of course it is. Max is an absolute diamond. Right, what can I do to help?'

Jesse smiled. 'Nothing. In a way, this whole . . . ridiculous thing you and Dylan have going on, it's convinced me. I can't be like that.'

Ridiculous thing. Ouch. Brushing aside the dig, Flo gripped Jesse's arm and squealed with excitement. 'Let me do something. I want to be in this! I can make a statement of support or . . . we can do a special show!'

'No.' Jesse firmly placed his glass on the table. He seemed, suddenly, wiser than his years. She could almost see new creases in his face, from worry, perhaps, not time. His eyes held a million secrets; he strained as he returned her gaze. 'You can't be in this. It's not about you, or Dylan, but me and Max. I want to do it my way. Properly, like set a date for it, get Tanya to set up an interview. Go big and proud.'

'*I'm* proud. Of you, I mean.' And she was. Also envious. Max and Jesse hadn't been together long, had much more at stake, and were braving a new frontier together. She and Dylan were . . . exactly where they'd been months ago, on their strange, fake hiatus.

Jesse's face lit up as he talked about Max, what form the reveal would take – morning television so all his aunties would see it – and who he wanted to interview him. She was thrilled for him, but couldn't shake a vague, yet palpable fear that set her trembling. Whatever it was, her mind wasn't ready to process what she was actually afraid of. The future, maybe.

Arriving at the arena, Joy texted to say they were in front of the TV, with a small glass of champagne, finishing with four words that almost floored Flo. 'I'm so marvellously proud.' Not we, so not scripted by her father, but from the heart, Joy's heart. Dylan had always mused she didn't have one. 'Probably just bats and out-of-date cans of soup in there,' he'd once said. That used to make her laugh; it didn't now.

Tanya had gone blond for the New Year and was puffing on a much slimmer, more sophisticated-looking vape than usual – one of the seven vaping apparatus she'd received from nieces, nephews, and godchildren for Christmas. 'I suppose it's better than the year they each bought me a bottle of gin and my brother staged an intervention, but I'd rather they spent their money on something interesting or useful, for themselves, like drugs or Invisalign.' She looked down at Flo, who was having her make-up done by what felt like a hundred people – her usual team bolstered by extras because this was a very big night. 'Still got that face of yours on,' said Tanya. 'Turn that frown upside down and all that. It's Queen of Heartbreak not Queen of Faceache. I suppose you'd rather be singing one of your own songs.'

It kind of *is* one of my own songs, thought Flo, as she tried hard to keep still as a shaky assistant attended to her lips. Flo hated it when it wasn't one of her usual girls. She held up her hand for the girl to stop. 'Do something else, do my eyebrows. Well, I have had quite a big year; a solo spot would've been nice.'

Tanya didn't say anything, just huffed on her vape and winked. Then, it was on: someone with a headset came for her, tapping a watch and grabbing her wrist – the rented jewels lording it nicely over her now slackening copper brace-let – as they garbled into a mobile phone.

'She's coming.'

Flo was whisked along grubby corridors. Members of her team scurried behind, prodding at stray curls and smoothing down creases. It was stressful, unglamorous and . . . everything she'd ever wanted. Fucking yes, she thought. She could still totally own this.

The plan was for Sonny to sing the first verse of 'Scarlett' on stage alone, before Flo joined him on the chorus, a line each on his second verse – now improved with her new lyrics – a line each on a reworked second chorus, together on the middle eight and then, the stage would plunge to black as Flo sang a verse of 'The Last Hello' alone, before they sang together on a mash-up of the two choruses. This meant she'd have to walk and sing at the same time – and this dress was complicated.

She still had mixed feelings about Sonny as she waited on the sidelines. She saw the hydraulics taking him up to the stage, Sonny looking small and nervous inside, turning at just the last second and blowing her a kiss. Smooth. Somehow, he made that verse sound beautiful – she got so lost in it she almost missed her cue, a production assistant prodding her on stage like she was a pig at the market. She glided on, drinking in the audience for a second. No nerves, only boundless energy and serenity, as she took the lyrics of that shitty, second-rate ballad and sang it to Sonny like she was making a promise. He came to her, eyes closing as he swooned to her voice. He didn't touch her at first, just hovered near. She could feel that heat though, the charge between them that she'd mistaken for food poisoning one night after a dodgy burger from backstage catering, but was, in the moment, something else entirely. Somehow it didn't matter that the lyrics to his song had the depth and sophistication of the terms and conditions on the back of a raffle ticket, because he was singing it to her, for her, about her, and then, when that gentle touch on her arm came, she realised the most important thing she had to do that night was have sex with Sonny. Then the stage went dark, and for a moment, she was alone. It was her turn. She sang the words that had made it happen, pulled from the debris of the broken heart that Dylan had given her. And she felt absolutely nothing.

Dylan knew people in TV were experts at saying one thing and meaning another, but his meeting with the producers was a new kind of cryptic. Thankfully, Priya did most of the talking and decoded it for him. They were 'persevering' with his storyline, despite the wider public reaction. Dylan had seen it online. 'Not the swell of support we expected,' were their words. Even those who liked the storyline had a few grumbles over two straight actors playing the roles and the portrayal of bisexuality as a shameful secret. Dylan understood, especially since his showdown with Max. It had been done, felt like old news. There was also the inescapable, non-existent sexual tension between Dylan and Montagu. On screen, they looked like two dining chairs trying to fuck. The answer, according to the producers? A near-death experience to bring the two characters closer together. Dylan had been around the block enough to know this would go down like a cup of cold sick with LGBTQ viewers – you shouldn't have to maim someone to make them sympathetic.

'If we do that, why can't it make them realise they're not right for each other?' Dylan found himself saying. 'Maybe Heath can come out properly but . . . he doesn't have to fall in love with Mario, the first guy he sleeps with, does he? That's not how it works.'

The producers were insistent. 'To gain acceptance, it needs to be about overcoming the odds, you know. Something heroic and beautiful. And we'll be cutting back on bedroom scenes altogether – the focus group can't handle more than one set of male nipples in any scene that's not in the locker room.'

Dylan was overjoyed he'd no longer have to pretend Montagu was ravishingly attractive, but felt some viewers were being cheated of the storyline they deserved. He and Priya walked to the canteen, feeling dejected.

Priya tried to find the upside. 'At least the storyline is continuing.'

Dylan stopped. 'Mate. Think about when they said the "near-death" stunt is happening. By then I'll have been in the show a year. Montagu not so far off.'

'Oh.'

'Exactly. Max told me about the "bury your gays" thing – it extends to bisexuals too. They're gonna kill one of us off. One year and out.'

Priya brightened. 'Montagu's an insufferable prick and as popular with viewers as gonorrhoea. It'll be him.'

Once he'd waved off Priya, he went in search of Ciara. She'd know what to do. He peeped round her dressing-room door. Ciara was curled up in one of her easy chairs – she had two, nobody else did. 'I might ask for a third at contract renewal,' she'd said on one of their late nights, cackling loudly. 'Not because I need one. I just want my room stuffed with armchairs because I can.'

She wasn't cackling now. Ciara had a copy of *Soap Suds* in

her hand and she looked exhausted. 'Every time I'm smash-ing it out the park, along comes a wrecking ball. You know that feeling?'

Dylan thought back to his meeting, and what he'd said about Heath and Montagu realising they weren't right for each other. There was a message in there somewhere, but he didn't want to look too hard in case he didn't like what he found. He zoned back in. 'Just had a rough meeting about Heath's storyline.'

Ciara laughed. 'Oh, ignore them. If you ask me, it's going really well. They just don't want you to ask for more money. I have a meeting later, that's why I'm still here.'

'Why, what's up?'

'I don't know where to begin. Something from my past has come back to bite me. A pretty high floor on my skyscraper of fuck-ups.' Ciara closed her eyes in dread. 'Years ago, to my eternal regret, not that I think about it often, I had sex with Montagu. Once. It wasn't very noteworthy.'

Dylan felt a strange heat rising. Jealousy. Someone as nice as Ciara, a man as disgusting as Montagu – it didn't make sense.

'Why didn't you tell me?'

Ciara shrugged. 'It didn't come up. Much like it didn't with Montagu – he was coked out of his dome.'

Imagining unctuous toad Montagu and his floppy penis made Dylan feel sick. 'So why's it coming out now?'

Ciara stretched out, forcing the bad news out of her body. 'Your friend and mine, Mick Dick, is running it. Even though it's ancient, and irrelevant.'

'Where on Earth has he dug it up?'

'Oh I assure you, there's been no digging.' Ciara rolled her eyes. 'Sit down, come on.' She patted the arm of her other easy chair. 'It was Montagu! King Shit himself. Who else?'

'Why would he do that?'

'My theory? Indirectly your fault. Your drugged-up walk in the park with your gay best friend . . . I think Monty is a bit jealous of the attention. Sadly he doesn't have a gay best friend to grope – I mean, what gay man would go near him without a hazmat suit?'

'But it's such old news. Who will care?'

'I know! A thousand years ago! I'd rather fuck a recycling bin! But now we're working together, everyone will think we've picked up where we left off. Like a low-rent Burton and Taylor. It's win-win for him!'

'Surely the producers will go nuts? They're always bollocking me for being in the papers.'

'But at least you actually get in them. Plus, he had his rough meeting yesterday, and according to the storyline team, he comes off a little worse than you.' She drew her hand across her throat.

No way. No fucking way. 'They're not! Hang on . . . How do you know it won't be me?'

Ciara laughed. 'The storyline team are basically koalas who only eat eucalyptus – except their staple diet is shots of tequila, paid for with my credit card. They tell me everything. Plus, y'know, you're actually great.'

Dylan felt a pain in his chest. The idea of being free of Montagu was exhilarating, but Dylan had been hired for this storyline – if it ended, would there be room for him? In a matter of seconds, Dylan imagined every scenario, making himself the loser of each one. He realised Ciara's problem was more immediate. 'This reflects badly on Montagu, not you.'

'Ah, sweetheart, have you never stopped a fan in a Team Dylan T-shirt and asked why they're wearing it? Women get the blame. I'll cop the flak for bringing the show into disrepute. Men are powerless against the Tigress, right? There's a market for my cast-offs. He gets notoriety, and sex with a few airheads who like licking the spoon from my mixing bowl' – Dylan winced, she'd definitely had a drink – 'and I'm left with the detritus, my bedpost and reputation whittled away to nothing.'

The mention of the Team Dylan movement made him remember all the awful things people said about Flo. Did they think he was like Montagu? 'I'll kill him.' Dylan punched an easy chair, and was rewarded with a cloud of dust and Ciara's bemused smirk.

'Don't get arrested on my behalf. Why are you mad?'

Dylan wasn't sure, but he was so angry, his temples throbbed. Just when he thought his hatred for Montagu had topped out, it found new heights. 'The Team Dylan stuff. I never put a stop to it, I let Flo suffer. It was wrong. This time maybe there's something I can do.'

Ciara shrugged. 'This is my battle and there's no need for you to get involved. And it's a bit late to stick up for Flo. She's got her own team out for your blood. I'm sure she's moved on.'

Dylan would say later, when asked about this moment, that for once, he wanted to cut through the bullshit. No more cowering under the threat of exposure. In a way, he wanted to see how she'd react.

'She hasn't moved on, and neither have I.' This sounded more dramatic in his head. 'We're . . . together.' Ciara didn't speak, her face didn't move. Botox, or shock? In TV, it was hard to tell. 'She's my girlfriend. Still. Always. But it's a secret . . .'

Ciara's eyes frosted over, her hands balled into fists, clawing at her own palms. 'I think you'd better go.'

'What? Let me explain. I wanted to tell you.'

'Please go.' She didn't look at him. 'I need to prepare to beg for forgiveness for one night of disastrous sex from before the pyramids were built.'

Dylan backed out. Ciara was staring into hell. Once the door closed, he heard the distinct sound of a fist slamming onto the dressing table, everything on it jumping and landing with a clatter. The sound of defeat.

Twenty-Six.

Once off-stage, a quick touch-up, then Flo changed into another ridiculous dress and was whisked to her table in the main arena. She sat between Jesse and Tanya, waiting to hear whether she'd won. Her onstage high started to wear off, and she reappraised the performance. Sonny had actually fluffed a couple of lines, and his harmonising on 'The Last Hello' told her she'd definitely been right to refuse a duet on tour. Looking at Sonny now, despite his expensive suit and the magic worked by hair and make-up, he looked worn out. His usual luminescence was dulled by nerves and a considerable amount of Dutch courage. This had been a big night for him; she felt bad for whinging that she didn't get to sing on her own. I can't save that terrible song, she thought, but I can fix this man, I can make everything better.

She read a text from her mother. Just one word: Wonderful. Flo started to well up. Then another. You looked glorious. Despite the colour of the dress. Flo smiled. Business as usual. Her tummy fluttered. It could be the sincerity of Joy's message, though it could also be down to the hit of booze on an empty stomach; she'd only eaten thirteen cherry tomatoes, a

Snickers and an energy drink because *dress*. When her categories were called, the thrumming excitement in her body was secondary only to the urge to get Sonny alone somewhere. Strangely, she didn't care whether she won. Which was lucky. Flo smiled politely and applauded when someone else's name turned out to be in the envelope. Should've known, she thought, it doesn't matter, I am still having the absolute time of my life. Jesse, of course, won his category.

The ceremony ended, tables started to mix with one another. Sonny stayed in his seat, looking straight at Flo. 'Well, we did it.'

Flo leaned over to him. 'Did we?'

'Yeah, it's definitely a top ten, isn't it? Amazing how fast it goes online. Boom and bust, one minute you're nothing, the next you're . . . well, still nothing, but you got a top ten.'

'Hmmm. Wanna come back to mine?'

He smiled and nodded, the inevitability of it hanging between them. They didn't speak in the car. At her flat, she showed Sonny round like an estate agent, pointing out tiles and wardrobe space and talking about anything other than what she was actually thinking. She poured them both a drink they absolutely didn't need, and went for it.

'It was an honour to share the stage with you tonight.'

Sonny smiled lasciviously. 'The honour was mine. We work well together, you and me.'

She blushed. 'I've never had anyone write a song about me before. It was so special, thank you.' She had ridden in enough rodeos when massaging a man's ego – you needn't go too granular with the details. Actions spoke louder. He need never know the lyrics made her want to donate her head to medical science. 'I should thank you properly,' she said, leaning into Sonny and putting her tongue very firmly, and quite forcefully, in his mouth. When she pulled back, Sonny wasn't smiling, he looked puzzled.

'This might be taking the plan a little too far,' he said, walking away to sit on the sofa. 'What's this about the song? I didn't write it for you. Or anyone. I didn't write it at all.'

Plan? Flo stayed completely still, lest she fall over. She carefully eased off her heels, just for something to do. 'You didn't write it? But . . . the lyrics, I mean . . . they're literally about me.'

Sonny scratched his head. 'Dunno. Ask Elijah. You know him, right, guitar . . .'

What? No. What?!? No. She didn't want to ask. She had to ask. No. 'Why?'

'He wrote it. It's all right, isn't it? For a beginner? Bit unrefined, but that really makes it stand out. Like your songs.'

Like *her* songs? Elijah wrote it? *Elijah?* Elijah who couldn't write a shopping list! She should've guessed from the fridge-magnet misogyny. It was nothing like one of her songs. She wrote and sang from the heart; Elijah wrote from the very bottom of his baggy, threadbare boxers. This was horrendous. The absence of a chair didn't prevent Flo's body searching for one, as a reflex. It found only the floor. 'Fuck.'

Sonny came and sat next to her on the floor. 'Look, the kiss was nice, but that's not what we're here for. We did our job, got ourselves a hit. Mission accomplished.'

But that hadn't been Flo's mission. There was no mission! What about surprising her in Morocco? Speeding her to London when her father was ill? How he looked at her, what he said . . . everything? She wasn't a beginner, she knew the signs.

Sonny reached for the bottle and filled their glasses.

'You're a very beautiful and exciting artist. I find you inspiring. You and me both got a lot out of it. It was the perfect pairing. You motivated me, got me revved up about my career again. Those songs, that energy. I got you lots of favourable coverage. I still have some friends in the media, you know. It's a good story, the new sensation and the old-timer comeback. Decent narrative. You did good, kid.'

Kid? Old timer? He was thirty-seven. And 'narrative'? That fucking word. Tanya! 'This was all for . . . promo?'

'Look, sweetheart . . .' Sonny became more avuncular before her eyes; the kindness she'd previously lapped up now seemed patronising. He spoke to her like he was tolerating her until she toddled off back to play in the sand pit, like his son. 'Tanya saw you and Jesse had no chemistry . . . understandable, he's gay, no judgement . . . and thought we could both do with a boost.'

'I thought you cared about me. You looked after me.'

'Sure I do, you're my little project. Tonight we delivered. I thought you'd be happy.'

'I didn't know anything about this! You knew I fancied you. Otherwise why come back here?'

'Yeah, I knew.' Sonny looked sheepish. 'It's just playing the game. Thought it would be a good photo for the papers tomorrow.'

'How could it? We came out the back way, there weren't any photographers.'

'Elijah knows that bloke, the guy who looks like a squished bag of Monster Munch, whatshisname, Mick Dick. He feeds him a lot of stuff, actually, I assumed you knew. Anyway, he sorted a photographer to be there. It'll be good for us!'

Flo wanted to throw her glass but she didn't want to spend

hours picking up shards. Elijah! The piece of shit. It made sense now, that first tabloid story about Dylan was way too close to home – it had to be Elijah. He really was as stupid as she'd feared – once it got out that Elijah was selling stories, he'd never work on a big-name tour again. He'd be back in Putney, sharpening his clichés. She'd make sure of it.

'Babe, it's just business.'

Babe. Disgusting. She tried not to gag. 'In Marrakech. There was a spark. I'm not dumb.'

'Thought it would be fun. Look, if I overdid it on the old charm . . . been a while, didn't know it still worked. I thought if I could get you interested, we could have a hit on our hands. It sounds like we do, you heard the crowd.'

He wasn't so much letting her down gently as dropping her hard, like a seagull dashing a crab on the rocks. 'You used me.' Like a one-night stand, she thought, but no wet patch to show for it. 'Just go.'

Sonny raised his hands in defeat, grabbed his coat, and made to leave. 'Don't take it personally. I had to make this work. We both win, really.'

Flo staggered to her feet, watching a daydream walk right out of her life. 'Sonny, wait . . .'

He turned back to face her.

'I just wanted to say . . .' She looked down at her feet, ashamed but not beaten. 'Your song is fucking awful and you sounded like shit tonight.'

The last scene of the day was a tense two-hander with Dylan and Ciara as Heath and Alessandra, arguing about Heath's affair with Mario – Montagu's character. There was lots of dialogue about honesty, and living a double life. While the scriptwriters' intentions were a heavy-handed message about infidelity and sexuality, and Dylan could practically hear viewers at home groaning at the clichés, Ciara's delivery made this feel very personal. They weren't Heath and Alessandra in this scene at all; this felt like a continuation of Ciara's dressing room that day. Ciara's final line was, 'Lying to everyone, making friends your accomplices in your deception, can you really live with yourself?' She spat it out like every word was a bullet. This was their first scene together in a while, and he hadn't seen her much off-set; she was riding out the storm of the Montagu revelations. Well, perhaps *storm* wasn't the best word. Moderate rain shower, perhaps. Nobody cared, after all – it was more a MontagWHO? moment. Priya said Montagu's contract was as good as cancelled. It was a hollow victory. Ciara wasn't feeling celebratory, either.

'Mud sticks, you know that. Sexy Snide Boy, lothario – they'll be calling you that for years. Difference is, it's like they admire you for it. With me, I'm hobbled a little more every time.'

He felt wrong for ever enjoying it, but would he have gained even half as many magazine covers or attention if they'd known he was in a monogamous relationship? He knew people wanted him to be like Heath. Sexually confident, with a dark side. He was in people's living rooms week in, week out. They thought they knew him. As Ciara said, being seen as a love rat had almost zero implications for him, so far. By osmosis, he kind of had become like Heath, in spirit. He felt reborn.

'Montagu will be as memorable as a fart in a lift in a few months' time, but he'll always be part of my myth.'

'Don't you feel like blowing the lid on it? Exposing the system?'

Ciara raised an eyebrow. 'Dignified silence is all I have left.' She left, the air where she'd been standing all the sourer and emptier for her absence.

When Dylan got home, Max was on the sofa, scrolling. They hadn't seen each other properly in ages; Dylan was always on set, Max out at work or over at Jesse's. They'd traded curt hellos and see you laters here and there, but their usual closeness was missing, and, Dylan now realised, being without it was like suffering radiation sickness; he was getting weaker all the time. Enough was enough; Max was his one constant and he couldn't lose him.

'What do I have to do to show you how much I love you? And how sorry I am? I'd do anything for you.'

Max finally glanced up. His eyes looked raw. Now Dylan looked closer, Max looked drawn and broken. His jaw was slack, like it was too much effort to close his mouth.

'I hate that I've made you feel like this, like you don't matter. You do,' said Dylan.

'It's not you, attention queen,' Max replied, softly. 'The date's in the diary. Jesse's coming out. There's gonna be, like, a statement, and a video, then he's gonna be on . . . oh what's that show that's on after the news? Anyway, that.'

Dylan hugged his friend tight and felt the tiniest of responses back. 'That's brilliant, isn't it? The big one! Why so unhappy?'

Max's pupils were glazed. 'What if they crucify me? Look into my past, dig up family members. Everything. I've seen what happened to you. It's how they work. I'm not famous and I don't wanna be, I just wanna work in my bar and be with my man.'

'It's gonna be great. Nobody's going to get crucified.'

'You don't know that.' Max filled the kettle, arranged cups, finding relief in the mundane.

Dylan looked at his oldest friend. He hadn't seen him this sad for years, not since the day they got on the train together, Max with just one holdall containing his entire life. Dylan had done his best over the last seven years to bring a smile back to Max's face that would never leave – a duty he'd neglected recently. 'Think how much better life will be when you can walk down the street with your guy, holding hands or being soppy and sickly on a blanket like the dickheads we always slag off in the park. You can be those dickheads.'

'That's if the world decides to give me permission. Two Black guys being open about their love for one another is going to raise a few eyebrows, even if people don't say anything out loud. They'll still type it, though. Online. Snide comments, you watch. Imagine your situation, times a hundred.'

Dylan felt a first jolt of fear for his friend, but did his best not to let it show on his face. 'Don't think about the bad stuff that might happen, concentrate on the good stuff that will definitely happen. I won't let anything bad happen to you.'

'You're not that influential. You can't protect me. You really have to get over your obsession with rescuing people. I appreciate it, though.'

Dylan felt tears in his eyes. The air was electric with fore-boding and excitement. He was scared for his friend, but thrilled they were talking properly again. 'You've always had this brilliant way of making me feel like a hero and a piece of shit at the same time.'

'You love it.'

'I do. When's it happening?'

'Week on Thursday. As long as my little sister is okay, I don't care. She'll die of excitement when she sees I'm shagging Jesse Ribeiro.'

Dylan nudged Max with his elbow and Max shuffled to sit alongside him. 'You're not just shagging. You're in love.'

'We are,' said Max. 'But if we were just shagging, or dating, or whatever, that'd be okay too.'

'Shame you can't act; you'd be a better Heath than me. You and Jesse are right to do this, you know. Honest. Open. Free.'

'Thank you.' Max smiled. 'I hope you're listening to yourself. You could do with taking your own advice.'

Dylan had been listening. Now he needed to talk to Flo.

Twenty-Seven.

Flo rearranged the cushions on the new sofa for at least the hundredth time, scattering them 'effortlessly'. She walked around the room, observing them from every angle. Perfect. Tonight was Estelle and Barnaby's first look at the new flat, and Flo knew a team of decorators had been hired, fired and rehired several times during their own renovations. Despite claiming they 'adored the personality' of the 'charming little cottage' (four-bedroom house) they'd bought on a quaint side street, they'd spent a year gutting it and giving it a new personality – Barnaby's, worst luck. When Flo went over, it was like being trapped in an interior-design magazine – glossy, perfect, but claustrophobic. A bit like their relationship. Estelle's inherited furniture sat looking lost and tired amid garish conceptual art and relentless colour-blocking; it wouldn't be long before these supposed 'heirlooms' Estelle 'could never part with' found their way to auction houses or the terrifying, huge shed in the back garden. Sentimentality was not legal tender at the bank of Barnaby.

The doorbell chimed just as Flo was on the verge of a minor nervous breakdown over the lingering smell of microwaved king prawn linguine from earlier. 'Oh, a kitch-enette, so utilitarian and chic!' she imagined Estelle saying. Flo gingerly peeked through the spyhole. It was Dylan, look-ing handsome, confident, and . . . glossy. It was like peering at a celebrity, a proper one she'd never met – Madonna, Cher, Beyoncé – and not her actual boyfriend. Arriving unannounced. Exciting! Except . . . Estelle and Barnaby. On their way. Now.

Dylan wished she'd stop saying 'you can't be here'. True, he hadn't phoned in advance, and no, he hadn't worn a disguise, and, no, he didn't care. 'We can't live like this anymore.'

'Ugh, I know. But can we "not live like this anymore" another time?'

When was the right time? It never seemed to be now, or even soon. Another two weeks, two months, eking it out another year? When had he last seen her properly, in a room with a ceiling, curtains open, not hiding? When had they last laughed about anything unrelated to how ridiculous their lives were? 'No. It's time.'

'Time?'

'To stop this. Tell people we're back together. Think of Jesse and Max and everything they're doing to live their truths – doesn't that make you wonder?'

'Live their truths?' Flo looked anxious, about to say some-thing she couldn't take back. 'You're right. I know you're right. Okay, say it's time . . . how do we do the reveal?'

'What do you mean?'

Flo walked to the window and peered out. 'The announce-ment, whatever you want to call it. How we doing it? Joint interview with Jesse and Max? That might be fun!'

Dylan ran his hands through his hair. What the hell was she talking about? 'No big reveal! No joint interview. We tell people we care about, and that's that. Maybe we should get it out of the way before Jesse and Max, let them have their moment. No thunder stealing.'

Flo spun to face him so fast he thought her head would snap. 'That's not how things work now. This takes planning. It has to be managed. We need to speak to Tanya and Priya.'

'It's not a business deal . . .' He paused as she winced. Toothache, or something else? 'It's our relationship. Us. We love each other.'

'Stop making me sound heartless! This will . . . might be a big deal to my fans. *Our* fans! Queen of Heartbreak this, Snide Boy that, whatever.'

'Only Mick Dick calls us that. I don't give two fucks about that sentient turd.' Dylan wouldn't be swayed on this. No bells and whistles. Nothing symbolic. It should be civilised, small, relaxed. 'We should get everyone together, a nice dinner, and tell them. Simple. Make it a celebration. We could do it here if you like, or get a restaurant.'

'Get a restaurant? You any idea how long it takes my friends to decide on somewhere to eat out? How do we get everyone there? We can't ambush them. My mother, your friends . . . Estelle.'

Then, clear and clean as a knife in the back, came her voice. 'Don't worry about that. I'm right here.'

Dylan and Flo whipped round to see Estelle in the doorway, looking meeker than usual.

'H . . . how long have you been there?'

Estelle walked in, carrying two bottle bags, each containing champagne. 'No idea. I didn't bring a stopwatch.'

Flo peeked out into the hallway. 'Did you leave the door open for Barnaby? Is he parking?'

'No. Why do you look so frightened?' She turned to Dylan. 'Hello. Last time I saw you, you were dressed like a steampunk Darth Vader.' She tittered emptily.

'Estelle.' Dylan smirked. 'It was supposed to be Death itself.'

Estelle shrugged. 'You carried off a cloak wonderfully. Happy to see you've kept your career out of the grave. I've seen you in magazines at my dentist.'

Dylan laughed, he couldn't help himself. He didn't care what Estelle thought anymore, so he could actually find her barbed tongue funny, and ridiculous. Why had he never seen this before? 'Flo's frightened you'll be upset, or angry, about us being . . . together.'

'That makes me sad.' Estelle ran her finger along the kitchen counter and reached up for champagne glasses. 'Do you only have flutes? No coupes?' Her smile was scar-tight as she poured. 'We're friends, my gorgeous girl. Nothing you do can make me angry.'

'That night at the show . . .'

'Ah, that.' The cork popped. 'I've been thinking about that a lot, how hurtful it must've been. Obviously you loved Dylan, and I should've respected that more.'

Dylan watched Estelle speak, confused. She was, it turned out, human.

'It made me think about Barnaby, too.'

Dylan held his breath. Estelle handed him a glass. 'People don't really change, I think, but what we're prepared to put up with does.' She thrust her own glass toward him. They clinked. It was a sharp siren – was it warning of danger or signalling the all-clear? 'I could kind of lock away what Barno really was and tell myself it didn't matter, but once you knew . . .' She handed Flo her glass. 'It changed everything. I hadn't been able to talk to you about it. I didn't think you'd understand. Then I thought of you not feeling you could talk to me about Dylan and that hurt me even more.'

Dylan watched them both, half-wondering what they'd be saying about him were they alone. 'So, is this a truce?'

'If you like. Do you like?' Her stare was sharp. If this was how she looked when surrendering, he never wanted to see her battle face.

'I do.'

'I don't want my best friend to find me unbearable. I don't want to lose her.' Estelle blinked slowly, like she was tired. 'I know everyone has a nightmare friend but . . . I didn't realise it was me.'

'It isn't!' said Flo. 'Honestly.' Then: 'Hang on, so who's your nightmare friend?'

'Midge.' Estelle pulled a face. 'She gave up anti-perspirant for political reasons just after sixth-form and always smells of falafel. And she's always talking about conspiracy theories off the internet. You, though . . .' Estelle paused. 'Remember the first time we met? I saw you fall over in the playground.'

Dylan saw Flo smile at the memory, then frown as if remembering the pain of the fall. 'I cut my knee. You pulled me up, took me to the nurse. I remember leaning on you.'

'I stayed and watched them bandage you up. Held your hand when you cried because the ointment stung.' She turned to Dylan. 'I've been trying to take her mind off all kinds of ointment hurting her ever since. Maybe she needed to feel it.'

Dylan had never been described as ointment before. He

sipped his champagne. The good stuff. Nothing but the best for Estelle. 'I'm not going to hurt Flo.'

'She's spent most of this last year you've been apart telling me how happy you made her. I should start believing her. Without you, she's become successful, confident, her own woman. And you're doing more than okay. Maybe it'll work better now. You're different people.'

There it was. A little sting of resentment he hadn't felt in a while. He was good enough now, he supposed, had a bit of money, was on TV. So this was what selling out felt like. But this wasn't the time to open up old wounds, not when he was winning. It was obvious that they'd got away with it; Estelle didn't know they'd been seeing each other all this time. Dylan mouthed 'Phew' at Flo; she suppressed a giggle.

Estelle sat on the sofa, wincing at the hardness of the seat, rearranging two cushions. Dylan joined her and held out his hand to shake. Estelle laughed. 'No need to shake on it. I'll still give you a hard time if I need to.'

'This time, I won't let it get to me.' Dylan retracted his hand.

Estelle reached inside her handbag and handed Dylan a paper tissue. 'Here, blot your forehead. You're sweating. I wish knowing that I scare people was more exciting than it feels.'

The air was heavy with something unsaid. Until Flo said it. 'Do you want to talk about Barnaby?'

Estelle leaned back on the sofa, opened her mouth and tipped the champagne right into it. She spluttered a little but didn't spill a drop. 'That's a story for another day. Let's focus on you tonight, but let's just say if anyone needs me, I'll be at Claridge's for the foreseeable.'

Estelle held her glass out for someone to fill, her favourite trick. Dylan obliged. Flo gasped. A new beginning. 'Can we restore some order? Get organising? Where are you having this cursed dinner? Let me arrange somewhere spectacular.' Estelle was suddenly bright-eyed, animated. 'If I know your mother like I think I do, gorgeous girl, then terrible news like this will require expert catering, surrounded by beautiful art.'

Twenty-Eight.

If there was one thing Estelle was good at, it was organising. She had, after all, been dishing out orders to the entire world for as long as Flo could remember. Estelle enjoyed phoning restaurants and barking at event planners the way some people loved spin class, and the next morning, as Flo watched a man on daytime TV explain how he found a rivet from a Lancaster bomber in his meat-free lasagne, Estelle called to say the restaurant was booked, as requested, on Wednesday night. This was real. Estelle had it all worked out: it would be small and informal – which for Estelle meant a restaurant with only *one* Michelin star. Flo's parents, a small clutch of pals, including Jesse and Max – their big reveal would be happening the day after, so it would be a chance to celebrate them, too. Oh, and Lois would be there. Dylan had insisted. Oblivious invitees would be told Estelle was hosting a dinner to celebrate Flo's success; her mother adored Estelle, and was fully aware of her innate pushiness, so this would feel perfectly normal, and would guarantee attendance. Max had been instructed to drag Lois along. Once everyone was settled, noses in menus and deliberating over aperitifs, Dylan would arrive. The additional, surprise guest, but not a 'crash boom bang' of a surprise, like a mistimed firework, but the 'oh it's you, how lovely to see you' kind. No jumping out of cakes, no dramatic announcement, just Dylan walking in, and taking a seat at the table, where he belonged.

'Estelle, you're so good at this. I almost believe it'll go smoothly.'

Estelle laughed, sounding lighter than she had in years. 'Trust me, gorgeous girl. Everything that stood in your way has gone. There's no reason for your mother, or anyone else, to be uptight.'

'Absolutely!' Flo replied, automatically, although the tiniest alarm bell ting-a-linged. Had everything that had stood in their way disappeared? After hanging up, Flo turned her attention back to the TV to see Sonny, all smiles and silken charm, singing that song.

The night before the big day – Dylan had asked her to stop calling it a 'reveal' – she couldn't settle. She tried for ages to get the lighting right, hopping from one lamp to another, flicking overhead lights on and off. Her phone vibrated. Dylan. One last run of their basic bitch intro text. (That superior nickname didn't sit right with her now – what was wrong with being basic, anyway?) She'd almost miss that buzz of knowing he was about to call. It used to be kind of thrilling, sneaking off to a toilet cubicle to hurriedly stab out a reply, letting autocorrect do its customary mangling. It was like being a spy. It even inspired a song she was saving for album two. That supposedly difficult second album, although she still had her debut to finish first. She couldn't wait. And neither could this. She called Dylan.

'Hey.'

'Hey.'

Silence.

'So . . .'

Dylan sounded tired. 'Our last clandestine call.'

'I know.'

'Let's make it a big one. What should our last words as secret lovers be?'

Silence. Flo looked round her flat for inspiration. 'Did you like that red wall?'

'Red wall?'

'In my living room. Should I paint over it?'

Dylan didn't say anything. Then: 'I like it.'

'You do? Everyone hates it!'

Dylan laughed. Flo imagined his raised eyebrow, his mouth right there, next to the phone. She was willing to bet he'd just licked his lips – he always did that when on the verge of saying something clever. 'I'm not everyone.'

'True. Look . . . better go. Big day.'

'Yeah, we ran over tonight. It was high drama. I got slapped seven times. Wanna get up early, go to the gym.'

'You? Go the gym early? You've changed.'

'You've no idea. I'm sure I saw an ab on my stomach earlier. Only five more to go. Night.'

After the gym, Dylan fancied scrolling through his phone aimlessly in the company of strangers, for an hour or so, give his traumatised muscles a chance to recover, so he went to a nearby café. He sat in a corner, near a window, with a choice of vistas, checking nobody was looking before he licked the frothy 'tache left on his top lip by his foamy cappuccino.

Skinny milk, no sprinkles, extra shot. He caught a look of recognition on the barista's face, but staff protocols prevented the poor guy from pointing out vaguely well-known men off the telly when he should be whipping up lattes or making the entire café jump out of their skin by banging the group handle on the knock-box. Dylan flicked through a paper, coming across a Mick Dick column about closeted celebrities and how they owed it to their fans to come out. That oleaginous roadkill lecturing anyone about honesty would've been funny if it weren't so pathetic, and genuinely harmful. Dylan moved onto a blog about how hot his *City Royal* character was (checking those was a favourite pastime) but felt a presence looming. A woman. In her forties, Dylan guessed. She had a bright, open face and was fiddling with her scarf, which was red – a shade her cheeks were racing to match.

'I hope you don't mind . . .' A fan, lovely. It was nice people felt they could approach, as long as they weren't brandishing machetes. This devotee carried only a flat white, spilling over into her saucer, and a phone. Dylan caught her glancing at the empty seat at his table, wondering if she should risk it. Dylan smiled, and said hello, without following her gaze to the seat; she took the hint. 'I'm such a big fan. I love Heath . . . and Holly.'

'Thank you.' Holly? Ciara would be livid. Dylan stayed seated; he'd learned it made them leave quicker, the difference in height becoming too difficult to ignore. You can't comfortably profess undying love for a fictional character with a cricked neck.

'It's so lovely Heath can be his true self, but . . .' She stopped herself. 'I know it's silly, it's not real, but . . .'

'Go on.' He sipped his cappuccino. Getting colder.

'Mario isn't right for him.'

'Interesting.' Which it was. And true.

'I'd love to see you and Ciara McLean together.'

Dylan laughed. 'You mean Heath and Alessandra, right?'

The woman's face went full, irrevocable scarlet. 'Um, you look great in scenes together. I see you're close in real life.'

She was pushing it now. Time to wrap up; he had a fool-proof plan. He stood up. 'Shall we get a selfie?' He took her camera and snapped two shots – teeth and dazzle in one, smirk and smoulder in the other. He watched her return to her table, where her husband, boyfriend or . . . significant other, was waiting. She excitedly showed him the photos. The man looked over at Dylan and nodded his thanks. He'd clearly watched this play out before. The comforting familiarity of knowing someone inside out. Dylan felt pleased he'd made someone's day. It would be nice if someone could make his.

Dylan did not finish his cappuccino.

'What are you doing here?' Her voice sounded brittle and unwelcoming as it crackled through the intercom. When she opened the door, he stepped over the threshold gingerly, his confidence rapidly depleting. She was wearing loungewear, and her 'no make-up look', which she'd recently told him actually took longer to apply than 'full red-carpet cement'.

Dylan stood in the middle of her living room, realising he'd never been here before, he hardly knew her. Her taste was less chic than he'd been expecting; some of her furniture looked like it had come from his gran's house. 'If you don't mind, I want you to listen for a minute. Two, tops.'

Ciara stood, hand on hip. 'You workshopping a new limerick?' But she knew. He could tell.

'Tonight . . .' Dylan's voice faltered, he took a deep breath. Every presentation day, every audition, every monologue he'd ever stumbled through – they all came back to him. He had to make it to the end. 'Tonight, I'm going out for dinner. Flo's family will be there, her friends, and Max, Jesse, Lois.'

Ciara nodded. 'My invite in the post, is it?'

'Stop . . . don't. So, we're gonna tell everyone we're back together. Not *back*, because we hardly broke up, but, we're telling them. It will be real. Again.' He paused.

Ciara raised her eyebrows.

'I'm starting to think . . . no, it's something I've been thinking for a long time, but only just admitted to myself. It's a mistake. You wanna know why?'

Ciara walked away, to the window, to stare out at nothing. 'Shoot.'

'I have feelings for someone else. I can't explain it, it's not the same way I feel about Flo. It's like it's cancelling out my feelings for her.'

Ciara turned to face him. 'Okay. Who is it?'

She was bluffing, right? His heartbeat boomed in his ears, almost drowning out his voice. 'It's you! I think you might feel it, too.'

Ciara narrowed her eyes as if squinting into a laser. 'I don't fuck co-stars. Had my pinky burned too many times.'

'I can fix that.'

She was glacially still. 'Really? How?'

The words that had been frothing inside his head came tumbling out. 'I'm quitting. I haven't earned the right to play someone like Heath. I don't want to be famous like this. So . . . if you don't want to be with a co-star, problem solved; I ain't your co-star. What do you say?'

Ciara sat on her sofa. She looked winded. 'Here's what I have to say. Don't be ridiculous! Don't put that on me. You're a brilliant actor, the show's lucky to have you. They know it; you should too. And as for the other thing . . .'

The way she called his declaration of love 'the other thing' made him realise this was not going to be the 'climactic scene of a rom-com' moment he'd imagined on the way over.

'I see it took a lot for you to come and say this. I get that you're having doubts about Floria and I'm not surprised. It's been a weird, high-pressure time for the pair of you.'

Dylan's face began to burn, his chest tightened. 'Please, am I dreaming this? It's . . . am I? Do you feel the same?'

She came to him, taking his hand in hers. He could smell her perfume, see the tiniest flaws in her skin, the stray hair over her face. 'No.'

No? But . . . hello? The connection? All those nights boozing and laughing? Posing for photos? Sharing confidences over restorative espressos in the murky light of dawn? Didn't they mean something? How could it be a no? 'Would it be different, if I were free? Tell me, I can take it.'

'They all say that. They never can.' Ciara laughed, but it was a nervous, anxious laugh that Dylan could tell had burned her throat on its way out. 'I did tell you. No. We're friends, wonderful friends. I adore you, you're funny and a bit . . . out of it, which is refreshing and sweet.'

Sweet. Nobody madly in love with you would ever call you sweet.

Her eyes searched his. 'You're my closest pal on the set, truly, I'd given up before you came along. But it's nothing else. You've read this wrong. You're a bit of a romantic, I get it, you enjoy playing the hero . . . but it's not on. It's

medieval. Kind of wet, as well. Drippy. You've some growing up to do. I get some women are into this but . . . nope.
Not for me.' She led Dylan to her sofa and held his hand as
he sank into it. 'Know what I think? You're panicking about
going legit with Floria and looking for an excuse. But I won't
be that excuse. Okay?'

He nodded slowly.

'Don't be hasty, you two have something special. You're
confused. My advice? Forget the last ten minutes. We never
have to speak about this again. Go to dinner, look at her face,
see where it takes you.'

'I feel like such an arsehole, and I'm sorry.' Dylan stood,
mortified, looking round the room, desperately, like he
couldn't find the door. 'And you're right.'

Ciara rolled her eyes. 'Of course I am. Happens to me all
the time.'

Dylan squinted at his phone, turning it every which way,
trying to get his bearings on the map. He finally reached the
restaurant, its warm light punching into the blackness, spilling across the road and fading at the dark parkland opposite.
The first traces of condensation on the windows, the low and
joyful rumble of chatter within. The clink of a plate, a fork
being dropped. Real life was happening inside, a few steps
away; time to join it. He stopped on the pavement, stepped
back, tried to see inside. He spotted Estelle straight away.
Joy was beside her, wincing as Max poured too much wine
into her glass and spilled it. He must've been nervous; he was
an expert pourer usually. Jesse next to him, checking his
watch anxiously. Everyone else oblivious. The calm before
the storm. Flo's dad, Bea, Vérité, Midge, another woman he

didn't recognise. No sign of Lois. Late as ever. No Barnaby either – in the bin, hopefully. Dylan smoothed down his coat, ran his hands through his hair, cleared his throat, and made to go in.

'Dylan.'

A voice from behind, somewhere. He looked toward the park, and saw a figure on a bench, out of the street-light's reach.

'Flo?' She'd been there a while; her eyes gleamed, watery from the cold. He hadn't even noticed she was missing from the table. 'What are you doing out here?'

'I can't go in,' she said, plainly. 'And if you think about it, neither can you.'

Twenty-Nine.

'I can't remember the last time I was here,' said Flo, tracing a finger along the back of the couch. 'Has Max painted?'

Dylan looked round the room, as if noticing it for the first time. 'Yeah, we had a leak. Landlord did it. Venetian cappuccino, apparently.'

'Lovely.'

They stood awkwardly, more like visiting dignitaries trying to be polite than . . . whatever they were now. Flo took her coat off and tossed it on a chair. Her phone buzzed.

'Estelle? Is she mad we're not coming?'

Flo concentrated on the screen. 'No. She's handling it, she says. I owe her one.'

'And boy will she make you pay, I bet.'

Flo turned her phone off. 'She won't. I don't think Estelle's ever called in a debt in her life. I owe her plenty.'

Flo sat on the couch and breathed in and out evenly and slowly, like she was meditating. 'Please, tell me you have wine.'

Dylan opened the fridge. 'Max has six bottles of Veuve

rosé in here. Should I pop one?' He turned to look at Flo.
'Are we celebrating?'

'Open one.'

'You said we needed to talk. We haven't said a word.'

Flo closed her eyes, took another sip of champagne. 'This
is so nice. Magical.' Her eyes opened. 'I mean, there's champagne all the time now, everywhere, if you want it, isn't
there? But to have it right out of the fridge, on a sofa, just
being yourself, it's lovely.'

Dylan, sitting on the floor below her, topped up her glass.
The bottle already looked miserably light. 'If you're going
for "relatable popstar", maybe don't say any of that in your
next interview.'

They both laughed. The central heating made a hearty,
lurching sound. Normality, everywhere, except between the
two of them.

'I was reading your Wikipedia page the other day. I do that
sometimes. Did you know someone's put your middle name
on there? Dylan Richard Fox. How do they find out this stuff?'

The warmth between them was like they were two old
friends catching up after decades apart. 'I didn't even know
I had a Wikipedia page. Maybe my mum set it up. Are yours
on there?'

'My what?'

'Middle names. You have got more than one, haven't you?'

Flo laughed so hard she coughed up champagne. 'Ooh, it's
been a while since we've had a good old class war. Just one,
actually.'

'Oh yeah, Scarlett.' Dylan paused for dramatic effect.
'Like that song.'

Flo shivered. How should this conversation get where it needed to go? If she kept her eyes focused on some point in the room and not on Dylan, she could get through it. 'It's been quite a year. This year will be even bigger. The album. I'm doing America. Then there's the year after that, and . . . you get the picture.'

Dylan's breathing was shallow, but measured. 'I'm so proud of you.'

'So am I, and that's hard for me to say out loud. It's been a big year for us, and for, like, *us* us as well, if you know what I mean?'

'All that sneaking around. Very Romeo and Juliet.' Dylan gave a tiny nod. 'But . . .'

'I don't think we're natural sneaks, are we? That made it harder. But what happens now, when we stop sneaking around?' She was getting there; she dared look at him for more than a millisecond, she was powering up. 'That's why I have to tell you . . .'

'You don't have to tell me anything. Tonight's supposed to be about starting afresh.'

'I do.' The finish line was within reach, just a couple more obstacles to go. 'I made a fool of myself. With Sonny, I mean.' Dylan looked back in alarm; weeks ago that reassuring spark of envy would've made her heart leap. 'Nothing happened, nothing nothing nothing, but I started to wonder what it might be like, you know, not necessarily with him, but anyone else . . .' He nodded like he understood. She continued: 'When me and you spent time together, it was like being pulled out of that . . . freedom, back into an old life I didn't recognise.'

'Sometimes it's been hard to enjoy the highs because I've been worrying so much about keeping everything secret.'

'Exactly.' Flo smiled, feeling warm and protective. This love, which she still felt, would get her through. Dylan hoisted himself up to sit beside her. He drained the last of the champagne into their glasses.

'You're trying to tell me it's over,' he said, softly. 'I'm trying to tell you you're right.'

The tears came from both so suddenly, it shocked them. They clasped hands. Dylan tried to do his brave face. Flo bit her lip. Tears of relief, she realised, not just sorrow.

'I want to feel that free all the time,' she said. 'I don't want to worry about what I'm saying, or singing, or it having to mean anything. I don't want to have to tell a man, "Oh sorry, no, I've got a boyfriend" when "I'm not interested" is the truth. I don't want to think about anything but my music. I know it's romantic, in a way, to think we could go back to how it was, but it was hard enough before . . .'

'It would be even worse now.' Dylan tapped the top of the bottle with his bangle. 'We'd kill it. Snatching moments together, trying to find gaps in our schedules. I don't want to get to a stage where we start resenting each other.'

'I think more than anything,' said Flo, her chest feeling lighter at the thought of it, 'I've learned that I want to be on my own. Think for myself. No responsibility to anyone else.'

'It was cute when it was me and you against the world but . . . I need to focus on what I've got going for me and I don't have much power but, y'know, I can use it to change the things I've been complaining about.' Dylan stood up, and went back to the fridge. 'I'm opening another. First one was the anaesthetic. Time to make the cut.' He eased the cork out and tossed it in the air.

'The red wall confirmed it for me,' Flo said, almost giggling. 'That's when I knew.'

'I was trying to be nice. It really is a fucking horrible wall.' He laughed. 'To be honest, once we had Estelle's approval, we were doomed. It wasn't natural.'

Flo laughed too, and leaned back in the chair and kicked off her shoes. 'That took a lot for her to do but yeah, Estelle's blessing, nope!'

Dylan poured. 'Total boner-killer.' He gave a sigh of satisfaction as he sat down. 'I made a fool of myself too . . .'

'Ciara McLean?' Despite herself, Flo still bristled. 'Figured.'

'The difference was, I actually was disappointed. She said I was . . . wet.'

Flo watched bubbles in her glass try to escape into the open air. 'Aw.'

'Nothing happened but I convinced myself I wanted it to. That's how I know this is the right thing to do. So I guess we're even.'

Flo took a sip and eyed Dylan coolly. 'Not quite. I have two number ones.'

Dylan gasped in mock horror. 'At least I won in my category.' He nodded to the mantelpiece; his Yuki award gleamed right on cue.

'Fix.' Flo looked round the room, recognising some of Dylan's things, and saw a poster that she'd never seen before, but knew was Dylan's taste. What did you do with all the stuff you knew about someone? Did it fade away? Might she need it some day? 'What will you do now? Go back to being a lad?'

'It didn't really suit me, did it?' It hadn't. 'I'll try being myself for a bit and see how I like it.'

'You know the worst thing?'

Dylan nodded. 'That everyone was right all along?'

'Yes!' Flo laughed. 'But not in the way they think. We worked fine then. We're just not right for each other now.'

'And they *were* wrong about us being more successful apart. Shame they'll never know we were together all along.'

'Oh God, we can never tell them! My mother will lose her fucking mind! As if that dinner tonight was ever a good idea?! Were we fucking high?'

'I know.' He stopped like he was about to say something. 'Shit. Just a sec.' He sprinted off into the bedroom, and returned with a very unwell-looking bunch of flowers. Definitely the last ones in the petrol station. 'Got these gorgeous blooms earlier, I was going to bring them to dinner but I wasn't sure they'd make it there alive.'

'I'm almost sorry not to see my mum's face as you handed them over. I love them.' She looked at him misty-eyed, like she'd come across an old photograph that had once meant the world to her. 'I thought we'd last for ever, y'know.'

'For ever's just for love songs.' Dylan winked. 'Please don't put me in another one.'

'You'll be lucky.' Flo raised her glass. 'Here's to being better off apart, telling the truth, and turning this fake break-up into the real thing.'

'Cheers! I couldn't have done it without you.' Their glasses chimed in celebration, and commiseration. 'But from now on . . . I will.'

Dylan saw Flo to the front door. They paused on the doorstep, the streetlight garish and unsympathetic. The street was silent, only the sound of Flo's cab purring in the background.

Dylan swallowed hard as he took in Flo's face, like he was trying to commit this moment to memory. There would never be another now, they would never stand so close again. This was really, really it. No going back. As he ran his eyes over her, he made peace with it. She read his mind.

'One last kiss to seal the deal?' she said, raising herself on tiptoes slightly.

'To remember for ever? This is high drama.'

Flo laughed. 'We *are* like Romeo and Juliet. Except we don't die at the end.'

Though it was cold, and the scene was lit like an operating theatre, there was an air of faded romance about it. They kissed like it was the very first time.

'That was a good one,' growled Dylan.

Flo leaned in. 'That voice doesn't work on me anymore,' she whispered, before taking off her bangle and placing it in Dylan's hand. 'Nice to hear it all the same.'

'Swap you.' Dylan gently pecked Flo on the forehead, removing his own bangle and dropping it into Flo's coat pocket. 'The Dylan Fox mangle is all yours. Worth a fortune one day.' She laughed. 'Goodbye, beautiful. See you on the red carpet.'

'I'll find you in a song.' Flo climbed into the car and it drove away. Dylan stayed on the doorstep until the sound of the engine faded to nothing, and he remembered it was cold, and shivered. He took one last look up the street and closed the door.

A few metres away, in a very cold Peugeot, Michael Richards' favourite photographer took one last look through the shots he'd taken, smiled, started the engine, and sped off in search of WiFi. This wasn't what he'd come for, but no matter: this was the exclusive *Snap!* never even knew they'd wanted.

'Hi Dylan, baby, it's Priya, sorry to call so early but I'm wondering if you've seen the pics on *Snap!* They're kind of . . . everywhere and . . . anyway wanted to check what's going on because that woman is definitely Floria and you seem to be . . . back together? Do I need to do a statement? I'm really happy for you and shit, but I'm getting loads of enquiries. While I'm here, I've had a call from LA. What are your feelings on pilot season? Maybe we can leave Heath on life support for a couple of months and get you in front of some studios. *City Royal* might get nervous and up your money, you never know. Winner winner, buy me dinner, baby. Call me!'

'Floria, angel. Well, you *are* the proverbial fucking dark horse I dunno what to say but I wanna know wheres, whens and absolutely fucking everything, sharpish. I'm not gonna lie I wasn't sure about this move at first, especially when my day today is supposed to be wall-to-wall Jesse and Max, but maybe this is the perfect narrative when we're thinking album promo – kinda like a Burton and Taylor vibe but without the divorces, and the death, obviously. Oh hang on . . . what? Tell her I'll call her back. Obviously Mick Dick is off every interview list, the fish-eyed poor excuse for a spunky Kleenex, where was I? Right, yeah, this is great, I need a couple of quotes. I'm thinking "no comment" right now till we come up with logistics and then we'll talk interviews. We'll do one of the glossies, nothing that prints on paper you can fold more than twice, yeah? But seriously, just imagining the material is giving me a hard-on. Have you been on Twitter yet? They're fucking lapping it up. From what I've seen so far, it's a toss-up between Team Dylia and Team Florian for the portmanteau; I'll be campaigning hard for Florian, obviously, good brand recognition. Oh, yeah, another thing, totally forgot, the live version of "Scarlett" is number one. Congratulations, angel, it's a hat-trick. Call me. Yeah? Okay, bye. Oh, it's Tanya, by the way.'

'Dylan? It's Lois. Are you *fucking* kidding me?'

Max was dreaming. He was about take a huge bite of an apple, then there was noise. A tune he half recognised. Was it a sign? Should he not bite the apple? When he looked again, he could see only the core was left. The noise was real, he was awake, and next to him, oblivious, lay his beautiful boyfriend.

'Jesse. Your phone's going. Also, you have one of your own songs as a ringtone? How did I not know this?' Jesse groaned and opened one eye, grabbing at the air and some-how managing to scoop up his phone and slam it to his ear. As he did, Max's phone began to vibrate. Max reached for it blindly, knocking a glass of water and a half-finished punnet of strawberries flying. Dylan, of course.

'If you're calling from your bedroom to ask me to put the kettle on, first of all, fucking hell pussycat, I told you no the last time and second of all, I'm at Jesse's. Hang on, what?'

Jesse sat up, trying to concentrate on his call. 'You what, Flo? Say that again.'

In her bright kitchen, Flo paced the cold marble floor, describing the photos, on the *Snap!* breaking news blog. Her and

Dylan together, headlined THE FIRST 'HELLO AGAIN'? A terrible headline; Mick Dick was losing his touch.

'So Dylan and I actually, uh, broke up last night, very, very amicably, I must say, but then we saw these photos and . . . well, we've both been talking about this, you see . . .'

A few miles away, in *his* kitchen, Dylan pulled a face as he lightly placed three empty champagne bottles in the recycling so Max wouldn't hear them clanging over the phone.

'I mean, even though me and Flo have decided to split up, draw a line under the whole fake break-up thing . . . now these photos are out, she and I are kind of wondering if it might be an idea . . .'

'I kind of wanted to run it by you first, Jesse, just to see if we're losing our minds.'

Jesse and Max looked at each other. 'Just spill.'

Flo took a deep breath. 'Well, what if we . . . pretended to be back together for a bit, you know, capitalise on the publicity? Would help keep interest going while I get the first album out, tour the States, record the second album. Yeah?'

Meanwhile, Dylan coughed awkwardly. 'Well, Maxy . . . stop me if you think this is weird, but we thought it might be kind of funny to play along for a bit.'

Max and Jesse looked at the phones in their hands. 'Put them on speaker,' said Max. Flo and Dylan's garbling filled the room.

'Hey, cool. Errr, hi.' Dylan managed to talk the loudest. 'See, I've got contract renewal coming up, there's maybe a pilot in LA. And it's a great story, right? It is. I know it is.'

Max smacked himself on the forehead, hard. 'If you do say so yourself.'

Jesse sighed deeply. 'Flo, are you sure about this? You . . . just broke up. Now you're wondering if you should pretend to be back together?'

'Yeah, Dylan, you've just spent a year pretending *not* to be together. Don't you do enough acting?'

'I know, Maxy, but think about it! It's so meta, it's genius!'

'Whoa! This is making my head hurt,' said Jesse.

'So guys,' said Flo, with fake cheeriness, 'tell us, honestly, what do you think? We should go for it, right?'

'Yes, boys, you'll back us, won't you? Won't be for long. How does that sound?'

Max resisted the urge to scream. 'How does it sound? You two nightmares do realise that today is supposed to be about me and Jesse going public, right? We have to get up and get ready for the studio in . . .' Max grabbed his watch from the bedside table. 'About twenty minutes.'

There was a brief, guilty silence.

'So I'll tell you how it sounds. Heterosexuality sounds absolutely fucking exhausting. I've got twenty minutes of calm left before my life implodes, so I'm going back to sleep.' Max nudged Jesse and they hung up at the same time, kissed, and both flopped onto their backs, side by side, hand in hand.

'We're not really going back to sleep, are we?'

Miles away, each in their kitchen, Flo and Dylan stood bellowing into their phones.

'Max?'

'Jesse?'

'Hello?'

'*Hello*?!'

Acknowledgements.

It takes more than one person to make a book happen. My name is on the front, but every author has an army behind them. I'm not just talking about the myriad talented people in publishing who keep the cogs turning, the pages coming, and the covers popping, but almost everyone I meet has a hand in this in some way. Little snatches of conversation, mannerisms observed, features and news articles read. Obviously, authors have their imaginations, and sometimes it feels like it comes from absolutely nowhere, but . . . it all comes from *somewhere*. Sadly, there isn't enough room here to thank individually every person I've ever encountered, so I'll focus on some key players.

First of all, people who read me. I usually leave you until the end for a 'Special Guest Star: Heather Locklear' kind of vibe, but you truly deserve top billing. Wherever and however you read what I write, I know there's a lot of competition for your eyes these days and I'm so grateful you choose to spend some precious time looking at my work. Thank you!

My incredible agent, Becky Thomas. One Wednesday in June 2019, we sat down for brunch – oh, I'm gay, by the way,

I'm a bruncher – and I ran the idea for 'the next one' past her, so we could decide whether it was terrible. And even though it was nothing more than a few garbled sentences in my Notes app, she said I should go for it. So here we are.

My editor Cal Kenny, for immediately getting it, and bringing fantastic energy – and a quite alarming obsession with my characters' arms – to the project. I like it when people say my jokes are funny, but I like it even better when someone says 'You could be funnier here, tbh'. It's good to be pushed! I hope this is the first of many books we create together. I'd also like to thank my previous editors Anna Boatman and Dom Wakeford for teaching me so much when we worked on my first two books. I wouldn't be here doing this were it not for the pair of you.

To everyone at Sphere, and Little, Brown for letting me carry on. Clara Diaz and Publicity, Lucie Sharpe and Marketing, Hannah Wood for the tremendous cover design, Thalia Proctor, plus my copy-editor Sophie Hutton-Squire for laughing at a joke on page one (score!) and generally sorting it all out.

To my friends, who are always so encouraging, enthusiastic and still genuinely impressed that I spend my life hunched over a laptop making shit up, and for making my book launches look busy, and forever giving it laldy. To the Sunday Club. To my partner Paul for surviving the daily endurance test that is living with me, and my family for general support and encouragement and reminding me how hard I am to buy presents for. Thanks especially to my sister Sophy for donating the phrase 'tic-tac teeth'. To Adam Kay for good advice and unwavering support.

Cheers to everyone who commissioned words from me